By the same author

Sleeping with the Blackbirds

The Clock Struck War (an anthology)

Random Ramblings of a Short-sighted Blogger

This edition published in the UK in 2019 by Fizgig Press, London

Copyright © Alex Pearl 2019

The right of AlexPearl to be identified as the author of this work has been asserted under the Copyright, Designs and Patents Act 1988.

All rights reserved. No part of this publication may be reproduced, stored in a retrieval system, or transmitted in any form, or by any means, electronic, mechanical, photocopying, recording or otherwise, without the prior written consent of the publishers.

All characters and incidents in this publication are fictitious. Any resemblance to real persons living or dead, events or locations is purely coincidental.

Cover design and photography by John Mac
Typesetting by Caroline Goldsmith

THE CHAIR MAN

Alex Pearl

In memory of the victims of the London 7/7
atrocity and all other terrorist outrages.

Does it take the harsh light of disaster to show a person's true nature?
Jean-Dominique Bauby

PROLOGUE

Michael had been sitting there for 40 minutes with the long plastic tubes, one of which he'd managed to insert into his back passage. Another was attached to a rubber pump mechanism, which he had already squeezed with his right hand to pump warm water around his bowel. The indignity of his daily routine was horrendous. Just as he began to think he'd wheel himself into the shower and try again later, his bowels evacuated and his ears were greeted by the sound of a mini Niagara Falls. *Thank Christ*, he thought to himself and pulled the bell cord.

Annie, the young Filipino girl had only been his carer for two weeks. She may have been young, but she'd been fantastic. You didn't have to explain everything to her 50 million times; you just told her once, and she'd get on with it. Better still, she'd smile and engage in normal conversation; not like those sour-faced bitches from the agency who moped around as if the world owed them a living and gave you the impression that they were doing you a favour by just showing up - even when they were half an hour late.

Within minutes Annie had wheeled him into the shower and was washing his hair. In truth, he could probably have managed it himself, even though his stomach muscles were clearly on their way out, and it was an almighty effort to sit up straight, but it was nice to get this kind of attention. Besides, it had been a long time since a woman had smiled at him.

'So what you do today, Mr Hollinghurst?' Annie asked while dousing his head with the shower as if watering a delicate flower that was in desperate need of a good drink.

'Oh, I don't know. Thought I might have a spin on the heath. Buy *The Telegraph* and catch up with the god-awful news. How about you?'

Annie smiled and shrugged. 'The usual. I go home to look after nan.'

She was a bright kid. She'd been to university back home and had a degree in economics, and now was only in the UK to look after her elderly grandma living in Golders Green. How many English teenagers would have the decency to ditch their lives and up sticks to look after an aged relative? Probably no more than you could count on the fingers of one hand, Michael surmised.

Annie wheeled him out of the cavernous wet-room, and through into the bedroom. 'Nice picture,' she said as they swept past the fireplace displaying the large framed shot of all four of them on the day of his daughter, Natasha's graduation ceremony at Durham University. They were all beaming; even that cow of a wife of his. Those days were long gone. Life had moved on. Though sometimes Michael felt like his life had just stopped moving and had come to a crashing halt on 7 July, 2005.

Part One

DEVILS & DUST

Bruce Springsteen, 2005

CHAPTER ONE

He could remember that morning very clearly now. It had been a day like any other. He'd just checked his email on his mobile and had stepped onto a train at *Edgware Road*. The train had barely left the station, and like everyone else, he was just going through the motions of the daily grind, hanging onto the handrail while someone else's elbow blocked his vision. This was the joy of commuting on London's electric sewer.

He could vaguely recall that deafening blast, but that's all. No white flashes; no screams; no pain; no dying passengers; no heroic paramedics; just nothingness. The media had been full of it, of course. Blurred CCTV images of those four demented individuals had appeared on newsprint the world over, and the whole ghastly business had acquired its own moniker; its own brand identity; its own soundbite: 7/7. London's very own *9/11*.

His clearest recollection was the face of that large black nurse bearing down on him. 'Hello there Mr Hollinghurst. You're at the Royal London Hospital.' He remembered hearing her chirpy voice very clearly, but it took a while before his eyes could focus properly.

He'd been there for some hours to undergo minor surgery to remove shrapnel from his right leg. And then he'd been transferred to Stanmore, the national hospital for spinal injuries.

The horror of it all came flooding back to him when he found himself in another altogether more claustrophobic tube. The MRI machine was a marvel of the technological world. It was also bloody uncomfortable. Lying there surrounded by whirring cold metal, he caught fleeting fragments of the moments before the blast. The attractive young woman sitting opposite applying eye mascara and pulling unflattering faces while doing so; the young guy with designer stubble reading the well-thumbed copy of *Our Man in Havana* by Graham Greene; the toddler with the pink headband sitting on her mother's lap. Their ghosts had come back to haunt him and his eyes had welled up with tears. What had given him the right to cheat death?

Some hours later he'd been wheeled back into his ward. There were three others sharing this utilitarian space with its grey flecked flooring, medical paraphernalia and lightweight dividing curtains that could turn your shared world into a private one in a mere swish.

The consultant had arrived with his entourage of student doctors and a dutiful nurse with an Irish accent had drawn the blue curtain, surrounding them in a calm oasis of nylon. Mr Hudson was your typical consultant, privately educated at some minor public school in the home counties, followed by a stint at King's College Cambridge and that long slog up the greasy pole that was the NHS. And here he was with his thinning grey hair and ruddy cheeks going through his file of notes. 'Well, I hope we're making you feel as comfortable as possible, Mr Hollinghurst. You've been through the most terrible ordeal. But the important thing now is to get you through this as best we can.' The rest of the one-sided conversation had washed over Michael. He could hear the pleasant and calming sound of Mr Hudson's dulcet tones and could understand the meaning of individual words but for some unfathomable reason hadn't been able to comprehend the sentences; to join up the dots. The word compression seemed to be one of the words that had cropped up quite a lot. Trauma was another. And then, rather ominously, surgery.

Once he was fully conscious and the full horror of a C3-C5 spinal compression injury began to sink in, the dark clouds had begun to gather and suicidal thoughts became the order of the day. He'd lost all sensation from the neck downwards, He'd lost bladder and bowel function; his legs were totally useless appendages that would lead a life of their own by going into uncontrollable spasms that would reverberate like a pneumatic drill on overdrive, through his entire body. It was just as well he had lost all sensation because that would have driven him nuts. Life was just about surviving. It wasn't much of an existence.

Things started to go downhill with Louise when they moved him to the rehab unit at Stanmore Hospital. In all honesty, their relationship hadn't been that great before all this happened. If he was going to be brutally honest, he'd tell you that they started to fall out of love a couple of years after their second child Ben had arrived. They'd grown apart like so many couples, and just held it all together for the sake of the children. But this; well this had changed everything hadn't it? He couldn't handle being the way he was and she couldn't handle him. And the implosion of their marriage, though inevitable, was still incredibly painful and ugly.

The day he received his first manual wheelchair, a lightweight Swedish little number with a blue carbon fibre frame, was the day his charming wife had announced that she was going to leave him in his hour of need. It was best to make a clean break and start afresh, she had said. She'd found a suitable three-bedroom flat in leafy Highgate. And she had already told the kids who were 'cool' about the whole thing. 'Look, Michael. We both know that this marriage has become a sham. It was only a matter of time before we were going to separate - go our own ways. Alright, I know it's fucking bad timing on my part. And I'm really sorry about that. But it's no good pretending anymore; going through the motions. The children are no longer children, and we've both got to live our lives.' She paused, and he wondered whether she had rehearsed the little speech. As a senior planner at one of London's most fashionable advertising agencies, she was always rehearsing her presentations. She'd spend hours getting the intonation of her voice just right and practising the art of leaving pauses in precisely the right places for dramatic effect. She was good at it, and she knew it. 'I know this whole thing feels shitty, so I'm going to make it as easy as possible. I'm going to forgo my share of the house. I don't want anything from you other than those two Rembrandt etchings, which I paid for.' Those dark, scratchy portraits of old men did little for him. He remembered the day she'd dragged him round that huge international sale of old masters in Regents Park. There were no prices on display; you had to ask for the catalogue, and most of the oil paintings had asking prices that ran into six figures, so those two etchings were a snip at just five and a half K. She was more than welcome to them.

The only saving grace was that both kids weren't going to abandon ship too. In fact, they had both decided adamantly to stay in the house with him, despite the fact that the place was obviously going to look like some kind of geriatric home with catheter bags, commodes, standing frames and enough wheelchairs to shake a stick at. If it hadn't been for his two well-grounded kids he might well have lost the plot. They kept him sane, and in a strange way, they had grown closer than they'd ever been.

Natasha had returned to the family nest having finished her geography degree at Durham with a 2:1, and Michael had helped her with the unenviable task of finding work and paying her way. He'd assisted her with her CV and personal statement in much the same way as he used to check her dissertations. Her writing skills were first class but were occasionally let down by a mild form of dyslexia. An affliction that meant that certain words like *where* and *were* would frequently get mixed up.

While her academic experience had come to an end, Ben's was just beginning. Unlike his sister who threw herself into her academic studies, Ben coasted through everything with minimum effort. He was naturally bright but incredibly lazy. His school wanted him to try for Oxbridge, but Ben had refused point-blank. He didn't want to spend all his time swatting for A stars when As would be perfectly achievable without the sweat and endless hours at his desk. After all, he could be doing more useful stuff like going down the pub with his mates, watching movies and playing computer games. His attitude really wound up Louise. But the more he stuck to his guns, the more Michael admired his son's attitude. And when he finally got the grades he needed to study Physics at Warwick Michael had been genuinely delighted; which irritated Louise no end. She still had Cambridge in her sights, and never forgave her son for not at least trying.

Some months after the terrorist attack, Michael had

discovered quite how lucky he'd been. Had he been standing a couple of feet to his right, he wouldn't be here at all. He had been protected to some extent by a plate glass partition and two other passengers, both of whom absorbed the full force of the blast and were killed instantly.

It was extraordinary how something as heinous as this asinine act of intolerance and hate could throw up so much human compassion and love in its wake. The doctors, nurses, paramedics, counsellors and members of the public who didn't know him from Adam, had restored one's faith in humanity. He'd received handwritten get-well letters from primary school children. And he'd been sent enough flowers to open his own florists, but ironically didn't get to see any of them as it was now a health and safety policy of the *NHS* not to have any flowers or plants on the wards for fear of cross-contamination.

The Royal National Orthopaedic Hospital in Stanmore was a rabbit warren of a place with endless corridors off its main arterial highway that sloped quite dramatically from one end of the building to the other. The irony of the steep slope wasn't lost on Michael. 'How the fuck are you meant to wheel yourself up and down this bugger if you're in a wheelchair?' he asked the hospital porter as he wheeled him into his new home - a relatively large ward with eight beds.

The porter, a young lean and extremely tall Caribbean laughed. 'Hey man, how am I meant to know. They shoulda thought 'bout that one before building this place. Know what I mean?'

In the three months at Stanmore he'd been shown how to manage his bowels with a system of pipes and a hand pump; he'd been taught how to use his wheelchair; he'd had countless sessions with physiotherapists to learn how to transfer from his bed to his chair with the assistance of a sliding board; how to transfer from his chair onto a car seat and toilet seat; he'd even managed to get himself into a standing frame with a motorised hoist; and he'd had intensive counselling with a psychotherapist. Throughout this period he'd been angry and depressed for obvious reasons. And although he hadn't been a great advocate for shrinks in the past when he'd been able-bodied, he could now see their value. When you've been through something as traumatic as this, you need to have someone you can share all your deep-seated feelings with; someone you can scream at or cry with. Because if you don't express your anger and frustration, you just end up internalising it; and the more you do that, the more it eats you up from the inside, and the more depressed and bitter you become.

The three months seemed like three years. He had hated the place with a passion, but at the same time, he knew that he desperately needed to be here to get his head straight and learn how to carry on living as a tetraplegic. He needed help with tackling all those *why* questions that continued to plague him, as they do with so many victims of terrorist atrocities. *Why me? Why that train? Why hadn't I gone to work five minutes later? Why hadn't I got into the carriage next door?* There were no answers, but the more you aired the questions to a sympathetic ear, the easier it became to move on. Not that it was ever particularly easy. This said, there was also that other very big question that lingered in the back of his head over the perpetrators themselves. Why on earth would they want to blow themselves and loads of innocent men, women and children to kingdom come? This in many ways was the most perplexing question of all. Try as he might, Michael just couldn't begin to understand this level of utter hate. How could a rational human being (and these guys were rational; they weren't clinically insane) want to kill innocent people in the name of Islam? For heaven's sake, some of their victims were also Muslims. History had thrown up plenty of evil monsters. Pol Pot was deranged enough to want to kill intellectuals; Hitler was deranged enough to kill Jews, homosexuals and people with disabilities; but this bunch of thugs seemed to want to kill everyone on the planet including their own lot. And every time there was some ghastly incident reported in the media, the radicalised perpetrators would fit the same profile. They would either be educated and perfectly polite citizens who kept themselves to themselves, or they'd be small-time crooks, losers living on the margins of society. They were the strangest of bedfellows.

The porter had positioned him in the vacant bay, and as he did so, the dinner lady appeared with her trolley and deposited a couple of plates covered with plastic covers on the adjustable hospital table that she neatly slid over his bed just above his lap. 'There you are my dear. Here's your haddock and cauliflower cheese, and rice pudding for dessert.' Michael forced a smile and removed the lid from the steaming plate of grey *NHS f*are.

The man in the opposite bed was doing likewise. 'Don't worry. You get used to the food here. I find it's not so bad if you don't actually look at it too hard. I leave my glasses off. Works for me.' And with that, he began to demolish the contents of his plate. 'The name's John by the way,' he managed between mouth-fulls.

Michael raised his hand in acknowledgement. 'I'm

Michael. I was at the Royal London before coming here. Nice to meet you John.'

John stretched over his table and recovered his glasses, which he propped on his nose. 'That's better. I can actually see you now. What are you in for then Michael?'

Michael tentatively placed the grey haddock in his mouth and chewed. It could have been worse. 'Oh, I'm in for rehab having damaged my spinal cord quite high up. So I've lost everything below the waist. How about you?'

'I'm here for rehab too. I've got what they call a lipoma, and it's also pretty high. So my legs are useless. They reckon I've had it since birth and that it's grown very gradually over the years. Woke up four months ago and just couldn't move. The surgeon here did the best he could but there's not a lot they can do other than relieve the pressure in the spinal cord.' He removed the lid on his dessert and spooned the contents into his mouth. 'So how did you damage your spine? You weren't horse riding were you?'

'No, not at all. I was riding a train. I was on the one that got blown up at Edgware Road.'

'Oh Lord. I am sorry. Those bastards need to be locked up.'

'No need for that. They blew themselves to pieces. Saved us the trouble.'

'Of course they did. Don't understand this whole suicide bombing thing. Course, the Japs started it didn't they?'

Michael was a little confused by John's line of argument. 'Did they? I'm not sure I follow.'

John removed his glasses and waved them in Michael's direction. 'They started it all with Pearl Harbour and their damn kamikaze pilots. They used planes as flying bombs, and Al Qaeda did the same when they flew those two airliners into the World Trade Centre.'

Michael reckoned John must have been in his seventies, so had probably been a schoolboy during the war. 'I hadn't thought of that,' he said. 'But at least the Japanese were targeting the military; not civilians.'

John nodded sagely. 'We can all be accused of targeting civilians during war I'm afraid; us, the Germans and the Americans. Look at Hiroshima and Nagasaki - well over 100,000 civilians were killed by those two bombs. But conflicts today are different. We're not just fighting nations with conventional armies; we're up against rogue states who operate across the globe through terrorist cells. Completely different ball game.'

Michael was pleased to be having a conversation with someone other than a doctor or nurse. Until now, the other patients he'd been sharing a ward with had either been comatose or too uncomfortable to talk. 'What do you think makes someone want to kill innocent civilians, John?' he asked, sensing that John would have an answer. He seemed to have an answer to everything.

'Well, that's easy. All boils down to ideology.' John paused and poured himself a glass of water. 'You see, if you believe that Allah is the only eternal being in the world and that your faith is the only true faith, and that all others denigrate yours, then you can come to the warped conclusion that everything the Western world stands for is inherently evil and threatens your very existence.'

There was a long pause as a nurse had checked John's temperature and blood pressure, and then drained his catheter into a grey cardboard bottle.

Some hours later they had continued their conversation over tea and biscuits. John had been a headmaster of a grammar school in Canterbury. 'Went there straight after leaving Birmingham University to teach history,' he'd explained. 'Ended up as headmaster, and spent my entire working life in that school. You become pretty attached to a place like that when it's become such a big part of your life, you know. Still miss it to be honest.'

Michael smiled and nodded. 'Job satisfaction is a pretty valuable commodity these days.'

'Best job in the world, teaching. Mind you, in my day it was different.' John finished his tea and placed his cup and saucer back on the trolley. 'Back then teachers could devote themselves to what they knew best: helping shape and inform impressionable young minds. Now you have to spend your time filling out paperwork, administering, playing the system and keeping the likes of OFSTED off your back.'

That phrase: *helping shape and inform impressionable young minds* struck Michael. Who, he wondered, was helping shape the impressionable minds of young Muslims?

As it turned out, this would be the first and last conversation with John. He was transferred the following day to an Intensive Care ward as his breathing had deteriorated dramatically during the night. His bay was soon occupied by an uncommunicative soul with all manner of tubes and wires protruding from orifices, veins and nerves.

It was a couple of days before Michael engaged in another conversation of any length. This time with an attractive young female doctor with long chestnut hair and tortoiseshell glasses. She had bounded into his space, introduced herself and smiled broadly while twiddling with her stethoscope as if it were a row of worry beads. 'Hello there Mr Hollinghurst. Nice to meet you. I'm Camilla and I'm one of the doctors in Mr Hudson's team. Now I know

Mr Hudson has already spoken to you at length about the compression to your spinal cord. The team here discussed your case this morning, and the general view is that surgery is something we might want to seriously consider to try and relieve the pressure to your spinal cord. But of course, at the end of the day, that won't be our decision, it will be yours. Mr Hudson is in theatre at the moment, but as soon as he's out he'll come and explain in detail what the operation involves, and how it might help. And you'll be able to ask him any questions you like. Is that ok?'

'Well actually, no, it's not ok. It's far from fucking ok, ok?' She clearly wasn't terribly used to this kind of verbal rebuke from patients and went visibly red while looking at her feet. 'Look, I'm sorry. I don't mean to be rude,' he added. 'It's just that... well, I'm not in a good place right now - and I'm not talking about this hospital. The idea of surgery frankly terrifies me.'

She looked up. 'There's no need to apologise, Mr Hollinghurst. I can perfectly understand your concern. As I said, you don't have to have surgery if you don't want to put yourself through the trauma. That would be perfectly understandable and acceptable. All we can do is offer you our professional view and advice. Whatever you decide, you can rest assured that we will do everything we can to help and support you.'

'Thank you doctor. There is actually one question I'd like to ask you if that's ok.'

'Feel free. Fire away.'

'The old boy who was in the bed opposite, John. Can you tell me if he's ok?'

'I'm afraid I don't know, but I can certainly find out for you. I'll get back to you as soon as I know. Is that all?'

'For now, yes.'

She smiled and turned, leaving a faint whiff of perfume in the air. Michael was feeling tired. He pushed the button on the bed's remote control until he was lying prostrate, and closed his eyes.

Mr Hudson didn't materialise for a whole day. And when he finally did, he did so with three young students, none of whom looked much older than Michael's son Ben. 'Hello Mr Hollinghurst. I hope you don't mind if my students sit in on this meeting.' He tugged awkwardly at the blue curtain. 'Now, we've had a good look at the MRI and we can see exactly where the compression in your spinal cord is taking place.' He produced a black and white print-out and pointed his pen at various sections that meant absolutely nothing to Michael. 'The tightness around your spinal cord here is causing all the problems. Now, we have two options: we can either sit tight and wait to see if the swelling and resulting compression in this area dissipates over time. Or we could carry out what we call a laminectomy to remove part of your vertebrae to try and relieve some of the pressure here. Personally, I think this has a good chance of helping, but the downside is that it's a fairly big operation and will require a longish hospital stay to recover. There are, of course, no guarantees that surgery will improve matters. And on top of this, there are obviously the usual risks associated with surgery of this nature to take into consideration. So it's not an easy decision for you I'm afraid. But it is an option that is worth thinking about.'

One of the students began to scribble notes in his notepad.

'And if I decide to do nothing, how likely is it that I'll see any discernible improvement?' asked Michael.

Mr Hudson screwed up his face and looked in considerable discomfort. Had he been a car mechanic about to give a diagnosis on a car, he'd have no doubt been sucking air between his teeth. 'That's hard to say. If the swelling within the tissues comes down and there is any improvement as a result, it could take anything between three and six months. But any possible improvement is going to be marginal I'm afraid. If there has been no improvement by six months, it's highly unlikely that you'll see any subsequent improvement.'

'And if I decide to have surgery, how long will it take to recover?'

'You're probably looking at three months, give or take a few weeks, assuming that there are no complications, infections or suchlike. It is, I have to say, a fairly unpleasant procedure to recover from. So to help your body cope with the trauma, you'll be on some pretty heavy-duty painkillers for the first few days following surgery. So let me make it absolutely clear that I wouldn't blame you in the least if you decided not to go ahead with it. But at this juncture, it is the only possible option open to us. So there you have it. You don't need to make any decisions for the moment. Just think about it; talk to your family, and sleep on it, and let me know in a few days.' And with that, he and his three acolytes smiled courteously and were gone.

CHAPTER TWO

As a young child growing up in East London, Mohamed Farik and his older brother Salah had a fairly normal Muslim upbringing. Their father had been born in British India and their mother in East Pakistan. Together they had worked hard to raise a family and to embrace the British way of life while remaining good Muslims. As far as Mohamed the child was concerned, Islam was a religion, pure and simple. His father had made it very clear to him that there was no place for politics in religion. 'Islam,' he had said to both his sons, 'was about purifying our hearts and drawing closer to God.' But the death of Mohamed's older brother Salah was to change all that.

Salah had been the most studious of the two boys, having completed a Masters in Mechanical Engineering at Leeds University. Following his graduation, he could have secured a good job with *Rolls Royce* for whom he did a placement over two summer recesses in succession. In truth, he could have worked for almost any successful engineering company, but instead decided to sidestep industry and use his knowledge to teach others. His first and, as it turned out, last job took him to Sheffield University, and it was here that he was to publish his first academic textbook - *The Aesthetics of Mechanics*. Following its publication, he became restless, left the university and announced to the family that he was taking a year out to travel. As a reasonably devout Muslim, he'd always wanted to learn Arabic.

Quite how he had ended up in Baghdad, nobody quite knew. But there he had remained for some months. While Iraq's dictator continued to taunt the West, the family had pleaded time after time for him to return to the security of the UK. And Salah had reassured them that he would return in good time. What he hadn't told them though was that he was gay, had fallen in love with another academic by the name of Imran, and was blissfully happy for the first time in his life. So while he could keep up the pretence of intending to return to the UK, deep down he knew that it would be almost unthinkable to do so. After all, his parents were elderly and frail; to introduce his partner and own up to his sexual orientation while his parents were in their twilight years, struck him as an act of gross insensitivity. They would be devastated; it would probably send his father to an early grave. At the same time, he didn't want to live a lie. But it had to be said that doing so from afar was a great deal easier. So all in all, staying put for the time being at least, was by far the most convenient option. One he could live with. And as for all this bluster and posturing from the American and Iraqi administrations, he, like so many others, were convinced that this whole pantomime would play itself out.

Sadly for Salah and countless thousands of Iraqis, the pantomime would turn into a tragedy of epic proportions. By the time Britain and the US had lost patience with Iraq's irrational tyrant and had unleashed their so-called *shock and awe* strategy of endless air sorties and continual bombardment of the city, the family were at their wits' end. All communications by then had broken down.

The family was eventually officially notified by the authorities of Salah's death months after his body had been recovered from the rubble and he had eventually been identified through dental records. He had been living in one of the buildings close to the Ba'ath Party's headquarters, which had been inadvertently hit by a cruise missile. The Americans called it *collateral damage*. And there had never been an apology from anyone for this heinous and senseless crime. From that day onward, Mohamed held America and the West in contempt. They had started this senseless war and killed his brother along with countless innocent men, women and children; and for what? Saddam had been bluffing all along. His weapons of mass destruction amounted to no more than a pile of rusty old chemical canisters that were well past their sell-by date. The inspectors had said as much.

Today, Mohamed's benign, rose-tinted childhood image of Islam was a very distant memory. The mosque he attended now was one his father would have baulked at. Segments within the mosque in Stepney harboured the view that Islam was in fact far more than just a religion, and many of its young members subscribed to this line of thinking. Here one could readily read the works of radical Islamists; men like Abul Ala Mawdudi, the founder of Jamat-e-Islami; the very same man who penned the following words: 'Islam is a revolutionary doctrine and system that overthrows government. It seeks to overturn the whole universal social order.'

Mohamed had become a key activist at the mosque, taking part in what was known as *Da'wah*, the Arabic word for *invitation*. It was in effect a call to Islam; a conversion programme aimed at winning over moderate Muslims. And over time, he had become friendly with a wide circle of young Muslims and his views had become increasingly extreme as a result.

One of his closest friends was George Caxton, a white Muslim convert who now went by the name Qssim El-Ghzzawy. His passion for Islam had been infectious. And his knowledge and eloquence made him a very popular public speaker. Years earlier he'd spoken out vociferously on the subject of the Balkan conflict. 'O *ummah* of Islam. Your sisters and mothers are being raped in Bosnia,' he had declared at a meeting in Tower Hamlets. 'And all you do is pray. You have a duty to protect your brothers in Bosnia. Together we must do everything we can to overthrow the existing political order in Muslim countries in order to establish an Islamic state. With a caliph in place, God willing, an Islamic army will assist our brothers and slaughter the Serbs. For we know only too well why the international community sits on its hands and refuses to arm our Muslim brothers... There is a conspiracy among the unbelievers; the Zionists and Christians to reduce the number of Muslims in Europe.' The atmosphere had been palpable, and Qssim's words had caught the imagination of his audience as effectively as a single match igniting a mound of dust-dry kindling.

Talk of jihad (holy war) and Khilafah (the worldwide leadership of Muslims) was now on the lips of many hot-headed young Muslims. This said, in-fighting and factionalism between the myriad of Islamist groups, which all held conflicting views in terms of theology and politics, was pretty bewildering.

But all this talk was beginning to sicken Qssim. Action spoke louder than words. And, he, Qssim El-Ghzzawy, was going to show his allegiance to Allah and his contempt for the stinking kafirs - the unbelievers of this world who had conspired against Muslims. 'Fight in the cause of God those who fight you, but do not transgress limits, for God loves not transgressors. And slay them wherever ye catch them, and turn them out from where they have turned you out; for tumult and oppression are worse than slaughter.' Were these not the divine words of the Quran?

He had returned home to the 70s tower block in the less than salubrious urban sprawl that was Ilford and took the lift up to his one-bedroom flat on the 5th floor. Here he removed a bottle of Stella Artois from the enormous American style fridge and took it out to the small terrace that faced northeast towards Mecca and sat at the grubby plastic garden table on the grey balcony. He may have fallen in love with Islam and the struggles of its people, but he hadn't embraced its religious strictures quite so rigidly. He wasn't going to banish alcohol from his life, and neither would he cease eating ham. Beneath the table was a leather case. He unclasped the fixtures and raised the lid slowly. The sleek lines of the sniper rifle lying neatly in its constituent parts never failed to move him. It made his heart race that little bit faster and caused a cold sweat to break out on the back of his neck. It was a thing of sheer beauty. Engineered by a master gunsmith from an off-the-shelf sporting rifle, it had been chambered for a .22 Magnum and had been fitted with a suppressor telescopic sight. He lifted it out from the dark cobalt sea of velvet and felt the precision of its cold steel barrel slide through his rough fingers. The telescopic eyepiece slotted into place with a reassuring click and he brought his right eye up to the glass lens. It was heavy, but not too heavy.

The church was no more than 500 yards away, on the opposite side of the busy A12. It wasn't an especially attractive red-brick pile and had probably been built in the

20s, but it was certainly large. Qssim trained the gun on a large modernist sculpture of Christ on the cross and lined up the crosshairs with the forehead and the bloody crown of thorns. Then he slowly brought it down past the attempt at mildly decorative Art Deco reliefs and stopped at the enormous arch housing two solid oak doors that remained decidedly closed.

Before long, one of the double doors opened and the congregants began to spill out. Qssim found the head of a portly balding man in a checked shirt and gently squeezed the trigger. The gun clicked harmlessly. Had it been loaded, that fat Kafir would now be dead meat splayed on the pavement. Within minutes he'd calmly pulled the trigger on no fewer than 25 unbelievers. This felt good. The anger that had been coursing through his veins had found an outlet, and he was feeling relaxed and sublime. He put the gun down and prised open the bottle with the edge of the table, and took a large swig.

✦

The whole Islam thing had originally appealed to him when he'd been serving time at Aylesbury's Young Offender Institution. He'd been banged up for almost two years of a four-year conviction for murdering his father. Not a long sentence for murder you might think until you consider the mitigating circumstances. George, as he was known before his stint behind bars, and his younger brother had from a young age been subjected to the most appalling sexual and psychological abuse at the hands of their father. The abuse continued until George's mother filed for divorce when her eldest son was just 13. And the boy's interest in guns had begun when he turned 18, and thoughts of retribution kept him up at night. Then, by chance, a friend had excitedly shown him an old Russian army issue Nagant MI 895 revolver and three bullets intact in their gleaming brass housings. He'd managed to steal them from his grandfather's safe. And George had persuaded his friend to let him have the gun for the princely sum of £50.

Tracking down his father hadn't been particularly difficult. He'd gone through the local phone directories and found that there was only one V. B. Caxton listed in the local area. He'd borrowed his mum's car on the pretext of going for a job interview and instead had driven over to Otley Way, a nondescript terrace of Edwardian red brick houses that had seen better days. Most no longer sported the original sash windows and leaded glass front doors. In their place were those ubiquitous double-glazed frames of the greying white plastic variety, and grubby net curtains. He'd found a space on the opposite side of the road and slipped on a pair of sunglasses. He felt like a complete prick. But it had to be done. It took forever for that front door to open, but open it did, and that fat bastard eventually stepped out into daylight. He hadn't changed, of course. Still had that ruddy red complexion, greased back thinning grey hair and pointed chin. George had seen enough, and turned the key in the ignition.

It was a whole week before he'd drum up enough courage to go back with the loaded gun. It was early evening. This time there were no parking spaces nearby so he'd parked further down the road and walked back to the house.

A young woman answered the door, and he'd asked if Vic was at home. He was apparently having a bath. 'That's ok,' he had said. 'I'll wait.' The girl had shown him into the communal lounge, smiled nervously and had then disappeared. He wasted little time, bounded up the stairs and could now hear the sound of running water. The adrenalin was pumping through his body. He was incredibly angry. He just wanted to get the job done. The bathroom door was half glazed with frosted glass. He tried opening it but knew instinctively that it would be locked. His father always locked the bathroom door. So instead he threw all his weight shoulder-first into the ageing woodwork, and the door surrendered feebly with the sound of splintering.

'What the fuck...' The pink figure of his father was discernible through the steam.

'Hi dad. Just thought it was time to pay you a visit.' And with these words he'd pulled out the gun, pointed it directly at his father and pulled the trigger. There was nothing more than a sickening click. And in an instant, that large pink frame had sprung from the water like an enormous whale. Before George knew it he could feel his father's filthy hands around his neck and the cold tiles of the wall pressing hard against his back. His strength began to sap, but before it did he summoned up all the energy he could muster and focussed on the trigger.

The crack of the gun was impressive in a confined space and its immediate effect was that the hands around his neck loosened like a taut tourniquet being cut. He could breathe again. And then he had fired the gun twice more for good measure and could feel the dead man's warm blood pouring forth as profusely as the hot water tap, which was still flowing.

He hadn't given any thought to the consequences of his actions. He didn't really care. Justice, as far as he was concerned, had now been done. He had eliminated his past; his demons could take a running jump; he could move on.

✦

His barrister had been a pretty cool black guy. 'The name's Charles but you can call me Charlie,' he'd said on their first meeting while shaking George's hand enthusiastically. Charlie turned out to be as charming and persuasive in the courtroom as he was in real life. He had argued convincingly that years of sexual abuse had been the sole motif and an overwhelming provocation behind George's act of violence on that fateful night. George's mother had broken down in tears and admitted that she had suspected her husband's vile crime, but had done nothing until she finally filed for divorce. Friends had corroborated George's experience at the hands of his father, and even one of his teachers had attested to his good character. The judge had taken it all on board, and despite the guilty plea, had passed a sentence of just four years of which he would only serve two.

The Aylesbury Young Offender Institution was a foreboding kind of place with its oppressive Victorian architecture; cold metal steps, rails and walkways; and its endless cavernous echoes of metal on metal. Some of the inmates were loners and didn't seem to speak to anyone if they could help it. George could easily have become like one of them had it not been for Ibrahim. Ibrahim was different to most of the others. He was relatively small and slight with wire spectacles and an infectious grin. George had met him in the library where Ibrahim had secured a place as one of the institution's librarians. Over a period of many weeks, George had struck up a friendship with Ibrahim who in turn had introduced him to his circle of mates or *brothers* as Ibrahim liked to call them. They were all Muslims, and were a tight-knit community, always looking out for each other and ready to come to the assistance of any of the brothers should the need arise. And there were times in this place where you really did need that kind of support. More importantly, it was a good thing to be seen to be part of such a loyal clan. It minimised the risk of anyone else picking on you in the first place.

Before long, George found himself becoming more and more interested in Islam as a result of hanging out with the brothers. He began to read books in the library. He learnt about Salah, the five daily prayer rituals and began to read the Quran. And then one afternoon he had greeted Ibrahim in the library and asked nervously if he could become a Muslim. Ibrahim smiled broadly and embraced his friend. 'Of course you can my friend. If you are sure and have the conviction to serve Allah, then it is the simplest thing in the world.'

George nodded eagerly. 'I am sure Ibrahim. I want it more than anything in the world.' His friend smiled once more and led George to a quiet corner of the library and removed a copy of the Quran from one of the shelves.

'Now my friend, to become a Muslim you have to recite what we call the Testimony of Faith in Arabic. The words simply mean *There is no true God but Allah, and Muhammad is the Messenger of God.* So if you are sure you want to do this my friend, simply place your right hand on the Quran and simply recite the following words after me: La ilaha illa Allah...'

George placed his hand on the holy book. 'La ilaha illa Allah...'

'Good. And now: Muhammad rasoolu Allah.'

George looked into the dark brown eyes of his friend. 'Muhammad rasoolu Allah.'

With these words, Ibrahim hugged his friend. 'Jazak Allah Khairan… May Allah reward you with blessings, brother.'

From this moment onwards, George found himself embracing Allah wholeheartedly and taking part in prayers with the brothers. He had become a fully-fledged member of the brotherhood, and that's when he changed his name.

◆

Following his release from the Young Offender Institution, George, now Qssim, began to regularly visit a mosque in Stepney, East London where he came into contact with individuals who passionately believed it to be the duty of all good Muslims to speak out on behalf of their oppressed brothers around the world and take part in jihad - a holy war against the Western oppressors. The greatest vitriol being reserved for the Americans and Israelis who had, according to the most radical among them, conspired to destroy Islam. He began to visit fringe groups and listen to the impassioned words of radical imams who praised the martyrs who had flown passenger airlines into New York's iconic twin towers. Men with their bushy grey beards and long flowing robes who now called for the establishment of an Islamic state to strike out at unbelievers everywhere. And he spent much time watching videos online of the suffering of Palestinian children in Gaza. The more he watched and listened, the more incensed he became, and the more his feeling of hatred that he had harboured for his father, came to the surface and reared its ugly head.

By the time he met Mohamed, Qssim was a passionate young man with a cause in his heart and a fire in his belly. To non-believers he was something entirely different; he was a seething, radical Islamist.

CHAPTER THREE

'Hi dad. How's it going?'

Natasha put down her mug of coffee and dived into the sitting room by the French doors - the only place in the whole house where you could receive decent reception on the mobile. 'Great to hear your voice... I was going to come over later. Is there anything I can bring?'

'Look Tash. I think the buggers are going to discharge me tomorrow. I'm going to have some kind of care package for six weeks. A District Nurse will come and visit us every day. It's going to be bloody hard. And I'm sorry I haven't given you more notice. I've only just found out myself.'

Natasha pulled the phone away from her ear and wiped away the tears that were streaming down the side of her cheek. She just couldn't believe what was happening to her father. He'd always been there for her. He'd been to all her school productions and open days. He'd taken days off to take her around all those universities including Edinburgh. He'd even driven over to Durham when she'd split up with her first boyfriend and took her for a lovely lunch to keep her pecker up. He was the best frigging dad in the world, and he didn't deserve all this shit.

'You still there gherkin?'

'Sorry dad. Just putting my coffee down,' she lied. 'Don't worry. Everything's going to be fine. I've got your bedroom set up downstairs. You're going to be much better off at home and out of that hospital environment.'

Within days Natasha had found a team of Filipino

carers, and Annie, the youngest of them had been Natasha's first preference. There was something about the girl that Natasha instinctively liked. You just knew that she'd be perfect, and her English was outstanding, which couldn't be said for the other candidates.

That morning had seen more deliveries to the house in a short space of time than Natasha had ever known. First there had been the *NHS* profiling bed delivered by two burly men in a huge lorry. 'You've got the latest model luv,' explained the larger of the two as he bent down with the heavy end of the bed, revealing a large swathe of builder's cleavage in the process. 'Our previous beds used to be powered by Chinese motors that were crap. Used to bloody break down all the flippin' time. But you shouldn't have a problem with this one.' He'd pulled up his jeans and got Natasha to sign the paperwork.

Minutes later, another man appeared at the front door. 'Hello dear. I have a standing frame from Mediquip for a Mr Michael Hollinghurst.'

'Fantastic. That's my father. He'll be home later today. I'll keep the door on the latch for you.' As the bed guys drove off, the new delivery man who was considerably older and smaller struggled with a very large unwieldy arrangement of ugly looking blue metal bars and levers with black padded cushions placed at strategic places to house ankles and hips. Thankfully, the large contraption was on casters, and could be wheeled into position. The man had explained how the straps for the hoist mechanism had to be attached and how to operate it. Then he went back to his van to collect the battery, which was as large and as heavy as a brick. 'I think your father has hit the jackpot,' he joked as he realised that there were several other items in his van that had to be dropped off here. First among these was a large commode on wheels followed by two adjustable hospital bed tables and a special sliding board designed to help her father transfer from his wheelchair to the bed or another chair. 'There you go, my luv,' he'd said as he produced the paperwork for Natasha to sign. 'There's about seven grand's worth of equipment there. Hope it all helps.'

'Let's hope so,' she replied and signed the pink sheet of A4.

She'd barely had time to boil the kettle and make a coffee before the doorbell rang again. This time a young lad in a grey hoodie carrying a toolbox stood on the doorstep. 'Hi there. I'm here to install an entry phone for Michael Hollinghurst.' The inflexion in his voice went up an octave on the last syllable of the sentence, as it does so often with the younger generation. Natasha found the trait mildly irritating; almost as annoying as beginning a sentence with the word *so*.

With much hammering and drilling, the young man went about his business and Natasha logged onto her laptop.

✦

By the time hospital transport had been free to take Michael home, it was 4.00 in the afternoon. The *NHS* had many virtues, but despite the perennial pledges of government support, it was clearly overworked and under-resourced.

It hadn't been a particularly good start to the day for Michael. After breakfast Camilla, the attractive young doctor with the horn-rimmed glasses had pulled the curtain around his bed. 'Good morning Mr Hollinghurst. I'm afraid I've come to deliver some very sad news.' She paused and focussed on the innocuous grey buildings through the window behind Michael's head. 'Mr

Partridge... John Partridge, the patient in the next bed to you in *Elm Ward*... Well, I'm sorry to say that he passed away earlier this morning.' She tentatively handed him a paperback. 'He asked me to give you this.' Michael took the book. The cover carried a photographic portrait of a young man in an *RAF* cap and the large type read *First Light*. The author was Geoffrey Wellum. Michael opened the first page and there in spidery writing, John had managed to write a short inscription.

> *Dear Michael,*
> *It was good to meet you, albeit briefly.*
> *Do take care of yourself.*
> *And have a read of this. It's a magnificent tribute to*
> *all those young men who gave their lives to*
> *preserve this great country of ours. It's also a*
> *rollicking good read.*
> *With warmest regards,*
> *John*

Michael closed the book and put it down. 'Do you know when he wrote this inscription?' he asked.

'Yes,' she replied. 'Extraordinary though it may seem, he wrote it no more than an hour before he died... He was such a lovely man... We are all going to miss him terribly.' She removed her glasses and wiped her eyes. 'I'm sorry Mr Hollinghurst... You'd think we doctors would get used to all this by now, wouldn't you? But we never do you know.' She apologised again and left.

His feelings of sadness for John and his family (assuming he had a family) were soon all too speedily overtaken by a vague sense that he needed to empty his bowels. Vague, because like anyone with this kind of spinal injury, it was always a bit difficult to know precisely when to head for the little boy's room. So he pressed his call button and a nurse materialised within a few minutes. Unfortunately, it took an entire hour for the same nurse to answer his call button the second time round to wheel him out of the toilet and back into his ward. To make matters even worse, Mr Hudson, the consultant was waiting with a couple of nurses by his bed.

'Ah, Mr Hollinghurst. Sorry to appear without warning as it were, would it be ok to have a quick word?' Michael nodded. He was still furious about having been left in the toilet for an hour. But he knew it would be pointless to complain to a consultant. He'd have to complete an official complaint form.

'Now, I know you've elected to have no further surgery and that's absolutely fine, but we are concerned about the spasticity in your legs, which we have been monitoring very closely. To be brutally honest Mr Hollinghurst, the spasms appear to be getting worse and are now really quite severe. And any kind of upset like a urinary infection is going to make them worse still. Baclofen, the medication you are on to control these spasms, is having a very limited effect chiefly because a tablet can't target the area of the spinal cord as precisely as we'd like. It's like using a blunderbuss to hit the bull's eye, and much of the drug will be dispersed to other areas of the body that don't need it. But the good news is that there is an alternative to the tablet. However, it does require a small operation…' Mr Hudson thrust both his hands deep into his trouser pockets and looked Michael squarely in the eye. 'Look, I know you want to avoid surgery at all costs. And that is your decision. But in this instance, surgery is relatively minimal. And there are no significant risks associated with this kind of surgery. Shall I continue?' Michael nodded. 'Good. Well, you see thanks to the latest advances in medical technology there is now such a thing as a Baclofen pump.' At this point, Mr Hudson produced a silver disk around three inches in diameter and no more than an inch thick, attached to a fine white wire and held it in the palm of his hand. 'Essentially, this is an ingenious mini computerised pump attached to the finest flexible catheter that can be surgically fed into the spinal cord to deliver a very precise dosage of Baclofen directly to the cord. We know from case studies both here in the UK and the States that those with Baclofen pumps fitted experience reduced spasticity and spasms in the legs as a result.' As Mr Hudson uttered the word *spasms* Michael's legs started shaking quite violently and one of the nurses gripped them tightly just above the knees until they eventually calmed down. 'And the other good thing about having a pump fitted is the fact that you'll receive a far smaller dose of Baclofen because it's being delivered directly to the area that needs it. So there's no excess Baclofen travelling around the rest of your body, and no chance of unwelcome side-effects.'

'If I were to decide to go ahead and have the operations, when could I have it and how long would it take to recover?' Michael asked.

'You're probably looking at between three and four months from now. As for recovery time? You should allow at least six weeks for full recovery. The pump can be positioned in the right or left side of your lower abdomen. Entirely up to you.' Mr Hudson removed his glasses and rubbed his right eye. 'I have no doubt that the benefit will be significant. Something for you to think about. But the first thing is to get you home and settled into a routine. I think hospital transport is being arranged, so you'll hopefully be seeing the back of us pretty soon. And if you would like to go ahead with the procedure, you can call my secretary, and we'll put you on the system.'

✦

It took three hours for hospital transport to eventually materialise. While waiting in reception, he'd picked up a copy of *The Evening Standard*. Inside was a big feature about the 7/7 bombers. According to the Standard, all four men had been 'ordinary' young lads growing up in Britain. Mohammad Sidique Tanweer, the eldest at 30, had a genial and placid looking demeanour. As a married man with one child, he'd worked as a primary school teacher and had been raised in Leeds. He was the youngest of four children born to Pakistani immigrants who had taken Pakistani citizenship. Shehzad Khan from Bradford was just 22, had been a sports science graduate and though very religious, seemed to get on with everyone. 19-year-old John Lindsay was a Jamaican-born British resident who had converted to Islam in 2000 and taken the name Jamal. In 2002 he'd married a white convert with whom he'd had a son. A daughter was born after his death. Hasib Mir Hussain at just 18 was the youngest of the four. A quiet student with few friends, he'd been living at home with his parents on the outskirts of Leeds. A second generation British subject, with parents of Pakistani origin, he'd been the youngest of four children.

Michael just didn't get it. Poor John had said it boiled down to ideology. But how could ideology convince anyone that it was perfectly acceptable to arbitrarily kill and maim ordinary, law-abiding men, women and children - and totally shatter the lives of every family member, friend and loved one associated with each victim? How the hell could someone who was a fucking teacher for pity's sake justify killing anyone let alone kids - kids who might very well have been in his own fucking classroom? He was angry that they had brutally killed innocent bystanders. And angry that they had had the audacity to kill themselves. Had they still been alive he'd at least have had the pleasure (if pleasure was the right word) of venting his anger at a bunch of loathsome, deluded scumbags. But those bastards had even deprived him of that.

✦

Mohamed sat motionless staring at his computer screen. The sender's name Alan Anonymous had caught his eye. The address read Anonymous@googlemail.com. The subject line had been innocuous enough. It read simply: *Please open,* and for some unfathomable reason, he had followed this strangely simple request rather than binning it. And now he found himself reading the message a second time while sensing goosebumps on his upper arms.

> *Dear Brother,*
> *We are impressed by your diligence and quiet*
> *demeanour and would be honoured to have you*
> *among our most trusted servants of Allah. We shall*
> *not be known to each other in person, but together*
> *we will (God willing) be able to carry out jihad and*
> *strike at the infidel where he least* expects *it.*
> *You will not communicate via this channel. For the*

*Kafir will try and trap us. But he will not succeed.
You will delete this email upon receipt and look in
the personal lonely heart ads in The Ham and High
next week. Rest assured that your IP has been
added to our access list.
Allahu Akbar*

Who was speaking so directly to him, and how had they managed to find him in cyberspace? He was, he realised, well enough known in the community, and his email address would have been known to several members of his mosque. Tracking him down like this wouldn't have been so impossible. In fact, the more he thought about it, the more he understood how easy it would have been. Anyone savvy enough could have found him through social media. Mohamed deleted the message as requested. Part of him was feeling flattered and excited, but the cynical side of him wondered if this could really be genuine. He'd read about so-called *honey-traps* in the US where American vigilantes had set themselves the task of posing as jihadists online, with the intention of duping genuine believers and handing them over to the authorities. But his gut feeling was that this was the real deal. And anyway, to get anywhere in this world, you had to take risks. It was a simple rule that applied to all walks of life - whether it was building a multinational business or spreading the word of Allah. For now, however, he would tread cautiously. He'd never heard of a publication called the *Ham and High* and was a little perplexed by the title. Not realising that the word *Ham* was a simple abbreviation for Hampstead, he'd wondered why any kind of publication should want to use the term given to a form of processed pig meat in its title. What was it with the British and their pigs - this cloven-footed beast with filthy habits that Islam had banished from the dinner table?

✦

The first thing that Michael now noticed about his new life was his lack of height. Before he was confined to a wheelchair, he'd seen the world from a rather different vantage point: around 5 foot 9 inches from the ground. Now he was the height of the average small child, and everyone other than children looked down at him. He didn't like it.

Aleksy the ambulance driver was a large, jovial Polish man who'd swapped Warsaw for London seven years ago. Now he was married to a teacher and lived in Kilburn. His English was impeccable. 'So you are going home for the first time since the explosion, Mr Hollinghurst.'

'Yes, Aleksy. I am indeed. Feels very strange.' Michael looked out of the window as the small ambulance turned up Hoop Lane past the large Jewish cemetery on the left and the imposing architecture of the nondenominational Golders Green Crematorium on the right: the avenue of dead souls. How easily he might have ended up here. The thought cheered him up. He was bloody lucky to still be alive.

The street hadn't changed. The same white stucco facades with their chirpy front doors and neatly trimmed privet hedges greeted them as Aleksy turned into Cedars Way. Luckily he was able to park outside with enough room to release the ramp and wheel Michael out. Natasha came to the front door beaming. 'Dad. Welcome home. It's been like a Marx Brothers film this morning; you know, the one when umpteen tradespeople are crammed into one small cabin.'

'*A Night at the Opera*, if I'm not mistaken, gherkin.'

'That's the one. I think we watched it together when I was no taller than you are now.'

He forced a laugh as Natasha stooped to embrace him as best she could. That was another thing that was to prove difficult - cuddles.

Aleksy carefully pushed the wheelchair over the small step and over the threshold into a large hall with cool terracotta floor tiles.

'Probably a good idea to get yourself a small fold-up ramp for that step, Mr Hollinghurst. You can find them secondhand on eBay. Much cheaper that way.'

'Good point Aleksy. We can add that to our shopping list, Natasha.'

She laughed. 'It's turning into quite some list.'

Michael wheeled himself into what used to be his study. Now it had been turned into his bedroom thanks to Natasha and several trips down to Ikea where she had purchased a number of flat pack wardrobes and drawers. The clean white units now stood neatly along the wall that his desk and shelves once occupied. And his newly delivered hospital profiling bed had replaced the leather sofa and the overgrown cactus.

'Where would you like me to put these, Mr Hollinghurst?' Aleksy stood in the doorway with two large suitcases.

'Oh, they can go here on my bed for the time being, Aleksy… And thank you for your help. I really appreciate it.'

Aleksy smiled an endearing toothy grin. 'That's alright Mr Hollinghurst. My pleasure.' Michael pulled a few notes out of his wallet and thrust them surreptitiously into Aleksy's palm. 'Here's a little something…'

'Oh no Mr Hollinghurst. Please. This is not necessary.'

'No, please… Take that wife of yours for a nice romantic meal.'

'It's very generous Mr Hollinghurst, but I can't accept this.' Aleksy placed the banknotes on the bedside table. 'It was lovely to meet you and your daughter, Mr Hollinghurst. I wish you all the very best for the future. Perhaps we'll meet again. I do hope so.' And with those words, the large man in his deep green uniform left the room, and Natasha showed him to the front door.

'He's a very decent sort you know? Not many would have turned down fifty quid. Protested, yes. But refused, I don't think so.'

Natasha smiled. 'Now, I hope you're hungry because I've just put two fish pies in the oven.'

'Absolutely famished, and it will make a nice change to have some decent home-made fare for once.' Natasha pushed her father into the kitchen diner and parked him at the large oak table where a place had already been laid for him. 'Thanks for arranging everything gherkin. I can't tell you how much I appreciate it.'

Natasha was peering into the oven and prodding the fish pies with a long fork. 'Don't be silly dad. It was nothing. All I had to do was put together a few sticks of furniture and make a few phone calls... Talking of which, after lunch I've asked Annie to pop over to introduce herself. I think you'll like her. She's very sweet and seems very sensible.' She uncorked a bottle of Rioja and poured two large glasses and offered one to her father.

'Thanks Tash. Haven't had one of these for months. But I'd better only have a half glass. I'm not really meant to have any with my medication. But sod that for a game of soldiers.' He raised the glass. 'Bottoms up!'

As she had imagined, the meeting with Annie went well. Michael seemed to get on with the young girl who clearly possessed a very wise head on such young shoulders. In fact, the idea of the dog had been hers. 'You should get yourself a friendly dog, Mr Hollinhurst,' she had said while sipping her tea. 'They can be trained, you know, to do all kinds of useful chores. And it might be good company for you.' Natasha had laughed, but Michael who had never been a great one for animals, suddenly quite liked the idea of a friendly dog loading the washing machine and nuzzling up against him when he felt low. It's funny how a dramatic change in circumstances can completely change your way of thinking. While able-bodied, the thought of going sailing or flying in a glider would have held little if any appeal to him. But now, as a wheelchair user, he found the prospect of taking part in such activities with specialist disabled charities, strangely liberating. And it wouldn't be long before he'd find himself signing up to go flying in a single-propellered Cherokee, and searching for a specially trained Labrador.

✦

Mohammed had asked the young girl at the till if they had a copy of the *Ham & High*. She turned to her colleague on the next till. 'Bob, do we stock the *Ham & High*?' Bob was giving another customer his change.

'Nah. This is Hornsey mate. Not Hampstead and Highgate. We're not posh enough here to sell the *Hampstead & Highgate Express* - more's the pity. We can offer you the *Hornsey Echo* though.'

Mohammed smiled. 'No thank you. I need the *Ham & High*.' So that was what was meant by *Ham* and *High*. It had nothing to do with pigs after all.

By the time he reached Hampstead, it had started to rain. The tobacconist sold cheap umbrellas, so he grabbed one on entering and then perused the plethora of mastheads on display; everything from serious politics and investment periodicals to car mags and lads' mags featuring buxom nubiles in over-revealing bikinis. The *Ham and High* was on the bottom shelf next to the *Jewish Chronicle*. He paid and let himself back out into the rain.

He didn't have to go terribly far to find somewhere suitable to take the weight off his feet. Suitable meaning independent. He couldn't abide those ubiquitous American owned coffee shops that turned over billions of dollars and stood for everything he detested about the West and its mindless decadence. This place had the air of a continental bistro about it with its wicker chairs that had seen better days and large politically-incorrect posters for *Gauloises* cigarettes.

'Can I help you sir?' The young man was carrying a tray and had a neatly folded tea towel over his shoulder.

'I'll have an Espresso please.' The young man bowed slightly and then made his way back to the bar.

The personal ads ran to two pages and were located after the classified ads right at the back end of the paper. All of them were written in some kind of code and were peppered with acronyms that meant absolutely nothing to Mohammed. GSOH, LDR, SBM, NS, SI, VGL, WLTM, and WTR seemed to crop up regularly. Interestingly, there was only one ad that didn't have a single acronym buried in the text. But in many ways it was also written entirely in code. A code Mohammed was able to decipher without even thinking.

> *Attractive and wise, I am in search of a God-fearing man with whom I can create a truly beautiful future. You will understand that this special relationship will require certain sacrifices. Material wealth is not what I am looking for. Our real rewards will be in heaven. Box 5678*

CHAPTER FOUR

The boy had always responded well to music, and had a gift for playing the piano by ear, even though he'd never received a formal lesson in his life. And there could be no doubt that it had a calming influence on him. The only other distraction that could hold his interest for hours on end was his PC. He'd happily spend days holed up in his bedroom trawling the net, creating his own computer games and hacking into accounts he shouldn't have been. But when it came to conversing with his family and those around him, life presented an insurmountable challenge.

In many ways, Alan Jenkins was a 15-year-old genius, but he was also severely autistic. It was a heavy price to pay, both for himself and his family. He had to go to a special school and would suffer terrible tantrums when feeling threatened by strangers or unfamiliar surroundings.

His parents, Brian and Hazel had done everything in their power to help their son. They had employed special private tutors, bought him a labrador puppy and taken him to Disneyworld in Florida. But nothing worked as well as J S Bach's *Goldberg Variations*. This discovery had been made by chance years ago when their friends Michael and Louise who lived across the road had come round for dinner.

Alan had worked himself into a frenzy over some seemingly innocuous detail that may have had something to do with the presence of additional members around the dinner table. While the boy's tantrum became increasingly vociferous, Hazel attempted to console her inconsolable son by hugging him. But the din from the child put everyone on tenterhooks, and Michael found himself excusing himself from the table and seating himself at the family's upright *Bechstein*. It was a lovely old piano that Hazel had inherited from her mother. He had opened the lid and began playing the Bach *Goldberg Variation* number one from memory. No sooner than he did so, Alan's tantrum dissipated into thin air, and in no time at all the boy had clambered off his mother's knee and sat next to Michael on the piano stool while intently watching Michael's fingers glide effortlessly across the black and white keys in some kind of elaborate dance.

From that moment onwards, J S Bach and Michael had become a big part of Alan's life. Within weeks, the boy had learnt to play by ear and replicate large parts of Bach's *Goldberg Variations*. And every time he became agitated, either Brian or Hazel would slip Glenn Gould into the compact disc player, and peace and tranquillity would descend as if by magic.

It was around the same time that the boy began to take an unhealthy interest in computers. Unlike other kids, he wasn't just content in playing games, he wanted to create his own, and use the computer as a powerful tool. On his 14th birthday he'd managed to hack into his own father's bank account and transfer £25 to the *National Autistic Society*; a fact that both alarmed and amused his father in equal measure.

And now some three years later, following Michael's return from hospital, Brian was sheepishly knocking on Michael's door with his son in tow. Michael pressed the entry buzzer and Brian pushed the front door firmly to enter.

'Sorry to disturb Michael, but Alan would like to make an apology, wouldn't you Alan?'

Alan looked at his shoes and handed Michael a sheet of A4 paper. 'Sorry Michael.'

Michael took the piece of paper and scanned down it. It was a long list of email addresses that looked very familiar.

'I'm afraid our boy has been up to no good, Michael. He's only gone and hacked into your email account... I found this list of addresses on our printer... No idea how he does it... Anyhow, he didn't mean any harm by it.'

Michael reckoned there were over 100 addresses on the page. 'Oh, I say. You have been busy, Alan. That's pretty bloody impressive.'

'Apologies, Michael. You can rest assured that Alan has wiped everything off his computer. You're no longer being spied on,' Brian laughed embarrassingly.

'I should hope not, young man. I daresay *GCHQ c*ould do with your services.'

'I won't do it again, Michael. I promise,' muttered Alan without looking up.

'Tell you what Alan, if you promise never to do that again, I'll promise to give you piano lessons. What do you say, eh? Need something to occupy my time now that I'm a man of leisure so to speak.'

Alan finally looked up and smiled a big, toothy, heartwarming grin. 'Wicked!'

'Look Michael it really isn't necessary. We should be teaching him some kind of lesson for this - and I don't mean piano lessons... And anyway you've got more than enough on your plate right now.' Brian was going to say something else, but Michael's right leg began to shake quite violently.

'Damn. These legs have a bloody mind of their own I'm afraid.' Michael clasped his right knee firmly with his right hand and pressed down very hard as if strangling a large snake, and the spasms eventually died down. 'Doctors reckon I'm going to have to have another operation to have some kind of computerised pump inserted into my stomach that feeds the anti-spasm drug directly into my spinal cord.'

'I'm sorry mate. You've already been through the mill. I guess the last thing you want now is another operation.'

'Too bloody right. But the thing is Brian, if I don't have it, these spasms are likely to get worse.'

Brian puffed out his cheeks, expelled air and gave his neighbour a look of sympathy. There was nothing he could say. 'Look, I'm going to have to dash Michael. I promised Hazel I'd make lunch.' With that, he grabbed his son's hand and let himself out through the front door.

✦

The decision to have the Baclofen pump fitted had been made by Michael months earlier. In the great scheme of things, it wasn't going to be a massive operation. Nowhere near as major as the other operation the consultants had considered and then dismissed as being too risky. The only irritating thing about this relatively minor procedure was that it had to be done in two stages. First of all, the very fine flexible catheter or tube that would administer the drug had to be precisely fed into the correct section of the spinal cord. This was a critical and skilful operation that could only be carried out by an experienced neurosurgeon. Once it had been completed, the follow-up procedure to attach the computerised pump would be carried out.

The letter from Stanmore hospital finally arrived on Michael's doormat a week later. Natasha had placed it on the breakfast table and Michael opened it nonchalantly as if opening a gas bill. 'Looks like D Day has arrived gherkin. I'm checking in on the 6th October - 3 weeks from today.'

Natasha had known from the envelope that it was from the hospital and had an inkling that it would be her father's date for the surgery. 'Ooh, that's good isn't it? The sooner you get it over with the better.' Secretly, she felt rotten for her father. She didn't want him to go through any more surgery. He'd been through his fair share of crap, and it just wasn't fair that he had to go through more. But she had to try and appear blasé about it all; brush it under the carpet; fight away the tears to make it easier for him to deal with. And by doing so, she'd be forcing herself to come to accept the simple fact that her father was going back to hospital.

Those three weeks passed swiftly enough. Michael hadn't returned to work since the atrocity even though his office had kept his job open. He worked as a solicitor for a medium-sized firm in Crouch End and Ken, the senior partner had been on the phone several times to see how he was getting on. They'd sent flowers, ready meals from some fancy company in Muswell Hill, and some of his colleagues had been to see him when he was in hospital. He'd been working there for the best part of 10 years and specialised in commercial dispute resolution - advising clients in the manufacturing, construction and technology sectors. He'd become a safe pair of hands, and knew his way round reasonably complex issues like shareholder disputes, commercial contract law, and professional negligence claims. He figured that he'd eventually become a partner if he played his cards right. After all, he was popular, diligent and had built up a solid and loyal roster of clients. But now his enthusiasm for work had waned, and his entire view of the world and the things he held dear had changed irrevocably. Fortunately, he had been financially prudent over the years and paid generous sums into several private pensions, which he had managed himself through an online portfolio. His slightly unconventional and cavalier approach to risk, which had led him to invest his entire portfolio in a handful of relatively volatile investment trusts investing in China, India and the Far East, had fared exceptionally well over the years, and would now provide him with an adequate income were he to retire tomorrow.

Be that as it may, his newfound freedom away from the office suited him. For once, he began to value his free time. He enjoyed spending time with his daughter and getting to know her better. He'd also found time for books. As a student, he'd studied English literature and had fallen in love with the war poets Wilfred Owen, Rupert Brooke and Siegfried Sassoon. Now for the first time in many years, he'd revisited those haunting yet strangely beautiful passages that had moved him enough to devote his final year's dissertation to them. But more significantly, and unbeknown to Natasha, he was now spending more and more time delving into the murky world of Islamic terrorism. He had started to collect press cuttings and read books on the subject. The more he learnt about the warped ideologies of Jihadists, the angrier he became. And the more the anger welled up inside him, the more he came to feel that he could no longer just sit still, and observe powerlessly from the sidelines.

♦

Mohammed stared at the white page for some considerable while. He knew that this was the ad he had to answer. The clues in the text were obvious. This special relationship will require certain sacrifices and Our real rewards will be in heaven said everything. But how was he to respond to Alan Anonymous at Box 5678? And then, it came to him. He would reply to this cryptic message that he perfectly understood with one that would undoubtedly resonate with the sender. It was a quotation from the lips of one of the greatest Roman philosophers and statesmen, Cicero. He began typing.

Dear Brother,

I have deleted your message as requested.

After all, a nation can survive its fools, and even the ambitious. But it cannot survive treason from within. An enemy at the gates is less formidable, for he is known and carries his banner openly. But the traitor moves amongst those within the gate freely, his sly whispers rustling through all the alleys, heard in the very halls of government itself.

For the traitor appears not a traitor; he speaks in accents familiar to his victims, and he wears their face and their arguments, he appeals to the baseness that lies deep in the hearts of all men. He rots the soul of a nation, he works secretly and unknown in the night to undermine the pillars of the city, he infects the body politic, so that it can no longer resist. A murderer is less to fear.

Marcus Tullius Cicero

> *I await your instructions in good faith.*
> *Allahu Akbar*

Something stopped him from sealing the envelope and posting it. Perhaps he shouldn't be responding at all. And if he were to, was this the best way to do so? He couldn't be sure. So he saved his message in draft form and logged off.

◆

The taxi arrived bang on time. Natasha had packed Michael's bag with Annie's assistance and was now helping her father negotiate the flimsy-looking fold-out ramp that some black cabs had fitted for wheelchair users. She pushed Michael into the cab and then somehow managed to squeeze past the protruding handles to get into the rear seat. It was incredibly tight.

Much of the journey was passed in silence. It was only 7 am and Natasha was never particularly chatty in the morning at the best of times. The taxi growled, bumped and stuttered its way through the grey light of London's North London suburban terraces.

By the time they pulled up in Queens Square, the light had improved and the streets had become more animated. The National Hospital for Neurology and Neurosurgery is home to the largest team of neurosurgeons and neurological specialists in the UK. Some of the finest brains dedicated to brains and the mysteries of the central nervous system. Like all other hospitals, Michael had known, this one sprawled across a hotchpotch of buildings, but unlike most, it did so in an orderly fashion around a neat if busy square. That other well-known cousin, Great Ormond Street for Children sat adjacent to

Michael's home for the next few days; which explained the regular stream of young mothers with children and buggies arriving in and departing from Queens Square.

At reception they were directed up to the Nuffield Ward on the fourth floor. This was a private ward - even though Michael wasn't using his private health insurance. Such was the need for beds that the hospital would often requisition rooms in Nuffield for certain procedures - Michael's being one of them.

An attractive nurse not much older than Natasha greeted them on their arrival and showed them to one of several standardised rooms. 'This is your room Mr Hollinghurst. It's number seven. My name is Alison and I'll be on duty here for the next few days. There's a drinks machine for tea and coffee outside, and I'll go and fetch you today's menu, as lunch will be served in an hour.' And with that, she was off. The room was bright and clean with a nondescript view over grey tenement buildings and the distant sprawl of slate roofs that punctuated the skyline with an assortment of chimneys, air ventilation outlets and television aerials set at jaunty angles. Like all hospital rooms, it could never look homely. The large hospital bed and endless medical contraptions with their wires and pipes and digital displays were a far cry from one's usual home comforts and hardly put you at ease. Neither did the bleeps and constant buzz emanating from them. But otherwise, it was a relatively quiet ward that would afford Michael his privacy, and for that, at least, he was grateful.

Natasha unpacked his bags and instinctively placed everything in their rightful places while Michael went in search of the coffee machine. By the time he returned, Natasha had made herself comfortable in an electric armchair by the window. 'Well, at least it's a decent room and you have your privacy dad.' Michael smiled and sipped his coffee.

'Thanks for unpacking Tash. I really appreciate it.'

'It's my pleasure dad. It was nothing.' She delved inside her bag and fished out her mobile and scoured the screen. 'I'll leave here at 12.00 if that's ok with you.' She replaced the mobile in her bag. 'I'm meeting Helen for lunch. You remember her don't you?'

Michael didn't have one of the best memories for names and struggled with this one. She could have been the quiet girl Natasha had known at university and had once stayed with them briefly. Or was it that other girl with freckles who had laughed at his terrible jokes at one of their summer barbecues? He smiled. 'Of course I remember. Nice girl, I seem to remember.'

'She says hi by the way.'

By the time Natasha took her leave, Michael was feeling distinctly tired. He pressed the call button and asked one of the nurses to help him onto the bed. Eventually, two nurses arrived with a mechanical hoist with which he was deftly raised from his wheelchair and gently deposited on the bed. He lay back on his pillow, closed his eyes, and tried in vain to banish the electronic bleeps from his senses.

CHAPTER FIVE

Alan had enjoyed the few piano lessons he'd had with Michael last month more than he'd expected. This was probably because Michael wasn't very strict with him. In fact, these lessons weren't really like lessons at all. They were certainly nothing like the lessons he had to do at school. These were much more relaxed. Michael would play a passage and all he had to do was copy it by ear. It was easy, and he was getting to play new stuff. Michael knew lots of pieces, and some of them made Alan feel really happy. One of his favourite ones was by the French composer Claude Debussy and was called Clair de Lune, which meant moonlight in French. He'd never heard it before, but now that he had, he couldn't get it out of his head; not that he minded. It was the kind of tune that put you in a good mood. And he wasn't always feeling in a good mood.

Then, of course, there had been their little secret. Michael had sworn him to secrecy, otherwise he wouldn't be able to continue the piano lessons. It was all a bit strange really. Why did Michael want him to do him this special favour? His father had told him numerous times that hacking accounts online wasn't a good thing to do. It was 'unethical'. That was the word that his dad kept using: 'unethical.' But Michael said that a little bit of hacking had never really done anyone any real harm, and that his dad had been overly concerned. And then he'd told Alan not to repeat these words to his dad or anyone else come to that.

Anyway, it wasn't much of a price to pay was it? All this secret mission required him to do was come up with a few more email addresses. Michael had given him an envelope and told him not to open it until he was in his bedroom alone with his door shut. Only then could he open the innocent-looking manila paper package, digest its contents and get to work.

If the truth be known, he'd felt a little let down when he finally did open the envelope. He'd been expecting Michael to want him to hack into something important and exciting like a police station or Downing Street, or possibly even the White House. Instead it had been the Whitechapel Shahjalal Mosque. He wasn't exactly sure what a mosque actually was, and how you pronounced it. Shahjalal certainly didn't sound very English did it? But it didn't take him long to work out that it was some kind of religious centre for those who followed the teachings of Islam - whoever he or she was. How incredibly boring. Still, it hadn't been difficult to get a few email addresses linked to this strange-looking building with its very peculiar green onion-shaped roof and slender towers.

It hadn't taken him very long. Nor had it proved particularly challenging. He had written all fifteen of the addresses in his best handwriting on a scrap of paper. The names had all been foreign-sounding and hard to say: Mohammed this and Abdul that. He'd folded the piece of paper and inserted it back inside the manila envelope and sealed it with sellotape. Then he'd placed it in his stationery drawer and forgot about it until his next lesson.

Alan's lessons always took place on Thursday evening after supper at exactly 8.00 pm. 'I know it sounds weird,' Hazel had said, 'but it's really important you turn up at exactly 8 o'clock. You see, Alan has a thing about time and numbers in general. If you are too early or too late, heaven forbid, he'll get very stressed. And we'll end up paying a heavy price for days on end. It's a common trait with autistic children. Their lives seem to be governed by numbers.' She'd given out a little laugh as a way of lightening the mood and saving any embarrassment. Michael had smiled sympathetically and assured her that he would synchronise his watch with Greenwich Mean Time and ring their doorbell at precisely 8.00 pm. And so it was that Alan's lessons had taken place every Thursday evening at 8.00 pm precisely. The first four lessons had gone really well, but it had been the fifth that had filled Michael with a sense of trepidation. It was during this lesson that he'd have to inform Alan of his impending surgery and the temporary suspension of his lessons until he'd made a full recovery. There was no telling how the boy might respond. A tantrum he could just about handle, but the thought of Alan blurting out in front of his parents that he'd been surreptitiously hacking into email accounts on Michael's behalf, was not one Michael particularly relished. Indeed, the thought of it made his legs go into spasms.

As it turned out, he needn't have worried. Having decided that it was probably best to explain the situation straight away, before taking his place next to the boy on the piano stool, he carefully and gently broke the news that lessons would have to be temporarily suspended. He then explained in perhaps more detail than was necessary, what the surgeons were going to do to him. Alan had taken it all in thoughtfully, and when Michael had finished, gave him one of his more quizzical expressions.

'So how big exactly is this computerised pump device?'

Michael made a round shape by joining together the thumb and forefinger of both hands. 'Ooh, about the size of a cricket ball I reckon, but reasonably flat, of course.' The answer seemed to satisfy Alan who reached deep into his trouser pocket and fished out a crumpled brown envelope.

'I have something for you,' he had exclaimed, and handed Michael the envelope. 'If I don't give it to you now I might forget.'

The news of Michael's impending hospital stay had, of course, been bitterly disappointing for Alan. He didn't like it when plans were disrupted like this. It made him feel insecure, knowing that the order, stability and predictability of his week had been altered, and worse still that it was completely out of his control. But disappointing though it certainly had been, it was made a tad more bearable by Michael's gratitude on receiving that innocent-looking manila envelope.

'I can't tell you how much I appreciate this Alan.' Then he had lowered his voice to a conspiratorial mumble. 'But you'll keep this between you and me won't you Alan?' He'd tapped his nose with his index finger. It wasn't a gesture Alan was familiar with, but he'd understood Michael perfectly well and nodded. Then he had looked at Michael directly and given him one of his inquisitive looks.

'Are you a religious follower of Islam then Mr Hollinghurst?'

Michael laughed. 'No… not exactly Alan. Well, in fact, not at all. I don't really believe in God or any religion. I'm what some people would call an atheist.'

Alan had looked confused.

'Look Alan, I know what you're thinking. Why have I asked you to hack into a mosque? And I can't give you an exact answer. All I can tell you Alan is that there are some people in this world who use religion as an excuse for doing inexcusable things. And I want to find these people Alan, before they hurt more innocent people.'

'Are these the same people who hurt you Mr Hollinghurst? Are they the reason you are in a wheelchair?'

The boy may have been autistic. But like so many autistic kids, he was nobody's fool.

'The people who hurt me are no longer with us, Alan... But there are others like them. And these are the people I need to find before they do more harm.' He had smiled at the boy warmly and then unclipped his briefcase and pulled out a couple of sheaves of musical manuscripts. 'Anyway... the thing is I've got a real treat in store for you this evening young man.' He had placed the manuscripts on the piano's music stand. 'Like Claude Debussy, today's composer is also French. His name is Erik Satie. In fact, he was friendly with Debussy.'

Alan giggled uncontrollably. 'Erik! That's a silly name.'

It hadn't occurred to Michael before, but Alan wasn't entirely wrong. Eric was one of those names that possessed a certain comedic quality. One inevitably thought of comedians like Eric Idle and Eric and Ernie. Perhaps the French version with a k had more gravitas. The footballer, Eric Cantona was French, after all. Ok, it was spelt with a C but Cantona wasn't deemed to be funny was he? But then on second thought, perhaps he was a bit of a clown. Michael had placed the score on the piano stand and began playing the deceptively simple yet hauntingly beautiful melody known as Gymnopédie No.1 that Satie had written at the tender age of just 21.

Alan had followed Michael's fingers over the keys, his chin cupped studiously in the palms of both hands.

It had been the perfect piece for Alan to grasp, and by the time the lesson had finished, the boy was playing it pretty perfectly by himself. He couldn't read a single note of music but somehow, he could replicate what he heard. It was an extraordinary gift that Michael had never witnessed until now. It was the kind of thing he'd read about in the Sunday supplements. But like all these things, it was always so much more impactful to experience something like this for yourself.

'My goodness. I thought that was you playing, Michael.' Hazel had stood in the doorway wearing an apron and clutching her Jamie Oliver cookbook. 'I love that piece. It's so evocative and mysterious. I can't believe you've learnt it so quickly, Alan.'

Alan had looked up from the piano and forced a grin. 'He's a smart boy, Helen. And this is a good piece for him to build his confidence. Not too many difficult chords.' Michael had reversed his wheelchair away from the piano to face Hazel.

'We can't thank you enough Michael. Alan loves your lessons.'

'It's my pleasure, Hazel.' Michael had said, thrusting his right hand into his jacket pocket and feeling the envelope nestling there. 'To be perfectly honest Hazel, I find these lessons very rewarding; very rewarding indeed.'

CHAPTER SIX

It was tea time by the time Michael came round. He was feeling exceptionally groggy and bleary-eyed when the young nurse arrived with the tea trolley.

'Can I tempt you with a nice cup of tea and a Jammy Dodger, Mr Hollinghurst?'

Michael forced a smile and muttered something unintelligible. The nurse opened the blinds onto the grey cloudless backdrop and soulless view of rooftops and ventilation ducts. His bed was gently raised by the whirring motor into the upright position and his bed table was wheeled across his bed, bringing the teacup and biscuits into view and within easy reach. The rest of the room was coming into focus. The paperback that he'd been given by the genial John, the headmaster who'd passed away all those weeks back, was sitting on his chest of drawers. He'd only just started it that morning and the makeshift bookmark protruding from its pages was the brown envelope that Alan had given him during his last piano lesson just days ago.

It had been a stupid idea writing that cryptic message and sending it to those strangers' email addresses. Even more childish had been his placing of the ad in the *Ham & High*. He had no bloody right to involve Alan. What the hell was he playing at? Nobody in their right mind was going to answer an ad like that in any event, even if they were a demented terrorist with a warped sense of right and wrong. They may have been scumbags but they certainly weren't stupid.

'Mr Hollinghurst. My name is Mr Underhay, your surgeon.' Michael's reveries were brought to an abrupt halt. The figure now standing before him was on the portly side, and his general demeanour wasn't what you'd immediately expect from an eminent surgeon. His shirt and buttons were straining to contain their owner, and Michael couldn't help noticing dark chest hairs breaking through the polyester-cotton like rampant weeds creeping through cracked concrete. 'Well, I'm pleased to say that your procedure went very smoothly this morning; very smoothly indeed. Both phases of your operation have been completed very satisfactorily. In other words, the very fine catheter, which will feed the pump has been positioned precisely where we want it, and the pump has been connected.' He tugged at the base of his shirt and scratched at the back of his balding pate while perusing the ceiling tiles and blowing out his cheeks and making little trumpet sounds. He was clearly one of life's great eccentrics, thought Michael, and took an immediate liking to this Mr Underhay. 'The pump has been inserted into the right side of your abdomen, so avoid lying on that side if you can. And I'm afraid it will feel sore for a few days once the anaesthetic has worn off. Having said all that, there really isn't much swelling - not much at all. So I think we can safely say that the chance of infection is minimal. Now I think the general consensus is that we'd like you to stay here for a couple of days, just to monitor you you understand, and make sure that the little clamps are working as they should. We don't want anything to dislodge. And of course, we'll also need to establish the precise dosage to administer to reduce the spasticity in your legs. But look on the bright side, eh. At least you're in a private wing with your own room; and tomorrow's Tuesday. If I'm not mistaken, bread and butter pudding with lashings of custard will be on the menu. My favourite. I'd certainly recommend it.' Without even waiting for Michael's response, Mr Underhay turned to open the door, and then hesitated momentarily in the doorway on noticing the paperback sitting on the chest of drawers. 'Ah, my word. I see you're reading First Light by Geoffrey Wellum. Had the pleasure of treating him many years ago when I was a houseman. Lovely man. One of The Few you know. Flew Spitfires at the age of 18. They don't make them like that anymore.' He exited and closed the door with a click.

Michael was feeling out of it. The anaesthetic was clearly still having its effect. Out of ghoulish curiosity he lifted his hospital gown to inspect the damage, but there was nothing to see other than a significant dressing firmly taped to the side of his abdomen. He closed his eyes and looked forward to seeing his son. He hadn't seen him for almost six months.

◆

As the grey, dreary railway sidings slid by slowly, Ben got up from his seat and pulled the nylon rucksack over his shoulder. From Waterloo he'd be home in around 35 minutes as long as the Northern line wasn't playing up. He'd unload his stuff at the house and take a shower before seeing the old boy. He'd missed him, and felt pangs of guilt for not coming home sooner. Truth was he had too much bloody work to get through, and coming back in the middle of exams would have been a disaster. He knew his own limitations only too well; and that if he failed to get his arse over to the faculty library every morning when he didn't have lectures, he'd procrastinate and put his work on the back burner. He wasn't one of life's natural students. He enjoyed physics but it was hard work, and there were times when he'd think he should have done something less taxing. Media studies or sociology would have been a walk in the park.

Being late morning, the underground wasn't too crowded and travelling North out of central London helped. By the time he arrived at Golders Green, he was ready for a brisk walk. He could have taken a hopper bus, but there was little point; according to the printed timetable the next one was 15 minutes away.

He paced along the main road from the station, turned up Hoop Lane and passed the cemetery. You knew you were in Hampstead Garden Suburb as soon as the streets became lined with neatly trimmed privet hedges shielding their Arts and Crafts properties designed by the likes of Unwin, Lutyens and Parker. The place was unreal: a leafy village in the heart of North West London. But to Ben it was nothing special; it's what he'd always known.

As he fumbled for his door keys, his mobile reverberated in his jeans pocket. It was a text from Natasha.

> *Hi Smelly, Hope your journey was OK. Car keys R in drawer in hall. Please take dad's mail on window ledge. CU there. Tash xxxx*

He plonked his rucksack unceremoniously in the hall and bounded up the stairs as he always did, two steps at a time. By the time he'd had his shower, stuffed his dirty washing in the machine and grabbed a piece of toast, it was almost 12.30. He picked up the small pile of envelopes in the hall and found the car keys. He and Natasha shared the old *Vauxhall Astra* between them. Ben smiled to himself as he opened the door on the driver's side and noticed fresh bumps and scratches to its tired bodywork. Natasha had a tendency to bash the car every time she parked. Ironically, she was a good driver; but clearly had a blind spot when it came to parking. He probably should have just taken the tube, but he couldn't face another cramped journey on the Northern line.

Queen Square was full of parked cars, but Ben found a meter on one of the side streets and parked without so much as scuffing the tyres on the pavement. 'Now that, my dear sis is how you bloody well park', he said out loud while looking at himself in the car mirror. Not that he'd ever say such a thing to his big sister's face. She'd wipe the floor with him, and remind him of his own failings, which were, of course, too numerous to number.

He worked his way to the lifts along the linoleum floored corridors and made his way up to the second floor. An attractive young nurse looked up from behind the reception desk.

'Hello there. I'm Ben Hollinghurst. I've come to see my father.'

The Nurse smiled broadly. 'Ah, Mr Hollinghurst. Let me take you to your father's room. I can see the family resemblance. You have your father's eyes.'

Room 7 was down the far end of the ward. She gently opened the door and let Ben in. His father put down the newspaper.

'The prodigal son returns.' Michael stretched out both

arms from his bed in a welcoming gesture, and Ben obligingly fell into his father's outstretched arms.

There can be few things in life quite as gratifying as embracing a son or daughter in your arms. This primal need to feel and protect your own flesh and blood is an instinctive human trait that Michael seemed to possess in spades.

'It's good to see you Ben.' Michael held his son by his shoulders and studied his features. 'Look at you. You're growing a beard.'

'Actually, my electric shaver doesn't work, and I couldn't be arsed to start using razor blades. Do you think it suits me?'

Michael laughed. 'It does as a matter of fact. But I shouldn't let it grow too long. Keep it trimmed.'

Ben extricated himself and unzipped his jacket. 'I've brought you something.' He reached inside his pocket and pulled out a small package that had been carefully wrapped in flowery wrapping paper. Michael carefully removed the paper and revealed a small olive green leather-bound volume. 'My word Ben. Where on earth did you find this? It's a first edition.'

Ben smiled. 'Bit of luck really. There's this grubby second-hand book shop near uni. Sells a lot of old crap including old porno mags. The guy who owns it doesn't know what he's selling, so when job lots come in, you can sometimes find some little gems.'

The volume was a collection of Siegfried Sassoon's War Poems published in 1919, and it was in remarkably good condition. 'Well, you've certainly hit the jackpot with this one, Ben. First editions of Sassoon's war poems are highly collectable and fairly rare. I will treasure this. Thank you.'

'It's my pleasure, dad. I'm only sorry I couldn't come

back earlier. But you know what it's like with exams and everything…'

Michael raised his hand as if holding back oncoming traffic. 'Don't be daft. I didn't expect you to. Your work must always take priority. Your future counts on it, Ben. I wouldn't want to screw that up for you. And you'd never get your work done when you're away from your desk. You know what you're like on that score.'

His father could read him like a book. 'Yeah, I know… Oh, before I forget, these are yours. I picked them up from the house.' He pulled the envelopes out of his other pocket and handed them to Michael.

'Oh thanks. Probably gas bills and bank statements. That's about as interesting as my life gets these days.' He placed them carefully on his bedside table. 'Tell me, has that mother of yours been in touch?'

Michael shrugged. 'The last conversation I had with her was a couple of weeks ago. She called to say that she was going to Chicago on some work thing. I haven't heard from her since.'

'Look, I'm sorry Ben that things have worked out the way they have. Truth be told, your mum and I would have split up anyway. And the fact that she and I don't exactly see eye to eye, doesn't mean you shouldn't call her once in a while. She is still your mum.'

Ben thought he was hearing things. Dad taking the side of the woman he clearly loathed. But then, that's what he loved about the old boy. He could always see the good in others, no matter how painful that might have been for him personally. 'Yeah, I know dad. I do try. I can't tell you how many times I've left messages on her damn answer machine and not heard a dickie bird back.'

Michael put his hand on Ben's shoulder. 'I know Ben. But it's good that you've tried. And no matter how distant she can seem, I'm sure that means a lot to her.'

Ben smiled. 'Enough about mum already. How are you doing?'

'Oh, I'm ok. Doctors here seem pleased with the operation... Should be home in a matter of days. They just need to get the dosage right for the pump. Then hopefully the spasms in my legs will improve.'

Ben was just about to say something when his train of thought was interrupted by the squeak of the opening door.

'Hi guys. Sorry I'm a bit late, but I thought I'd grab us some lunch from M&S.' No matter how busy and flustered Natasha could be, she always managed to look as if she was about to be whisked off for lunch at The Ivy. She placed the shopping bag by the door and hugged her brother. 'I'm loving the beard. Can't believe you're my baby brother... So how's our invalid?' She pecked Michael on the cheek.

'I was just telling your brother here that everything seems to have gone well. Doctors reckon I'll be home in a couple of days.'

'That's brilliant. I've asked Annie to give the house a good clean tomorrow, so it should look spic and span by the time you come home.' She retrieved the bag from the floor and began laying out various packages of salads, pasta and cold meats.

'Thanks Tash, you're a star. I'm famished.' Ben stretched across and helped himself. 'So how's the job going?'

Natasha removed her orange cashmere Epsom coat and hung it on the back of the door. 'Well thanks. I've been there a year now. Can you believe it? So next month I get the promotion they promised me at the interview.'

Natasha had done well after her graduation. She was a grafter and had never been one to wait for things to happen. She'd always been passionate about environmental issues, which was primarily why she had studied geography in the first place. And after graduation, she'd got herself a job for an organisation called *Green Routes* that promoted recycling in Lewisham by literally knocking on doors and informing residents of the benefits and potential rewards for recycling waste. Natasha had been one of 55 door knockers, most of whom were recent graduates. It was a tough job that paid very little and relied entirely on the candidates' interpersonal and communication skills. But because Natasha felt so passionately about the subject, and had a natural flair for getting on with people, she had in her first month alone, signed up twice as many residents as anyone else. So it had been a huge disappointment to the company when she finally left after two months to take a fast track graduate role at *Landmark plc*, London's largest recycling company. In truth, she may not have got the job had she not already worked for *Green Routes*. Her experience and sheer force of personality got her through four rounds of interviews to win one solitary place. What she didn't know was that over 400 graduates had applied for the role, including some very impressive candidates from both Oxford and Cambridge. The deal was that in year one, she'd learn all about the business from the ground up. This meant she'd have to work within Customer Services, deal with customers' issues while also becoming familiar with the business model, customer audits and billing systems.

In addition, she'd be required to take part in presentations and attend conferences. After completing her first year, she would then be promoted to an Account Manager, dealing with and managing her own designated clients. The company had originally been set up in 1974 as an offshoot of the conservation charity *The Countryside League*, and was later taken over in 1990 by two young entrepreneurs with green credentials. Every year since 1990, the company had managed to turn over a profit. Today it was a public limited company, employed 500 people, owned its own paper recycling plant in Essex and had a fleet of more than 200 vehicles.

Natasha poured three tea mugs with Buck's Fizz. 'Here's to less shaky legs, great exam results, and no more angry clients shouting at me down the phone.'

CHAPTER SEVEN

The cafe in Alexander Park was fairly animated for a Thursday afternoon, probably due in large part to the school holidays and the cloudless powder blue sky. Mohammed looked at his watch anxiously. Where was his friend? It was almost three o'clock and they had agreed to meet at half-past two. This dump was no good for them anyway. They needed somewhere quiet. Somewhere private where they could talk freely without worrying about prying eyes and ears. He took a look at his mobile and as he did so, the chair beside him was pulled away. Qssim lowered himself into the red moulded plastic. Mohammed could recognise that distinctive and expensive aftershave of Qssim's anywhere.

'What time d'you call this brother?' he asked pointedly while gesticulating with his watch.

'Looks like three o'clock to me. And that's a nice watch by the way… Oh, and it's nice to see you, too.'

'Look, I'm sorry if I'm tetchy. I just needed to talk to you, ok?'

Qssim looked at his friend. He could see something was troubling him, and he knew from the phone call that had been unusually curt, that something was up. 'Apology accepted. But before you say another word, can I get you something? I could murder a coffee.'

Mohammed shook his head. 'No thank you. But you go ahead.'

Qssim languidly rose and joined a queue of mothers with buggies laden with the kind of brightly coloured paraphernalia that middle-class families buy by the truckload, only to eventually give away to Oxfam once their little darlings had outgrown nappies.

Outside large black and white plastic swans moved inelegantly across the manmade pond. These hideous pedalos were occupied by young kids in T-shirts and trainers, munching on chocolate bars and packets of crisps. By the time Qssim got back with his coffee, Mohammed was standing up and ready to go.

'Hey brother. What's going on? I've only just arrived.'

'This place is too busy. We're going on a boat ride. Nice day for it. And you can bring your coffee with you.'

Mohammed led the way to the edge of the pond towards an old boy in a grubby woollen cardigan and an equally sorry looking pair of polyester trousers that were shiny at the knees. He handed the man a ticket. The man took it and gestured towards one of several empty swans. 'Number five mate. You've got half an hour.'

The two men stepped carefully into the precarious craft and sat themselves side by side on the bench seat and together began pedalling.

'That's what I like about you brother. You have class... Real class.' Qssim looked at his friend trying to sip his coffee while peddling. And instinctively, the two started giggling.

'Well it's not every day that you get invited to ride a swan, is it?' Mohammed pointed towards the island. 'Let's park ourselves over there.'

The craft gently drifted towards a thicket of trees overhanging the island. There were no other pedalos nearby.

Mohammed's mood changed once the vessel had come to a halt. 'This is the reason I wanted to talk to you:' He pulled a piece of paper out of his trouser pocket and handed it to

Qssim. 'I received this email message last week.'

Qssim read the note slowly:

> *Dear Brother,*
>
> *We are impressed by your diligence and quiet demeanour, and would be honoured to have you among our most trusted servants of Allah. We shall not be known to each other in person, but together we will (God willing) be able to carry out jihad and strike at the infidel where he least expects it.*
>
> *You will not communicate via this channel. For the Kafir will try and trap us. But he will not succeed. You will delete this email upon receipt and look in the personal lonely heart ads in The Ham and High next week. Rest assured that your IP has been added to our access list.*
>
> *Allahu Akbar*

'Have you shown this to anyone else?' asked Qssim.

Mohammed shook his head. 'You are the first to see it. And I have permanently deleted it from my PC.'

'And the *Ham & High*? Is that some kind of code?'

'No. Neither is it anything to do with pig meat… It's an abbreviation for the *Hampstead & Highgate Express*, a local newspaper for that wealthy part of North West London.'

Qssim read it again. 'Did you buy a copy of this Hampstead Express?'

Mohammed pulled the page from his pocket and unfolded it. He had circled one of the classified ads with a red felt tip. 'Here, look at the one I've marked.'

Qssim took the piece of newsprint and studied it.

Attractive and wise, I am in search of a God-fearing man with whom I can create a truly beautiful future. You will understand that this special relationship will require certain sacrifices. Material wealth is not what I am looking for. Our real rewards will be in heaven. Box 5678

Qssim studied the words closely. 'This is definitely a cryptic message designed to resonate with the likes of you and I. The question is, is it genuine?'

'My thoughts exactly,' replied Mohammed. 'There have been a few cases in America where individuals have posed as jihadis online,' he continued.

Qssim nodded sagely. 'Honey traps. That's the term now used for such filthy schemes... You need to tread with great care... On the other hand, if it is from one of our brothers, it may well represent a very significant opportunity to carry out jihad - particularly if there are resources and finances in place... Were you going to respond?'

Mohammed nodded. 'I wanted to show you my first draft. I thought I'd quote Cicero.'

Qssim screwed his eyes up and looked in pain. It was his way of questioning something without saying a word.

'Don't tell me you don't know who Cicero was.'

'What is this, fucking University Challenge? No I don't know who Cicero was.'

'Well, he was a Roman... Never mind. It doesn't matter. It's of no consequence.' He pulled a final sheet of paper from his pocket and handed it to Qssim.

Qssim read the third piece of paper:

I have deleted your message as requested.

> *After all, a nation can survive its fools, and even the ambitious. But it cannot survive treason from within. An enemy at the gates is less formidable, for he is known and carries his banner openly. But the traitor moves amongst those within the gate freely, his sly whispers rustling through all the alleys, heard in the very halls of government itself.*
>
> *For the traitor appears not a traitor; he speaks in accents familiar to his victims, and he wears their face and their arguments, he appeals to the baseness that lies deep in the hearts of all men. He rots the soul of a nation, he works secretly and unknown in the night to undermine the pillars of the city, he infects the body politic, so that it can no longer resist. A murderer is less to fear.*
> *Marcus Tullius Cicero*
> *I await your instructions in good faith.*
> *Allahu Akbar*

Qssim started to shake his head as he read. 'No, no, no... You mustn't send this... You mustn't acknowledge your understanding of that message so openly. By doing so you are implicating yourself... No, you must answer as if you are answering a personal ad.'

Mohammed felt stupid. Of course Qssim was right. He always was. He nodded in agreement.

'Tell you what. Why don't we find a nice quiet corner and draft this letter together?'

Mohammed smiled broadly. 'That would be good. Thank you brother. I know the ideal place. I hope you're feeling hungry.'

CHAPTER EIGHT

'Hello dere, Mr Hollinghurst. Sorry to wake you.' A middle-aged woman with silver-white hair and a distinct Southern Irish twang had wheeled in dinner. She placed it on Michael's table and pushed it across his bed. 'There'll be a nice piece of salmon under dere, Mr Hollinghurst. It'll help build your strength up.' She lifted the perspex lid and Michael could discern steam rising from the plate. The advantage of being in a private wing other than having your own room, was the food, which was actually rather good.

He focussed on the name label pinned to her lapel... 'Thank you... Miss O'Neil. This looks terrific... While you're here, would you mind passing me those envelopes on the side there?'

She happily obliged. 'There you go Mr Hollinghurst. Now you enjoy dat dere meal of yours. And don't let it go cold.'

There were only four envelopes. The first one was a bank statement. He could see that without even opening it. The second had the well-known logo of a cruise line emblazoned across it. And the third was by far the bulkiest and looked a great deal more promising, particularly since the postmark was NW3 - the London postcode for Hampstead. He opened it. Inside were three sealed envelopes on which the PO Box number and postal address of the newspaper had been written by different hands. Michael tore open the first to reveal a handwritten note.

Dear Box 5678

You sound like one serious dude. I am a vivacious 40-year-old petite redhead with a passion for life and possess a GSH. Love country walks, open fires and fine dining. If you'd like to meet up, contact me at sclarkson42@sc.co.uk Come on - lighten up already! And let's have a blast.

Look forward to hearing from you,
Sam

Michael smiled to himself. She sounded like she'd probably be a lot of fun. He put the note back in the envelope and opened the next.

Hi 5678,

I am an attractive 45-year-old hard-working professional. I lost my husband to cancer 13 months ago and am looking for a kind-hearted soul mate for companionship and possibly more.

In the first instance, you can call me on 08678 564367.

Deborah

There was certainly a fair number of lonely people out there, thought Michael, while also feeling a tad guilty for raising these women's hopes of meeting Mr Right.

He opened the last envelope with little enthusiasm. But as he began to read, goose-pimples stood to attention across his shoulders and lower arms.

I am looking for a deeply committed and passionate partner with whom to build a trusting relationship

and a better world. A world in which our children can have real faith.
ghadleigh@yahoo.co.uk

Michael read the message again. There could be little doubt that this individual was responding to the cryptic call for jihad. The references to 'a better world' and 'real faith' were fairly blatant clues. And as if to make it totally obvious, the first four characters of the email address spelt ghad. This was no accident. The bait had been well and truly swallowed.

Part of Michael felt elated and triumphant, but there could be no denying that part of him also felt deeply disturbed and upset that he had somehow managed to tap into this potentially dark and menacing undercurrent in British society.

✦

Alan sat at the piano. He'd been playing the Erik Satie pieces over and over again until they were note-perfect. He had to get them right. It was important. He couldn't explain why exactly. All he knew was that he couldn't let anything distract him from his playing until he was completely satisfied that he had done the pieces justice. His mother had called him twice for lunch and his mobile phone had buzzed, indicating a text, but he couldn't let these distractions hinder him.

It was around 4 o'clock by the time he finally sat down at the kitchen table and tucked into his fish finger sandwiches. They were cold, of course, but it had been a price worth paying. His Erik Satie repertoire was now sounding pretty good; good enough at least to impress his mother. Besides, fish fingers tasted better cold - everyone knew that. So it was a win/win all round. He squirted a dollop of tomato ketchup on his plate and then dug his Nokia mobile phone out of his pocket. It was the bright red one that he found vaguely embarrassing, but he wasn't too bothered by it. He hadn't been so keen to have one in the first place, but his parents had thought it good that he be contactable when out of the house. His father had one of those fancy *BlackBerries*, which were pretty cool, but nothing could replace his PC. As far as he was concerned, mobile phones were just very second rate PCs.

He wiped some excess ketchup from the corner of his mouth with his sleeve and looked at the text.

Hi Alan,

Hope everything's ok. I'm fine. I've had my operation and should be home any day.

Just a quick question for you: If you were going to disguise an email message, how would you do so without using some very complicated code or software?

Hope you're looking forward to your next piano lesson.

Michael

Alan smiled. There were loads of ways you could hide messages. Planting them in jpeg image files was fun, but it was a bit complicated. Unless you used *JP Hide and Seek* software. But it sounded like Michael didn't want to go down the software route. The simplest and most effective method was probably to use *Spam Mimic* - a free website that allowed you to encode and decode emails at the click of a mouse. It was a pretty neat site, and not that many people knew about it.

✦

Andrew Underhay lifted Michael's right leg gently under the knee joint and the nurse and student doctor both looked studiously at the useless appendage as it twitched involuntarily. He put it down and repeated the procedure on the left leg. The reaction was identical. 'Hmmm… There is some improvement there. I don't think we should increase the dosage of Baclofen, seeing that the spasms are certainly less pronounced than they were. And over time, we may very well see further improvement. I'd just like to check the strength of your hands and arms If I may, Mr Hollinghurst. If I could just ask you to push with all your strength against my outstretched palm with your right hand please?' Michael happily obliged. 'That's very good. And now with your left… Excellent… Absolutely no loss of strength there.' The nurse scribbled notes dutifully. 'Well Mr Hollinghurst, I see no further reason to keep you here any longer than necessary. Nurse Richardson will outline a few more details about this ingenious piece of medical technology; including all those do's and don'ts. Then Nurse Richardson, I suggest you arrange Mr Hollinghurst's discharge notes.' Sue Richardson smiled and nodded, while the older man rose from his chair. 'You'll have to excuse me… No rest for the wicked… All the best, Mr Hollinghurst.' And with that Andrew Underhay left the ward.

The nurse gave Michael a run-down of situations to avoid. Scanning machines at airports were apparently a no-no, as were MRI machines. If he needed an MRI, the pump would have to be deactivated beforehand. He'd be issued with a special card in due course that he should keep with him at all times. And he'd have to have an appointment every six months to have the pump refilled with Baclofen. 'Everything you could possibly need to know about your Baclofen pump is in here, Mr Hollinghurst.' Nurse Richardson handed him a small folder, which Michael flicked through. It seemed to be crammed with information graphics, reams of technical details and a lengthy question and answers section. It would no doubt take its place with those other seemingly useful tomes that were now collecting dust on his bottom bookshelf. He closed the file and placed it precariously on a mound of detritus that was already building up on his bedside table. As he did so, he felt a distinct vibration in his trouser pocket. Michael's automatic reflex was to thrust his hand deep into the offending pocket to fish out his mobile.

The text was short, but seemed like it might be all he needed to know:

> *Hi Michael,*
> *I'm good thanx. Can't wait for our next lesson.*
> *Just go 2 www.spammimic.com It's pretty cool!*
> *C U soon.*
> *Alan*

Michael brought up the website on his mobile. *Spam Mimic* did precisely what its name suggested; it turned your emails into vast chunks of meaningless spam. All you had to do was type your message into a white panel and then click the *Encode* button and the website instantly turned your message into gibberish. To reveal the message, you just had to paste the chunk of spam in the white panel and press the decode button and, hey presto, your message was revealed.

Alan was right; it was pretty cool. Out of interest, Michael did a quick search for more details about *Spam Mimic*, and within a few clicks came across an academic paper on the subject. The piece itself needed decoding. A few seconds of perusing was enough to turn his brain to jelly.

> *Spam Mimic works by using context free probabilistic grammar to derive its output. Each production of the grammar is translated into Huffman tree based on the probabilities assigned to each variable or terminal symbol in the production.*
>
> *For example:*
>
> *S -> A(.25) | B(.75)*
>
> *A -> aS(1.0)*
>
> *B -> bS(.75) | b(.25)*

It was clearly a pretty clever piece of software written by a boffin. But more importantly, you didn't have to be some kind of digital genius to use it.

Michael brought up the message from GHadleigh on his mobile. Could this have been from one of the original names he'd emailed from Alan's list? His hunch was that it was, but there was, of course, no way of knowing; not for someone of his limited technical abilities at least. Without any further thought, he began to compose another message. This time there'd be no need to be cryptic. It could be simple and instructional.

◆

The idea of creating an email address in the name of GHadleigh had been Qssim's. He was the one who was good with words, and he'd composed the letter. And now Mohammed was on tenterhooks. He'd been checking the account every hour or so for the past couple of days. But so far, he'd received nothing but junk mail from companies trying to sell him something. The last one carried the subject line: Male Erectile Dysfunction? Dickheads, thought Mohammed as he deleted the post, and then smiled to himself on realising the unintended pun.

He'd given up looking by the time, some days later, the innocuous email arrived. He had just finished rolling up his prayer mat, and had flicked on the kettle when his mobile on the kitchen worktop had pinged in that familiar though slightly irritating fashion. He pulled the phone out of its charger and peered at the illuminated screen. There was a new email message and the subject line looked promising. It read:

Instructions for GHadleigh. The sender was
indeed Alan Anonymous.

Mohammed opened the email, and his heart immediately sank. His entire screen was full of unreadable verbiage. 'Shit bags,' he cursed to himself as he scrolled down.

Dear Friend, We know you are interested in receiving red-hot announcements. We will comply with all removal requests! This mail is being sent in compliance with Senate bill 1916, Title 3; Section 306! This is NOT unsolicited bulk mail...

The text went on and on in this vein. What the hell was going on? Why had some arsehole sent him this garbage? But seeing that it had come from Alan Anonymous, he kept scrolling down without reading and was about to give up and bin the whole message, when the text came to an end, and the final words suddenly appeared in caps:

TO DECODE THIS MESSAGE, GO TO SPAM MIMIC.COM AND CLICK ON THE GREEN DECODE LOGO. THEN PASTE THIS ENTIRE MESSAGE INTO THE WHITE PANEL AND CLICK DECODE. FINALLY AND MOST IMPORTANTLY, PERMANENTLY DELETE THIS EMAIL AND ALL SUBSEQUENT EMAILS FROM YOUR PC. ALLAHU AKBAR.

Mohammed's heart suddenly went into fifth gear. 'Shit sticks' he cursed to himself, and could feel a cold sweat break out on his forehead and a bead of salty sweat roll into his left eye. He tentatively scrolled up to the top of the page and then highlighted the entire piece. Then he brought the *Spam Mimic* website onto his screen. It was a fairly simple, uncluttered blue page with the words *Encode* and *Decode* in the top left-hand corner. He clicked on the word *Decode* and a white screen popped up along with a prompt to paste the encoded message. He placed the cursor on the white box and pasted the text. Then he stared at it for some considerable while. He was feeling unbelievably nervous. A simple click would draw him inexorably into this clandestine operation. Did he really want this? Did he really know the full ramifications of his actions? Then he saw the image of his brother smiling nonchalantly at him from a framed photograph on his desk. He looked stately with a mortarboard balanced on his mop of thick, black hair and the black and green university gown draped across his shoulders. Salah Farik had his whole life in front of him; the world was his oyster. He was kind, sensitive, funny and clever - so very clever. But he wore his cleverness lightly. Never looked down on anyone else and never professed to know better than anyone else, despite the fact that he was clearly far more eloquent and better informed than most mere mortals. Mohammed missed his brother. He missed his generosity of spirit; his calm, placid nature; his reassuring voice. He'd been a good brother, and his only brother. As Mohammed's eyes began to well up, he wiped them with the back of his hand. He looked away from the screen and his eyes inadvertently fell on his bookshelf and the only book he couldn't bring himself to read - not that he'd have understood a word of it anyway. Its red spine displayed the title in white sans serif type: *The Aesthetics of Mechanics*, and its author Salah Farik. Mohammed turned back to his PC and clicked on the icon that read *Decode*.

✦

'Ah, Mr Hollinghust. How nice to see you again.' Aleksy the Polish ambulance-man strode into the reception area, and Michael looked up from his newspaper.

'Aleksy. This is a nice surprise. How are you?'

The large man shook Michael's hand firmly and placed his muscular tree trunk of an arm affectionately around Michael's shoulder. 'Im very well thank you. It's nice to see you Mr Hollinghurst, but not so nice to see you back in hospital so soon.'

Michael smiled. 'I know. I think my kids were a bit cut up about it too if the truth be known. But it's for the best. They've planted this piece of high tech wizardry inside me that's going to improve the spasms in my legs.'

Aleksy raised his eyebrows. 'That's amazing. Medical technology is so advanced now. These doctors can work wonders.' He walked around to the back of Michael's wheelchair, unlocked the brakes gently with his foot and pushed Michael through the double doors and out onto the forecourt where a small fleet of ambulances and other hospital vehicles sporting fluorescent yellow stripes had parked.

'You know Mr Hollinghurst, you should get yourself a dog… Not any old dog you understand.'

'I know what you mean, Aleksy. One of those assistance dogs.'

'Yeah. That's exactly right. They are incredible… I sometimes pick up this lady in Hampstead who is a wheelchair user like you, and her dog… he carries her bag…' He strapped Michael's chair in place, closed the tailback and swung his large frame into the driving seat of the small converted Volkswagen. They were off down the bumpy, pot-holed piece of tarmac that could barely pass as a road, and Michael felt relieved at least that Aleksy had strapped him in firmly as the vehicle lurched every which way. Few able-bodied people ever quite understood how unbelievably bumpy a bumpy ride actually feels to a wheelchair user. The bumps always seemed to Michael to be magnified tenfold. He wasn't entirely sure whether this was down to his altered physical state or the laws of physics. Ben would no doubt have the answer, but it would almost certainly be one he'd never begin to understand.

'It's funny you mention a dog, Aleksy; my carer made the very same suggestion a while ago. I never used to be much of an animal person, but I have to say that the idea is growing on me. Particularly if the dog in question can put my washing in the machine and fetch my newspaper.'

Michael could see Aleksy's brown, expressive eyes in the mirror, and could tell from these alone that this large and immensely likeable man was smiling.

The traffic was unusually light and before long they were heading along the A1 and through the rare stretch of greenery otherwise known as Mill Hill Park before emerging into the land of nondescript, grey suburbia that could pass for anywhere.

'If you're interested, I can ask the lady in Hampstead where she went for her dog.'

'That would be very helpful, Alexy. I'll give you my email address when we arrive.'

Within 20 minutes the reassuring sight of endless walls of neatly clipped green privet were sliding past Michael's window seat. But it looked as if the road was about to be dug up as countless orange plastic barriers could now be seen standing guard around the driveways of all the houses in the road, Michael's included.

'Oh bugger! You won't be able to park in our driveway or outside, Aleksy... Looks like they're laying cables or pipes.'

'That's ok Mr Hollinghurst, I'll just put my hazard lights on and park in the middle of the road.'

Aleksy unstrapped Michael's chair with military precision and wheeled it deftly down the ramp, across the road and up the gentle incline of the dropped curb and carefully negotiated the plastic barriers.

'Here's the front door keys Aleksy. If you wouldn't mind doing the honours. It'll be a lot quicker and easier for you to open.'

On entering the hallway, Michael could tell instantly that Annie had clearly done a first-rate job cleaning the place just by the pleasant smell of furniture polish and slate oil, which she used for polishing the fireplace hearth. Aleksy placed Michael's bags in the hallway while Michael scribbled his email on a notepad on the telephone table. 'Here you go Aleksy. If you could email me the details about the dog, I'd be very grateful.'

'No problem, Mr Hollinghurst. I should be seeing her sometime this week, so I'll make a note to ask her.' He paused by the front door. 'Well, you take care of yourself, Mr Hollinghurst.'

'You too Aleksy. And thank you.'

The large man turned and let himself out.

Michael wheeled himself into his downstairs bedroom and opened his laptop on his bedside table. He gingerly tapped at the keyboard and brought up his Alan Anonymous email account. There were quite a few emails in his inbox since he last looked. Several from financial advisers touting for business; one from a national children's charity; and a load of really dull junk mail selling everything from double glazing to self-help courses and budget funeral plans. There was nothing that looked remotely like gibberish produced by *Spam Mimic* from a certain GHadleigh. Not yet at any rate. It was, admittedly, something of a relief.

The house was quiet. Natasha was at work and Annie had obviously left earlier. Michael wheeled himself into the kitchen; it was just gone one o'clock; time for a bite and to catch up with the news. He switched on the kettle followed by the radio, which immediately sprang to life.

The man's voice emanating from the speaker was reasonably youthful sounding; it had a confident air about it, but wasn't in the least bit formal or stuffy. He sounded like the kind of decent bloke you could have a pint with.

'I want to give this country a modern compassionate Conservatism that is right for our times and right for our country.

'I'd like to thank all of the other participants in this election for the very civilised and decent and reasonable way it has been conducted. It has been good for our party.

'It has shown talent, it has shown ideas, and above all, it has shown optimism about the future of our party and the future of our country…'

Good old-fashioned empty platitudes coming out of the mouths of babes, thought Michael and wheeled himself back to the kitchen. Annie had left a smoked salmon sandwich on the bottom shelf and there was a half-empty bottle of Rioja that was just about reachable. Sod it. He knew he shouldn't, but he was going to have a glass anyway. He balanced the sandwich and bottle and glass tumbler on his lap and wheeled himself back into the bedroom.

'Now that I've won we will change.

'We will change the way we look. Nine out of 10 Conservative MPs, like me, are white men. We need to change the scandalous under-representation of women in the Conservative party and we'll do that.

'We need to change the way we feel. No more grumbling about modern Britain. I love this country as it is not as it was and I believe our best days lie ahead.'

There was a pause and then an almighty applause.

'I'll drink to that my old chum,' Michael said to himself, as he poured a generous tumbler of wine and brought it to his lips. So, it looked like the Tories had got themselves a new leader in the form of this young lad called David Cameron who liked to be called Dave. First it was Modern Labour under chummy old Tony with his acoustic guitar, open shirt collars and rolled-up sleeves. Now it looked like the new Tories under this fresh-faced young Etonian had taken a leaf out of New Labour's book. There seemed to be very little to distinguish one party from the other. They were both doggedly claiming to own the central ground of British politics. But maybe that was a good thing.

He gulped down a large mouthful of Rioja. The unmistakable tannins and oaky backlash on his palate were most acceptable. This was a bloody decent drop of vino. He picked up the bottle and studied the label. No wonder - it was a *Gran Reserva; a Campo Viejo Gran Reserva 1999*, no less. His daughter had expensive tastes. That would have set her back at least thirty quid, if not more. He took a bite out of his sandwich, and as he did so, his mobile reverberated in his pocket.

CHAPTER NINE

The message had been disappointingly short considering how incredibly long the spam garbage that concealed it had been. It was a bit like posting a tiny watch battery in a huge package large enough to accommodate a double bed. But it made sense to be very prudent. And this was certainly a very prudent way of going about things.

Mohammed read the message slowly.

> *Brother,*
> *The hour has come. We must strike fear into the hearts of the unbeliever. You must waste no time in finding at least one accomplice. A loyal and committed follower of the faith. Someone you can trust. And together, with our assistance, you will obey the commandments of the prophet. You will carry out Jihad.*
> *Acknowledge receipt of this message via our special channel along with the email address of your accomplice. Further instructions will follow.*
> *Allahu Akbar*

Mohammed printed out the message and then deleted the email from his PC.

✦

Michael pulled his mobile from his pocket and brought up his email.

Dear Mr Hollinghurst, I send you the details about dog:
Mrs Susan Appleby
sappleby@cleverdogs.co.uk
020 7433 7492
She is very nice lady. I think this will be good, no?
Aleksy

Michael smiled and finished the remains of the Rioja in his glass. He'd never been a big fan of dogs in the past and had always thought them rather smelly. But now the thought of a special and super-intelligent canine helping with the day-to-day chores filled him with a certain degree of excitement, even if the creature did turn out to be a tad pongy.

He wheeled himself into the hallway, picked up the cordless phone and punched in the numbers. The phone rang for a while before it was answered by a well-spoken lady of indeterminate years.

'Hello. Susan speaking.'

'Hello, Mrs Appleby. My name is Michael, and I was given your number by Aleksy, the ambulance-man from the hospital in Queens Square... I hope you don't mind me calling you like this.'

'Oh, hello there Michael. Not at all. It was about assistance dogs, wasn't it?'

'Yes... I understand you have one.'

'Absolutely. Wouldn't be without my Horace... You'll need to get in touch with a company called *Helping Paws*. They are a wonderful charity that trains these fabulous animals. If you'll bear with me one moment... Horace my precious, would you be a good boy and fetch my diary?'

Michael could hear the distinct sound of dog whimpers and much tapping of canine paws on what he presumed was parquet flooring.

'Ah... excellent. Here we are... Do you have a pen and paper to hand, Mr Hollinghurst?'

'Yes.'

'You'll need to speak to Marjorie Hawkins. She's the founder of the charity, and I know her very well. Tell her that you spoke to me, and I'm sure she'll pull a few strings. You see, there is a waiting list, and you will, in the first instance, be assessed. But at least Marjorie will get the wheels in motion once you've spoken to her. Her number is 0207 879 9542.'

Michael jotted down the number. 'That's very kind of you, Mrs Appleby. I really appreciate this.'

'Not at all. Always happy to help fellow chair users... Oh, and do let me know how you get on... Goodbye, Michael, and best of luck.'

Michael put down the receiver and then spent the next half hour speaking to Marjorie Hawkins. He had the sense that he was almost being interviewed by the woman. She wanted to know everything about his spinal injury, his surgery, his wheelchair, his home and garden, and his predisposition to animals and dogs in particular. And then, rather unexpectedly she posed that question few had the temerity to ask: 'Mr Hollinghurst, I hope you don't mind me asking, but how did you sustain your injuries?' Michael was a little taken aback. He wasn't usually asked that question so directly, primarily he thought, because your average Brit was far too reserved and buttoned up to probe. And he certainly didn't like to publicise the fact that he was a victim of an atrocity. He paused for a moment and wondered whether he should be facetious and say he'd been bitten by a shark. But then dismissed the thought.

'Oh… I was one of those poor sods who shared a train at Edgware Road with a demented jihadist with explosives strapped to his back on 7/7… I was one of the lucky ones.'

There was a pause on the other end of the line. 'Oh my goodness… Mr Hollinghurst, I am so very sorry to hear that… I think in the circumstances, we can place you at the very top of our waiting list; and forego the official assessment.'

'That's very kind of you Mrs Hawkins but I really don't want to receive special treatment and deprive someone else…'

Mrs Hawkins was having none of it. 'No, no, no. Mr Hollinghurst. I insist. Your level of spinal injury makes you a high priority case in any event. I have all the details I need, which I will pass on. And one of my colleagues will be in touch shortly. These dogs are wonderful animals, Mr Hollinghurst. They can make a world of difference to their owners in so many ways. With any luck, you will see what I mean very soon.'

The call had put Michael in a good frame of mind and he immediately tapped a text to Ben and Natasha.

Hey, guess what. We're getting a dog!

Within seconds Natasha called him back.

'I can't believe you dad… For over 20 years you and mum never let anything with four legs anywhere near this house. Ben used to beg you for a dog when he was much younger. And you always used to say that it would make the place smell, and that animal hairs would be bad for Ben's asthma and mum's hayfever.'

'I know Tash… But look, things have changed. Mum's no longer here and I'm not as mobile as I once was. And I'm sure we'll get used to any smell.'

'Don't get me wrong. I'm not criticising you dad; I'm just saying it's kind of ironic… Of course it's a good idea. Bloody great idea. And hey, I want to be the one who takes it for walks.'

Michael laughed. 'He or she will, I'm sure, be the ideal companion when you go jogging round the Heath extension.'

'So where are we going for this dog, and more importantly when?'

'It's a charity I've got onto through Alexi the ambulance driver. They've got a rather cheesy name: *Helping Paws*. They train dogs specially for wheelchair users. And they've put me at the top of their waiting list. So I suppose it could be fairly soon.'

✦

'Look brother. The answer is no… that's final. '

Mohammed was looking hurt; like a schoolboy whose best friend hadn't picked him for the football team at school.

'But I don't understand man! You are as passionate about the cause as anyone I've ever known. You get up and preach to others. You speak so movingly about the injustices done to our brothers. OK, so you weren't born a Muslim and you're white…'

Qssim didn't want to hear any more. 'I've given you my answer, brother. And whether you like it or not, you have to accept it with good grace.' Qssim mopped perspiration from his brow and forced a smile. 'Perhaps you've hit a nerve or something... I don't know... Yes, I am a Muslim convert. But unlike you, I don't have any members of my family who've been killed by the US military. So I don't share that kind of pain. Yes, I am passionate about the cause of Muslims around the world. But no, I am not prepared to die in the name of Jihad. If I'm perfectly honest with you, I'm not even a devout Muslim. I drink beer and wine. I eat pig. I listen to Western music. And I shag girls who aren't even fucking Muslims, OK?'

Mohammed knew his friend wasn't as devout as most Muslims he mixed with. So it wasn't these simple facts that shocked him so much as the blatant admission by his friend.

'I guess I see myself as a mouthpiece for the cause... A passionate mouthpiece maybe... But nothing more.' This was the first time Qssim had entertained his friend in his flat in Ilford. 'Look around this place,' he added. 'You won't even find a prayer mat,'

It was a pretty spartan flat admittedly. There were indeed no prayer mats, prayer books or other religious paraphernalia to speak of. There were a couple of framed prints on the wall. One had a strange stylised portrait of an effeminate looking man with a lightning flash graphic painted across his face, including his right eye. And the other carried the words *Led Zeppelin 1973* against a grainy black and white shot of an exploding airship. There was no shortage of books on his shelves, none of which were devoted to Islam. Most seemed to be well-thumbed paperbacks. It didn't look like the kind of flat lived in by any kind of Muslim. But then again, Qssim wasn't any kind of Muslim. He was a bit special. A one-off.

'Thing is I am far more useful to the cause of Jihad as a voice, not as some kind of martyr… You know that… Everyone knows that. And if I'm brutally honest with you, I'm not even a great believer in the whole martyrdom thing. It's a waste of resources. Then again, maybe I'm just a bit of a coward.'

Mohammed laughed. 'Come on man. You a coward?… A coward wouldn't have had the guts to do what you went and did to your old man.'

'That had nothing to do with guts… That was all about justice.' Qssim rose from his seat and slid open the sliding doors onto the small balcony, letting in the distant roar of traffic commuting on the busy A12, either towards East London or deeper into Essex - the land of Mondeo man and Essex girl clutching her infamous white handbag. Qssim leaned on the balcony rail looking pensive. 'Look brother. Don't get me wrong. I'm not saying Jihad isn't the right path. I'm just not a big fan of suicide missions OK?'

Mohammed joined him on the balcony. 'I hear what you're saying.'

Qssim looked at Mohammed intently. ' Tread carefully my friend… If you have any suspicions or doubts in your mind that these messages are not genuine, pull out immediately, do you hear me?'

Mohammed nodded.

'And I want copies of all the communications you receive and the corresponding email addresses… If this mystery emailer is anything other than genuine, he will have me to answer to.' Mohammed wasn't too clear how his friend was going to track down Alan Anonymous, but he felt distinctly reassured, at least, that there was some kind of back-up in place, should he decide to go ahead.

There was a silence as both men contemplated the grey urban sprawl amid the incessant throb of traffic. It wasn't what you'd call picturesque, but this constant flow of humanity seen from this vantage point was, if nothing else, mesmerising.

'Can I offer you some tea or coffee?' Qssim asked.

Mohammed raised a hand. 'No thank you. I'm fine. I have already outstayed my welcome.'

Qssim smiled and put his hand on Mohammed's right shoulder. 'Before you leave, I have something for you.' Qssim went back inside and was gone for a few minutes. When he returned he was holding a folded piece of paper, which he firmly pressed into the palm of Mohammed's right hand. Mohammed opened the scrap of paper on which was written an email address for someone by the name of Ibrahim Choudhury.

Mohammed gave Qssim a quizzical look.

'He's a good man... One of the best... I met him in prison, but he's out now. If it wasn't for him, I wouldn't have converted to Islam, and wouldn't be standing here talking to you. You can trust him implicitly. He's the perfect accomplice. And unlike me, he's a good Muslim.

'Speak to him. Promise me.'

CHAPTER TEN

'Ziggy! Here, fetch!'

Natasha threw the fluorescent yellow tennis ball as far as she could and let the dog off the lead. He immediately gave out a little yelp in appreciation and went bounding after the ball. She'd often come on to the Hampstead Heath Extension of a morning before the daily trudge to work on London's unsavoury Northern line.

The dog had been a brilliant move. He was so clever; he could help her dad move his feet on the bed and roll over onto his side; he could even load and unload the washing machine; and he was good company too, particularly when she wasn't around, which was proving to be more often than not. But despite all this, Natasha couldn't help noticing that her father wasn't quite himself. She couldn't put her finger on it, but he was just a tad more distant these days. You could tell him stuff and he just wouldn't take it in; he didn't seem to engage with you like he used to. His head seemed to be somewhere else.

The one-year-old golden labrador jumped up at her with the bright yellow ball in his mouth.

'Good boy, Ziggy. I think Natasha needs to get ready for work now.' She took the ball from his mouth, and he stood still obediently while wagging his tail and letting his owner clip the lead back onto his collar.

By the time they returned home, Annie had arrived and had already wheeled her father into the wetroom on his commode. Ziggy instinctively made his way to his owner's bedroom and sat patiently by Michael's bed while Natasha darted upstairs to get her work bag together and swap her trainers for work shoes. As she ambled downstairs, she could hear the distant rumble of the boiler, which meant that Annie would now be showering her father. How life had changed for her dad, and how swiftly he had somehow managed to adapt to his far from perfect daily routine that robbed him of his dignity. He'd proved to be so much more resilient than she had ever imagined, and she was so incredibly proud of him. If it had been her in that position she was sure she'd never have coped anywhere near as well. Now she could hear the water cascading and Annie laughing, presumably at one of her father's terrible jokes. She'd refrain from shouting 'goodbye.' She'd text him instead.

◆

He considered himself a good Muslim, but unlike many good Muslims, he preferred to pray from home. As far as he was concerned the Prophet (peace be upon him) had said himself that we should offer some of our prayers in our homes 'so as not to make these homes like graves.' And anyway, wasn't it generally accepted that the whole world was considered by Islam as a suitable place of worship? Ibrahim was pretty sure that this was the case. Any place, of course, other than somewhere totally unsuitable and disrespectful like a bathroom, rubbish dump or cemetery.

Ibrahim rolled up his prayer mat and placed it in the corner of the room. Then he pulled off his wire-framed spectacles and rubbed the lenses furiously with a lens cleaner.

He was a reasonably shy and quiet individual, was on

nodding terms with his neighbours, and would attend mosque only on Fridays. As an only child to hard-working parents born in Pakistan, Ibrahim was brought up in Leeds where he'd attended South Leeds High School, and from here had gone on to study Computer Science at Liverpool University. His mother's sister was very involved in education and worked as a council liaison officer at a school in Bradford and had been one of the first Asian women to be invited to a Buckingham Palace Garden Party where she was introduced to the Queen in recognition of her work among the Muslim community in Bradford.

Ibrahim himself was a primary school teacher and had involved himself in a community-run drop-in centre that professed to be some kind of youth outreach project until, that is, he got himself a criminal record in the summer of 2001.

In essence, it had been no more than a stupid student jape. There had been this perfectly ordinary terraced house in Leeds that happened to have in its front garden an impressive collection of garden gnomes; and for some unearthly reason Ibrahim and his mates had one evening joked about knocking the heads off the gnomes. And then the fantasy had turned into something of a dare. Ibrahim being the quietest and most introspective of his peer group, became the focus of the stunt. If Ibrahim had the guts and initiative to carry out a clandestine attack on the gnomes, the group would reward him handsomely by clubbing together and presenting him with £350.

It wasn't really the money that had appealed to him. It was the seemingly insurmountable challenge the others had set him. After all, nobody ever expected quiet Ibrahim to do anything daring. And if the truth be known, none of his friends seriously expected him to rise to the bait. It was this sudden desire to surprise everyone, including himself, that spurred him on and made him utterly determined to carry out this ludicrous mission - and carry it out in style. He would take it upon himself to reshape this miniature sculpture park by physically removing as many bearded heads from their shoulders as he could. He had always been keen on chemistry at school and had remembered a simple experiment that demonstrated the extraordinary explosive force achieved by combining water and dry ice.

Under the cover of darkness, and armed with a glass bottle of water, a small container of dry ice and an old mallet, Ibrahim made his way to the terraced house with the gnomes. Here he set to work.

Two heads were easily removed with a deft tap of the mallet. But next would come his piece de resistance. He pulled on a pair of thick gardening gloves and placed a pair of goggles over his nose. Then he carefully unscrewed the bottle of water and poured in the dry ice, screwed the lid up tight, and took cover behind the garden wall.

As far as he could remember, the chemical reaction would take in the region of 30 seconds. But that admittedly was with a plastic bottle, not a glass one. And he was certain that the outside temperature would also determine the timing of the explosion. Of course, he could have just scarpered there and then, but like all good science students, he wanted to see the result of his experiment.

It felt like a ludicrously long wait; certainly longer than 30 seconds. And he was contemplating what to do if it didn't work, when the explosion finally made him jump out of his skin. It had certainly been more powerful than he'd anticipated. Perhaps he'd used too much dry ice, and perhaps the glass bottle had been a mistake.

On raising his head above the garden wall, he could now see that his homemade device had left a small crater in the earth and several gnomes had been seriously damaged. But before he could discern the full extent of his handiwork, a burly middle-aged man with bulging biceps and tattoos, arrived on the scene of carnage. Ibrahim dropped his tools and made for the street, but he didn't get far before being pinned to the pavement and undergoing the humiliation of a citizen's arrest.

Some weeks following his act of madness, Ibrahim found himself standing before Judge Stevens at Leeds Magistrates Court. Stevens wasn't recognised for being particularly soft and, unlike some district judges, has never been known to break into anything remotely resembling a smile, in the courtroom. The Bradford Gnome Decapitation case may have been a farcical affair, but Stevens took a pretty dim view of the defendant's reckless behaviour despite his otherwise good character. And although criminal damage had amounted to little more than a few hundred pounds, it was Ibrahim's use of an explosive substance that made this case particularly worrisome in the myopic eyes of Stevens. There was, after all, the criminal handling of explosive material and the potential risk to the public at large to take into account. And for these reasons, Ibrahim came away with a criminal record and a sentence of three months at Her Majesty's Young Offender Institution Aylesbury. Much to Ibrahim's relief, his case hadn't been deemed serious enough to be referred to the Crown Court.

The final irony was that Ibrahim, until this point, hadn't harboured radical, Islamist views. He was what most people would call a 'middle-of-the-road Muslim.' But while in Aylesbury, he would fall under the spell of Abu Anjem al-Masri, a young radical preacher who had deliberately got himself into Aylesbury for minor offences, with the express purpose of spreading his warped but impassioned view of Islam to his literally captive audience.

Upon his release, Ibrahim learnt that his employer, Brookland Primary School had decided, in the circumstances, to make him redundant. He hadn't been in the least bit surprised. How on earth was a primary school going to justify to the parents of 11-year-olds that their little darlings were being taught by a crazed lunatic who had been found guilty of blowing up garden gnomes and putting the general public at risk? But in the great scheme of things, it was, in Ibrahim's mind at least, a small price to pay for the enlightenment he had received at Aylesbury. Al-Masri had opened his eyes to the persecution of Muslims across the globe. And the need for all Muslims to unite in the name of Jihad.

'Everything happens for a reason. And in his infinite wisdom, Allah has willed you to blow up those garden gnomes and to cause criminal damage in order to bring you here,' al-Masri had said. And Ibrahim had believed every word of it.

While at Aylesbury, Ibrahim had become a librarian; a role that had become vacant when the institution's previous librarian had received parole. Here Ibrahim could lap up the teachings of radical imams like Wasil ibn Maturidi and Malik ibn Hanbal - men that al-Masri had introduced him to. And it was here, too, that he had converted his friend Qssim to Islam on that fateful day.

He hadn't seen or spoken to Qssim since his release six

months ago and had no idea if his friend was still incarcerated. Now he had other things on his mind like the unenviable task of trying to get back into employment with a criminal record that would stay with him for at least two years.

As a matter of habit, he flipped open his laptop and opened his email. The subject line at the top of his mailbox immediately caught his attention as it read: 'From Qssim's friend.' He opened it inquisitively.

Dear Ibrahim,
I hope you don't mind me contacting you like this. My name is Mohammed Farik, and I am a very good friend of Qssim El-Ghzzawy's. In fact, it was Qssim who suggested I contact you. I would like to discuss a proposition with you that may be of interest. So please do get back to me with a convenient time and place we can meet where I can elaborate further.
Qssim sends his best wishes and apologises for not contacting you sooner. He will be in touch shortly.
Speak soon,
Allahu Akbar

How very strange. Ibrahim had only just been thinking about his good friend Qssim, and now, out of the blue, he receives this message via a third party. He could only put it down to divine providence. This was clearly meant to be.

CHAPTER ELEVEN

They called it the *Polo* simply because it was round in shape and had a giant hole in the middle - much like the famous peppermint Polo mint that first appeared in the UK in 1948. Since 2003, this vast piece of modern architecture comprising swathes of hi-tech glass and steel had housed no fewer than 5,500 members of staff, most of whom had previously been at the Oakley and Benhall sites nearby in the suburbs of Cheltenham. It was, in short, the largest building designated for secret intelligence gathering built outside the United States of America. Its official name, of course, was *Government Communications Headquarters* or *GCHQ* for short.

The big hole in the middle was occupied by a rather lovely and well-tended garden large enough to house the Royal Albert Hall. And directly below the garden lay the giant brain of this extraordinary operation. The brain itself occupied as much space as the employees above ground and took the form of endless banks of supercomputers that hummed away gently and incessantly. The lifeblood to the brain was supplied by an astonishing 1,550 miles of fibre optic cable and 1,850 miles of standard copper wiring.

The entire operation of *GCHQ* is understandably shrouded in much secrecy and mystery. Indeed, thanks to the *Serious Organised Crime and Police Act* of 2005, it was now a serious criminal offence to merely trespass onto the site's grounds. And access is very rarely granted to any other organisations including the media.

A large part of *GCHQ*'s work is focussed on monitoring, sifting, analysing and assessing communications via the internet and telecommunications in order to defend the homeland from terrorist and criminal activity. Its other primary raison d'etre concerns the protection and security of the government's own internal communications. Work that requires the collective skills of some of the country's finest mathematicians, engineers, IT and computer science graduates and linguists.

Lelah Hasan was a very small cog in this giant machine. Interestingly, she was also one of a growing number of Muslims to be employed by *GCHQ* in the area of counter-terrorism. Having studied maths at Warwick University and graduated with First Class Honours, she could have taken a role as a junior analyst or fund manager at any one of the giant American investment banks in London, but instead she chose to work for the government for a considerably smaller salary. Ever since the atrocities of *9/11* and *7/7*, her sense of patriotism had grown enormously. She was a British Muslim who was proud to be British. She loved her country that had given her everything, and she loathed with a vengeance the wilful manipulation and distortion of Islam by a few bad apples who committed murder in the name of Allah. As far as she was concerned, they were the world's biggest sinners. They were nothing more than despicable, heinous thugs who were bringing her faith - the faith that she loved - into disrepute. They certainly weren't Muslims. And she wanted to hit back at them in any way she could. Joining *GCHQ* seemed like a pretty good way of doing just that.

The application process for a maths graduate to join one of *GCHQ*'s Technical Projects Team had been rigorous to say the least. First she had had to sit a Mathematics Aptitude Test. This was split into two papers - the first of which took the form of questions requiring short answers; and the second, requiring longer and more considered answers. The second paper also posed more questions than could realistically be answered in the time allowed, so candidates were encouraged to read all the questions before deciding which ones they could answer most confidently and thoroughly. This way GCHQ would be in a good position to assess the strengths of each successful candidate and match these core strengths to specific roles.

Those applicants like Lelah who passed the test were invited back to an Assessment Centre two weeks later for another full day; this time to take part in several group activities in the morning, followed by lunch and an interview. Immediately after the interview, she had to complete a series of *Developed Vetting* forms that delved into every aspect of her life to assess whether she'd be at risk of financial inducement or blackmail. These tests would be followed up by a six-month investigation and a further personal interview by a Vetting Officer who would come to her home.

Following this lengthy process, Lelah didn't hear anything back from *GCHQ* for some months and blithely assumed that she hadn't been successful. And then, one morning, the official-looking letter arrived on her doormat. It was short and to the point:

Dear Ms Hasan,
Thank you for your application to join the Technical Projects Team at GCHQ.
I am delighted to inform you that your application

has been successful.

If you would like to accept this offer of employment, please complete the enclosed paperwork and return it to me in the enclosed envelope.

Once we receive your formal acceptance, we would like to invite you to attend a special induction on 5 December with a view to you starting the following week commencing 9 December.

I look forward to hearing from you in due course.

Yours sincerely,

Angela Lansbury

Head of Personnel

Lelah was initially shocked by her success. She didn't think that she had come across terribly well at the interview; nor had she been especially happy with her contribution to the group activities. But she had obviously done enough to tick all the boxes. She was perfectly aware that she wasn't one of life's natural extroverts, but perhaps that had been in her favour. After all, it was generally accepted that some organisations steered clear of hiring individuals who displayed supreme confidence and charisma, on the basis that such candidates can often be too headstrong, lousy team players and generally less compliant. And the culture of *GCHQ* certainly seemed to be one that fostered an air of collective responsibility, judging from the open-plan layout of the place. Anyway, in her own quiet way, she'd done it. She'd achieved what she had set out to achieve. And for once in her life, she was actually feeling pretty proud of herself. In fact, part of her was feeling the sudden urge to share her good news with all and sundry; to shout it from the rooftops, but she knew full well that this was something she'd never be able to do. One of the many things made abundantly clear from those intensive few days in Cheltenham was that secrecy was of paramount importance to those fortunate enough to work for *GCHQ*. Besides having to sign the Official Secrets Act, all employees were forbidden to let anyone outside their immediate family know where they worked, let alone what they worked on.

✦

As a Muslim and an outstanding mathematician, it wasn't entirely surprising that Lelah ended up being placed in the *Bletchley 5* counter-terrorism unit. *Bletchley 5* represented one of thirty sizeable technical teams designated to analyse internet data with possible terrorist associations. She would be required to hone her cryptography and steganography skills and work with specialist filter programs like *Paragon* and *Jayne* that had been devised to trawl internet traffic for certain words, phrases, acronyms or encrypted text with possible terrorist connotations. *Paragon* and *Jayne* had been part of a massive joint initiative with the Americans, had taken over five years to develop at a cost of more than 150 million dollars, and was constantly being modified and updated. The two programs would eventually evolve into one, allowing *GCHQ* to access the fibre cables that carried the world's web traffic and telecommunications, and store captured data for up to 30 days.

Bletchley 5 dealt primarily with internet traffic in the South West including London, so it was regarded by many as one of the most prestigious if not important filtering units within *GCHQ*. And since *9/11*, it had been instrumental in foiling at least 20 significant terrorist plots on the homeland, including the infamous boot bomber Richard Green.

Every piece of data that Lelah analysed had to be classified into one of four risk categories: Extremely High, High, Medium, or Low. Most would inevitably fall into the Low or Medium categories. Those that made it onto the Extremely High or High rankings were apparently almost always encrypted, and these golden nuggets would be verified and ultimately shared with other intelligence services, including *MI5* and the American intelligence-gathering agencies. There was a tendency for genuinely disturbing traffic to be buried away in digital image and audio files through fairly sophisticated use of steganography. And messages would almost always be cryptic, using code words and euphemisms. References to marriage or weddings would, for instance, very often mean bombing or detonating. And the use of girls' names would commonly stand for bomb-making chemicals.

The whole tangled web of Jihadist terrorism would become clearer, though increasingly complex to Lelah, as time went by. But on one level, carrying out her work was not very different from getting stuck into her academic assignments at university, which she loved. Only with this work, she had the added bonus of knowing that it would help protect her homeland; the country that she adored, and would hopefully stifle the despicable, criminal plans of those twisted minds she so despised.

✦

Mohammed had discovered this 18th century neoclassical Palladian style house on the outskirts of Hampstead Heath on the day he'd ventured into Hampstead for that day's edition of the *Ham & High*. Once the rain had eased off, he had strolled around the village and then walked along Heath Street, which lead into Spaniards Road and passed the infamous Spaniards Inn where Highwayman Dick Turpin was reputed to have been born in the early 1700s. Continuing on down Hampstead Lane, he eventually spotted the impressive double gates and gatehouse to Kenwood House. Both people and cars seemed to be coming and going, so he thought he'd take a look. He walked through a small car park that was full to the gunwales with smart Germanic 4-wheel-drives and rubbed shoulders with middle-aged women with expensive-looking, well-groomed dogs in tow. He followed them down a path that curved through a thicket of mature rhododendrons and came out onto a large expanse of verdant grass to one side and an impressive forecourt and palace to the other. A gravel path continued down the side of the house through an enticing arched pergola clad in climbing vines that brought you out onto a magnificent vista of Hampstead Heath and the ornamental lake. The back of the house looked very different to the facade. For one thing, it was white in colour and shimmered in the sunlight; and it seemed to go on forever.

A little way past the house, the gravel path swept down to what would have once been the service wing to the house. Now it served as an animated tea room with tables and chairs both inside and out. And it was here that Mohammed had suggested to Ibrahim that they should meet.

Being a weekday, it wasn't as busy as it had been when he'd first discovered it. And despite it being a pleasantly mild day for April, most of the tables outside were vacant, so he took one that was well away from the house and sitting in its own isolated space.

Ibrahim shuffled into the forecourt no more than five minutes after Mohammed had arrived, his round wire spectacles glinting in the sunlight. Mohammed had already checked out his profile on social media and knew what he looked like. He raised his hand and Ibrahim acknowledged this friend of a friend.

'As-Salam-u-Alaikum.' Ibrahim smiled at Mohammed and repeated the same greeting back, and the two men shook hands.

'Thank you for agreeing to meet like this.' Mohammed paused and then lowered his voice. 'I know from Qssim how committed to the cause you are… I too am committed. Ever since my beloved brother was murdered by British and American bombs in Iraq, I have sworn to avenge his death.'

Ibrahim nodded and placed his right hand on Mohammed's arm. 'I feel your pain, brother. I know what it feels like to lose loved ones. Two of my Palestinian cousins were killed by the Israelis in Jenin in 2002. They were innocent civilians. They weren't armed fighters resisting the Israeli incursion.'

Mohammed fumbled in his pockets. 'I'm sorry… May peace be upon them.' He pulled out a photograph of a young man. 'This was my brother. His name was Salah. He had a glittering future ahead of him. He was a brilliant engineer… I can't tell you how much I miss him.' Ibrahim took the photograph in his hand and studied the benign smile and the dark mesmerising eyes that seemed both knowing and compassionate.

'May peace be upon him. He looks like he possessed a beautiful soul...'

'He did… I can assure you my friend, he did…'

A couple of young women sat down at a table close by. One was clearly of the faith and was wearing a headscarf. Her friend was a blonde and was in Ibrahim's eyes, at least, a classic 'English rose.' The girl with the headscarf caught Ibrahim's eye and smiled. She had a beautiful smile. He imagined she also had a beautiful soul.

◆

Lelah hadn't seen Nicola since graduating. They'd met in their first year when sharing college halls, and despite the fact that Nicola was a white Catholic studying History of Art and had little interest in maths, the two had hit it off from day one. They had remained best friends throughout university, had shared houses, and had confided in each other over everything from boyfriends to family relationships, so it was going to be difficult for Lelah not to say too much about her new job.

Lelah had come down to London for the weekend to stay with Nicola at her parent's house in Hampstead. Nicola's father was retired now and had run his own successful direct marketing agency in Covent Garden in the late 80s and had sold the company to the Slattery brothers during the pair's infamous buying spree in the late 90s. The family home was a rambling old Georgian pile that boasted five floors and a well-stocked wine cellar that sat in one of Hampstead's most popular locations for film crews, due to its proliferation of cast-iron railings and Victorian gas lamps.

'So tell me all about this new job that you've landed,' Nicola probed while pouring two cups of organic lemon and fennel tea from an elegant glass teapot.

'There's nothing much to tell really...' Nicola was looking distinctly disappointed. 'Well, that's not entirely true... Thing is I'm not at liberty to tell anyone. Suffice it to say that I'm employed by the government, everything I touch is classified, and I'm based in Cheltenham... And I'm not even supposed to tell you that much. So please keep it to yourself.'

Nicola put her cup down. Lelah chuckled to herself as she could literally see the penny dropping by the expression on Nicola's face 'Oh my God... How exciting, Lelah... You can rest assured that my lips will remain sealed.'

Lelah nodded appreciatively and smiled.

'Bloody hell Lelah, that's amazing. You've done incredibly well to get there.' And then as a conspiratorial whisper, she added: 'I've heard that it's notoriously difficult to get through the application process. I know Oxbridge graduates with Firsts who were weeded out in the early rounds.'

'I know. To be honest Nicola, I don't know how I did it. My interview was terrible, but I guess they probably liked the fact that I didn't come across as arrogant and full of myself.' She poured more tea in both cups and topped up the pot with hot water.

'Do your parents know?... I mean, are you allowed to tell them?'

'Oh yes. We can tell immediate family where we're working, but that's about all we can tell them. We can't talk about what we actually do... But, you know the really great thing about this job is that I'm not allowed to take my work home with me for obvious reasons. How cool is that?' The two girls laughed in unison.

'But hey, that's enough about me. I want to know more about your new job.'

'Well it's nothing as exciting as yours, but it is quite interesting in its own quiet way… I'm working for a small gallery in New Bond Street owned by this charming old buffer called Matthew Anstruther-Gough who inherited the business from his father. They specialise in Italian Renaissance, Flemish and Dutch portraiture from the late 15th to 16th centuries. There are some lovely pieces in the collection including a fab portrait attributed to the world's first recognised female Flemish portrait painter Catharina van Hemessen who leant her trade from her father in the mid-1500s. I could bore you for hours about this woman, but don't worry, I won't.

'But the really interesting piece is an enormous portrait of a young boy that Matthew picked up in New York some years ago, which he's convinced is one of a pair by Caravaggio. The other one, according to Matthew, hangs in the Hermitage in Moscow. Thing is the experts in London can't agree among themselves over its authenticity. If it is ever verified by the London experts as a genuine Caravaggio, its selling price would be astronomical, as Caravaggios are incredibly rare.'

'That's incredible. I wonder what your Mr Anstruther-Gough paid for it.'

'I asked him that very question, and didn't expect him to give me such a candid answer… Apparently, he paid £150,000 from a private collector in Manhattan on the basis that the piece was attributed to the 'circle of Caravaggio.' Now that may seem like a huge sum of money to the likes of you and I… but if it were a genuine Caravaggio, then he'd be sitting on a painting worth in excess of £50 million.'

'Wow. So what does he plan to do with it?'

'Well, he's talking to the Hermitage with a view to lending it to them to exhibit alongside their own. As far as the Russians are concerned, it is the genuine article. And Hugo reckons that an airing at the Hermitage will seriously strengthen his case and put pressure on the London cynics to reconsider.'

✦

The two girls on the table nearest to them were making Mohammed feel a little uncomfortable. He certainly couldn't hear what they were talking about, so they were clearly out of earshot, but their mere presence put him on edge.

'I think this place is getting a little too busy for my liking. Shall we go for a walk across Hampstead Heath?'

Ibrahim was thinking the same thing. 'Yes, that would be a good idea. I've never seen Hampstead Heath before.'

The two men rose from the table as the two girls seemed to be laughing at something. Something no doubt frivolous like clothes or pop music, Mohammed thought to himself.

'It's new to me too. I came here for the first time myself only a week ago,' Mohammed explained. 'You see I had to buy a copy of a weekly publication called the *Ham & High* - it's shorthand for the *Hampstead & Highgate Express*. I don't live around here. I actually live over the other side of London in Forest Hill in South London. Where have you come from?'

Ibrahim was distracted momentarily by a series of high-pitched squawks as a flock of distinctly green feathered birds flew overhead. Parakeets had just started to colonize Hampstead Heath, and their plumage was unmistakable.

The two men continued up a steep incline. 'I'm currently living in Peckham, but I was brought up in Warrington, up north. You can probably detect a slight Northern accent.'

At the brow of the hill, the two paused for breath. Before them lay a lush carpet of green and ochre, and nestling behind the treeline you could discern London's recent landmarks. The huge white hula-hoop that was the London Eye peeked out from the grey cityscape, its glass pods twinkling like little diamonds on a bracelet. And Canary Wharf could be seen further back, standing solid and majestic - a beacon for the City and the resurgence of the East End.

Mohammed pointed to a solitary bench. 'Shall we park ourselves here?'

Ibrahim looked relieved. 'I wouldn't say no. My legs aren't what they used to be.' This was all perfectly pleasant, he thought, but when was Mohammed going to explain what all this was about?

Mohammed removed an envelope from his jacket, slid out several sheets of paper and handed one of them to Ibrahim. 'This was an email I received some while ago, completely out of the blue. I have no idea who it was from, but I was intrigued nonetheless. Read it.'

Ibrahim reached for his lens cleaner and rubbed the lenses of his spectacles. Then he brought the typed sheet into focus.

The message urged Mohammed to 'carry out jihad and strike at the infidel.' It was written in a tone of voice that was more than familiar to Ibrahim. He could imagine any one of the many committed imams preaching in London, writing it. The message concluded with a request to purchase a copy of the following week's *Ham & High* and look in the personal lonely hearts ads.

Ibrahim looked up from the page. 'I am intrigued… And did you manage to get a copy of this *Ham & High*?'

Mohammed nodded and produced a second piece of paper, which he unfolded and handed to Ibrahim. 'This was the wording of one of the ads in the lonely hearts section.' Ibrahim studied the typed text. It was short and cryptic - written in the style of a personal ad, not that he was particularly familiar with such ads. But there could be no mistaking the hidden message. And the final words: 'Our real rewards will be in heaven' would have resonated with any Islamist worth his salt.

'You responded to the Box number?'

'With Qssim... He wrote the reply. Here…' Mohammed handed Ibrahim the third message. He studied it. It was another cryptic message in the style of a personal ad. It was signed off with the email name GHadleigh. Why GHadleigh? he wondered. And then it suddenly dawned on him why.

'Nice touch that - signing off GHadleigh - as in jihad.'

'Yeah. We were quite pleased with that. It was Qssim's idea. Wondered if you'd spot that.'

'Nice one…' Ibrahim handed the sheets of folded A4 back to his new friend. 'And did you get a reply?'

Mohammed produced yet another printout. 'It took a little while to get a response, but then this finally came through.' He handed Ibrahim the sheet. The subject line read: Instructions for GHadleigh. And the sender was the same Alan Anonymous that had sent the previous messages. But then there followed reams of gibberish that looked like spam. It filled the entire page. Ibrahim gave up reading it after the first line and just flipped the page over. There was more of the same on the reverse. But then at the foot of the page in caps was a simple instruction to cut and paste the spam into a decoding website. It was encrypted.

'Bloody hell. This is serious shit.'

'I know. I wasn't sure if I should have continued.' Mohammed paused. 'I just felt the more I got involved, the more difficult it would become to withdraw. But then I also felt somehow privileged, honoured even that they should choose me of all people. And then I thought this could be the one chance I'll ever get to avenge the murder of my brother - may peace be upon him...

'So this is the message I received once I'd pasted the spam into the *Spam Mimic* website.' He produced a final sheaf of paper, and Ibrahim studied it carefully. This was clearly a call to arms. Mohammed was now being urged to appoint an accomplice. To do what exactly wasn't entirely clear. But what was clear was that further instructions would follow in due course.

Another flock of noisy bright green parakeets made their way from the husk of an ancient gnarled oak to another nesting place further afield, and shafts of sunlight formed a patchwork of bright yellow puddles on the grass. The sun was setting now, and casting long shadows across the heath while the distant skyline of the city had turned into a less well-defined grey smudge.

'So the question, my friend, is will you be my loyal accomplice?'

Ibrahim felt honoured. It was his calling to serve Allah and carry out jihad and avenge the persecution and murder of Muslims across the globe. He knew that. And he also knew that the West was the biggest threat to Islam. Everything the West had in its sights could only ever be accomplished by the elimination of Islam. It was either us or them. That, as far as he was concerned, was an irrefutable fact.

He didn't need to answer. Instead, he looked into the dark brown eyes of Mohammed.

'Allahu Akbar… Allahu Akbar… Allahu Akbar...'

✦

As the sun began its slow descent, burnishing the edges of a ragged cloud formation and creating narrow bands of pale orange and magenta, a cyclist in a dark green hoodie freewheeled from the top of the hill. Cycling on the Heath was strictly prohibited, but Clive was willing to take the risk occasionally. He couldn't understand why you couldn't cycle freely here but could do so in Richmond Park. It didn't make any sense. Anyway, he figured he'd get away with it more readily at this time of day when the light was beginning to fade.

As he sped down the path, he admired the landscape that had enticed the artist John Constable to set up his easel on the Heath and complete his oil sketches from life over a hundred years ago. The large expanse of land and sky was a rare sight so close to the city.

As he turned down the home straight, he was distracted by an unusual sighting. Two men were hugging each other on a park bench, and he was quite sure that one of them was visibly crying.

CHAPTER TWELVE

You could call it beginner's luck, but Lelah had always possessed that lucky streak. Ever since she was a child, she had won competitions and prize draws. She had even won £10,000 on the *Premium Bonds* with no more than a £50 stake. And now after just two months into her job, she'd struck gold.

It hadn't been a particularly sophisticated piece of encryption. The message had been simply buried in a block of fake spam generated by the *Spam Mimic* website. So she didn't even have to employ any of her considerable steganography skills to unpick the code. It had quite literally fallen into her lap.

Barry Gardener, her line manager sat at his desk looking like the cat who'd got the cream. 'As we suspected, it's good news, Lelah.' He paused, placed his reading glasses on his nose and took another cursory look at the printout. 'It's been verified by *Vixen 5* as high priority. As you know, high priority finds aren't exactly everyday occurrences in this department. Last one was over 5 months ago. *Bletchley 13* have had slightly better results than us of late - not that we're in any kind of contest you understand. But even they haven't picked up anything of significance recently.'

Lelah smiled nervously. Barry had been at *GCHQ* for five years and in this time had worked his way up to manage *Bletchley 5*. But then he was your classic A star candidate, having achieved a First in Applied Mathematics at King's College Cambridge. He had scored so well when applying to *GCHQ* that he had been automatically selected for the Fast Track Programme. He fitted the English boffin stereotype to a tee: being well-spoken; from middle home counties stock; with a minor public school education; and was definitely old before his time. There was an air of confidence about him that some would mistake for conceited arrogance. Give him a tweed jacket with leather buttons and elbow pads and he'd look every bit a Bletchley Park Enigma code-breaking boffin from the 1940s. Lelah actually got to like his slightly shambolic manner and his sonorous Radio 4 voice. Besides, he'd been particularly nice to her from day one, and was generally very supportive of the entire team under his wing.

'Anyway, the upshot to all this is that *MI5* is now on the case and our boys and girls over in *C Wing* will be tracing our prime suspects… Excuse me one moment Lelah. I'm gasping for a coffee. Can I grab you one?'

'No, I'm good thanks.'

'Don't go away. I'll be back in two secs.' And with that, he sprung from his ergonomically designed swivel chair and made his way over to the open plan kitchen area opposite.

While he was gone, Lelah cast her eye over the printout.

> *Brother,*
>
> *Following your request, I can report that I have a loyal accomplice with whom I can trust. Together we await your next command. We look forward, God willing, to carry out jihad and obey the commandments of the prophet, Alayhis Salam. The*

> *unbeliever cannot be allowed to oppress our brothers any longer.*
>
> *The name of my accomplice is Ibrahim Choudhury, and his email address is I.Choudury@yahoo.co.uk*
>
> *Allahu Akbar*

These 74 words were fairly direct. There had been no attempt by the sender to disguise their meaning and intent once the spam cover had been broken. It had apparently been very unusual for a message of this nature to be so blatant, and suggested to Barry that they were dealing with some kind of naive chancer.

Barry returned to his desk with his coffee, which he placed well away from his keyboard, having already written off two.

'As I was saying Lelah, it's been verified. So that means it will now be shared with *MI5* and the boys in blue.' He gingerly sipped at his coffee. 'So I think we can safely assume that there'll be a surveillance operation triggered and a fair bit of delving into bank accounts and the like. *C Wing* should have details for us on the sender and recipient any day; and with any luck, they'll be unearthing further threads sent from that IP address. But I can already tell you in confidence that we know that Ibrahim Choudhary has a criminal record. He served three months at Her Majesty's Young Offender Institution in Aylesbury for criminal damage to garden gnomes, would you believe.'

Lelah thought she was hearing things. 'I beg your pardon.'

'Yep, that's right. It's a pretty bizarre one admittedly. Why anyone would want to go and destroy garden gnomes beats me.'

'And three months inside sounds a tad harsh doesn't it?'

'Ah... Well, it would have been, had it not been for the manner in which these bearded little men met their demise.'

Lelah raised her eyebrows and gave Barry one of her quizzical looks.

'He used an explosive device... Well, not exactly a serious device, but a crude dry ice bomb. As far as the judge was concerned, his was "a gross act of indiscriminate recklessness that put the lives of innocent members of the public at risk." It was enough to put him inside - albeit for a relatively short period of time.'

Barry opened a drawer in his desk and pulled out a red file and handed it to Lelah. 'These are the case notes if you're interested. Reads a bit like a Tom Sharpe novel if you ask me... Anyway, what I wanted to say was congratulations on landing this one. Our Mr Choudhary may seem like a small fish, but from my experience, it's very often the small fish that surprise us the most. They should never be underestimated... Small acorns and all that. Anyway... in light of all this, I think a working lunch is in order. Can you do next Friday?'

Lelah smiled. 'Yes, that should be fine, Barry.'

'Excellent. It will give me a chance to fill you in on the department's training programmes, and some exciting new software that's now in the pipeline.' He paused, brought up his diary on his screen and entered the details. 'Naturally, this would also be a good opportunity for you to share any concerns or queries you may have... So put it in your diary. And I'll keep you posted on developments as and when I know more.'

'Thank you Barry.'

'My pleasure. All part of the service.'

CHAPTER THIRTEEN

'Oseh shalom bimromav, hu yaaseh shalom aleinu v'al kol Yisraeil, v'im'ru: Amen.'

The word 'Amen' was repeated by everyone else in the room; all of whom were standing. There must have been well over a hundred people here - both men and women; though women, Michael noticed, were for some curious reason at the back of the room. There was a pause, and then the elderly rabbi looked earnestly at the five mourners and closed his prayer book as well as his eyes. 'The Lord who heals the brokenhearted and binds up their wounds, may He grant consolation to the mourners. O strengthen them and support them in the day of their sadness and grief; and remember them and their children for a long and good life. Put into their hearts the love and reverence for You, that they may serve You with a perfect heart; and let their end be peace. Amen.'

Again the word 'Amen' was repeated by the congregation.

The rabbi continued. 'As a mother comforts her son, so will I comfort you; and in Jerusalem you shall find comfort. Your sun shall no more set; your moon shall no more withdraw itself, for the Lord shall be your everlasting light, and your days of mourning shall be ended. He will destroy death for ever; and the Lord God will wipe away the tears from all faces, and remove the reproach of His people from the whole earth; for the Lord has spoken it.'

The three men and two elderly ladies standing close to the rabbi then recited the Hebrew mourners' prayer once more until the room once again resonated to the word 'Amen.'

At this point, everyone seemed to close their prayer books, and the rabbi turned to the assembled congregants. 'That concludes the shiva service. You may now pay your respects to the family.' No sooner had he uttered these words than waitresses appeared with silver platters laden with lovingly made canapés, and the discrete hubbub of hushed conversation began to fill the room.

This was the first time Michael had experienced a Jewish memorial service known as a shiva. He was here to support one of his best friends, Danny Grunberg. He and Danny had been good friends since primary school, and had both ended up in the law. In Danny's case, the bar where as a successful criminal barrister, he had eventually taken silk and was now head of Chambers in Gray's Inn.

Danny's father Helmut had lived with leukaemia for almost 20 years, so had done exceptionally well to get to 82. As a German Jewish child growing up in Hamburg in the 30s, he and his two sisters had been lucky enough to have been among the first tranche of Jewish kids to be transported to England by their parents on the *Kindertransport* in February 1939, before the rest of the family were transported by the Nazis to their eventual deaths at Neuengamme concentration camp in northern Germany. Michael had met the old man many times and had admired his tenacity in embracing a new life, building a successful property business and raising a family. While Helmut had still been able to speak German fluently, there had been no trace of a German accent when he spoke English, and he had been a fiercely patriotic Englishman first and foremost. Like so many refugees who came here during the war, he loved his adopted homeland with a passion and strived to be more English than the English.

Michael last came to Danny's house before the terrorists had put him in a wheelchair. It was a charming Edwardian home with an abundance of original features, generously sized rooms, high ceilings and large sash windows. It was just as well it was capacious judging by the number of people who now wanted to pay their respects to the old man. Though the one thing the house certainly was not was wheelchair friendly. Despite this, Danny had clearly gone to great lengths to install impressive ramps at both the front and back of the house that provided the perfect gradient for a manual wheelchair user. Michael was touched by his friend's thoughtfulness but not in the least bit surprised. Danny was that kind of person; always thinking about the needs of others over himself. It was probably why he was such a good barrister. It was little wonder why all his clients in the criminal fraternity seemed to love him.

One of the waitresses bent down and thrust a silver platter of delicious fare under Michael's nose. Before he knew it he had a veritable plate of goodies on his lap. It was a pleasantly warm evening, so he pushed himself through to Danny's library at the back of the house and through the open French doors and down the second ramp. The terrace looked out onto a pretty, well-tended walled garden. A manicured lawn with its ornamental sundial was the centrepiece, ably assisted by herbaceous borders, rose beds and mature trees and shrubs of every description.

There were a couple of groups sitting at a table, and Michael thought about joining them, but before the thought had activated his arms to set his wheels in motion, he was distracted by footsteps directly behind him.

'Friend or family?' A tall and ungainly looking man with distinctive sideburns and a moustache leant down and offered Michael his outstretched hand.

'Oh… friend. Very good friend as it happens. Danny and I go way back… Since we were in short trousers. And yourself?'

'I'm a friend, too. Though our friendship isn't as long-standing as yours. The name's Alastair by the way. Alastair McCleod… First time I've been to one of these… Not of the faith, I'm afraid.'

Michael picked at his finger food. 'Me neither. Moving service though, even though I don't understand a word of Hebrew. And Danny's eulogy was touching wasn't it?'

Alastair nodded. 'He's a first-rate speaker is our Danny. But then, that is his bread and butter after all. Have you ever heard him in a courtroom?'

Michael shook his head. 'Regrettably, I haven't. But I should imagine he's formidable.'

'He's one of the best… There aren't many defence counsels out there that can have both the judge and jury eating out of their hand like he does.'

'So are you in the law?' Michael probed tentatively.'

'You could say that. I'm a copper. Detective Chief Inspector with *CID* to be more precise.'

Michael wasn't expecting that as an answer. For some strange reason, he assumed that he'd been another lawyer. But the fact that he was now talking directly to a senior detective also seemed fortuitous. Michael had been busking with this whole terrorist fishing malarkey, and if the truth be known, he was beginning to feel a little out of his depth - particularly since he had now received an email from what journalists might describe as a potentially active terror cell. One half of him was itching to offload everything he'd been up to to this Alistair character. But the rational side of him didn't want to spill the beans, and wanted to stay in control, and remain perfectly calm.

'Oh, wow. That must be an exciting job if all those detective shows gracing our TV screens are to be believed.

'It has its moments.'

'So how do you know Danny?' Michael asked.

'Cricket... We both open the batting for The Bluebottles. We're a bunch of coppers mainly. But I knew Danny well before that, through my work. That's how I got him roped into the team... Bloody good batsman. Has one of the sweetest cover drives I've ever seen.'

Michael had forgotten about his friend's love of the noble game. 'Ah yes. He does love his cricket. He once dragged me off to a Test Match at Lords. I'm afraid I don't share Danny's passion for the game; any game come to that. I have two left feet and absolutely no ball sense.'

'At least you know your limitations. Had a new chap join us for one game who reckoned he was a pretty decent minor counties level seam bowler. And when we brought him on he proceeded to bowl ten wides in his one and only over... Anyway, that's enough about cricket. How about yourself Michael? What's your line of business if you don't mind me asking? ... No, don't tell me, you're an accountant aren't you?'

Michael laughed. 'No, I'm afraid not. But you're not a million miles wide of the mark. I'm a solicitor. At least I used to be one until I ended up as a tetraplegic.'

Alastair gave him a look of sympathy and for a moment wished he hadn't gone there. 'Oh, I'm sorry

Michael, I didn't mean to pry into…'

'No, it's ok. I'm one of the lucky ones. I actually survived. 52 poor sods didn't.'

'Oh my God. You are one of the victims of the 7/7 bombing aren't you?

Michael nodded. 'Yep. That's me. And to be honest, there's not a single day that passes when I'm not haunted by the faces of those other poor buggers - including a young girl - who were sitting and standing right next to me. Completely innocent people who didn't make it.'

Alastair put his hand on Michael's shoulder. 'I'm really sorry Michael. If there's anything I can do to help…'

'Thanks Alastair. As it happens, there might be at some point… Do you have a business card?'

Alistair rifled through his jacket pockets and pulled out a worn-out old wallet from which he plucked a business card and then proceeded to scribble something on the back of it. 'Here you go. I've written my mobile number on the back. It's best to catch me on that, as I'm rarely by my desk these days. You can call me anytime. And if I'm not picking up, just leave a message. I'll get back to you. That's a promise.'

Michael took the card and placed it in his pocket. 'Thanks Alastair. I appreciate that, and may very well take you up on that. Anyway, I must make a move… Very nice to have made your acquaintance. I hope the next time we see each other is in happier circumstances.' He shook Alastair's hand for the second time and wheeled himself back inside through the library and down a tessellated passageway that led past an elegant dining room and sitting room, and back to the large drawing-room. The numbers were clearly decimated now, though the waitresses were still circulating with their silver platters. Danny and his two brothers and his father's two elderly sisters were sitting in the bay window on low chairs as is the Jewish custom. Michael shook their hands in turn and muttered his condolences. Danny was last in the line-up. He took Michael's hand warmly in both of his. 'It's really good of you to make the effort Michael. I really appreciate it… Dad really liked you, you know.'

Michael smiled. 'I liked him too. He was an incredible man.'

Danny wiped away a tear. 'Tell me, how are the kids doing? I haven't seen them in ages.'

'Ben's in his final year and seems to be coasting and Tash is enjoying her job.'

'And how's it been without Louise?'

'Do you really want to know?… Bloody marvellous… blissful. Trouble is, the kids don't have much to do with her either. As much as I try to get them to at least call her, they just don't seem to want to.'

'Well, it's down to Louise too to make the effort. You always said she was a bit of a cold fish… Are you going to be alright getting back? Can I order you a cab with wheelchair ramps?'

Michael raised his right hand in protest. 'No it's fine Danny. I'm driving again. I've been on a training course to learn how to use hand controls, and slide from my wheelchair into the car and then pull the wheels and frame separately from the pavement and onto the passenger seat. It's not as difficult as it sounds because I've got this super light wheelchair made from carbon fibre.'

'That's fantastic Michael… Look, I'm sorry I haven't been in touch recently. I've been worked off my feet, and things at this end haven't exactly been a bed of roses. But I will give you a call next week. Perhaps you'd care for a spot of lunch. I've just joined the Athenaeum. Dad would have loved it. Quintessentially English. Charles Dickens, Benjamin Disraeli and Charles Darwin were all members, so heaven knows why they've let riff-raff like me in.'

Michael laughed. 'They haven't met me yet… I'd love that. We'll catch up then. Speak soon.'

Danny patted his friend affectionately on the shoulder and bid Michael farewell, while an elderly gentleman stooped down and wished him a long life.

✦

One of the few good things about being disabled, and there weren't many, was that you could park pretty easily with a blue badge. In Camden, for instance, you could even park on double yellow lines, so long as there were no yellow kerb dashes present. So parking outside Danny's place in the heart of Hampstead had been a doddle.

Tash had been fantastic as usual. She had done all the research online to discover which model gave you the most space between the top of the steering column and the back of the driver's seat to pull the wheelchair frame and its wheels from the driver's side to the passenger's side. The *Honda Jazz* fitted the bill perfectly, so Michael had ordered a new one to be adapted with hand controls. It was a lovely little car, and strangely enough, he didn't miss the old *Mercedes*, which in retrospect was far too large and far too thirsty for his liking.

Driving back, his mind now turned to his encounter with Alastair. He seemed like a genuinely likeable bloke. And he was keen to speak to him. But it felt too early. He had to work out in his own mind his next plan of action. It wasn't for him to make suggestions to potential terrorists. No, any foul plans had to be initiated and carried out by them. All he had to do was provide some kind of spark or incentive; a carrot to dangle in front of their filthy noses before laying the trap. And only when he had laid the trap could he speak again to Alastair. But for the moment the carrot was eluding him. As he turned into Hoop Lane, it suddenly dawned on him. He was being a complete fool. The carrot had to act as bait. It had to engender trust. And it had to be irresistible. There could only ever be one kind of carrot like that. It was bloody obvious. Why had it taken him so long to work it out?

He punched the air and then switched on *Classic FM* and turned Mozart's Requiem to full volume. Make no mistake. He was going to screw those bastards good and proper He was going to screw those bastards if it was the last thing he did.

CHAPTER FOURTEEN

It may have been the oldest trick in the book, but it always worked a treat. It was one of the most effective ways to gain access to a property without arousing suspicion. Dennis placed the lanyard pass with the *British Gas* logo and personal details on show, around his neck and got out of the van. He'd been with *MI5* as an intelligence officer, which was just another title for spy, for seven years now. It wasn't in the least bit glamorous. Nothing like being James Bond. In fact, he hadn't planned on joining the service. He'd originally been recruited when applying for a job at the Foreign Office, which he didn't get. Instead, he'd received a letter back from the Ministry of Defence suggesting he might consider other 'more interesting' positions by contacting the phone number at the foot of the letter. He had been intrigued and flattered, and ended up going for a four-hour interview in an unmarked building, at the end of which he'd had to sign the Official Secrets Act. The recruitment process continued for another seven months after that initial interview, until he was eventually officially assigned to *H Branch* that investigated and infiltrated extreme left-wing political targets in the UK. You tend to get moved around every two years, so he'd done stints for various other branches including *T Branch*, which monitors militant Irish republicanism. The money was crap, but the job was certainly interesting; far more interesting than his previous job as Head Librarian at Belsize Park's public library.

Now he'd been moved to the notorious *J Branch* responsible for monitoring homegrown terrorism, and this had been the first case he'd been assigned to. *GCHQ* had intercepted an encrypted conversation between two suspected jihadists and had tracked down three physical locations. Now it was down to J Branch to get their hands dirty.

Forest Hill wasn't an area he was particularly familiar with, but then South East London wasn't somewhere he had reason to visit. As an East Ender brought up in Wanstead, he knew the East End and West End like the back of his hand. Venturing anywhere south of the river was like visiting a foreign country. This said, this terrace of late Victorian houses could easily have passed for any road in Wanstead. Dennis couldn't help noticing that number 16 was a bit tattier than its neighbours - and even they weren't exactly showhomes. He opened the rusting front garden gate and pushed his way past overgrown laurel bushes. The place clearly needed a lick of paint and a fair bit of TLC. He pressed the doorbell, but this was greeted by silence. It obviously wasn't working. So he used the feeble excuse for a door-knocker that hung apologetically below the letterbox. But this produced little in the way of noise, so he finally resorted to the crude approach of thumping on the door with his fist. Eventually, a young girl with dyed red hair and a pierced nose came to the door in a dressing gown. She looked as if she'd only just got out of bed.

'Hi there. Can I help you?'

Dennis took hold of his lanyard pass and showed it to the girl. 'Good morning. I've come from *British Gas* to service the boiler and carry out safety checks to the property. You should have received prior notice by post.'

'Oh yeah. We did. Come on in... The boiler's through here.' She led him through a narrow corridor and into a small lobby area behind the staircase.

'The boiler's here.' The girl opened a white melamine cupboard and revealed an old Potterton boiler that would have looked more at home in a museum.

'Thank you very much. I'll just check that everything's in order here, and once I've done that, I'll need to run our Carbon Monoxide safety tests in all the rooms.' Dennis paused. 'How many people are living here?'

'Five at the last count. Used to be six, but Maureen's moved out. Had a blazing row with her boyfriend last week, and we haven't seen her since.'

Dennis opened his toolbox and fumbled around. Every room in the house bar the communal bathroom had been turned into a bed-sit by the landlord to eke out as much rent as humanly possible, and he'd obviously spent diddly squat in the process. The house was a disgrace, and almost certainly broke every health and safety rule in the book. It was a disaster waiting to happen.

'Ok. And is everyone at home?' he asked.

The girl gave him a pained expression. 'Not sure to be honest... Ibrahim upstairs is in. I know that because I saw him only ten minutes ago. But if the others aren't I'm sure they'd be ok with you doing your safety check... Better safe than sorry, eh?'

Dennis nodded. 'Absolutely. It's shocking how so many rented apartments fall below the safety standards these days.'

The girl stood there watching him as if she had nothing better to do, which she probably didn't. Should he wait for her to sling her hook before planting his bugging devices? He knew the answer to that one.

'I don't suppose there's any chance of a cup of tea luv, is there? I ran out of the house without breakfast this morning, and I couldn't half do with a cuppa if that's alright.'

The girl smiled, happy that she could assist. 'Yeah. Course. No problem. How do you take it?'

'White with no sugar. I'm sweet enough.'

'Coming up… Ooh, tell you what I'll even rustle up some toast and jam. How does that sound?'

'Bloody marvellous. You're a star. Thanks so much.'

The girl turned and disappeared into one of two downstairs rooms. As soon as she had gone, Dennis set to work. He planted one bugging device at the top of the cupboard housing the boiler, and then took his small stepladder to the front of the house where he'd spotted a smoke detector on the ceiling near the front door. He looked up the stairs. The coast was clear. He'd have to be quick. He stood on his stepladder and prized open the smoke detector with a screwdriver and placed the bugging device under a couple of wires. To the untrained eye, it would look as if it were part of the alarm. He snapped it closed and resumed his place by the boiler. By the time the girl returned with tea and toast, he'd closed the boiler cupboard and produced some paperwork.

The girl handed him a mug and a plate of toast in exchange for which Dennis gave her a *British Gas* Inspection form. 'That's lovely. Thank you.' Dennis took the plate and mug. 'And if I can ask you to sign this please?' The girl looked at the form and Dennis handed her a pen while munching on a piece of toast. 'Everything seems to be working as it should, despite its age. But we will be writing to your landlord in due course to recommend a new boiler because, to be honest, this one is well past its sell-by date, and once it goes, it will be beyond repair.'

'Fair enough… Hope that little shit of a landlord takes notice… He was meant to have the place painted last month and he still hasn't sorted out the damp in my room.'

Dennis gave her one of his sympathetic, knowing looks. 'Well, if it's ok by you I'll just check your room for any gas leaks.'

The girl led him into a cramped bedsit that was strewn with all manner of detritus; mainly clothes plus CDs, magazines, trashy paperbacks, dirty coffee mugs and stuff that rightly belonged out of view in the bathroom.

'You'll have to excuse the mess I'm afraid,' she said while making a token gesture of picking up a couple of paperbacks, as if that made any difference.

'That's alright, you haven't seen my daughter's room.' He removed a handheld device and pointed it in the air while taking readings. 'All looks good to me… I'll just check the back of your oven.' He tipped the old piece of iron forward and surreptitiously placed a bugging device on the wall. She clearly wasn't a prime target, but it was always protocol to bug entire premises that harboured primary targets. With this completed, he made his way out. 'Many thanks for the tea and toast. Very much appreciated.'

'You're welcome.' The door clicked behind him as he climbed the stairs.

A noticeably short Asian young man in his mid to late 30s wearing wire-framed spectacles and a black t-shirt answered the door of one of two rooms upstairs.

Dennis went through the same procedure again. Ibrahim smiled politely and showed the stranger into his room.

Unlike his neighbour downstairs, Ibrahim's room was spotless and tidy; almost too tidy for Dennis's liking. There was a prayer mat in the corner and a desk with the ubiquitous laptop. Other than a single bed and a bookshelf housing a solitary row of books on Islam, the room was spartan.

'I'm just going to check behind your gas oven for any possible leaks.' He repeated the exercise of inspecting the pipes while placing the bugging device behind the oven. 'All looks fine... I've already checked the communal boiler, which is fine for the moment. I explained to your neighbour downstairs that it should be replaced soon by your landlord, as it is extremely old.' Ibrahim nodded. As Dennis spoke, he noticed the gas heater on the opposite wall. 'Do you use the heater much?'

'Only in winter, as we don't have double glazing.'

'Well, I'll check that, too.' He knelt down with his back to Ibrahim and on turning the gas tap, discreetly placed a bugging device just between the gas pipe and the skirting board. It was the perfect place. The two devices would pick up everything including the proverbial pin dropping. He was bloody good at this. 'That all looks good, too. Can't be too cautious with these appliances... Thank you. I'll see myself out.' Before closing the door behind him, he turned. 'Oh, is it ok if I use the little boy's room?'

Ibrahim looked perplexed. 'I'm sorry?'

'The loo. I presume there is one. Is it alright if I use it?

Ibrahim laughed. 'Yes, of course. There's a bathroom across the passageway. Goodbye.'

Dennis slipped into the bathroom and locked the door. The bathroom, like much else in the place, was well out of date, and the toilet cistern was high up on the wall, so he stood on the toilet and reached for the top of the dust-ridden porcelain where he placed another bugging device. Then he pulled the flush and ran the taps for a few seconds before making his departure.

There were just two more rooms to complete. Sensing that the girl was probably right, he tapped on the door of Ibrahim's neighbour. There was no response, so he gently turned the handle and let himself in.

Within five minutes he was back in the van and bringing up his email on his mobile. He needed to file a status update to the technical backup team. He tapped out everything they needed to know.

Branch: J
Project: Orion
Primary location J - 567
No. of active devices: 6
Primary targets: 1
Collateral targets: 4

Then he pressed send - a simple action that would immediately require a three-man team to conduct 24-hour monitoring of every sound emanating from primary location J - 567.

He turned on the new *TomTom* satnav on his windscreen and keyed in the postcode for his next assignment of the day: location J - 742. This would require him to drive back across the river and head for north London's Alexandra Park; an area he was pretty familiar with, having once rented a flat in Muswell Hill. With a twist of the ignition key, he started the engine, pulled out from the kerb and punched the radio's on button. The radio was set to one of London's phone-in stations.

'Hello James. You're live on air. What would you like to say about this media storm we're now witnessing over this prank telephone call by Floss and Bland ?'

'Hi Colin. Many thanks for taking my call. Well, I think it's nothing short of a disgrace quite honestly. I mean these guys are beyond the pale. It wasn't in the least bit funny… I mean, how would you feel if you were called by a radio presenter and told live on air that your daughter was sleeping around?'

'I wouldn't be happy, that's for sure... But do you think the BBC was right to suspend them?'

'To be perfectly frank, I'd have gone further. They should have been fired and fined for bringing the broadcasting corporation into disrepute.'

'Thank you for that James. There certainly seems to be a pattern emerging here… And now I'm going to have to hand over to Gordon Kay for a news update. But don't go away...'

Dennis pressed one of the pre-set buttons and the calming sound Bach's Goldberg Variations wafted through the van. It was one of his favourite pieces of classical music. And if he wasn't mistaken this was one of his all-time favourite performers. The strange human mumblings and grunts behind the exquisite fingering of the *Steinway*'s keys were unmistakable.

'Take it away Glenn, you mad bloody genius. Take it away my son.' As far as Dennis was concerned, the world could go and take a running jump. Glenn Gould, one of the world's finest, most brilliant and most troubled and misunderstood interpreters of that other great genius, J S Bach, was weaving his magic on the airwaves. How on earth could anything else compete?

CHAPTER FIFTEEN

'Hi there Natasha. It's Danny here. Danny Grunberg. How are you doing?'

It took Natasha a few seconds to put a face to the name. 'Oh… Hello Danny. I'm fine thanks… I was sorry to hear about your dad.'

'Thanks. It's been a tough week… Dad was 82, but these days that's not considered so ancient. And he was young at heart, and a big part of my life…' There was an awkward pause. 'All part of life's rich tapestry I suppose… But look, what are you doing with yourself now you're home? You've finished uni haven't you?'

'Oh yeah. I finished a year ago, and I'm working for a recycling company as an account manager.'

'That's fantastic Natasha. You've done well to land on your feet. It's difficult for you kids to get jobs. Never used to be this difficult in my day… Look, you take care of yourself and keep your head down. I'm sure I'm going to hear great things about you in the coming years.'

'Thanks Danny. I'll find dad for you.'

'Thank you - nice chatting…'

'Likewise…' She put the receiver down and went in search of her father who she found in the sitting room wearing a pair of headphones with his eyes closed.

She nudged him gently and he opened his eyes and removed one of the ear cups.

'Sorry to disturb you dad, but Danny's on the phone for you.'

Michael took the earphones off completely and placed them on a coffee table next to the book of Siegfried Sassoon's war poems, which now seemed to have brightly coloured post-it notes poking out of various sections.

'Hi there Danny. Thank you for calling. I wanted to call you but wasn't sure whether you'd still be in mourning. And I don't know what the etiquette is.'

'Don't worry Michael. I'm not especially religious. Dad was less so… Look, it's been a while. Why don't we have lunch next week at the Athenaeum? It's wheelchair friendly, and I think you'll like it. Besides, it will be really good to catch up.'

'I'd like that Danny.'

'Splendid. How about Wednesday at 1.00?'

'Wednesday at 1.00 is good for me.'

'Terrific. I'll reserve a table now… Oh shit, I'm afraid the senior clerk is gesticulating wildly at me. I suspect I'm late for a meeting. I'll have to go. I'll see you next Wednesday.'

'Look forward to it Danny.'

The phone went dead at the other end and Michael returned the handset.

✦

Michael logged into his bank account and brought up his current balance, which was just shy of £50,000. Then he checked his stocks and shares ISA, which he'd religiously paid the maximum into every year. That was now standing at a very healthy £200,000, having more or less doubled over seven years. In addition, there were his pensions that he hadn't yet touched. These were currently valued in excess of half a million. He was by all accounts pretty rich, certainly rich enough to dangle a sizeable carrot in front of a couple of terrorists.

He wheeled himself into his office and parked his knees under his old writing desk on which his laptop sat open beckoning him to tap at its keys.

He brought up the *Spam Mimic* website and sat for some considerable while just staring at the blank screen.

The faces of those poor passengers who had been close to him were haunting him again. He closed his eyes and the words of Sassoon rang in his ears:

> *Who will remember, passing through this gate,*
> *The unheroic dead who fed the guns?*
> *Who shall absolve the foulness of their fate,-*
> *Those doomed, conscripted, unvictorious ones?*
>
> *Crudely renewed, the Salient holds its own.*
> *Paid are its dim defenders by this pomp;*
> *Paid, with a pile of peace-complacent stone,*
> *The armies who endured that sullen swamp.*
>
> *Here was the world's worst wound. And here with pride*
> *'Their name liveth for ever', the Gateway claims.*
> *Was ever an immolation so belied*
> *As these intolerably nameless names?*
> *Well might the Dead who struggled in the slime*
> *Rise and deride this sepulchre of crime.*

The tears welled up in his eyes. There was no way he was going to just sit on his hands. He owed it to that poor kid with the pink ribbons in her hair and the young guy with the Graham Greene novel.

He started to tap manically at the keyboard. Without so much as a pause for thought, the words just flew from his fingertips

He didn't even read it back over to check for errors. Instead, he encoded it straight away and copied the chunk of spam generated by the website and pasted it in an email to Mohammed. Then he pressed send, blew his nose and wiped away the tears from his eyes.

✦

It was around lunchtime by the time Dennis arrived at his third location. The flats in Alexandra Park had been a doddle. All the residents had been at home including the primary target, Mohammed Farik who seemed like a quiet and polite sort of bloke - the kind of individual neighbours would no doubt describe as someone who kept himself to himself. He fitted the standard lone terrorist profile, despite the fact that he had no previous history of radical behaviour or a criminal record. He certainly wouldn't be the first in that respect. Dennis had managed to lay ten bugging devices throughout that property in record time.

Now he sat in his van in a quiet leafy residential street of Arts and Crafts whitewashed properties with steep gables and attractive front gardens shielded by neatly trimmed privet hedges. He'd been well briefed. The target was Michael Hollinghurst, a white lapsed C of E professional living in middle-class suburbia in North West London. The strangest thing was that this Hollinghurst character had been a victim of the 7/7 bombing himself and was now a wheelchair user as a result. So it was quite possible that they were dealing with what J Branch liked to call an 'amateur fisherman' looking for retribution. It wasn't unheard of. But all known cases to date had been in the US rather than the UK. As ever, the department was keeping an open mind, and as Dennis sat there admiring the mature cherry trees with their fading cherry blossom, Michael Hollinghurst's history was being gone through back at HQ with a fine-tooth comb.

Dennis pressed the door intercom and within seconds the voice of a well-spoken man emanated from the speaker. 'Who is it?'

'It's *British Gas*. I've come to check the boiler.'

'Are you sure you have the correct address? I'm fairly certain it was checked quite recently.'

Dennis bit his bottom lip. 'Is this Mr Michael Hollinghurst I'm talking to?'

'Yes it is.'

'Well, it's quite possible Mr Hollinghurst that there's been an administrative error. In which case I'm very sorry to trouble you. But seeing that I'm here, I can double-check the boiler for you if you like and carry out safety checks throughout the house, too.'

There was a pause and the speaker made a crackling noise. Then it sprang to life again.

'Oh alright. You may as well do that. You'll need to push the door quite hard when you hear the buzzing sound.'

The buzzer was fairly loud and Dennis pushed the door with some force and it opened onto a large terracotta tiled hallway at the end of which sat its owner in a wheelchair. Mr Hollinghurst was probably in his mid to late 50s and had a vaguely creative look about him thanks to a grey cashmere cardigan over a black T-shirt. 'Come through. I'll show you where our boiler is.' Dennis followed him down a corridor past a sitting room and into a spacious kitchen cum morning room with an old farmhouse style table and Aga. 'The boiler's here.' He pointed to one of many oak faced cupboards. Dennis pulled it open and revealed a gleaming white Vaillant combination boiler. 'I'm putting the kettle on for coffee. Would you care for one? I can recommend it. It's an excellent Kenyan dark roast. The only slight problem is that I have to leave for an appointment in half an hour. Hope that's alright.'

Dennis took an instant liking to the man. He had an air of old-world charm about him. Some would no doubt use the term 'old school.'

'That's not a problem. I won't need more than 20 minutes max. And as for coffee, how could I resist? That would be very nice indeed. Thank you.'

As Dennis feigned to make fine adjustments to the boiler, he placed a bugging device behind the boiler's pressure tap, but as he did so, he felt something brush up against the side of his lower right leg. He stopped in his tracks. It was alright. It was only a golden labrador peering up at him inquisitively.

'Ziggy. Fetch my slippers please.'

The dog immediately lost interest in the man fiddling with the boiler, obeyed its owner's voice and trotted out of the kitchen. 'Here you go.' Michael removed the mug of coffee that was on a tray balancing on his lap. 'Help yourself to biscuits; they are on the table.'

Dennis closed the boiler. 'Thanks, that's very kind of you. The boiler is absolutely fine...' He was about to say something else, but the reappearance of the dog made him lose his train of thought. The dog had two grey slippers in his mouth, which he carefully dropped on the floor in front of Michael's wheelchair. He then did something quite extraordinary; he pushed Michael's right foot off the footplate with his nose and carefully picked up one solitary slipper, which he now somehow managed to slide and tug onto Michael's right foot. Then he took Michael's foot in his mouth and pushed it gently back onto the footplate. This completed, he repeated the procedure for the left foot.

'That's one hell of a clever dog you have there.'

Michael lovingly stroked the back of Ziggy's neck as the dog rested his head on his owner's knee. 'Yeah. He's amazing. Helps me turn over in bed; opens and closes the front door; loads the washing machine; he could probably fix the boiler too come to that.'

Dennis laughed and sipped at his coffee. 'See what you mean about the brew.'

'Good isn't it? It's from a terrific coffee shop in Muswell Hill. You can't get stuff like this from the supermarket.'

Dennis finished his coffee and then proceeded to carry out safety checks to the rest of the house. It was the kind of place he'd give his eye-teeth for. Generously proportioned rooms, parquet flooring; original fireplaces by the looks of things; furniture straight out of Ideal Home magazine and a garden to die for. But on his and Hilary's salary, there seemed little chance of them ever moving out of their two-bedroom maisonette in Wanstead for something a bit grander - let alone a five-bedroom pile like this in Hampstead Garden Suburb. Truth of the matter was that he worked his bollocks off to keep his country safe from the scumbags of this world, but he was still fighting an uphill struggle to pay off his mounting debts. And no amount of overtime seemed to make an iota of difference to his bank balance. God help them if they were to ever have kids.

'I've checked all the rooms for any carbon monoxide traces but everything is as it should be. Thanks for the coffee, Mr Hollinghurst. I'll see myself out.' He'd managed to place eight bugging devices around the house, but he couldn't help feeling that this was a complete waste of time. There was no way this guy was a terrorist. But that wasn't his call, was it? All he was required to do was carry out his orders without arousing suspicions. And as far as he was concerned, he'd just scored 11 out of 10.

By the time he got back to the car and switched on his covert radio, he'd received a message to call base.

'Base zero five...'

The radio sprang to life. 'Roger, zero five... third target identified. Proceed to IG1 4KG Flat 23. The target is a male white Muslim convert. Name: Qssim El-Ghzzawy, previously George Caxton. He has form. Served time for manslaughter. Shot his father who had abused him as a teenager. Proceed with caution. Repeat proceed with caution.'

'Roger base zero five.'

In this game, and it was a bloody game, nobody ever addressed you by name over the radio. And when you were addressed by name in person, it was never your real one. Secrecy was the name of this particular game. Christ, the hurdles he'd had to overcome to get here. Looking back at it all, he was still pretty amazed he hadn't failed miserably. After all, he didn't have an army background like some of the guys he'd trained with. And getting selected for *Special Operations* had been a pretty big deal.

The training programme had been a real bastard though. He'd never forget the bloody expedition to Cape Wrath, the most North Westerly point on mainland Britain where they had camped for God knows how many nights in sub-zero temperatures; and the Commanding Officer waking them every fucking night at 3 in the morning to watch a documentary, after which they were led to a hut and given an hour to write a detailed essay. It happened for four consecutive nights, and each night the fan heaters were set at higher temperatures, making it increasingly difficult to stay awake. To cap it all, at the end of each session, the essays were ceremonially shredded in front of their noses. By the time this had happened three times, most of the guys had virtually given up. But for some strange reason, he hadn't. And his fourth essay had been longer and more detailed than any of his previous attempts, and of course, that was the only essay that didn't get shredded. Of the 28 hard nuts that had originally been selected for the programme, only two had managed to come out the other end, and he'd been one of them.

Dennis turned the ignition key and set the satnav. It was back to his old stomping ground in North East London. Oh what joy.

CHAPTER SIXTEEN

The cab had arrived ten minutes early and had managed to park right outside the imposing double doors of the private clinic in Wimpole Street.

Michael had considered asking Natasha to accompany him to this private consultation but had made the firm decision not to for obvious reasons. He'd put her through more than enough emotional trauma. It simply wasn't fair to lumber her with this as well.

The cabbie, a jovial sort who lived in Billericay, hadn't stopped talking for the entire journey. Michael wondered if his name was 'Dickie from Billericay' and smiled to himself. As a student, that song had been a favourite of one of his flatmates. That would have been the late 70s - another bloody age.

He wheeled himself up the perfectly designed slope that had been recently added to the exterior of this handsome Edwardian edifice and pressed the ivory button housed in a smart brass plate that had been thoughtfully placed at precisely the right height for wheelchair users.

'Good afternoon. Welcome to the surgery of Matthew Loveday. Can I help you?'

'Hello. Yes… it's Michael Hollinghurst. I have an appointment to see Mr Loveday at 1.00. I'm a little early.'

'That's fine Mr Hollinghurst. I will open the doors for you.'

There was a clicking sound and the doors opened automatically and Michael wheeled himself across a marble-floored lobby and parked himself by a swish reception desk. The girl he'd just spoken to was far younger than he'd imagined.

'Good afternoon Mr Hollighurst. Mr Loveday's surgery is on the second floor. You can take the lift, which is just to our right down the passageway. Can I arrange tea or coffee for you?'

'That's very kind… A strong black coffee would be perfect. Thank you.'

The entire building had been given a very expensive facelift by the looks of things. The style was contemporary; almost minimalist, but the elaborate use of white marble, glass and steel would have come with a hefty price tag. But then, this was Wigmore Street and the fees, like every other surgery in the road, would have been astronomical.

He'd barely scanned the newspaper headlines when a ruddy-faced man with surprisingly long white hair emerged from behind the solid-looking surgery door.

'Ah, Mr Hollinghurst… Sorry to keep you waiting. Do step this way.' Then he realised what he had just said and went a shade redder out of embarrassment. 'Oh… I'm sorry Mr Hollinghurst… How stupid of me.'

Michael laughed. 'Think nothing of it. I'm always being asked to "step this way" and to "take a seat." I'm not the least bit offended. In fact, I rather like it… Makes me feel normal.'

The consultant smiled in relief as Michael wheeled himself into Loveday's surgery that looked out onto the street below.

The consultant sat on the corner of his desk and looked at his patient with compassionate eyes. 'Well, Mr Hollinghurst, I've got various x rays to show you and I'm going to talk you through the current position, and then we'll speak to one of my colleagues about future treatment.'

It was obviously going to be a long session.

CHAPTER SEVENTEEN

Mohammed hated travelling on the London Underground. It was filthy and horribly overcrowded, so he was relieved when the King's Cross platform slid into view. He'd soon be above ground breathing fresh air again, if you could call London's air fresh. But aside from this, he was feeling excited for an altogether different reason. In his pocket was a left luggage locker number and a six-digit code. He had deleted the email on his PC back at the flat as usual, but had made a note of the numbers. The email from Alan Anonymous had been brief, curt almost. He couldn't remember the exact wording, but it just said that he should make his way to Kings Cross Left Luggage and locate locker number 59 and remove the package. Inside he'd find a significant sum of money with which to plan jihad. The word 'significant' had certainly intrigued him. But the last part of the email, which required him to divulge his plans through *Spam Mimic* did not appeal to his common sense. He would keep those details to himself, Ibrahim and Qssim. There was absolutely no reason to share them with anyone else - let alone this anonymous figure, no matter how much money he was donating to the cause.

He had no idea where the Left Luggage section was at Kings Cross, but within minutes had inadvertently found it close to the public lavatories. How very convenient. The station was still pretty busy, despite being well past the morning rush hour. He had read in *The Evening Standard* that there were plans afoot to transform Kings Cross and

St Pancras into a world-class transport hub by transferring the Eurostar service from Waterloo. It could do with a thorough face-lift because the place, like much of Kings Cross, was tired and dishevelled. The Left Luggage section was no exception. The dark blue metallic lockers with their peeling paint looked about as secure as your average brown paper bag. Number 59 actually had no number as its disc had come away and had left two small screw holes where it had once sat. But its neighbours 58 and 60 still had theirs. Mohammed pulled the piece of paper from his pocket and lined up the cogs on the chunky combination padlock to read 171059. As he twisted the last digit into place there was a reassuring click and the padlock sprang open. Mohammed tentatively took a look over his right shoulder. Half of him wondered if he was being observed by the mystery emailer. The place was a hive of activity. There was no one obviously watching him as far as he could tell.

The package was a sealed A4 padded *Jiffy* bag. He swiftly removed it and placed it in his holdall, and then slipped into the Gents next door. He chose the cubicle at the furthest end and locked the door. Once inside, he closed the toilet lid and sat on it. Then he placed the holdall on his knees, removed the sealed envelope and carefully unpeeled the sealed flap. Inside were several wads. He pulled one of them out. Fuck! They were £50 notes. He counted 100 notes. That was £5,000 in this wad alone. He put his hand into the envelope and ran his fingers over the other wads. There were at least eight of the fuckers inside. Shit - that was £40,000 in total. His hands trembled as he re-sealed the envelope and pulled a plastic Tesco carrier bag from his holdall. This done, he placed the envelope in the plastic carrier bag and then proceeded to remove his trousers and jacket. From his holdall he pulled a set of new clothes. He wasn't a fool. If he was being watched by anyone, whether it was this Alan Anonymous or anyone else, he wasn't going to make it easy for them. He changed into a smart suit and tie, and then he did something he hadn't done for over 20 years. He fumbled in the holdall and recovered an electric razor, and proceeded to shave off his entire beard.

✦

Dennis pulled up in a side street just off the A12. He could see the tower block from the van. He switched on his covert radio. 'Base zero five…'

'Roger, zero five…'

'Have arrived at primary target 3. Am going in. Do you read?...'

'Roger… You are there to carry out safety checks to the flats and fit carbon monoxide detectors… Kid gloves please, zero five… No silly tricks.'

'Roger…'

He got his box of tricks together and locked the van. It wasn't every day that you went and planted bugging devices in a murderer's home. But then this was no ordinary kind of job. And in truth, that's why he liked it. It got the old adrenalin running. He felt alive. And above all, he was doing something worthwhile - protecting this green and pleasant land from a bunch of psychos and undesirables.

It was a typical 70s tower block. Dull, uninspiring and grey. Very grey. He took the lift to the fifth floor. Flat number 25 was just a few steps along the newly laid carpet from the lift that reeked of stale beer and urine. It's not the kind of place you'd want to make your home, but then most of its residents wouldn't have had a great deal of choice in the matter. Dennis stood outside the flat for a few seconds studying the uneven dark varnish applied to the surface of the door. His palms were feeling distinctly sweaty now. He tentatively pressed the doorbell, but there was no discernable bell or buzzer sound coming from within the flat. Why did this keep happening to him? He tried again by pressing harder, but there was still no response, so he resorted to rapping at the badly varnished wood with his knuckles. He waited patiently for an inordinate length of time, but there were still no sounds of life coming from the other side of the flat. The only sound was coming from the lift and Dennis froze. Thankfully, its doors failed to open as it continued on its journey upwards.

It looked like he'd come all this way for nothing. It was one of those occupational hazards, and he should have just walked away. He knew that perfectly well. He'd been briefed and trained to do exactly that. Particularly in circumstances like this. But Dennis didn't always play by the rules and enjoyed the thrill of going off-piste. He removed his lock picking pouch from his pocket. He was a dab hand at picking locks and within a few minutes had located the five pins with his bent paperclip while applying the right level of pressure on the lock with a wrench. One at a time, he pushed the five pins upwards with the paperclip into their unlocked positions, then he gently turned the wrench with precisely the right amount of pressure and the door opened easily. He stepped into the nondescript flat and closed the door behind him. Other than the David Bowie poster on the wall, there was nothing particularly distinctive about the place. He didn't have time to mess about, so he got to work. He got down on his knees and applied the first bugging device beneath the utilitarian table. And that's when he heard the sound of the toilet flushing and the unlocking of a door. Shit!

Before he had time to get to his feet, the figure of Qssim was in the room looming over him and staring at the intruder with incredulity.

'Who the fuck are you? What the hell do you think you're doing in my flat, man?' Qssim took hold of a baseball bat that was on the bookshelf.

Dennis didn't have time to think. The baseball bat came crashing down and Dennis had managed to avoid it at the last moment. And in that split second had succeeded in getting the first punch in, hitting Hasan squarely on the jaw. It sent Qssim reeling, and Dennis saw his chance to make it for the door. He yanked at it desperately, but the bloody thing wouldn't yield. He'd somehow managed to lock himself in. He tried again, but it was no good. The baseball bat now struck him on the back of the head with a sickening crack, and Dennis felt his legs buckle like a stack of cards and he fell to the floor. He was still conscious but his body had given up the ghost as he felt Qssim drag him by the legs across the room. There was a sound of a metallic door latch and he felt cold air on his face, and the cold, unforgiving surface of ceramic tiles on the back of his head as he was unceremoniously dragged across an outdoor patio. Then he felt rough, unmerciful hands pulling him up by the collars of his jacket with great force onto a wall of sorts. He opened his eyes. All he could see was the sky through a thick pink fog; pink sky and pink clouds, which he knew was caused by blood trickling into his eyes. Now he could feel himself being pushed further over the wall, which scraped the skin on his back, and could see the world upside down. Trees, cars, people… He was being held upside down by his legs. He was powerless, and he knew he was going to die.

'Who the fuck are you, man?'

The voice was coarse. It was clearly the voice of a victim.

'Father fucking Christmas...'

And with those words, Dennis felt the hands let go of his feet and his body falling through the air like a limp sack of potatoes to a certain death on the pavement five stories below.

Qssim had to get to work quickly. He donned rubber gloves and started removing the blood from the floor with a detergent and a mop. He ran the baseball bat under a hot tap. Then he threw the gloves, the bat and the mop into a plastic bin bag. Finally, he grabbed the case under the table on the patio and stuffed his passport into his back pocket.

He was out of here. And he wasn't coming back.

CHAPTER EIGHTEEN

Michael arrived early at the Athenaeum in Pall Mall and was greeted in the grand lobby by a smartly dressed middle-aged woman seated behind an antique desk.

'Good afternoon. I'm here for lunch with Mr Grunberg. My name is Michael Hollinghurst.'

The lady smiled and delicately placed a pair of reading glasses on an equally delicate nose. 'Welcome to the Athenaeum, Mr Hollinghurst.' She consulted a large leather-bound tome with ruled pages and fountain pen jottings. 'Ah yes. I see Mr Grunberg has booked a table for one o'clock in the Coffee Room. Lunch is served in the Coffee Room upstairs on the first floor. Our guests are a little confused by that title, since it is, in fact, the grandest room in the house.' She chuckled to herself. Then she tapped a small button on her desk and within seconds a smartly attired butler appeared magically from the wings 'Ah Charles, would you be so kind as to show Mr Hollinghurst to the Coffee Room? ... Enjoy your lunch, Mr Hollinghurst.'

Charles nodded majestically and gesticulated towards a passage behind the desk. 'This way Sir.' Michael wheeled himself across the marble floor and followed Charles to the lift. It was a confined space lined with polished walnut, that trundled slowly through the lift shaft to the first floor. Charles was waiting dutifully on the other side when the doors finally opened.

The Coffee Room, as it turned out, did seem to deserve

a more exotic moniker for such a magnificent space. Large silk curtains draped the eight enormous windows that lined two sides of the room and three elaborate Victorian glass pendant lights were suspended from long ceiling chains. The ceiling itself was a work of intricate geometric plasterwork and elaborate gilding. And at the far end of the room, stood a handsome black marble fireplace above which hung an enormous gilt-framed mirror. Michael was shown to a table by one of the windows looking out onto the Mall. As he did so, his mobile phone vibrated in his jacket pocket, and he discreetly pulled it out. It was a text from Danny. He was running a little late and suggested he order a bottle of Merlot.

By the time the waiter had poured a glass and had been back with the menu, Danny appeared looking a little flustered.

'Michael. So sorry about this… Sod's law I'm afraid. Bit of a crisis back at the ranch… One of our clients decided to throw a wobbly 24 hours before his big day in court… Still, worse things happen at sea as they say.' He plonked himself down with his back to the window. 'Anyway, it's good to see you Michael… It's been far too long.'

Michael raised his glass. 'Likewise.'

'Looks like we are in good company.' Danny shifted his gaze momentarily to the opposite side of the room where the distinct figure of the white-bearded Archbishop of Canterbury in a dark grey suit and dog collar, took his seat.

'Now this gaffe may seem very grand and all that, but let me manage your expectations, Michael... Put it this way, one doesn't come here for the food. Talking of which, if I were you, I'd certainly go for rainbow trout. Less for the chef to cock-up.' He laughed and took a swig of wine. 'But that, I have to say, is a very decent drop of vino.' Danny topped up Michael's glass and ordered a second bottle. 'Tell me Michael. How are things, honestly? Do you need any help?'

Michael smiled. 'Things are... just about tolerable, I suppose... And thanks for your offer of assistance, but I'm fine financially. In fact, I don't even need to draw on my pension yet... All those years of being frugal have paid off handsomely. I did toy with the idea of going back to work part-time, but frankly, I don't need to, and I don't really want to. Early retirement suits me down to the ground.'

'How about Louise? Don't you need to buy out her share of the house?'

'She may be a cold-hearted bitch in many ways, but strangely enough, she's been incredibly generous financially. In fact, she didn't want her share of the house. I think she felt guilty about leaving me when she did, and giving up her share of the bricks and mortar was her get-out clause.'

'Your circumstances are exceptional. But even still, that's pretty unheard of these days Michael; particularly with London property prices as they are.'

Michael nodded and took a sip of wine. 'I know. And I offered to sell up. I'd have been prepared to downsize and move into a purpose-built flat with a couple of spare rooms for the kids. But she wouldn't hear of it. All she wanted was a couple of Rembrandt etchings that were hers anyway... That said, she inherited a fairly large sum from her late father a couple of years ago and is earning a fortune at that trendy advertising agency where she's a partner. So I suppose she can afford to be a bit cavalier.'

'So where's she living now?'

'Highgate... She didn't mess about... Bought a swanky apartment that's probably worth as much as the house. And I'm pretty sure she bought it outright - though I don't know that for a fact.'

A tall young waiter arrived at the table, topped up their glasses and then took their orders. No sooner than he had taken the order back to the kitchen, another figure approached the table. He was in his late fifties and was wearing a fawn raincoat that had seen better days and underneath this was an open-necked shirt. Not wearing a jacket and tie in a place like this was a cardinal sin, yet he'd clearly been let in.

'I'm sorry to interrupt your lunch gentlemen. I am Detective Inspector Dickinson.' He flashed his ID badge. 'And I need Mr Hollinghurst here to accompany me to Scotland Yard as a matter of urgency.'

Danny could barely believe what he was hearing. 'But this is absurd. Are you arresting my colleague who only a matter of months ago was a victim of that bloody ghastly terrorist attack?

'I'm afraid Sir that we require Mr Hollinghurst to help us with our enquiries... I am not at liberty to say anything else at this moment in time... But I should add that anything you do say, Mr Hollinghurst, may be taken down and used in evidence against you.'

'So you are arresting him. What the bloody hell's going on Michael?'

Michael was almost as taken aback as his friend. How had they tracked him down so swiftly? He'd been a complete idiot not telling the police what he was up to. Now he was a suspect.

'Don't worry Danny. I think I know what it's about. I'll explain later… Don't get up. I'd better go… I'm sorry…'

Michael followed the Inspector out of the dining room, and Danny slumped back in his chair, perplexed and saddened by this sudden turn of events.

'Fuck my old boots!' Danny downed the wine in his glass. 'What the fuck is this world coming to?'

An old boy at the next table turned and scowled at him. 'There's no need for that kind of language in here.'

Danny scowled back. 'That, Sir, is where you're wrong. Fucking wrong!' And with that, he got up and made his way out of the dining room as the waiter arrived with two plates laden with sizeable rainbow trout and a selection of vegetables.

✦

The tramp sprawled ungainly on the floor at Kings Cross in his urine drenched trousers that stunk to high hell and had watched Mohammed intently. He'd seen him take the package out of the locker and then slip into the Gents next door. That was a little while ago. But it only occurred to him now that the smart businessman who had come out five minutes earlier may well have been Mohammed in disguise having shaved off his beard. He'd been a complete pillock. The guy had walked right past him. Truth was it was hard to keep track of everyone who'd gone in and come out, while acting the part of one of life's no-hopers. There was only one way of being sure. He'd have to go in and check, so he picked up his half-empty beer can and dragged himself into the Gents. There were now only four males in the urinals, and with his appearance and rancid odour, they didn't stick around for long. He counted ten cubicles in total; all of them empty, and in the corner of the one at the far end was a black bin bag stuffed with clothes; Mohammed's clothes.

He remained in character and dragged himself back to his place and began muttering to himself.

'Zero ten to base. Target has given us the slip. No longer bearded. Has a change of clothes. Now wearing a dark suit and red tie. Headed towards Exit 4 five minutes ago. Do you read?'

'Roger Zero ten… All stations from Base. Target now clean-shaven and wearing a dark suit and red tie. Repeat, dark suit and red tie. Heading towards Exit 4.'

Now a female voice made its presence felt on the radio: 'Base Zero five. Got him. Target in control.'

'Roger Zero five. Good work. Stay with him.'

◆

Like so many car showrooms these days, this one was all glass and steel. It was a bit like sitting in a giant greenhouse, only there were no exotic palms or cacti on display; just shiny new cars.

'Sorry to keep you waiting Mr Farik. I've just sorted out all the paperwork for you. MOT and servicing are included for the first two years, as is AA membership and comprehensive insurance. If you'd just like to sign the paperwork here…'

The young man placed the relevant forms on the glass table and Mohammed signed them.

'My colleague will just bring the car round for you. Here's the key. You'll find the logbook and manual in the glove compartment. Many thanks for your custom, Mr Farik. I do hope you enjoy many years of trouble-free motoring.'

Mohammed made his way to the forecourt and lowered himself into the driving seat. It may have been an ex-showroom model, but it had that distinctive new car smell. He opened the glove compartment and placed the *Jiffy* bag of money into it, and then turned the ignition key, started the engine and put the automatic transmission into Drive. He reckoned he could be in Forest Hill in around 40 minutes.

As he drove out of the showroom, a solitary figure standing in a bus shelter watched him and then mumbled something to himself. To the old lady who was passing by with her shopping bag on wheels, it sounded like *Yankee two five three Alpha Bravo*. He was obviously a nutter. So she made a mental note not to make any eye contact. You just couldn't be too careful these days. It never used to be like this. She blamed it on all those foreigners that were flooding into the country, including those evil Muslim fundamentalists. It was a disgrace. Her country bore no resemblance to the one she had grown up in as a girl.

CHAPTER NINETEEN

Caroline Sharp was an inspector for the Healthcare Commission, the public body set up by the Department of Health to oversee the state of health and social care in the United Kingdom. She'd had a particularly arduous day assessing a nursing home in Ilford that fell well short in so many areas of healthcare provision.

It was now 4 o'clock in the afternoon and she hadn't had any lunch, so before hitting the road back to her middle-class existence in Putney, she had stopped off at an Israeli bakery for a smoked salmon and cream cheese bagel, and on her way back to the car, had received the shock of her life.

Sprawled across the roof of her *VW Golf* estate was the broken body of a man. His bruised head dangled over the back windscreen and had created dark red rivulets of blood that flowed freely across the glass; and his arms and legs were splayed out like a deranged daddy longlegs on marijuana.

She dropped her bagel and fished her mobile out of her pocket and instinctively called 999.

Dennis was a lucky man. That *Volkswagen* that was now a write-off had been parked at precisely the right place and exactly the right time. It had broken his fall. And its owner had arrived on the scene just at the right time. Her call had saved his life.

◆

'Tash. It's dad here… Look don't be alarmed… I'm at a police station…'

'Are you ok dad? What's going on?'

'Yeah. Everything's alright…They just want to interview me over something I've been doing.'

There was a pause. 'What do you mean dad?… You haven't been planning a bank job behind our backs have you?'

Michael laughed nervously. 'No I haven't been planning to rob any banks, but I have been a bit stupid…' Natasha sat pensively on the kitchen chair. She knew instinctively that this was more serious than her father was letting on. But she wasn't going to say a word. She'd let him fill the gaps.

'You see, ever since coming home, I've been trying to find potential terrorists online by posing as one of them, and I've been talking online to a couple of extremists, with the aim of setting them up and getting them put away. And to cut a long story short, this online dialogue has been picked up by our intelligence services before I have had a chance to explain myself to anyone, including the police.'

'Bloody hell, dad. They've arrested you haven't they? They think you are a bloody terrorist, don't they?'

'They haven't come to any conclusions, Tash. They are just doing their job. They need to question me and establish exactly what's going on… It's a process, and it may take a fair bit of time.'

'So how long are they going to hold you for?'

'That, Tash, is the million-dollar question… Under section 41 of the Terrorism Act 2000, I think I'm right in saying that I can legally be retained here for up to 14 days.

The government is trying to extend that to 90 days... But anyway I've explained about my daily routine with my bowels and the catheter, and my daily need for specialist care every morning and evening. And the DCI said he'd get back to me on that one.'

'But dad, if you've been talking to a bunch of looney tune Islamists, are you in danger of becoming one of their targets?'

Natasha was always quick to spot the most apposite questions that struck at the heart of an issue. It was a question that was beginning to plague him at night. The police had managed to track him down. How hard would it be for a terrorist cell to do likewise?

'I don't think there's any chance of that Tash. These guys don't have the resources of our intelligence services. They are amateurs.'

Natasha wasn't convinced. Those maniacs that flew the two airliners into the Twin Towers on 9/11 had plenty of resources. Ok, they probably were higher up the food chain, but if these headbangers had connections, who knew what they would be capable of? She chose to say nothing.

'I'm going to have to go now, Tash. They want to interview me... But can you do me a huge favour? Can you call Danny? He's been texting me. Just tell him what I've just told you. And say that I'll call him as soon as I can - when I have a chance.'

'Sure dad... And please keep me in the loop. If you have to stay overnight, I'll drive Annie over with all your gear.'

'Thanks Tash.'

'No problem... Love you dad.'

Christ on a flipping bicycle, what had her father gone and done? Now she knew what he'd been up to in his office while she was at work. Part of her could understand his actions. If she had suffered at the hands of those monsters, she'd probably want to do something about it, too. It was clearly an effective way for him to channel his anger and frustration; maybe even his guilt for surviving when so many others in his carriage hadn't. So she wasn't angry with him, but she was certainly scared. Scared that the police wouldn't believe him. And scared that these vile individuals he was in communication with would somehow track them all down and murder them in their beds.

◆

Danny was in his car on his way back from the office when his mobile rang. He'd pulled up into a side road and put his mobile into speaker mode, and listened to Natasha explain everything she knew. He had an inkling that it had been something like this. He'd seen this desire in victims to hit back at their tormentors before. It was only human nature. But from his own experience, there was usually a huge gulf between the wish to do something and the actual act of doing it. But it seemed his friend had bridged that gulf, and if he had indeed managed to tap into a genuine terrorist cell, then he'd be playing with fire. He'd need the full support of the police and the intelligence services. He hated to admit it, but as a wheelchair user, the odds were stacked against his friend. He'd be a very easy, sitting target - quite literally. But these concerns had to be brushed aside for the time being. The immediate challenge was to get Michael released. And to do that, he knew he'd have to throw his weight around and pull a few strings, but as one of the country's leading criminal QCs with some very useful high powered connections, he was in a pretty good position to do exactly that.

✦

Michael couldn't believe the amount of personal details his file contained. The police knew where he had lived at university. The societies he had joined. The political movements he had been sympathetic to. CND marches he'd been on. They had been particularly interested in a PLO rally he'd been on in Hyde Park in 1976. The details were breathtaking. In fact, he'd forgotten about most of these events. As an idealistic student back in the 70s, it had been normal practice to get involved in these kind of activities. It was 'cool' and 'right on' in the same way as listening to Bob Dylan and wearing flared trousers were the done things back then.

They had wanted to know his views on Palestine and the plight of the Palestinians. Did he view their cause as a just one against Israel? And was Israel in his view, an apartheid state?

He had gone to considerable lengths to make his position clear. The whole Middle East situation regarding Israel and Palestine was, and always had been, as far as he was concerned, an incredibly complex one. Both sides had the right to self-determination, and both sides had behaved badly. The PLO had refused to accept the existence of Israel and Israel had built settlements on disputed land.

Detective Inspector Brian Dickinson was a quietly spoken and mild-mannered man. Had he been anything else, Michael may well have shown his irritation a little more. But instead, he took the questioning in his stride and did his best to fully cooperate.

'I'm sorry to have to ask you all these questions Mr Hollinghurst. But we have to follow a fairly rigid procedure in these circumstances and piece together the most comprehensive picture we can. I'm sure you understand.'

Michael nodded. He appreciated the Inspector's candour. 'No. I fully understand, Inspector. I blame myself entirely… I should have involved you guys in all this from the start… And to be perfectly honest, I feel reassured that you are now in the know because I've clearly got myself into this thing far deeper than I would have liked… In truth, I suppose I never really thought my amateurish efforts would actually lead to anything.'

The only other person in the room was a young female police officer named Deborah who sat listening and didn't say a word.

'Well, I suggest we take a break here for fifteen minutes.' Detective Inspector Dickinson turned and spoke into a concealed microphone. 'Interview suspended 16.05.' Then he switched off the recording device, and the female officer rose. 'Can I get you a tea or coffee Mr Hollinghurst?'

'Yes. I'll have a coffee if I may. Black with one sugar.' The officer left the room and the Inspector rose. 'While you do that, I'm going to get my fix of nicotine if you don't mind. We'll continue in fifteen.'

✦

'Look Andrew, I know the counter-terrorist boys have to go through their procedures. But I can personally vouch for Michael Hollinghurst. As you already know, the man has suffered the most appalling injuries as a result of the terrorist atrocity. I know him better than most people.

We've known each other since school. There really is no need to treat him as a potential terrorist. He's been reckless, yes. But who's to say you or I would have behaved any differently in the circumstances?'

Andrew Sullivan grunted, set the telephone to speakerphone and finished the remnants of the 15-year-old single malt in his crystal tumbler. 'I hear what you say, Dan. But look, as Deputy Commissioner, I simply don't have the clout or indeed the inclination to interfere with the internal workings of the counter-terrorist unit. That's hardly my remit.'

'Of course not. I'm not suggesting that for one moment… You know me better than that, Andrew.'

'You're asking me to put a good word in for your man? You'd like me to create a little bit of… mood music?'

'You always were a dab hand at the old violin, Andrew.'

The older man chuckled. 'Now flattery, my dear boy, will get you absolutely nowhere.'

There was silence, broken only by the sound of another wee dram departing from the bottle and pouring into Andrew's glass. 'Leave it with me Dan. I'm not promising anything mind. So don't go raising your man's hopes.'

Danny punched the air. It was as much as he could realistically expect. 'No, I realise that. But thank you for hearing me out, Andrew. I really appreciate it.'

'Don't mention it… Now, more importantly, when are we going to have that game of squash? I hear on the grapevine that you have a very mean forehand.'

◆

Michael had finished his coffee well over fifteen minutes

ago, and there was still no sign of Inspector Dickinson. He'd told them pretty much everything he could that was relevant. He hadn't wanted to mention Alan Jenkins, his neighbours' autistic son, but he had little choice when the Inspector started probing about his methodology when it came to hacking. He had to be completely honest and open now. Everything he had told them would be verified, so the Jenkins family would in due course receive a knock at their door, and questions would undoubtedly be asked. Friends, acquaintances, work colleagues, anyone in fact who knew him reasonably well would no doubt get dragged into all this. Intelligence were probably going through all his mobile contacts right now. He only hoped he wouldn't lose friends over it. Out of nervousness, he checked his mobile for any messages, and as he buried his head in his phone, the door clicked open, and the young female police officer appeared in the doorway clasping a blue file.

'Chief Inspector Dickinson apologises for keeping you waiting, Mr Hollinghurst. He won't be long now. Can I get you another coffee?'

Michael switched off his mobile. 'No thanks. I'm fine.'

She smiled and then disappeared.

A few minutes passed, and the door clicked open once more. The Chief Inspector reappeared and Michael's nostrils were greeted with the distinct odour of stale nicotine.

'I'm sorry to keep you Mr Hollinghurst. I am, it seems, the proverbial bringer of good news and bad. What would you like me to divulge first?'

Michael was intrigued. 'Let's have the good news.'

'Fair enough... It seems, Mr Hollinghurst that we have been instructed from on high to accept your account of events, in light of your impeccable record and, of course, the injuries you have already sustained at the hands of terrorists. On a personal note, Mr Hollinghurst, I would also like to apologise for the trouble this station has put you to. But from now on, we can cease any further questioning, and this interview can now end.'

Michael knew instinctively that this must have been Danny's doing. He was the only person he knew that had high powered contacts. And the fact that Danny had stopped texting him spoke volumes.

'So what's the bad news?'

'The bad news, Mr Hollinghurst is that you can't go home.'

'What do you mean? That's absurd. I have to go home. I have all my medical paraphernalia at home… You have no idea what my routine is every morning and evening… I'll spare you the details…'

The Inspector understood better than Michael might have realised. He had a cousin with a spinal injury and was well aware of the everyday needs of a tetraplegic. He gave Michael a look of sympathy. 'I'm sorry Mr Hollinghurst, but you and your immediate family are now potentially at risk. Our intelligence has revealed that a very close contact of your Mr Mohammed Farik is, in fact, now wanted for attempted murder, having already served a sentence for murdering his own father. These are very dangerous individuals driven by fanaticism and ideology. And we don't as yet know the extent of this cell's tentacles.' He paused and took a deep breath. 'What we do know, Mr Hollinghurst, is that we will need to move you and your family to a safe house, while we have one known murderer on the loose and two of his associates being closely monitored by intelligence services.'

Christ! This was worse than Michael could possibly have feared. 'So this murderer... Who did he try and kill?'

The Inspector raised a slat in the Venetian blind that hung across the only window in the room. Outside a couple of kids were kicking a crushed can noisily along the kerb. 'He came very close to killing one of our own intelligence operatives... Came remarkably close by all accounts... Threw him out of a fifth-floor apartment. Fortunately, someone had parked their car below, and he fell on the roof.' The Inspector moved away from the window and observed Michael's face, which now looked a shade paler. 'Dreadful business, I'm afraid, Mr Hollinghurst... It's normally seat belts and airbags that save lives, but in this instance, it was the car roof that saved our poor bugger. But I'm afraid he's not out of the woods yet. He's in intensive care with a broken back... So this, as you can imagine, has now become a fast-moving investigation.'

CHAPTER TWENTY

He wasn't used to wearing a suit and tie. It made him feel like an insurance salesman. Neither was he used to being clean-shaven. But Mohammed would get used to his new image soon enough. He parked, took the *Jiffy* bag out of the glove compartment and made his way to Ibrahim's house. The doorbell didn't seem to work, so he called him on his mobile.

'As-Salam-u-Alaikum, brother. It's Mohammed. I'm outside. So get your arse down here. I have something to show you man.'

Ibrahim was surprised to hear his friend's dulcet tones on the mobile. 'You're kidding me, man. What's going on here?... I'm coming... Don't go away.'

'Don't you worry. I'm not going anywhere.'

Ibrahim opened the door and on seeing what appeared like an apparition before him, laughed.

'Hey man. What's happening here?... You gonna sell me some life assurance or something? What's with this look? I barely recognise you, brother.'

Mohammed smiled and pointed to the shiny dark blue *BMW*. 'Do you like my new set of wheels?'

'Holy shit, man. Have you just won the lottery?'

Mohammed opened the passenger door and gesticulated to his friend to get in. 'You could say that, brother. Why don't you and I go for a little drive, and I'll explain everything... It seems the prophet, in his infinite wisdom, is smiling at us benignly from upon high, my friend.'

Ibrahim slid gently onto the leather seat and closed the door with a reassuring heavy clunk. Mohammed looked at his friend, turned the key in the ignition and laughed. And without really knowing why, Ibrahim laughed with him.

◆

Qssim had known instinctively that the guy in his flat hadn't been some regular burglar, and was convinced that it must have been connected in some way to Mohammed's mystery emailer. He could have been an undercover pig or intelligence services. It's partly why he acted as he had. But in retrospect, he wished he hadn't. After all, the bloody police had a file on him as long as his arm, and tracking him down would be a piece of piss. He'd been an idiot. He knew that, but at least he had the good sense to at least acknowledge it. That fact alone gave him a chance to slip the net.

In no time at all, he had managed to disappear among the hordes of London's travellers on the underground and take the Northern line to Euston where he headed for the ticket office to purchase a single to Edinburgh. The train was in the platform, so he boarded it and made his way to the toilet compartment and locked the door behind him. Once safely inside, he removed his mobile from his jacket and switched it on. Thankfully, it had been fully charged. Then he placed it carefully in the sanitary towel bin and let himself out. If that bastard had been an intelligence officer, they'd probably be tracking his mobile, so this was his insurance policy. If he could throw them off his scent, this would buy him valuable time.

The train was due to depart in five minutes, so he stood by the doors waiting patiently. He had no idea if anyone was following him. Nobody else was standing by the doors in the carriage. But that meant absolutely nothing. He couldn't assume anything.

The electronic beeps were bang on time and the doors slid closed. But Qssim's right foot had blocked the left-hand door where he was standing, leaving a sliver of daylight through which to force his ample body and holdall. It had only taken a matter of seconds but it had felt an awful lot longer. His mobile was now heading to Edinburgh while he was travelling in the opposite direction. His mission was accomplished.

◆

Mohammed parked the car outside a row of four lock-ups close to a railway line that carried London's Northern line trains with their distinctive red, blue and silver carriages.

He turned off the engine and looked earnestly at Ibrahim. 'Before I say anything, I need to know for certain that you are 100% committed to jihad.'

Ibrahim looked mystified. 'You know I am, brother.'

There was a long pause. Mohammed looked directly into his friend's dark brown eyes. 'And are you prepared to give your life to your Muslim brothers in the name of the Prophet?'

Ibrahim nodded. 'Yes.'

'You see, if you have any reservations or doubts, I need to know now, and you'll be free to walk away. But if you are sure, well then there is no turning back, my friend. We will both be set on a course. A one-way course to martyrdom. Are you sure that's what you want?'

Ibrahim was quiet. It was the first time his friend had uttered the 'M' word. Until now, neither of them had discussed dying quite as overtly as this. The romantic notion of giving your life to a cause was arguably more attractive than martyrdom and the thought of wearing a suicide vest that would blow your head clean off.

'Perhaps I do need a little time to take in what you say, brother. Particularly when you say it like that.'

Mohammed smiled. 'Yes. I had a feeling you needed more time… But not too much time, brother.' Mohammed opened his door and got out. I was thinking of renting this lock-up. What do you think?'

Ibrahim let himself out of the passenger seat and followed Mohammed to the lock-up with its blue shuttered pull-down door.

'This my friend will be the nerve centre of our operation… Come here…' Mohammed opened his arms, and the two men hugged.

Ibrahim felt his friend's clean-shaven cheek against his beard. Then he felt something altogether more unpleasant as his friend's grip tightened. He felt a cold and sharp sensation at the back of his head, and before he could even utter a single word, his vision and all his senses simply gave up the ghost.

'I'm sorry, my friend. It is for the best. For the sake of Allah, I must have 100% commitment. Nothing less. Allahu Akbar.' Mohammed coldly removed the sharpened screwdriver from the base of Ibrahim's brain and let his body slump to the floor. There was a lot of blood. Far more blood than Mohammed would have liked. But it was all confined to the floor as far as he could tell.

There was no time to lose. He jumped back in the car and set off.

✦

As soon as Mohammed's *BMW* had disappeared, a figure in a dark grey hoodie appeared from the lock-up next door. He ran over to Ibrahim's body and checked his pulse. Then he spoke sharply into his collar button.

'Base Zero Three. Target Zelda 2 dead. Do you read me? Target Zelda 2 dead.'

The tinny electronic voice of his radio responded immediately: 'Roger Zero Three.'

The grey figure continued his monologue. 'Our murder suspect is Target Zelda 1 driving a dark blue *BMW Yankee two five three Alpha Bravo*. Repeat, *Yankee two five three Alpha Bravo* - travelling north on Archway Road. Executive action required.'

'Roger Zero Three. Cease and withdraw.'

✦

Mohammed was shaking. He had never killed anyone before. And it was scary how shockingly easy it had been. He hadn't wanted to do it, but he had been left with little choice. He couldn't afford to team up with someone who wasn't totally committed, and something told him instinctively that Ibrahim was lightweight; a chancer; a freeloader. And he'd been right. He'd have been a liability; a dangerous liability. He'd have put any plans to carry out jihad in jeopardy.

He needed to speak to Qssim urgently. But he wouldn't tell him about killing Ibrahim. After all, Ibrahim had been Qssim's friend who'd introduced him to Islam in the first place. Qssim might never forgive him for acting as he had. But whether he liked it or not, he was going to have to speak to Qssim because Qssim was the only person he knew who could help him acquire guns; powerful and magnificent guns. He'd already tried calling his mobile but the fucker wasn't picking up his calls, so he'd left messages.

As he indicated to turn right, he inadvertently noticed tiny dark freckles on his left wrist just below his watch strap. How strange. He didn't have freckles. He rubbed his wrist and the freckles left dark red smears on his skin. It was dried blood. In disgust, Mohammed spat on his wrist and wiped it on a tissue, leaving just one hand on the wheel. As he did so, a car on his right side suddenly rammed him hard with a deafening crunch, throwing Mohammed's head violently against the glass side window with a sickening crack. His car mounted the pavement and was brought to an abrupt halt by a solid iron bicycle stand that had been cemented and bolted to the pavement.

The whole thing happened so quickly that Mohammed wasn't given a second to react.

It was an exemplary example of a clinically precise response from the *Special Forces Strike Team*. They'd been trained to take out terrorist targets in the most efficient and ruthless manner known to man. And this was just one such method.

Mohammed was badly bruised and stunned but fully conscious as his windscreen was smashed to pieces and thick chunks of glass rained down on him. Then he was physically dragged through the windscreen and thrown like a lump of meat onto the steaming bonnet of his car while his hands were zip-tied and a black hood thrown over his head.

◆

The train pulled in at Milton Keynes Central and an armed

counter-terrorist unit comprising six heavily armed officers entered the train from two ends of the carriage adjacent to the toilet cubicles located at the far end of the train.

Mark was a good friend of Dennis. They'd trained together and had been the only two to make it through the special training at Cape Wrath, which had almost bloody killed them. And now, it seemed, his mate had actually come pretty close to death. Mark didn't know the full details yet, other than the fact that his friend had got into some kind of scrape with a potential terrorist, and had come off worse. Much worse.

Thanks to *GCHQ* and state-of-the-art digital mobile tracking technology, Mark now had the opportunity to come face to face with Dennis's attacker. *MI5* even had the ability to track a mobile phone when it's switched off.

As the men boarded the train, the passengers took fright at the sight of the enormous guns and one young woman screamed.

'It's alright. Everything is under control. Please stay calm and evacuate this carriage as swiftly as you can. Nobody is going to get hurt.' Mark made sure his gun was pointing at the floor as he gestured to the far end of the carriage. The passengers obeyed like sheep and the carriage was emptied in a matter of seconds. While two officers sealed the two entrances to the carriage, Mark and one other officer focussed on the one cubicle that was occupied. According to their tracking device, the target was behind that door.

Mark whispered into his radio.

'Base T44. Target zone cleared. Target isolated behind locked toilet cubicle… awaiting instructions.'

His earphone came to life. 'Roger T44… Prepare to force an entry… Shoot to kill if necessary.'

Mark felt the trigger of his *SIG Sauer* semi-automatic. He'd dearly like to finish off the bastard given half a chance. He motioned to the officer next to him to position the battering ram to strike just below the door's locking plate.

'Ok T44… Permission granted… Go for it!'

'Roger.'

Mark gestured to his officer, and with one hefty swing the battering ram destroyed the lock with a loud smack and the red door flew open. Mark stepped in and pointed his semi-automatic at the target's forehead.

It was an elderly man sitting on the toilet with his trousers around his knees. The poor man was ashen-faced and utterly terrified.

Part Two

BRILLIANT MISTAKE

Elvis Costello, 2005

CHAPTER TWENTY-ONE

'Welcome to The Retreat, Mr Hollinghurst.'

The ruddy face of a middle-aged and softly spoken Scotsman appeared from behind the solid rustic front door painted in a delicate shade of duck egg blue. Michael couldn't help noticing the extraordinary level of security features to the inside of the doorframe, which seemed to be coated in steel plate. It was clearly a door that wouldn't succumb easily to a crowbar or battering ram.'I'm Sergeant Bolzwinick, but you can call me Alexander. I'm afraid it's not entirely wheelchair friendly here, but as you'll see, we've done our best with the odd ramp.' He ushered Michael into the cosy interior of the 17th century cottage. Michael encountered the first of the industrial metal ramps as he wheeled himself across the threshold and into the hallway that was considerably lower. The hallway was large for a cottage of this kind and its original flagstones, while attractive and authentic-looking, played havoc on his wheels by causing sharp vibrations to set off spasms in his legs.

Alexander led him into a spacious bedroom with a single bed, a sofa, and a writing desk below a sash window that looked out onto an attractive view over a small garden and a patchwork of rolling hills.

Alexander stood in the doorway. 'This used to be the morning room, sir but we converted it into a downstairs bedroom... I hope you'll enjoy your stay here... It's a lovely part of the world.'

'Thank you... Alexander. And I insist that you call me

Michael.' He took in the view. He could get used to this place, though he wasn't sure that he could say the same for Tash and Annie. They would join him later with all his usual paraphernalia that had become part and parcel of life as a tetraplegic. 'Funny thing is, I always wanted to live in the country. But my wife - ex-wife now - would never hear of it. As far as she was concerned, we had to live as near to the old smoke as money would allow... Crazy really, when you consider how much healthier and attractive somewhere like this is.'

Alexander nodded. 'Let me show you the rest of the property on the ground floor, Michael.'

It was deceptively spacious. A large wet-room across from the bedroom was perfect for Michael's needs and an attractive sitting room complete with an oak-beamed ceiling, real fire and two wide recesses lined with an assortment of leather-bound volumes and paperbacks, looked most welcoming. At the far end, a strikingly attractive young police-woman with short dark hair rose from one of the armchairs.

'Let me introduce you to PC Hetherington.'

The young woman extended her hand. 'Hello Mr Hollinghurst. Good to meet you. I will be on duty here during the day.'

'PC Hetherington will be relieved of her duties at 5.30 each day by PC Mann, ' Alexander interjected. 'I am here 24/7 - so you're going to have to get used to my ugly mug I'm afraid. There will be two of us on-site at all times. And security here is, as you'd imagine, is state-of-the-art.'

'I'd noticed the reinforced doorframe.'

'Oh, that's nothing. The really impressive stuff is naked to the human eye.'

Michael surveyed the bookshelves. It was an eclectic mix of titles. Everything from trashy potboilers and the works of Dickens to dry volumes of *Gray's Anatomy* and old *Archibald Criminal law* volumes. Probably several joblots from the local auction house in Bury St Edmunds, he surmised.

'As you know, your identity has been changed. You'll find your new passport and driving licence in the name of Peter Baldwin in the office next door, where we've also set you up on a PC and encrypted mobile phone. Your old IP address is being monitored and managed by intelligence services. And your house in North London is now occupied by plainclothes officers. To all intents and purposes, it will look as if you've rented the place out. If there are family and close friends you'd like to inform, we can do that for you… It will be safer for you to stay off the radar for the time being.' Alexander tapped Michael on the shoulder. 'Everything is being taken care of. You and your family will be safe with us, Michael.'

'Thank you, Alexander… My kids are everything… They are all I have…'

CHAPTER TWENTY-TWO

The bolts and locks were opened from the other side of the door, and Qssim pushed it impatiently.

'What's the rush my friend?' An old man with a white beard and benign countenance let his friend barge past.

'Praise the Prophet - peace be upon him... It was a fucking miracle that I was able to remember where you lived.'

The old man looked mystified. 'You look troubled brother... And your clothes are a complete mess. What has happened to you? And how can an elderly imam help his friend in need?'

Qssim sat at the base of the stairwell and looked at his elderly friend. Anwar al-Banna was one of the East London Mosque's three imams. Here was a man held in high regard and indeed adored by a sizeable community.

'I had to sleep on the street last night... I can't go back to my flat...'

The imam raised an eyebrow. 'And the reason for such a state of affairs?'

Qssim looked directly at the old man. 'I killed a man yesterday... It wasn't planned... It just happened... I had just come out of my bathroom... only to find this complete stranger in my flat. I challenged him and he punched me really hard in the face, so I hit him with a baseball bat... We struggled, and I eventually threw him off my balcony... I'm on the fifth floor, so he didn't stand a chance. ' Qssim paused, fumbled in his bag and pulled out an issue of *The Evening Standard*. 'But that's not all.' He threw the copy of the paper and it landed by the old man's feet. The front-page headline read: Islamist murder suspect arrested, and below the headline sat a large photograph of a familiar looking face smiling at the camera. It was Mohammed.

'Mohammed had been talking to a stranger online who called himself Alan Anonymous. Said he was looking to recruit Jihadists… They spoke in code… I told Mohammed to tread carefully… He had no proof that this Alan Anonymous was genuine… And the person he's accused of murdering is a good friend of mine who I introduced him to… Ibrahim Choudary. Sounds to me like Mohammed's been set up. He's not a murderer. And he wouldn't have murdered Ibrahim… I'm also convinced that the man in my flat was no regular burglar. He's got to be connected to all this.'

The elderly imam listened intently. And now his face seemed to shed its soft and magnanimous features. 'Where is your mobile?'

'It's okay. I'm not stupid… I planted it on a train heading for the Scottish highlands.'

'Good. Let's pray that nobody followed you here.' The old man paused for thought. 'You're going to have to stay here with us for the time being until I can get you to a safe place. When you do leave this house, and you will, you'll have to wear my wife's burka. But you won't be able to leave the country. All airports and ferry ports will already have your identity and be on the lookout for you. So for now, you'll just need to lie low.'

Anwar al-Banna was a wise old boy. Qssim knew that. If there was anyone who could help him give the police and intelligence services the slip, Anwar was that person. Qssim smiled at his friend. 'Thank you brother. I appreciate that.'

'It's the very least I can do in the circumstances… But one thing's for sure. We're going to have to track down this Alan Anonymous character. If he infiltrates our network, it could jeopardize everything.'

✦

'Good news dad.' Natasha appeared in the Kitchen doorway with Ziggy in tow. 'Annie has arranged care for her grandmother and will be able to join us in this little getaway tomorrow.'

It was a huge relief for Michael, not that he wanted to share his concerns with Tash. The thought of having to take on a new carer had filled him with dread. And the last thing he wanted was for his daughter to have to fill in while a new live-in carer was sought.

'That's great news Tash. But I'm worried about Ben. He has insisted on staying in Durham to finish his degree… I can't say I'm surprised, and I don't blame him… I'd have probably done the same had I been in his shoes. But it doesn't stop me worrying.'

She gave him one of her sympathetic looks. 'To be honest, I'd have probably done the same dad. And frankly, this whole thing feels a tad over-egged if you ask me. I mean, this potential terrorist won't know which city you live in - let alone your name and address.'

'I know… And with one of them dead, and another one behind bars, there's only one bugger on the loose to worry about... I do wonder if I'm getting special treatment because I'm a victim of 7/7, or that intelligence services know more than they're letting on.'

Natasha poured two mugs of coffee and placed one in front of her father. 'There's no point speculating… At least you're safe here.'

'Yeah, I know, you're right. And I'm sure this third character will get picked up soon enough. It's nigh impossible these days to evade detection for long… Anyway, it's great that you've been given the time off at work… They've been incredibly understanding.'

Natasha had explained the situation to her boss and the company hadn't flinched. They had said she could have as much time off as she needed, and that her job would always remain open to her when she returned. 'I'm one lucky girl, that's for sure.'

'Rubbish. Nothing to do with luck, Tash. You work bloody hard, and you're brilliant at what you do. They value you. And so they should.'

'Thanks dad. It's only a shame they don't acknowledge that with my remuneration. Hey ho…'

Michael laughed. 'Money isn't everything in life, Tash… My first ever job was for a bunch of criminal defence lawyers. The pay was lousy, but the work was really interesting… I loved that job. Loved it so much that I used to get in early every morning bright-eyed and bushy-tailed. There's something about criminal law that really does get the old adrenalin flowing. But then I gave it all up for the world of commercial work, the daily grind and filthy lucre. It may have paid for the trappings of a middle-class existence, but that's about all you can say for it. The work was mind-numbingly dull, Tash… So don't lose sight of job satisfaction. It's a rare commodity.'

Her father was right. He usually was.

CHAPTER TWENTY-THREE

'This may tickle a bit.' Anwar's daughter Asma was in her early twenties and vivacious. She was clearly a bit of a dab hand with a mascara brush. 'Best if you look up at the ceiling.' She giggled as she applied the dark dye to Qssim's eyelashes. 'You know, you have long eyelashes for a man.'

Qssim wasn't in the mood for small talk. He didn't want to go through with this farcical plan in the first place, but he didn't have an alternative suggestion. 'What makes you such an expert when it comes to men's eyelashes then?'

'I'm a hairdresser aren't I?... I get to see loads of blokes' eyelashes. And none of them are as long as yours… I'm telling you, yours are long.' She stepped back to admire her handiwork. 'Not bad… Not bad at all. Here, take a look at yourself.' She held up the mirror and Qssim inspected his own face. He was barely recognisable with his hair tied back and those dark eyelashes and very slight pinking of the cheeks. Asma had managed to give his lips a subtle emphasis with a natural skin tone, and had made him look feminine without looking as if he was wearing makeup. The last thing any Muslim woman ever did was wear makeup in a public place, so it was absolutely crucial that he looked right.

Anwar inspected Qssim's face at close quarters. 'It's good. Very good indeed Asma… I think we can try the wig now.'

His daughter smiled in acknowledgement of her father's compliment and selected the straight, black, mid-length wig made from human hair. It was the most natural-looking, and as luck would have it, fitted Qssim perfectly.

'Look at him now… A real beauty to behold!' Anwar handed Qssim the mirror and was a little taken aback by the feminine visage that peered back at him. His hands may have been a dead give-away, but this face framed by silky black shoulder-length hair that hung naturally, was totally convincing.

Whether he liked it or not, there was no denying that Qssim had now become a not unattractive woman to look at, at any rate.

◆

Wearing a burka and seeing the world through a fine gauze is a strange experience. For Qssim it was made even more bizarre by the fact that he was also made up and dressed like a woman underneath.

Anwar had given him strict instructions, which he had to commit to memory. The pickup point would be on a relatively quiet country road that snaked through the sleepy village of Leeds, three miles from Maidstone. He was to head for the Ten Bells public house situated at the northern end of Upper Street and wait on the opposite side of the road. He'd be picked up at 1.00 pm by a man by the name of Hasan to whom he would hand a sealed envelope from Anwar containing a short note in Arabic confirming Qssim's identity. This aside, Qssim knew very little other than the fact that the old man was obviously well connected. He also knew that being a white Islamist made him a little bit special in the eyes of his Muslim brethren. But he had no idea where he'd be taken and by whom.

✦

He'd managed to get the train from Victoria to Maidstone East without any major incidents. He sensed that people were generally unfazed by the appearance of a woman in a full burka, but his journey hadn't been totally unsullied by the English capacity for racism. Some yob in a white van had wound down his window and called him a 'fucking bitch', and an elderly woman had tutted the words 'shouldn't be allowed' under her breath as he passed her; none of which surprised him in the least.

The train at Victoria wasn't particularly full and he had managed to find an empty space in the rear carriage. Interestingly, other passengers had decided not to sit in close proximity, and he was certain that this had everything to do with the burka.

When you're concealed from the world, it's remarkable how much more observant you become. Qssim became acutely aware of prying eyes as well as the abundance of CCTV cameras. He had little doubt that if it hadn't been for the flimsy piece of fabric covering him up, he'd be on the anti-terrorist radar and would have been arrested by now.

By the time he'd got out at Maidstone East and made his way up the steep hill to the bus stop, it was 12.30. He was cutting it fine. He could have ordered a cab, but he didn't want to speak to anyone for obvious reasons, and so far he hadn't had to. Luckily, he hadn't had to wait long for a number 13 bus, which trundled up the hill and carried him out of the town on the A20 and eventually turned off down a leafy B road. The bus terminated at Burgess Hall Drive, just a couple of minutes' walk from Upper Street. It was five to one, so he'd have to walk briskly.

The Ten Bells stood on the outskirts of Leeds village. It was a traditional looking pub with crumbling old brickwork and a distinctive pub sign that swung gently in the afternoon breeze. Qssim's feet were feeling sore from the ladies' footwear, which Asma had acquired for him. But at least he'd made it with a couple of minutes to spare. There was an old weathered public park bench that had clearly seen better days, bolted to the pavement, so he took the weight off his feet and perched like an exotic bird on the rotting hardwood.

Traffic was fairly light and consisted mainly of women in hatchbacks and small tradesmen in small vans. This was presumably their lunchtime, so they'd soon be munching their BLT sandwiches and salt and vinegar crisps.

Qssim envisaged Hasan sporting a beard and driving an old *Volvo* estate.

He was wrong. A smart black *Saab* saloon finally appeared at ten past one and pulled in to the side of the road. It wasn't beaten up, nor was it an estate, but it was *Volvo*'s Swedish cousin, so he'd been thinking along the right lines. A tall gaunt-looking man with a distinctly Middle Eastern countenance and designer stubble got out of the car and strode over to where Qssim sat, his leather brogues crunching asphalt underfoot.

Qssim rose and handed Hasan the letter. He took it without saying a word, tore it open and digested the contents. Then he simply grunted and gesticulated in the direction of the car. Qssim got into the passenger seat and was surprised to see a woman in the back seat dressed in black with a black headscarf.

'Welcome Mr Caxton.' Nobody had called him that since he'd been in prison. And now he felt insulted.

'My name is Qssim. Nobody calls me that.'

Before he knew it, the cold barrel of a revolver was pressed hard into the side of his head.

'We can call you what we like, you stinking piece of shit… Now listen to me Mr fucking Caxton. I'm going to drive round into the car park here and you are going to get your arse out of that seat and get into the boot. Do you understand?'

Qssim nodded. 'Yeah… No problem.'

It was some introduction. Hasan drove the car into the empty car park and ordered Qssim out of the car. The boot had been emptied and smelt of petrol. There was barely room for him to get in, but once he had, he managed to somehow lie in the foetus position, and Hasan slammed the boot shut over his head with a resounding clunk.

Qssim's world had suddenly turned completely black.

CHAPTER TWENTY-FOUR

Michael could access his old email account, which was now being closely monitored 24/7 by intelligence. There were all the usual suspects: bank account alerts, mobile phone statements, countless standardised messages from enterprises he'd never heard of and the occasional message from the few friends and family members who had been informed about his predicament.

There was one from his neighbour Brian Jenkins that Michael couldn't bring himself to open. He scrolled down and then felt pangs of guilt... He couldn't just ignore it. That would be cowardly. He owed the Jenkins family an apology. Tentatively he scrolled back up to the message from B Jenkins. The subject line: *What the hell!* gave Michael a foretaste of what was to come and a pretty good hint of the general tone of Brian's email, so it was hardly surprising for Michael to cast his eyes over the following:

> *For crying out loud, Michael. What in heaven's name have you been playing at?*
> *You've completely betrayed our trust. Dragging Alan into this whole sordid scheme of yours is unforgivable. I know you've been to hell and back, but it doesn't give you the right to ride roughshod over the trust and emotions of your friends and their severely autistic child. I can't begin to tell you how all this has affected Alan's behaviour. We're*

now having to pick up the pieces. And it's all your bloody fault...

Michael could hear Brian's voice as he read. It wasn't often that Brian got angry, but when he did, he'd use the word bloody and he'd give the word extraordinary emphasis. Michael closed the email. It was too painful to read, especially as he agreed with every word of it. He had no excuses to give. He was guilty as charged.

He continued scrolling down and stopped at an email from Danny.

Dear Michael,

I've no idea where this email will find you. I only hope that it's comfortable and affords a decent view. The one thing it undoubtedly will be is safe. And that my friend is the most important consideration at present.

Once this thing blows over, as indeed it will, you'll be able to look back at all this and laugh it off. It'll certainly be something to tell your grandchildren about.

Don't worry. I don't expect you to write back for obvious reasons.

By the way, I bumped into Hugo Manningtree yesterday. He sends his best wishes and is very keen to get you up in his latest two-seater. It's a beautiful bird. Like an adoring father, he pulled photos out of his wallet and showed off his new baby. He has just acquired a state-of-the-art hoist for wheelchair users. Apparently, two of his flying

students are tetraplegics. As soon as you're back in London, I suggest we take a trip up to St Albans and pay him a visit. Says he'd love to give you free flying lessons. Food for thought methinks. Might be just what the doctor ordered.
Must scoot.
Speak later,
Dan

Michael smiled to himself. Danny's email had cheered him up no end. Hugo was the only other person he still kept in contact with from school days. Unlike everyone else he knew, Hugo didn't end up going to university but was quite possibly the brightest person Michael knew. There were few people in this world capable of teaching themselves aeronautic engineering and building their own aeroplanes, or for that matter, learning five languages fluently including Japanese. If truth be known, there weren't many things Hugo Manningtree couldn't turn his hand to. He was one of life's polymaths. So it was hardly surprising that his working career had taken so many twists and turns. Having inherited his father's publishing business back in the late '80s, he'd been a successful publisher of scientific journals for a couple of years before becoming bored, selling the business and turning to sheep farming just outside Tideswell in the Peak District where he became a dab-hand at dry stonewalling. This kept him occupied for three years until he met Rebecca. The farm was eventually sold and the couple returned to London where Hugo decided to set up a vegetarian restaurant in Notting Hill. Heavily influenced by Moroccan and Mediterranean cuisine, the business slowly but surely began to win rave reviews, and before long was attracting the likes of Paul McCartney and his then-wife. And it was during the restaurant's success that he somehow managed to find time to take flying lessons. The hobby became a passion that turned into an obsession. By 2001 he had handed over the reins of the thriving restaurant business to his younger brother and bought a 50-acre site in St Albans on which he established the Manningtree Flying School, and it was this same year that this handsome couple tied the knot.

The thought of flying with Hugo admittedly had a certain appeal. On one level, it might prove to be a good way for him to forget about his disability and do something liberating for once. If nothing else, it would be one hell of a laugh.

He'd been to Hugo's place a couple of times before he'd become disabled. It was an impressive set-up. Back then Hugo owned three fixed-wing lightweight two-seaters that were classed as microlights, and he'd built two of them himself from kits. To the untrained eye, they looked just like planes, but their lightweight construction meant they were technically classed as microlights. In addition, he had three flex-wing microlights with the classic fabric handlebar wings. These machines may have looked like glorified flying lawnmowers, but they were deceptively powerful and quite capable of hitting 70 mph on the runway in around eight seconds and cruising happily at 2,000 feet. Danny had been up in one of them with Hugo, but Michael had taken one look at the flimsy-looking devices and declined the offer of a free ride on the spot. But that was then. Sod it! Now there was absolutely no reason why he shouldn't throw caution to the wind.

He'd played it safe all these years, and it hadn't exactly saved him from his current predicament, had it?

'Once you've been through that lot, you might want to go through these.' Sergeant Bolzwinick popped his head round the kitchen door and then appeared in the room with a postbag of letters, which he gently tipped onto the table. 'We're forwarding all your mail to this address... Took a little while to set up I'm afraid, hence the backlog.'

Michael looked up from his laptop. 'Oh, that's alright. I'm sure that most of it is just junk mail anyway. It's criminal the amount of trees marketeers are happy to destroy in order to flog us crap none of us need or want.'

'Tell me about it... But there is a fairly effective way of removing yourself from mailing lists you know.'

'I'm all ears.'

'Well, it's very simple. You just cross out the address and write: Wrong address. Return to sender and pop it back in the post. The sender will then have to pay the postage to receive their own junk mail. Keep doing that and you'll soon find that your junk mail will start drying up, and you'll probably save a small forest in the process.'

'That's a neat trick. I'll have to remember that one.' Michael wheeled himself over to the other side of the kitchen and filled the kettle and put it on the hob. 'Can I get you a coffee?'

The sergeant pulled up a chair. 'You must have been reading my mind, Michael. I'd love a strong black one with one sugar. Thank you.'

'I hope you don't mind me asking, but your surname... Is it Eastern European?'

Alexander chuckled. 'No I don't mind in the least. And you're by no means the first to ask that question I can assure you… My father was a Lithuanian Jew and my mother a reasonably devout Scottish Presbyterian, so I'm quite a mixture. Dad was one of six and was something of a rebel by all accounts. He and his younger brother fled their homeland some years before the war and somehow ended up in Glasgow where he and his brother were taken in by a Presbyterian minister and his wife and four daughters. Lucky he got out when he did because the rest of his family perished in the Holocaust… Anyway, that explains my distinctive surname. Dad toyed with changing the family name by deed poll, but my mother never let him… Said he owed it to his family to keep their name as a way of honouring their memory… She was right of course.'

'It's a sad story…'

'Yeah… And it wasn't my father who recounted it to me either. He never spoke about his background. I guess it was too painful… It was mum who told me everything. She knew it all like the back of her hand.'

'It's a great name.'

'It is. Dad didn't speak a word of English when he showed up on these shores. So it was only the immigration officials' interpretation of his Lithuanian pronunciation we have to go on… But dad always said that Bolzwinick was a close phonetic match to the original Lithuanian. And before you ask, no there are no other Bolzwinicks in the phone book or online.'

'Are your folks still alive?'

'No. My father died over 20 years ago from a sudden heart attack. He was 75. My mother told me everything she knew, which was a lot, after his funeral. And sadly, she passed away last year. She was 95.'

'I'm sorry…'

Alexander gesticulated with his right hand as if swatting a fly. 'It's ok… She was an incredible woman. Fiercely independent, she refused to live in a care home when I suggested it on her 90th birthday. Said it would be the death of her, and she was probably right. She and my father were very close. In so many ways, she was his rock. Thanks to her, he was able to move on and lead a reasonably normal life without dwelling on the past.'

'I don't mean to pry, but can I ask what became of his brother?'

Alexander smiled. 'His story doesn't have a happy ending I'm afraid. He never found a soul mate and found it difficult to adjust to life in this country after the war. As a result, he suffered with bouts of very deep depression. My parents were very good to him, but there was little they could really do. And following my father's sudden death, he took his own life.'

'Oh my lord, this really is a sad tale. I'm sorry. It's all my fault… I should never have asked.'

Alexander finished the last dregs of coffee and licked his lips. 'Not at all. It's good to talk about these things… Life can be a real bitch at times.'

Michael took the empty mugs and wheeled himself over to the dishwasher.

'By the way, I'd like to take you and Natasha through some security procedures this morning, if that's alright… It's something we do as a matter of course, you understand.'

Michael nodded. 'Of course. I think Tash is in the land of the living. I just heard footsteps. Shall we say 11 o'clock?'

'Perfect… Gives me time to catch up on paperwork… I've enjoyed our little chat. But now you'll have to excuse me.'

CHAPTER TWENTY-FIVE

He had no idea how long he'd been in the boot of the car. When you're being thrown around in the pitch black and every part of your body begins to feel bruised, you lose any sense of time. It felt like perpetuity, and it wasn't helped by that bastard Hasan's reckless driving. Every bump and every swerve left its mark on him and made him curse.

When that boot was finally opened and daylight flooded back into Qssim's world, he shielded his eyes until they readjusted.

'OK my friend it's time to remove that burka and get your arse out of my boot.' With these words, Hasan's rough hands pulled Qssim's legs out of the boot. Qssim noticed Hasan's chunky gold signet ring on the small finger of his left hand and an even chunkier gold *Rolex* that caught the light and threw light patterns on the lid of the boot.

They had parked in a field close to a clapboard cottage that had clearly seen better days if its peeling white paint and nicotine-stained net curtains were anything to go by.

Qssim removed the burka and pulled the wig from his head.

Hasan pushed him through an unkempt front garden of cracked concrete and weeds, and they entered the premises through a backdoor into a basic looking kitchen with dirty plates and a collection of tin foil takeaway dishes piled up in the sink. At first glance, it looked like your typical rundown student pad. But Qssim knew that this was far from the case. The fact that he was here at all was down to the old man.

Anwar's trusted position as imam to the community was the perfect foil for his other more sinister role in the world. It was a role that was never overtly spoken of in public or in private for that matter. But Qssim knew enough. He knew that Anwar had set up several charities in the UK that successfully raised money; significant sums of money. These charities had innocuous names like *The Islamic Relief Project* or *The Enterprise for Islamic Studies*, and he also knew from diligent investigations of his own that only a very small proportion of the money found its way to the professed beneficiaries of these charities. But he had a pretty good idea where most of the funds would have ended up. They'd almost certainly have been siphoned into the pockets of radical causes that promoted jihad and financed groups that the West would no doubt describe as terrorist organisations.

'Ok Mr Caxton, you can stop here.' Qssim felt Hasan's gun press into the small of his back. They were standing in a narrow passageway and to his right was a door. 'Raise your hands please.' Qssim did what he was told as Hasan ran his hands down the side of his body and legs checking for a concealed weapon. 'Now open the door and go inside.' He obeyed his orders once more and stepped into a distinctly cold garage with bare breeze block walls and a couple of metal shelves. A bare light bulb hung from the ceiling above one solitary wooden chair. This was obviously the interrogation room. Hasan followed close behind him. 'Please sit on the chair, Mr Caxton.' He wished he'd stop calling him Mr Caxton. It was pissing him off big time, but he refused to be visibly riled and took his seat in the middle of the garage, and Hasan immediately took his hands, placing them behind the back of the chair and handcuffed them to the struts forming the backrest.

◆

He could hear the distant sounds of laughter and what he thought may have been Arabic being spoken. Then the sound of the door handle being turned.

She emerged from the shadows, and now he could see her more clearly thanks to the light bulb. She was older than he had first thought when he caught a glimpse of her in the back of the car. Fifty perhaps, well-groomed in a smart black trouser suit and headscarf, she was Middle Eastern in appearance. But she looked very out of place here. Her sophistication and the fact that she was a woman didn't seem to fit. But then, come to think of it, neither did he.

'So Mr Caxton, we have it on good authority that you are a committed member of our… ' She paused and looked at him. '…. our cause.' She reached into her jacket's breast pocket and pulled out a packet of cigarettes and offered him one.

'Thanks. But no thanks.'

She pushed the cigarette between her bright red-lipsticked lips and lit it with a match. As she inhaled hard and exhaled a cloud of smoke, the door opened and a large figure entered the room carrying two chairs.

'Ah, good of you to join us Ahmed. This is Mr Caxton. Perhaps you'd like to unlock his hands.' Ahmed appeared from the shadow. He was balding, had biceps the size of watermelons and wouldn't have looked out of place at the entrance of any glitzy West End nightclub. Without saying a word, he turned a key in the handcuffs and the metallic click released his hands. Then he placed the two chairs in front of Qssim.

'First of all, I must apologise for your ordeal in

advance. But you have to understand our security procedures. We have to ensure that you are who you say you are.' She took another drag on the cigarette and seated herself in one of the chairs. Ahmed did likewise.

'Whoever applied the makeup, did a good job... Here, use this.' She handed him a pack of moist disposable face towels and Qssim started to self-consciously wipe away the traces of makeup and mascara.

'Anwar's daughter is a professional makeup artist.'

'Anwar is a good man.' She flicked ash from the cigarette onto the floor and took another long drag. 'Tell me... How long have you known Mohammed Farik?'

Qssim felt more relaxed now that she had at least apologised and given him some kind of explanation, albeit brief, for his shoddy treatment. He cast his mind back. 'I've known Mohammed for about eleven, maybe twelve years now... Met him at the mosque in Stepney, and we became good friends.'

'You knew his brother Salah?'

'No. I never knew him, but I knew all about him, and that he had been killed in an American bombing raid in Iraq.'

'You say you knew all about him?'

'Sure.'

'So you knew he was gay?'

There was a pause. Was that possible? Mohammed had never said as much. But then, if it were true, Mohammed wouldn't have let on. 'No, as a matter of fact, I didn't know that... Mohammed never mentioned it.'

'No, I don't suppose he did... I don't suppose he ever told you about his own history of mental illness either?'

'Mental illness?' Was this some kind of game? He could call Mohammed plenty of things, but a mental head case wasn't one of the labels that immediately sprung to mind.

'No… No… I'm not aware of that… It's absurd…'

She took a final drag and deliberately dropped the butt on the floor where she unceremoniously stubbed it out underfoot. 'How about Mr Ibrahim Choudary who Mr Farik is alleged to have murdered… How did you know him?'

Qssim still couldn't believe that his old friend had been murdered. There was simply no way Mohammed could have been in any way responsible. 'We met in prison in Aylesbury. Ibrahim was the Head Librarian. He loved that library… It was Ibrahim who converted me to Islam as a matter of fact.'

'And do you know what Mr Choudary's crime was exactly?'

Qssim laughed. 'Yeah… He blew up a couple of garden gnomes. Used a homemade dry ice device apparently.'

She smiled. 'He also had a tattoo, did he not? Just here.' She pointed to the right side of her neck. 'Can you tell me what that looked like?'

'Bullshit… He had no such thing… If he did it was invisible.'

'How about his birthmark. He had one of those, didn't he? Where exactly was it? And can you describe it?'

'Yes he did. It was on his hand. His right hand that he used for writing, and it was just above his middle three knuckles. It looked kind of gross. Purple and blotchy.'

She got up and stepped towards the door. 'There is one other thing you didn't know about Ibrahim, of course.' She turned and looked Qssim in the eye. 'He was one of us… He was a highly valued member of this cell. And I can assure you that we don't take this matter lightly. Thanks to Ibrahim, we were getting quite close to tracking down your

Mr Anonymous. But now Ibrahim's murder has become a direct threat to this organisation and our future plans. If we are to succeed in our operations, we need to know who is responsible and eliminate this threat immediately.'

Qssim began to sweat. This was serious. He had no idea of Ibrahim's involvement in a truly radical activist cell like this. He had played the part of a mild-mannered Muslim with slightly radical tendencies. And he'd obviously played that part brilliantly to cover up his real motivations. It was quite a lot to take in. But it was even more difficult to believe that Mohammed had murdered Ibrahim. There was no possible reason for him to do so, unless he really was a psycho. 'Look, I don't begin to understand how and why Ibrahim was murdered... I did warn Mohammed about this Alan Anonymous character. I said that it was possible that he was an undercover agent posing as one of us. And I told him to tread carefully. Those were my precise words. But Mohammed is naive. He's never cautious. I think he's been set up. Whatever happened, he fucked up. He fucked up big time.'

'On that, Mr Caxton, I think we can agree. You'll excuse me. I won't be long.' She let herself out of the door and was gone.

Ahmed folded his sizeable arms across his chest and chose to remain silent. Qssim didn't have long to collect his thoughts, as she re-appeared at the door, this time clasping a blue folder. 'Now Qssim'... It was the first time she had addressed him by his correct name. 'I'd like to know some details about the man you discovered in your apartment. The man you managed to throw off your balcony... Can you describe him please?'

Qssim. Closed his eyes. 'He was around 5 foot 8 inches tall. White. Slight build. Clean-shaven. Dark brown, slightly wavy, unkempt hair. Squarish jaw... '

'Do you remember what he was wearing.'

'Fairly casual zip-up jacket and jeans and a long-sleeved sweatshirt. Grey…'

'And did he have a lanyard around his neck?'

'Shit. Yes he did… How did you know? I completely forgot about that… Didn't get to see what was on it. Think it was probably the reverse side that was showing.'

'Would have been a fake lanyard for some utility company. It's one way these intelligence officers get into the premises of unsuspecting occupants. But it's very strange that he forced an entry. That would have been breaking with protocol.'

She pulled a photo from the blue folder and handed it to him.

'That's him. That's the fucker. Who is he?'

'We don't know his real name Qssim. But we do know that he works for *MI5*'s counter-terrorism unit, or at least he used to. Thanks to you, there's one less… fucker, to use your charming technical expression, for us to have to worry about.' She fumbled in her jacket and produced another cigarette. 'But we are going to have to deal with your Mr Farik, and more importantly this Alan Anonymous. Mr Farik can be dealt with very easily. Mr Anonymous, on the other hand, will take a little longer. But we do have the means to locate the area for his IP address and an account name. Once we establish these key facts, it will be down to you to track him down… The bad news for you is that you are now high priority on the counter terrorist's so-called hit list. Hit one of those bastards, and you can be sure that they'll do their very best to hit you even harder.'

Qssim knew instinctively that the guy in his flat hadn't been a regular burglar, and this confirmation from the woman in black didn't surprise him one bit, but it still made him feel uneasy. 'How safe am I going to be here?'

'We selected this part of the world for its lack of CCTV cameras. It's not your journey here that worries us. It's your route from your flat to Anwar's that is the immediate problem. There will be CCTV footage on public transport and high streets. It's only a matter of time before they figure out your journey from Ilford to Anwar's. We are in a race against the clock Qssim.'

'What about Anwar and his wife and daughter?'

She looked at her wristwatch. 'They should be cruising at 2,000 feet as we speak. We arranged a private flight from Blackbushe airfield in Hampshire. They'll be in Islamabad by midnight our time… At times like this, it can be very handy to have dual citizenship.'

'Qssim sighed a sigh of relief. 'Thank God for that… By the way, I deliberately planted my mobile on a train to Glasgow en route to Anwar's.'

She laughed. 'Oldest trick in the book. But a trick worth playing… If *MI5* were tracking your mobile, which they probably were, they may well have fallen for it without checking CCTV. They simply wouldn't have had the time to go through hours of material… Where did you plant the mobile?'

'In the toilet.'

'Good… You may have bought Anwar and his wife and daughter vital extra time to slip away. But this is no time to grow complacent. Never underestimate the ability of intelligence services in the UK. These bastards are very good. They have foiled many of our brothers' plans, and they pride themselves on being the best in the world. And to be fair, they probably are.'

'What now?'

She took a particularly long drag on her cigarette. 'My instinct is to get you out of the country on a false passport. And that's exactly what intelligence services would expect you to do. So for this reason, I think we should just keep you here.

CHAPTER TWENTY-SIX

It didn't take long for him to end up here.

He had been shown photographs of Ibrahim's body lying in a dark puddle of blood. They showed him the screwdriver in a plastic bag. It still had Ibrahim's dried blood all over it. And his clothes had been sealed in plastic bags. The evidence was overwhelming. But still, his lawyer said that his client wished to exercise his right to remain silent. And that's when Mohammed had chosen to ignore his puny, bespectacled lawyer. He told them that he had killed Ibrahim. That he had had little choice in the matter. That he had heard the voices again. The voices he used to hear. He couldn't ignore them. They had to be obeyed. Whether he liked it or not, Ibrahim had to die. And that's when they went through his medical records, and he was assessed by more men in suits and asked more and more pointless questions. Why couldn't they just leave him alone? Eventually, they did.

He was now remanded in custody in B Wing - the remand wing of Winchester prison. And it was here that his fate awaited him.

✦

For the first few days, the cause of death was unknown. There were no visible wounds or bruising to his body that would suggest foul play. One of the prison wardens had discovered him that morning lying prostrate on the cold floor of his cell. And the initial, though inaccurate, conclusion was that it must have been a heart attack.

The pathology report said otherwise. There had been significant concentrations of aconitine found in both the femoral blood and urine results of the post mortem. Aconitine is an alkaloid toxin produced by the Aconitum plant, also known as Devil's Helmet or Monkshood. Its deadly properties have been well known for many centuries. Indeed, the emperor Claudius is reputed to have been poisoned with the crushed leaves of the plant by his wife Agrippina who sprinkled the powder over a plate of mushrooms.

How the substance had found its way into Mohammed's bloodstream remained a mystery. He had received no visitors and rarely came into contact with other inmates. Despite a thorough and forensic investigation into the unexplained death, there was absolutely no evidence to corroborate the authority's conviction that Mohammed had been unlawfully killed by someone on the premises.

The cause of death on his death certificate read simply asphyxia caused by the ingestion of Aconitine.

CHAPTER TWENTY-SEVEN

To all intents and purposes, Qssim had become a house prisoner. He was confined to using the downstairs rooms, these being the kitchen, sitting room and bathroom. He slept on an ancient-looking sofa in the sitting room and was constantly in the company of at least one other. There seemed to be four men in the house at all times including the mean spirited Hasan and the solid frame of Ahmed, all of whom were armed with semi-automatic pistols - *Glock 18s* by the looks of things. They were, without exception, men of few words. The woman in black who he knew by no other name had disappeared after day one.

'Thought you'd like to see this.' Hasan threw a copy of *The Daily Mail* onto the sofa. The headline read: 'Terror suspect dies behind bars.' The grainy photograph was of Mohammed in a grey sweatshirt looking neither happy nor especially sad. It must have been an official prison photograph. How incredibly surreal. This was the second time Qssim had seen the face of one of his comrades staring back at him from a national newspaper. He scanned the article:

> *Terrorist suspect Mohammed Farik who had been charged with murder and was on remand at Winchester prison awaiting trial was yesterday found dead in his cell by one of the wardens.*
> *The prison's governor Stephen Richards was*

visibly shaken by the news. 'I am very disturbed by this incident,' he said. 'We are very proud of our track record here at Winchester when it comes to prisoner welfare. And this is the first time we have had a fatality on my watch in our remand wing.'

There were apparently no signs of injury to Farik's body. And when asked about the cause of death Mr Richards was keeping an open mind. 'At this juncture, we have to wait for the findings of the pathology report. But as I said earlier, there are no obvious signs of foul play, or indeed suicide. This could very well be a tragic case of death by natural causes. We will just have to wait and see.'

Qssim put the paper down. He'd read enough. Then he recalled the words of the woman in black. Mr Farik can be dealt with very easily. Those had been her precise words.

'It was you lot, wasn't it? You had him killed, didn't you?'

Hasan smiled. 'I couldn't possibly comment. But I can say that I for one won't be shedding any tears for your friend. He murdered our brother.'

'Ibrahim Choudary, peace be upon him, was my brother, too.'

Hasan looked at him intently, and then muttered, 'I know… '

Qssim was mystified by Hasan's response. 'What do you mean? How could you possibly know?'

Hasan averted his gaze from Qssim's face. 'My name is Hasan Choudary…'

'You were Ibrahim's brother?'

Hasan nodded and lit himself a cigarette. 'He was my younger brother - peace be upon him.'

Of course. Now it made sense. That's how Ibrahim had got involved. 'I'm sorry... But I still don't understand how your brother could have been murdered by Mohammed...' Hasan shrugged and exhaled a cloud of smoke. 'Did he really have a mental health problem?"

'Everything you heard in that room was true, except for the tattoo. That was to test you... We had his medical records... Antisocial personality disorder was the official diagnosis back in the early 1990s.'

Qssim wasn't entirely sure what that meant. But Mohammed could certainly be antisocial at times. And he'd sometimes wondered if he'd been on the autistic spectrum. Perhaps he had been less than stable mentally. And perhaps he had flipped and killed poor Ibrahim in a fit of paranoia. Now he'd never know.

Hasan took a final drag on his cigarette before stubbing it into an olive dish. 'Benazir who interviewed you wants you to grow your beard. She will be back tonight. She wants to talk to you.'

Qssim nodded. It was the first time the woman in black had been given a name. So she was called Benazir. It suited her. He was glad that Hasan had spoken as he had. Now he could understand his anger and could feel some kind of connection with at least one of his captors. He was, after all, Ibrahim's older brother. He couldn't be all bad.

✦

The sound of wheels on the gravel outside woke Qssim from a doze. The light outside was fading.

She was pulling slender leather gloves from her hands as

she entered the room. 'Sorry I'm late. I wanted to get here sooner. Could someone grab me a strong black Turkish coffee please?' Hasan rose from the armchair in the corner and put his newspaper on a side table. 'No problem.'

She turned to Qssim. 'I'm liking the designer stubble, and I'll like it even more when it's a proper beard. But we're going to require a little more work to your face. I have spoken to one of our close associates who runs a cosmetic surgery off Harley Street. He's one of the best. We're going to have to do some work to your nose, cheekbones and jawline. He has slotted us in at the last minute for tomorrow afternoon.'

Hasan returned with the coffee.

'Thank you, Hasan. Did you manage to order those false number plates?'

'Yes. They'll be here tonight, and I have taken the extra precaution of getting the car resprayed silver.'

'Excellent. You can never be too cautious. CCTV is everywhere. It's becoming the bane of our lives.'

She turned back to Qssim. 'I'm afraid you'll have to travel in the boot again. There's an underground carpark without CCTV at the surgery, so we can safely transfer you to the clinic where I suggest you stay until you have made a full recovery and your bandages can be removed. Mr Noorani, the surgeon will also work on your lips employing the very latest techniques using collagen. At the end of all this, you'll have a new identity including a passport and driving licence.'

It wasn't quite what Qssim was expecting. 'I don't suppose I have much choice in the matter.'

'Not if you want to evade British intelligence and the full force of the British criminal justice system.'

'You seem to be going to a lot of trouble to protect me.'

'Qssim, I needn't tell you that white Muslim converts are a valuable asset to us. In short, you raise fewer suspicions for obvious reasons. You can operate under the radar, so to speak. And in your case, you have already earned your stripes by eliminating a member of *MI5*... Then, of course, there is the matter of our Mr Anonymous who has already managed to alert *MI5* to Ibrahim. They will have trawled through his mobile and PC files by now. Fortunately, they will find nothing linking him to us, as we forbade any direct contact. It's how we operate here. And it's why you can count yourself safe as long as you're under our wing. But having said all this, it's vital that we get to Mr Anonymous before he does any more damage. Spies are potentially lethal to our network. If we allow them to infiltrate our system, they will spread like a malignant cancer.'

'What do you have in mind?'

'Once we know roughly where he's located you can start putting pressure on him - assuming, of course, that he's a man. You can send him threatening emails. Name the area where he lives. We'll know that pretty soon from his IP address. Tell him you're closing in on him, and that it's only a matter of time before you'll track him down. Once we have his username and his geographical location, you can go through the phone directories and election registers.'

'How are you going to get his username?'

'We have ways and means, Qssim. As I said earlier, we have long tentacles. You don't need to know how we access this kind of information. You just need to know that we can.'

'And once I know who he is and where he is, how do I go about eliminating him without leaving a trace? I wouldn't like to make the same mistakes I made last time.'

She lit a cigarette. 'Don't worry Qssim. We won't let you make a dog's dinner of this one. You won't be alone… You'll just be the point of contact… the deal maker.' She inhaled deeply.

'Deal?'

'Yes. We'll offer him the chance to buy his freedom with cash.'

'You're kidding. That's ridiculous, He's not going to fall for that. He'll go straight to the police.'

'Not necessarily… Not if we make it clear to him that by doing so he'll be putting his entire family in jeopardy. He's bound to have dependents. We'll know by then, God willing, who each and every one of them is.' She stubbed out the cigarette. 'And if he does go to the police… we'll still be able to take him out when he's least expecting it. at a time and a location of our choosing.'

Qssim nodded. 'And if he does play ball, how do you propose we pick up the cash and dispose of the body?'

'That's something we can finalise nearer the time… Have faith Qssim… Have faith.'

CHAPTER TWENTY-EIGHT

They must have looked a strange sight.

Natasha usually walked Ziggy, but Michael couldn't see why he shouldn't attach the dog lead to his wheelchair and take himself for a spin while the dog got a bit of exercise at the same time.

The pavements around here were generally fairly narrow and difficult for his wheelchair but the saving grace was that they were at least reasonably flat - a great deal flatter than those in Hampstead Garden Suburb and Muswell Hill.

The village, like all quaint English villages, boasted a post office, a butcher and a small grocery store. At the far end of the early Victorian parade, sat The Fox and Hounds public house run by an affable and jovial old cove who used to own his own photographic retouching studio in London's Soho, until digital technology and Photoshop came along and put him out of business. They served a very decent drop of bitter, but tempting though it was to drop in, Michael thought better of it. He didn't want to stay out long, and if he did show his face in that place, he'd almost certainly get collared by the landlord and end up drinking too much. Besides, he could tell that Alexander wasn't keen for him to stay out too long.

Both he and Natasha had been given tracking devices to pin to their underclothing as a precautionary measure, so their whereabouts were known at all times, and they had both been issued with panic buttons that could be activated in the event of an emergency. Alexander had also shown them the security features built into the cottage. The place was easily as secure as any high street bank by the looks of things. The wooden front door, for instance, wasn't just an innocent-looking piece of timber. It actually encased a solid 5 millimetre steel plate and sported four 3 inch deadbolts and three hinge-bolts, all of which sank with a satisfying clunk into the deep recesses of a very solid steel door-frame with a reinforced concrete core. All the sash windows housed double glazed bulletproof laminated glass. And there were passive infrared sensors and high definition CCTV cameras with automatic night vision all over the place. It was, in short, a burglar's worst nightmare.

Michael wheeled himself into the post office and gesticulated towards the stack of newspapers. 'Fetch me The Telegraph, Ziggy.' Without flinching, Ziggy wagged his tail and gave a little whimper before sniffing out the piles of newspapers and tugging at one of the larger broadsheets and depositing it on Michael's knees. It was *The Times*. Oh well, that would have to do.

'Good boy. I can live with that. At least it's not *The Sun*, eh?'

The newsagent looked in disbelief. 'That's one well-trained dog you have there, even if he can't distinguish between *The Telegraph* and *The Times*.'

'Oh yes. He's a bit special, aren't you Ziggy?' The dog put his head affectionately onto Michael's knees and gave its owner one of his knowing looks, and Michael obligingly stroked the top of his head. 'He was specially trained for a whole year to help me, so there's not much he can't do around the house. He can even put clothes in the washing machine and help me turn over at night. But he's also fantastic company and incredibly affectionate. I'm very lucky to have him.'

'That's remarkable. They do say that labradors are particularly intelligent don't they?'

'I think that's right.' He paid for the newspaper while Ziggy tugged at the door handle and pulled it open causing a bell to jingle.

'You just moved into the area have you?'

Michael had a feeling that someone would ask them that question sooner or later. That was the only problem about being in an isolated village like this - pretty though it was. You stood out like a sore thumb to the locals, and everyone wanted to know your business.

'Yes. My daughter and I have just taken a holiday let following my divorce... Good opportunity to blow the old cobwebs away and start afresh with a complete change of scenery and all this fresh air.'

'Well, you've certainly picked a nice spot here... But don't let me keep you. I can see that your faithful little helper is straining at the leash.'

Michael smiled and waved as he wheeled himself through the front door.

By the time he returned, Natasha had materialised from her room upstairs and was sitting in the living room and chatting to PC Hetherington. Michael wheeled himself into the kitchen and spread his newspaper on the table.

Two stories seemed to dominate the day's news. On the home front, the discovery of a dead swan in a sleepy backwater on the East coast of Scotland not a million miles from St Andrews, had come to the world's attention. The bird had apparently tested positive for the deadly H5N1 strain of avian influenza commonly known as bird flu.

While the virus didn't pose an immediate threat to humans, there had been a great deal of speculation by experts over the possibility of the virus evolving and becoming a serious risk to human health by triggering a flu pandemic. Such an outbreak could put the lives of millions at risk. It was enough to make some local authorities cordon off their wildlife parks, and large swathes of the population to question the wisdom of consuming chicken. To assuage the growing fears, the *Secretary of State for Health and Social Care* had said repeatedly on air that public health was not being compromised and that every precaution was being taken by the government to minimise the risk. And to reassure readers even further, he had been photographed as a PR stunt at a well known fast food outlet eating chicken drumsticks with his eleven-year-old daughter.

Further afield in the US in the city of Boise, Idaho, a young girl of 29 by the name of Karyl Fisher was being reunited with her family having been abducted from her home back in 1991. Fisher had been originally taken by a man and woman close to her home in Boise, and police could confirm Fisher's identity as she walked into the police station 18 years after the event. She had apparently been held in an underground cell for all these years and neighbours had suspected nothing. She had only been able to escape when her captor had suffered a heart attack.

Michael was halfway through the article when the kitchen door opened and Sergeant Bolzwinick appeared with a stack of mail. 'I'm afraid it's taken a little while to have your mail redirected here, which will explain the volume... So apologies for that.' He stacked the post on the table, forming a leaning tower of envelopes of varying size and hue. 'But the one package that you'll be most eager to receive is this one.' He produced a small manilla padded envelope that had been re-sealed with sellotape. Michael immediately recognised the envelope he'd placed in the locker at King's Cross. 'All the notes have been traced back to your bank branch in Muswell Hill. There's about 7K missing, but there's still around 37K there.'

Michael opened the envelope. It was surprising how much money you could fit in such a confined space. 'Thank you… I didn't think I'd ever see this again.'

'My pleasure, Michael.'

'Don't suppose we'll ever know what he spent the missing £7,000 on will we?'

Alexander grimaced. 'Thought you might ask me that… As a matter of fact, we do know. Virtually all of it was spent at a car dealership in Southgate. It paid for a second-hand *BMW* that's now a complete right-off.'

Michael nodded.

'Under normal circumstances, intelligence services would have held fire and waited for the suspect to purchase bomb-making equipment, guns, anything that would have implicated him. But Choudhary's murder changed all that. Mohammed Farik was assessed to be too dangerous and unstable not to bring in, which was a bit of a bugger as far as *MI5* were concerned. They like to play the waiting game because they know as a general rule of thumb that the longer they monitor and track their targets, the more invaluable information they can glean.'

Michael nodded. 'That figures… Do you think he was murdered?'

Alexander filled the kettle with water and placed it on the hob. 'Almost certainly.'

Michael was taken aback by the Sergeant's answer. 'Really? What makes you say that?'

There was a long pause before Alexander spoke again; this time slowly. 'It's not public knowledge, but the pathology report found traces of the deadly poison aconitine in the blood and urine… You're not to repeat this to anyone, you understand?'

Michael nodded. 'So he didn't die from natural causes?'

'No. It could only have been murder or suicide. But everyone back at the ranch is convinced that it was murder… Problem is there's not a shred of evidence to support this theory. Forensics have been all over that prison like a rash, and there's nothing to suggest foul play on CCTV either. Whoever did it knew exactly what they were doing, and went to exceptional lengths to completely cover their tracks. To do this in the confines of a prison is no mean feat…' He sighed. 'The press will have a field day when they get hold of this.'

CHAPTER TWENTY-NINE

Qssim was feeling incredibly drowsy.

He had no idea on initially opening his eyes, where he was. Then it all started to come back to him. The uncomfortable journey in the boot of that fucking car, and the arrival in the underground car-park. The face of Mr Noorani and those gleaming white teeth revealed by an artificial smile.

The whiteness of the place was what immediately struck him now. It was so damn white it hurt your eyes. Everything was white. Even the ceramic floor tiles, which looked pristine enough to eat your supper off.

The door clicked open. 'Hello Mr El-Ghazzawy. Good to see that you are in the land of the living. How are you feeling?' The figure of a woman in a blue nursing uniform lent over him and placed a belt around his right forearm, which was then inflated.

Qssim wasn't used to being addressed by his Muslim surname. He moved his lips but nothing seemed to come out.

'110 over 70. Excellent blood pressure Mr El-Ghazzawy.' She removed a clipboard from the end of the bed and made a few notes. 'I'll be back shortly with the menu.' And with that she left the room, closing the door behind her.

Tentatively he raised his hands to his face and his fingertips were greeted by the sensation of fabric. Bandages. His entire face was covered in the stuff. In fairness to her, she had said that he would be bandaged and that he'd have to stay here until they could be removed. But he hadn't really thought too much about it. The idea of acquiring a new identity had obviously appealed to him in his present circumstances. There was even a faint whiff of glamour to the whole thing if he was being completely honest with himself. It was usually Hollywood stars who'd check-in for this kind of treatment. And yet it was exactly this kind of decadence that Islam would have condemned. How ironic was that? But this aside, the extent of this bandaging wasn't something he had bargained for. *Shit!* The bloody things even went round the back of his head. He took his hands away before they discovered something else, placed them on his chest and closed his eyes. At least he wasn't in any pain. In fact, he had very little sensation in his entire body. That had to be down to the anaesthetic.

◆

It must have been a couple of hours later when the gentle rapping on the door woke him.

Mr Noorani's beaming face appeared from the side of the door followed by the substantial bulk of his body. 'My dear Mr El-Ghazzawy. I do hope we have managed to make you reasonably comfortable.'

Qssim slowly nodded and made a guttural noise that could have been interpreted any way you liked. 'I'm checking on all my patients that have been in theatre today, and am starting with you since you have had multiple procedures, all of which I'm pleased to say went very smoothly.' Mr Noorani took a seat and straightened his tie. 'Would you like me to raise your bed?'

'Please.' Qssim had found his voice though speaking

felt very peculiar and something of an effort.

Noorani pressed a button on a remote control and the back of Qssim's bed gently moved into an upright position. 'Multiple procedures?' Qssim asked. He could barely pronounce the words.

'Indeed… Or to be more precise six procedures, which is a fair number to have in one session.' The surgeon let out a little lighthearted chuckle, which seemed to be a nervous trait. Then he did his best to adopt an altogether more serious tone. 'But I always recommend my patients to have all their procedures carried out together to reduce the recovery time. There is nothing worse than having to suffer six separate recovery periods, believe me.'

Qssim tried to smile.

'In your case, Mr El-Ghazzawy, we carried out surgery to reshape both your upper and lower eyelids. Then we reshaped your nose, making it narrower and shorter. This was followed by work on your ears, which we have reshaped and pinned closer to your head; your eyebrows, which we have elevated; and your lips, which we've made fuller. Finally, we did some fairly major reconstruction work to your mandible. That's your jawbone. This used to be fairly wide, but is now far narrower, and changes the overall shape of the lower half of your face.'

No wonder his mouth was so difficult to move.

'Recovery time varies from patient to patient. But we're talking several months. Maximum - six. And the bandages are usually removed after 6 weeks. Bruising and swelling may take a little while longer to come down completely, and the same goes for scarring.'

There was a knock on the door.

Mr Noorani rose from his chair. 'Come in.'

The door opened and a nurse wheeled in a trolley.

'Ah, this will be your supper Mr El-Ghazzawy. Perfect timing nurse Stanley. I have just finished.' He turned to Qssim and smiled even more profusely. 'Good evening Mr El-Ghazzawy. Enjoy your supper.'

◆

He was horribly overweight. And he had the irritating trait of stretching his fingers and making the knuckles crack. But they were minor flaws in the great scheme of things.

They had arranged to meet at the usual place, an innocuous curry house with a distinctly 80s feel. Its tint of peach Artex and faded prints of the Taj Mahal were about as appealing as the food itself, but that was a good thing. It meant that it was never particularly busy. In fact, it was surprising that it had managed to stay in business at all.

'Can I take your orders?' The elderly waiter stooped over the table with his pencil poised over his notepad.

Benazir glanced at the laminated photocopy of the menu. 'I'll have the Vegetarian Thali, thank you.' The waiter scribbled on his pad and turned to her unlikely looking dinner date.

'I'll go for your excellent Tandoori chicken with pilau rice, onion bhajis and naan bread.'

As soon as the old man had trundled back to the kitchen with the order, Benazir reached for a cigarette and lit up. 'So Rami. I take it you now have everything we need?'

The large man looked disapprovingly at her as she exhaled. 'It's a filthy habit. You should give it up. ' He unfurled the napkin and spread it over his lap. 'Who do you take me for? Of course I have the information. I wouldn't have called you otherwise.'

She nodded. 'I know... but it was far swifter than I'd have expected... Usually, these things take time, to coin a phrase.'

Rami smiled. 'Very true, sister. But on this occasion we got lucky. Very lucky. We didn't need to rely on hacking thanks to a little mole.'

Benazir stubbed out her cigarette. 'A new source?'

Rami tapped the side of his nose. 'My lips are sealed, sister. Let's just say you'll find this book particularly rewarding, particularly page 83.' He placed a slim blue paperback on the table. The title was *The Diving Bell and the Butterfly* and its author, Jean-Dominique Bauby.

'That's very kind of you Rami... I haven't read it.' She nonchalantly turned to page 83 where Rami had written neatly with a pencil in the fold of the spine: M. Hollinghurst NW11. 'Insightful Rami. Most insightful. For once, I think I'm going to enjoy this meal.'

CHAPTER THIRTY

This was the very same ward that Michael had been in almost eight months ago. Like so many NHS hospitals in the UK, the Royal National Orthopaedic Hospital in Stanmore looked tired and rough round the edges. Parts of it looked almost makeshift, yet this was one of the finest hospitals in the country for spinal injuries. People travelled from all corners of the country to be seen by its specialist consultants. And nobody ever had a bad word to say about the place.

Dennis lay on his back on *Elm Ward* and was gently snoozing. There were all manner of machines monitoring him with varying bleeps and flashing displays via an array of plastic tubes that were physically attached to him, including a catheter and a full looking bag of pink urine. Pinned to the wall behind a modestly proportioned cabinet on wheels were an assortment of colourful paintings that had clearly been produced by the hand of a very young child. They were happy paintings of people, and houses, and cats, and flowers. They all possessed blue skies and giant orbs of golden sunshine. Their young creator would have been blissfully unaware of the truly sad and tragic circumstances in which these chirpy paintings now found themselves.

Dennis had broken his spine fairly high up, and as a result, was now paralysed from the neck downwards. He'd lost all control of his legs, bladder and bowels, and virtually all sensation below his shoulders.

On the table were a selection of cards and various boxes of chocolates, all of which remained unopened with ribbons and packaging intact. There was a bowl of green grapes and a small pile of pristine paperbacks that hadn't been opened. Above his bed, a small television screen was suspended by a metal arm that resembled a miniature crane. On the screen, a presenter was hosting an inane daytime quiz show. The colour was turned to the highest and most painful volume, making the presenter's face luminous orange, to compensate for the sound that had been turned off.

In the corner by the bed sat the petite figure of a young woman, her face buried in her hands. Her lithe and delicate body was bent over double, and convulsing as she sobbed.

CHAPTER THIRTY-ONE

There was something addictive about flying just before sunrise. He couldn't really put his finger on it. But it gave him the most extraordinary feeling of elation. Nothing else came remotely close, including sex, which he had never rated particularly high on his list of human endeavours - not that he had a definitive list, of course.

As far as the flying itself was concerned, there was absolutely no point in taking off in one of his beautifully streamlined fixed-wing numbers that cosseted you in a snug airtight cockpit, concealing you from the elements. That was no good at all. No… it had to be seat-of-your-pants stuff - flying in a bog-standard but bloody powerful canvas flexi-wing that let you feel the wind in your hair - what little he had left. He'd learnt to fly in one of these little beauties yonks ago, and had caught the bug from that very first day. If he ever went bankrupt and had to sell off his worldly possessions, he'd rather sell his house than bid farewell to this machine; not that he'd ever admit as much to Rebecca. She'd throttle him. He laughed at the thought. Then the word *throttle* lingered momentarily in his brain and nudged him into automatic mode.

He strapped himself into the harness, placed the helmet over his head and went through the safety procedures, talking to himself as he did so. 'Untie the wing… Jolly good… Check brakes are on… Yup… Check the throttle is working and is now free closed… Excellent. Check the fuel tap is on… Good. Engine ready to engage… Nobody in front or behind... Splendid.' He paused and then shouted 'Clear the prop!', and then resumed mumbling to himself. 'Fab... Take the brake off... Check oil pressure... Good. Check fuel range... Check harness... Gloves on... Check engine... Revs up to 3,000... Now idling... Fuel tap on... Set the trim... Taxi out... Apply full power. ' At this point, the light aircraft with its wobbly canvas wing started bouncing along the grass and began to pick up speed. By the time Hugo had yelled 'Geronimo!' into the cold, biting air, he was travelling at 70 miles per hour, and all three wheels had left the ground. He was airborne.

The adrenaline pumped through his veins as the tiny speck of a craft made its steep ascent into the vast early morning heavens.

Within ten seconds he had climbed to 2,000 feet and had levelled off. The patchwork of fields formed a sea of midnight blue beneath him and the world felt a million miles away. He never really felt the cold once he was up. His whole body clock seemed to slow down up here. It was his form of yogic bliss; a nirvana of sorts that allowed him to relax in a way he simply couldn't on the ground. It also gave him space to think and collect his thoughts. And it wasn't long before those thoughts turned to the conversation he'd had the previous day with Danny.

Danny and Michael were the only school friends he'd stayed in touch with, but he hadn't seen Michael since he'd been out of hospital. And it was something that gave him pangs of guilt. It was a tragic bloody business. Could have happened to anyone, of course. Danny had told him everything about the aborted lunch at the Athenaeum, Michael's arrest and the lengths to which Danny had gone to release their friend from police custody.

He didn't blame Michael one bit for behaving as he had. If he had been in his friend's shoes, the idea of posing as one of those heartless bastards to get back at them, would have struck him as a bloody good idea. Nevertheless, he'd been surprised that Michael had had the balls. It wasn't like him to hit back like that. There wasn't an aggressive or vindictive bone in his body. Michael was simply the nicest, most laid back and charitable bloke he'd ever known. But then there was no accounting for the ways in which seismic events like getting blown up could affect anyone's behaviour.

The morning sun peeped its head above the parapet that was the horizon line and the inky silhouettes of the surrounding trees and hedgerows slowly came into sharp relief.

Hugo had a couple of flying students who were wheelchair users, but he wasn't sure if he'd ever have the chance to bring Michael up here. Danny had been informed by the police that Michael was now enjoying special protection at the taxpayers' expense. It could be years before he'd get to see his friend. What a godawful world they were living in.

Hugo moved the control bar to the left and brought the aircraft into a steep bank to the right. Then he brought the control bar back to the centre in line with the horizon line and straightened her up. The entire view was now drenched in golden sunlight and long shadows were being thrown randomly across the landscape as he flew over the distinctive crucifix form of St Albans cathedral with its elongated nave and green leaded roof that glinted in the morning sun.

According to Danny, Michael wasn't contactable for security reasons. It was apparently standard procedure when one's life is seen to be threatened by a recognised terrorist group.

Danny reckoned that Michael would eventually contact one of them by mail. It seemed strange, but these days, the old fashioned method of communicating with pen and paper could be deemed more secure than the electronic equivalent. That was certainly something Hugo could relate to. He for one certainly wasn't a keen advocate of online banking. To him, it seemed like a bloody recipe for disaster.

He took his hands off the control bar and let the microlight fly herself.

Before the accident, Michael had been adamant that he wouldn't come up, even in one of Hugo's more sturdy fixed-wing aircraft. But Hugo was convinced that his friend would eventually change his mind. There were plenty of wheelchair users who'd taken to the sky. It hadn't stopped Douglas bloody Bader had it? No… he'd eventually win his friend round. It would do him the world of good to see the world from this angle; to fly like a bird; and to gain a real sense of bloody liberty.

CHAPTER THIRTY-TWO

Qssim was feeling as if he'd just stepped out of a boxing ring having gone ten gruelling rounds with a world-class heavyweight. His face felt like nothing on earth, and the painkillers seemed to do little to numb the pain. He'd been in this place for some weeks already and still, the bandages had remained on and were now beginning to irritate his skin around his cheekbones.

The only good news to shout about was that piece of paper that sat on his bedside table. There were just two names and a postcode written on it in blue biro: *Michael Hollinghurst NW11*. But it was all the information he'd need to nail that bastard who'd caused such havoc and continued to pose a massive threat to their operation. Benazir had dropped by that morning to check on his progress, and just before leaving, had nonchalantly slipped him the piece of paper while giving him one of her knowing looks. Little did he know that Hasan was already on the case.

The way Benazir saw it, there was no point in hanging around for Qssim's face to heal. She had the information she needed far earlier than she had expected, and Hasan was a reliable pair of hands. She could trust Hasan implicitly. He'd already proved himself by dealing efficiently with Mohammed. She hadn't asked any questions. It was better that way. And now Hasan had the information, she knew he'd have an address fairly soon.

✦

Hasan had found a copy of the telephone directory for the North West London postal area in the public library in Golders Green. He sat in the reading room and flicked through the pages until he came to surnames beginning with *H*. There was a whole column of *Hollinghursts* and quite a few *A. Hollinghursts*. He ran his finger down the column. There weren't many *B*. or *F. Hollinghursts*. And as luck would have it *M. Hollinghursts* were also light on the ground. There were only five of the bastards. He surreptitiously jotted down the five addresses in his notebook, but only two of them had NW11 postcodes. There was always the possibility, of course, that their *M. Hollinghurst* was ex-directory, which would present something of a challenge - but not one that was insurmountable.

Now he'd do a quick search on one of the library's clunky old PCs. He typed in the library password and waited patiently for the machine to bring up the internet. After an infuriatingly long wait, the machine eventually made some peculiar internal whirring noises and finally displayed the *Google* search engine page. Then he typed *192.com* into the search bar and brought up the online directory. This database held around 700 million residential and business records for the entire UK. Much of this information had been trawled from the *Electoral Rolls*, *Companies House* and the *Land Registry*. *M. Hollinghurst* and *NW11* brought up exactly the same names as the telephone directory. Better still, it also named all the other occupants. Hasan duly added these extra names to his notes, slipped his notebook back in the breast pocket of his jacket and nonchalantly strolled out of the library's 1930s Neo-Georgian style edifice.

◆

Qssim couldn't bear the irritation behind the bandages in the region of his right cheekbone and scratched it furiously with the blunt end of a pencil.

He pulled a piece of scrap paper from his pocket that Benazir had handed him earlier and stared at the handwriting in blue biro. At least he now had something to occupy his brain; something he could get on with. This place was driving him nuts.

He sat at the laptop and typed the name *M. Hollinghurst* into the search engine, which brought up 372,0000 results. Fuck! Where the hell was he going to start?

He brought up the Facebook page and searched for *M. Hollinghurst*, which unveiled an endless stream of beaming faces. For no apparent reason, *Max Hollinghurst* sat at the top of the page. He was a young college kid from Chicago in a checked shirt and displayed the early onset of adolescent acne. Qssim scrolled down further. The first *Hollinghurst* he could find from London was a *Mandy Hollinghurst*. Another young kid at university by the looks of things. This was hopeless. It didn't tell him anything useful. He left the web page and scrolled down the references to the bottom of the page and then loaded another page. He'd got through all the social media garbage and was now into the world of blogs and obituaries. He scrolled through another couple of pages. More obituaries and stuff about *Hollinghurst Foundations* and *Hollinghurst* the author. Mindlessly he forwarded 20 pages at a time before he noticed an article in a publication entitled Suburb News. The headline caught his attention: *Life goes on for Suburb survivor of 7/7*. A shiver ran up his spine. He knew then instinctively that he'd inadvertently stumbled onto something. He scrolled down further without reading a single word of the text and a photograph at the bottom corner of the page came into view. A middle-aged man in a wheelchair stared out of the photograph with a young girl by his side. The caption read simply: *Michael Hollinghurst at home with his daughter Natasha*.

◆

Hasan opened the window slightly and lit a cigarette. He'd been here an hour now, and there had been no sign of activity behind the net curtains. He'd parked opposite the house. It had simply been the first NW11 address on his list of five, and had been a stone's throw from the library. The property was a typical thirties semi and like most properties in the road, had been well maintained.

He took a deep drag on his cigarette and tapped it on the edge of the open window, causing the newly formed ash to scatter to the ground and disappear like virgin snow. It was 5.45 and there seemed to be a few more people passing the house - no doubt on their way home, he imagined, from work. A young lad in a suit and tie stopped just behind the car and fished a mobile from his trouser leg. Hasan watched him intently in his driver's mirror as the young man glued the phone to his ear and engaged in an animated conversation.

He was just about to switch on the radio when his newly stolen mobile began to vibrate on the dashboard.

'Hello.'

'Hasan. Where are you?'

It was Benazir. She was calling from a call box. She

never introduced herself on the phone. She didn't have to.

'I'm outside 43 Wyndham Gardens NW11.'

There was a pause. 'It's the wrong address, Hasan.'

'You sound confident… How do you know?'

'Qssim found an article online. Michael Hollinghurst is a survivor of the 7/7 attack. He lives in Hampstead Garden Suburb… You're in Golders Green. And get this: he's a wheelchair user.'

'Shit… No kidding… A *chair man*.'

'That's right. A *chair man*.'

Hasan laughed heartily and at the same time instinctively ran his hand inside his jacket and felt the cold metal of his *Glock 18* couched neatly in its holster. Then he felt inside his right jacket pocket for the silencer.

'That's the best news I've heard for a long while.'

'I thought that would cheer you up.'

'Certainly has sister. Wow… Mohammed was a pretty straightforward nut to crack, but this guy; he's a fucking sitting target.'

Hasan laughed again and Benazir hung up.

She never liked people laughing at their own jokes. But in Hasan's case, it was a small price to have to pay. *The Chair Man* may have been a neat moniker, but Benazir had the distinct feeling that they wouldn't be needing to use it for a great deal longer.

CHAPTER THIRTY-THREE

So this was Hampstead Garden Suburb. A little piece of idyllic country living in North West London straight out of the pages of *Homes & Gardens*. It was the kind of middle-class England that Hasan detested. You wouldn't find any mosques or halal butchers in this neck of the woods. But you'd find plenty of Christians and Jews - Israel lovers the lot of them.

The house was an attractive whitewashed semi-detached cottage, and like the rest in the road had steep gables and well-tended hedges. There were no signs of CCTV, which put him at ease, and it was eerily quiet. There were a couple of lights on inside, and a fairly new *Honda Civic* sat on the driveway in front of the garage, which was festooned with Wisteria.

Hasan calmly screwed the silencer to his trusty *Glock 18*. It was a thing of beauty. Chunky, solid and reliably efficient. It had already saved his life on more than one occasion.

The light was fading. Now was the time to act. He felt a cold sweat break out on the back of his neck as he opened the car door and stepped purposefully into the front garden. A security light automatically clicked on as he made his way to the front door. He stood there and waited for his hand to stop trembling, then he rang the doorbell and stepped back from the door. He could discern the sound of footsteps treading on a hard floor and eventually an internal porch door was unlocked.

A young man in a grey fleece opened the door. 'Hi there. Can I help you?'

'Oh. Hello. I'm sorry to trouble you. But can I ask you to fill this with water for my car? It's completely run dry.' He handed him a plastic bottle.

'Yeah. No problem. Just wait there. I'll be back.' The young man disappeared back into the house and soon returned with a full bottle. 'There you go.'

'Thanks a million.' Hasan took the bottle. 'Oh… don't suppose I could use your little boy's room while I'm at it, too… I'm dying for a pee.'

The young man hesitated for a moment and then found his voice. 'Yeah… The loo… That shouldn't be a problem. Do you want to see to your car first and I'll show you where our bathroom is.'

Hasan smiled, carried the bottle to the car, opened the bonnet, and then proceeded to pour the water into the already full water tank. This done, he closed the hood and made his way back to the house.

'Thanks a lot. I really appreciate this.'

'That's fine. If you'd like to follow me, I'll show you to our bathroom.'

He followed the young man through a terracotta tiled porch and across swathes of parquet flooring. There were several rooms off to both sides of the house, but irritatingly all the doors were closed. 'Here you go.' Hasan was led down a few steps to a mezzanine level. He opened the door and stepped into the cloakroom. He could sense that there were others in the house, but he couldn't fathom how many. The young man would have been in his late thirties, possibly even forty. He was too old to be Hollinghurst's son surely. Something just didn't feel right.

He could tell.

He flushed the loo and then turned to face the handbasin. And that's when his eyes fell on it. He froze. *Shit!* How could he have been so fucking stupid?

Lying on the windowsill and staring right back at him was a police warrant card wallet. It was open and revealed the young man to be police officer Raymond Maurice warrant number 2821A6. The place was probably crawling with the fuckers. There were no signs of wheelchairs or ramps. Michael Hollinghurst and his family had clearly been moved. So he was going to have to be calm and collected. He took a deep breath and then opened the door.

Maurice was waiting for him. 'Thanks very much for that.'

The young man nodded and showed Hasan to the front door. 'No problem. Have a safe journey.'

CHAPTER THIRTY-FOUR

This was as close as they were obviously going to get to their so-called *Chair Man*. Benazir had probably been right in thinking that Hollinghurst would have been moved to a special safe house. It was the only possible explanation for Hollinghurst's house being manned by pigs. Their only hope of making contact was going to be by conventional mail to his old address in the hope that it would eventually get forwarded to the safe house.

There was still a possibility though that they'd be able to call his bluff, make him feel insecure and vulnerable, and make out they could track him down, even though they had about as much chance of doing so as drilling for oil in Alaska. But none of that really mattered. Their biggest trump card was this: they knew the names of his kids, and thanks to social media they even knew what they looked like and where they worked. If they could get to him by threatening the lives of his kids, he might just want to talk. It was a big gamble. And it wasn't without risk. After all, if their *Chair Man* went to the police with the letter, the full force of British intelligence would be bearing down on them. And Benazir knew only too well what that would entail. It would mean that the very best forensic wireheads would be looking in minute detail at any internet, mobile and CCTV leads that had their fingerprints on them. She was confident though that they were pretty clean in this respect. None of them had used their mobiles to communicate with each other except for

Hasan who'd steal mobiles to receive occasional calls. Otherwise, emails would be sent and received from random libraries and internet cafes. And with the exception of Ibrahim who was now dead, and Qssim, none of them had criminal records. Qssim did worry her though. He was known to intelligence and may well have been monitored before he'd chucked the *MI5* operative off his balcony. But after Hamid Noorani's handwork, nobody was going to recognise the old Qssim.

As far as the letter was concerned, they were going to have to tread exceptionally carefully. Any letter would have to be written with surgical gloves to avoid leaving fingerprints or any trace of DNA. And they obviously couldn't send it directly. Instead, they'd have to use a mail forwarding service set up by a third party. And this, in turn, would have to be linked to a PO box in London set up by another associate who would collect and deliver the mail to a predetermined location.

It was ironic that in the age of technology and digital communication they now found themselves resorting to pen and paper. Paradoxical perhaps, but in a world where the stakes were high, they couldn't afford to take unnecessary risks.

CHAPTER THIRTY-FIVE

Ever since her husband Robin had died from Parkinson's disease, Nicola Walker had toyed with the idea of moving out of the family home in Oban on the west coast of Scotland and moving into a self-contained flat. She knew it would make sense, but she was simply too attached to this place. They'd brought up all three kids here, and they'd been blissfully happy for all those years. Then there was the garden that she and Robin had tended. She couldn't just let it go. There were too many wonderful memories ingrained in the fabric of the place. And in truth, she loved the house; always had done - even if it was now too large for a single person of her mature years. As long as she had the strength to get up those stairs, she was going to stay put.

The one and only plan she had set herself after Robin's death was to keep herself busy, and she'd stuck to that more rigidly than a limpet to a rock. She had set up her creative writing classes in the back room of The *Intrepid Smuggler* public house, which met every month; she had become an active member of the local choral society; and there was her small business, the confidential mail forwarding service. She had initially started this for a friend who had suffered domestic abuse and had fled the family home to get away from her violent and alcoholic husband. The friend had eventually been placed in a special hostel in Aberdeen, and had desperately wanted to write to her daughters without giving away her whereabouts to her estranged husband, so Nicola had offered to forward the letters by setting up a PO Box at her local post office in Oban - 180 miles from Aberdeen, and sending and receiving mail on her friend's behalf. The arrangement worked well, and it wasn't long before other women from the refuge came to Nicola for the same service. There was something about the handwritten letter that continued to have universal appeal. It was so much more personal and emotive than an email. And as a result, Nicola now had a growing list of customers, which besides occupying her time also brought in a small income to supplement her modest pension. She had even gone as far as placing classified ads in *The Lady* magazine to expand her customer base.

All her customers to date were women, and she blithely assumed that they had all suffered domestic abuse or violence of one kind or another. Some were open about it and others were not. And it was certainly none of her business to probe. So it had been something of a surprise to receive an account request that morning from a man. Stranger still were the very specific requests from this new customer to remove the letter from the envelope, and to destroy the envelope.

CHAPTER THIRTY-SIX

'I don't fucking believe it. You complete fucking scumbag. Look what you've gone and done to me!'

Mr Hamid Noorani wasn't used to this kind of foul-mouthed abuse from his patients. But this, of course, was no ordinary patient. He'd been introduced to him by Benazir who he had known through her charming husband, the eminent neurologist Mr Aalee Assad, as well as his associations with Islamic charities to whom he had made several large donations over the years.

Benazir had asked him for this favour. It was to be a discrete operation for twice the usual fee paid in cash in advance. In return, he had agreed not to ask any questions and keep all records of the clinical work strictly off the books. There had also been the strange request to turn off the CCTV system in the underground car-park on arrival for half an hour.

Qssim was looking at his bruised face in the mirror. There were dark purple patches around both eyes and his jawbone, and much of the remaining skin had a distinct yellow pallor. He looked like something out of a horror movie.

Mr Noorani smiled. 'Please don't be alarmed Mr El-Ghzzawy. The results of surgery always look far worse than they really are. And recovery will be a great deal swifter now that your skin is being exposed to the air.'

Qssim wasn't convinced. But there was little point shouting at this guy, even if he had been incompetent and done a lousy job.

'How long is it going to take for this mess to heal?'

'You should begin to look far more presentable in four to six weeks. But you have to understand Mr El-Ghzzawy that everyone is different, and some people heal faster than others. You may, God willing, be one of the fortunate ones.'

Qssim stared more intently at his reflection in the mirror and half-closed his eyes. He could see now that his face had an entirely different shape. His jawline wasn't as square; his nose was shorter, and his mouth looked different; fuller perhaps. Bruising aside, he didn't seem to be in as much pain as he had been before now.

'I could murder a cup of tea if there's one on offer.

Mr Noorani looked up from his mobile and smiled. It seemed to be an automatic response to everything, and it irritated Qssim no end.

'I will ask the nurse to arrange a pot of tea to be brought to your room... You are making good progress Mr El-Ghzzawy. You will excuse me now. I have other patients to see this morning. Good day.'

Three days before those bandages had been removed, Qssim had spoken to Benazir. She had seemed pretty pleased with the letter he had laboured over but had made a couple of small amendments here and there. 'Nothing major' apparently. And it had been sent via an associate to a mail forwarding service somewhere on the west coast of Scotland. She'd found it in a small classified ad in a publication called The Lady that Qssim had never heard of. 'All we have to do now is wait and hope,' she had said confidently. Her perfume had had a distinct whiff of musk about it. It was alluring, and for once he had felt suddenly drawn to her. He'd had sexual encounters with plenty of girls, but they'd all been the same: shallow, submissive, and easy lays. But Benazir was different. She was strong, smart and totally in control. He'd never encountered any other woman quite like her. She was one hell of a turn-on, and she knew it. He had approached her and taken in that intoxicating perfume, and she had fixed her gaze through those dark brown eyes on his finger as he gently ran it across her cheek. He had felt her warm breath on his lips as he slipped his hand like a conjurer under her blouse and felt the smooth warm contour of her right breast. And that's when she had kneed him hard in the testicles, and he had doubled up in pain and fallen to the floor. The pain in his face beneath those bandages had suddenly paled into insignificance.

CHAPTER THIRTY-SEVEN

The forwarded mail would appear as if by magic on the kitchen table every week or so, and usually first thing in the morning. Once Annie had got him dressed and completed his foot stretching exercises, she'd wheel him into the kitchen, put on the kettle and hand him the pile of mail that was irritatingly always out of his reach.

This morning, the pile of mail was smaller than usual. As Annie made tea, Michael went through the motions of opening the letters.

As she approached the table, he gave her a look she'd never seen before. He looked like a little boy who had got himself hopelessly lost, and didn't seem to be quite with it.

'Are you alright Mr Hollinghurst?'

He suddenly composed himself and brought himself back into the real world with a smile. 'I'm perfectly fine thank you Annie… In fact, I was just wondering... Do you think it would be more sensible to bring the standing frame in here? It would save you the hassle of pushing me back into the living room, and the light is so much better in here for reading the paper.'

She wasn't at all convinced that he was fine. And as he spoke, she couldn't help noticing that he had folded one of the letters and placed it in his pocket.

'Yes. We can do that Mr Hollinghurst. No problem. We have plenty of space in here. And you have a lovely view of the garden.'

'Indeed Annie… You and I are on the same

wavelength… Sometimes I think you can read my mind.'

They both laughed. But in truth, the last thing Annie could do right now was read his mind.

✦

That first letter hadn't really surprised him. He'd been half-expecting it. And he'd already decided how he'd respond in the event of receiving the news. But it was the second letter that took him completely by surprise. That was the last thing he was expecting. And Annie had picked up his sense of alarm.

He wheeled himself back into his room and closed the door. How had those bastards worked out his whereabouts? He removed the letter from his pocket and unfolded it. Then he reread it carefully.

> *So Mr Michael Hollinghurst,*
>
> *We finally caught up with you. You didn't think you'd be able to escape so easily, did you? Wheelchair users like you are very easy to track down Mr Hollinghurst. You must know that. In fact, your entire family has been very easy to track down. We know your son Ben is studying Mechanical Engineering at Durham and that your daughter is an environmental consultant here in London. So you see, there really is no escaping us Mr Hollinghurst.*
>
> *You must also understand that we are not very happy with you. Thanks to your deception, two of our brothers are now dead and buried. Such despicable action on your part can not go*

unpunished. But we really have no desire to do you and your family any physical harm. You have already suffered enough. Instead, we think it's right and proper that you should pay a considerable financial price, Mr Hollinghurst. In this case, £2 million in cash delivered in person by you. It is, we believe, a fair price. In return, we will not seek retribution. You see, Mr Hollinghurst, we are very fair people.

Should you fail to comply, however, or worse still, share the contents of this letter with the police, we will be unable to keep to our side of the bargain. This deal will be null and void - and you will, I am afraid, be placing you and your family in grave danger.

You have five days in which to respond to this letter. If you are agreeable to our terms, and I do hope you are, you will need to send the following message: 'The chair man plays ball' by first class mail to PO Box 3, St Andrews Lane, Oban Argyll PA33 4JK.

Further instructions will follow. But in the meantime, you will need to raise the £2 million, and seek a good friend who can help you travel undetected to the west coast of Scotland.

We look forward to hearing from you.

PS: If you do show this letter to the police, I assure you that you will be wasting your time. You will fail to find any traces of DNA other than those left on the envelope by Her Majesty's postal services.

There was no name or signature. And the envelope had his North West London address typed on a label. The postmark was Oban, Argyll.

Christ! There was no way he could get the police involved now. It was simply too risky. These bastards already knew too much. They knew where they had lived. They even knew the names of the kids and where they worked. All he had to do was put a foot wrong, and it would be curtains for all of them. As for the two million quid, it would have been difficult, but not impossible to raise. His pension and investments would raise most of it, and he'd be able to take out a loan for the rest. But it was ridiculous. The money was never going to guarantee anything. They were going to kill him whether he had the money or not. That was as plain as day.

There was only one way forward as far as he could see. He'd have to play them at their own game. But first of all, he'd have to talk to the only man in the world that could help him.

He wheeled himself to the desk and took out a pen and notepaper. Within minutes he was in full flow, and by the time he came up for air, he'd filled six sides of lined A4 paper with neat, tightly spaced handwriting. Fortunately, he had a good memory for addresses. It was odd because he could never remember birthdays.

He folded the letter and pushed it into one of the envelopes that had sat in a desk tray. Then in his neatest handwriting addressed it to: Mr Hugo Manningtree, Wisteria Lodge, Abbey Mill Way, St Albans AL1 5GN.

CHAPTER THIRTY-EIGHT

He may have been 15 years older than her, but she still found him incredibly attractive. It wasn't his looks, because he couldn't be described as handsome in the conventional sense. It was his whole presence; his manner; his demeanour; his physicality; his unbridled confidence; his joie de vivre; and his voice; that inimitable, deep, sonorous bloody voice that had all the traits of an upper class, privileged background; a background that would have been filled with nannies, polo and cucumber sandwiches. It was a life she had secretly pined for as a young girl, and now she had entered that world with a man she genuinely loved.

As far as he was concerned, he'd been a bloody lucky bugger. Rebecca or Becks as he liked to call her was a damn fine filly. Young, funny, warm-hearted and drop-dead gorgeous. Quite why she had fallen for him was a mystery to most people, including himself. It would, he'd offtime quip, remain one of life's great conundrums. At first, he thought it was his money she had fallen in love with, but over time he'd come to realise that she wasn't the least bit materialistic. Alright, she enjoyed the lifestyle they had both become accustomed to, but that wasn't the basis of her feelings for him, which he now knew were genuine and heartfelt, despite the fact that he was lousy in bed. She, on the other hand, had an insatiable appetite for sex.

It wasn't that he didn't enjoy the act; of course he did. But he just couldn't raise his game to match hers. And that was something that obviously troubled him, particularly when coupled with his infertility, which had denied them both of a child. For a prematurely born boy, infertility was very often par for the course. It was something Hugo had come to accept. And to her credit, Rebecca had never complained or shown the least bit remorse. It wasn't in her nature.

He traced the outline of her spine with his index finger and felt her soft breasts gently nestle in the hair on his chest, and they kissed. As his nostrils filled with her perfume and her golden locks tickled his face, his mobile sprang to life.

'Oh, hell's bells.'

She giggled and kissed his forehead. 'Can't we just ignore it?'

'We could, but I suppose it might just be important.'

He propped himself up on his pillow and Rebecca rolled off him.

He pulled himself off the bed and parked his bare buttocks on an antique Chippendale and scooped his *BlackBerry* from the mahogany dressing table.

'Hello. Hugo here. This had better be good.'

'Huge. It's Michael…'

CHAPTER THIRTY-NINE

Iqbal Masood was 14-years-old and had a sweet cherubic face that wouldn't have looked out of place in a large composition by Rubens. He also had mild learning difficulties. He stood in line at the post office clasping the card that his father had given him and waited patiently.

Eventually, he was standing before the officious middle-aged woman behind the counter who had served in this post office for more years than she would happily own up to.

'Can I help you sunshine?'

He placed the card through the glass window and the woman's eyes, magnified by the angle of her bifocals, focussed on the number.

'Cat got your tongue, has it?'

Iqbal didn't like her. She didn't look friendly and she certainly didn't sound it. He just stood there and looked at his shoes while she disappeared round the back.

This wasn't the first time his dad had asked him to pick up letters from the post office. He enjoyed running these errands. They made him feel important. And his dad had implied as much when he said that these trips to the post office were more than just simple errands. The letters he had to retrieve carried very important information. And it was 'imperative' (that was the word his dad had used) that he kept the letter safe in his inside pocket with the zip done up. And if anyone asked him questions, he was to say nothing.

The woman reappeared at the window with her bifocals balanced on top of her lined forehead. In her hand was the usual manilla envelope. She slid it under the glass window along with the box number card. 'There you go sunshine. Just the one item. Anything else I can do for you?'

Iqbal shook his head and took the letter and stuffed it into his pocket. Then he looked at her and forced a smile. 'Thank you miss.' Now he had to walk to his aunt's house and she would take him to school. This was the usual procedure when he picked up a letter from the post office. He would never go home, and he would keep the letter safe in his pocket for the entire day.

Once he was back in the street and on his way, Iqbal could relax. Nobody had asked him anything difficult other than that unintelligible question about cat's and tongues, which may just as well have been in a foreign language. Everything was alright. Everything had gone to plan - apart from the fact that he was feeling distinctly uncomfortable down below. He'd wet himself.

CHAPTER FORTY

Nestling amid the classy coffee bars and bookstores on London's frenetic Piccadilly, St James's Church was a beacon of tranquillity. It had occupied this spot since 1684 and owed its existence to Henry Jermyn, 1st Earl of St Albans who had commissioned the great architect Christopher Wren to construct a parish church on the site. It was in many ways the perfect place for lunchtime concerts. It was also the perfect place in which Hasan could discreetly receive communications.

As was usually the case, there were only a handful of grey-haired people sitting in the oak pews waiting for the musicians to appear. Hasan placed himself in the middle aisle seven rows from the front.

Directly in front of him, an old boy was rummaging around in his knapsack and eventually produced a sandwich, which reeked of mackerel. A few rows in front and to his right sat a large woman knitting something in red.

'Good afternoon ladies and gentlemen, and thank you for gracing us with your presence this afternoon.' The vicar was an affable man of the cloth, and most probably two decades younger than most of the assembled audience. 'As regulars to this church's lunchtime recitals will know, we at St James's are passionately committed to playing our part in helping homeless youngsters who for no fault of their own now find themselves living on the streets of this fine city. So to assist us in raising funds, we have placed small envelopes on each of the pews, and I would urge you after the recital to make a contribution, no matter how small, for which I would like to thank you in advance. Thank you very much... And now, we are very fortunate today to have two very talented musicians who have only just graduated from the Royal College of Music. So without further ado, please give a big welcome to Dmitri Barzinsky on violin and Isobel Perry on piano.'

As the small audience broke into an applause of sorts, the two musicians resplendent in black evening gown and tails appeared from the wings.

The young man with the violin stepped forward. 'Good afternoon. Today we'd like to play two very romantic pieces. The first by Beethoven is his sonata for violin and piano number 5 in F major Opus 24 - often known as the *Spring* sonata, which Beethoven wrote in 1801 when he was 31. And the second piece by César Franck was written in 1886 when the composer was 63 and was a wedding present for the 31-year-old violinist Eugène Ysaye.'

The young man stepped back to his music stand and glanced at his accompanist at the *Steinway*.

There was a pause as a figure shuffled his way down the centre aisle and parked himself next to Hasan. He handed Hasan a folded programme.

'Ah, thank you my friend. How thoughtful. I thought you'd never come.'

'And miss Beethoven? It's a wonderful piece you know.'

Hasan smiled in incredulity and opened the programme as the pianist began to play the opening bars to the first movement of the Franck sonata. Inside was a manilla envelope secured with a piece of sellotape.

CHAPTER FORTY-ONE

Qssim couldn't believe that he was now travelling in the back seat of the car, rather than that damn boot.

Mr Noorani hadn't been quite as incompetent as he had feared. His scars and bruising had virtually disappeared, and he now looked like a complete stranger. It was remarkable. He couldn't quite believe that the person staring back at him in the mirror was actually him. First, he had changed his name; now he had changed his physical identity. He was a fucking human chameleon. Admittedly, his mouth and jaw still felt a bit strange, but that wasn't surprising considering the amount of surgery he'd undergone.

Hasan turned off the main road and they were now traversing open countryside; a patchwork of fields; the occasional pub; strange-looking oast houses. It was the first time he'd seen where they were taking him. But now things were different. They seemed to trust him.

The car swung off the road and across a sea of gravel. He knew from the sound alone that they had arrived.

◆

The curtains were drawn, barring what little light there was outside the room's interior.

Benazir sat centre stage smoking pensively. There were some new faces here unless they'd all had plastic surgery, too. Qssim chuckled to himself at the thought, and Benazir gave him a look of disdain. She clearly hadn't forgiven him for his clumsy advances.

She stubbed out her cigarette and motioned for the door to be closed.

'OK... Thank you everyone for arriving here on time. I'll make this meeting as swift as I can. We have succeeded in making contact with our *Chair Man*, and he has agreed in writing to our initial plan. Better still, he says that he can rely on a friend to fly him by microlight to a rendezvous point of our choosing. This is the best news we could have hoped for because it means that he has a very good chance of giving the police and intelligence services the slip. It also means that we can arrange a pick-up point that is off the mainland, very remote and out of the range of prying eyes.

We don't know his current location. The letter we received from him carried a St Albans postmark, but it's highly unlikely that this is his location. We do know, though. where his son and wife are located. And he knows that we know. So if he were to make one false move and go to the police, he knows also that he can kiss goodbye to at least half his family. Unfortunately, we don't yet know where the daughter is but suspect that she's holed up with him in a safe house. He has agreed to hand over £2 million in cash in return for which we have offered him and his family freedom from retribution. He's no fool though. He probably doesn't believe that we'll spare him, but he does probably reckon we'll leave his kids alone if he hands over the cash. It's the only shot he has at safeguarding his loved ones. So this is in all probability the most likely scenario.' She paused and took a long drag on her cigarette. 'There is, of course, the possibility that he'll involve the police and special forces. So we're going to arrange a very remote pickup point off the west coast of Scotland. Anything suspicious within a five-mile radius will be picked up by our monitoring team on the ground. So we'll be in a good position to abort the operation...

'But have no illusions. This is an operation that comes with its fair share of risks. Though the biggest is, I believe, the risk of letting our *Chair Man* act with impunity. To do so would be to risk everything this cell and our brothers across the globe stand for. It would risk the future cause of jihad. We cannot let one pathetic cripple undermine the word of Allah and our Brotherhood. We can't allow his actions to encourage other infidels to follow in his filthy footsteps.'

'Footsteps? Don't you mean wheel tracks?' There was nervous laughter at Hasan's attempt at a joke. Benazir chose to ignore it and waited patiently for the silence to resume.

'Failure to act now would be a gross sign of weakness and would send out the wrong message.'

All the men in the room listened intently to her every word. The mood had become sombre once more.

'However, if our *Chair Man* does go to the police, we won't necessarily have to abort the operation and flee with our tails between our legs. We will actually be well equipped to deliver a decisive blow... And the reason I say this is because I now have some good news... The consignment of weapons we were promised six months ago, has finally got through.'

There was an almost palpable sense of relief as she uttered these words.

'So given the choice, who would rather stand and fight than flee? Can I ask for a show of hands please?'

Without exception, all the men in the room, all ten of

them, raised their right arm without any hesitation.

'Good. I thought as much... It is, as I say, an unlikely scenario, but one we must prepare for. And for this reason, I'm going to require all ten of you to take part in this operation. We will charter two light-weight aircraft from two separate airfields. Needless to say, you will all need to carry your own personal firearms. The heavy-duty stuff will be stashed in sealed travel cases split between the parties. The pick-up time and location will be finalised nearer the time. On the day of the pick-up, the money will be handed over and examined by Iqbal, our counterfeit specialist.' Iqbal a diminutive balding figure stood cross-armed at the back of the room and smiled as Benazir acknowledged him. 'Following the successful exchange of the money, Hasan will accompany *the Chair Man* back to his aircraft where he will dispatch him and his pilot with two single shots to the head. The aircraft will be torched and the remnants dumped into the sea. The bodies will enjoy the same fate. We will clean up thoroughly in the usual fashion, so there will be no traces of DNA... Any questions?'

A tall man standing next to Iqbal at the back of the room put his hand up.

'Yes, Aamir.'

'What makes you so confident that he won't go to the police? And how is he going to raise £2 million?'

Benazir nodded while stubbing out her cigarette. 'Very reasonable questions... In answer to the first one, I'd say it was my gut feeling that he will probably cooperate. But I can't be 100% certain. If he doesn't play ball, he has a lot to lose. My guess is that he'll do everything to save his family.' She paused. 'Even if he were to succeed in getting us all put away, he'd know that others within our network will seek retribution… You wouldn't wish that on your worst enemy, would you?' Nobody answered. The room remained silent. The only discernible sounds came from a couple of distant crows arguing loudly over territory. 'As for your second question, the answer is a simple one… We know that his house is worth around £3 million and that there appears to be no mortgage on the property. He will undoubtedly have a pension fund and investments. I wouldn't have thought two million quid would be too difficult for him to raise one way or another… Any other questions?' You could have heard the proverbial pin drop.. 'Good. In that case, be prepared for our little excursion sometime next month. I'll keep you posted. This meeting is now closed.' She gestured to Hasan and the two left the room deep in conversation.

CHAPTER FORTY-TWO

This was the first time Qssim had ventured out on his own since the operation. Besides looking like a complete stranger, he also possessed a new name: Bernard Underwood. Thanks to Benazir, he had a driving licence, passport and bank account in his new name, as well as an address somewhere in East London. Christ knows how she had secured the documents. They certainly looked authentic. He wasn't going to ask too many questions - particularly after the incident that ended with her kneeing him so unceremoniously in the groin.

Irritatingly, the money machine on the street wasn't working, so he ventured inside the bank and took his place in the short queue.

He'd only been standing there for a couple of minutes when a couple of hard nuts in black balaclavas closed the door and another head case brandishing a sawn-off shotgun screamed at everyone to get on the floor. And then for some crazy reason, this nutter decided to pick on him.

He felt his collar being tugged from behind. 'Come on. Get your fucking arse off the floor!' Qssim did what he was being told only to have the gun rammed hard into the side of his head and his right arm twisted behind his back. He was manhandled to the glass partition behind which sat a terrified young cashier. 'Ok, darling. You're going to listen carefully, and do exactly what I tell you, otherwise this nice gentleman's brains will be all over your lovely counter. Do you understand?'

The girl froze as if she was a hare caught in headlights. 'I said do you fucking understand?' She nodded. 'Good... Well, you're going to hand me 50K pronto without playing any stupid tricks.'

Before she had a chance to act, someone in a green hoodie leapt from the floor and delivered a ferocious karate chop to the side of the gunman's neck. It all seemed to happen so incredibly quickly. The gun fell to the marble floor with a loud clatter, but before its owner followed suit, the man in the green hoodie who was no youngster and not especially large, yanked the gunman's right forearm forward and in a flurry of quick successive moves forced the arm back against the elbow joint until it cracked. Then he retrieved the gun and waved it at the two other thugs in balaclavas.

'Ok... Now you two are going to remove your masks and smile nicely for ze cameras, you understand? One false move and those kneecaps of yours aren't going to look too good, believe me. I have to tell you I am very good with one of these things.'

The men obeyed their orders. One was an old boy with grey hair. The other one could have been his son. 'Good. Now place both hands on ze head togezer and sit on ze floor wiz your legs crossed... And while they are doing zat, can one of ze nice cashiers please raise ze alarm?'

Within seconds the piercing sound of the bank's alarm was ringing in everyone's ears.

'I think everyone should just stay sitting on ze floor until ze police arrive.' He patted Qssim on the arm while training the gun on the two thugs. 'How are you doing my friend?' Qssim smiled.

'I'm ok thanks. That was a pretty impressive performance.'

'Well, it's not something I make a habit of, thank God.'

To Qssim's ears, the accent was distinctly Middle Eastern. And then it caught his eye. On the guy's green hoodie was a familiar-looking enamelled badge with a green, black, red and white design. It was the Palestinian flag.

'You are Palestinian then?'

'You are very observant, my friend… But no I am not Palestinian… I'm an Israeli.'

What the hell was an Israeli doing wearing a Palestinian flag? Qssim was confused.

'It's ok. I know what you're thinking… but look, you people have to understand zat we Jews… we don't all hate Palestinians. Many of us - thousands of us, in fact - actually like those guys. One of my best friends is a Palestinian ok. And thousands and thousands of us Israelis hate how our government is behaving right now. You understand what I'm saying?'

Qssim hadn't ever thought that such a thing was even possible. Before he had a chance to think any more of it, a whole army of armed police spilled into the bank and placed handcuffs on the three would-be bank-robbers including the gunman who was now crying in agony, his right arm a redundant, lifeless appendage.

'Here my friend, take thees.' The Israeli handed Qssim a clean white handkerchief. 'For the head. You have a nasty gash there.' Qssim took the handkerchief and the Israeli picked himself up from the floor and dusted himself off.

A police officer stepped forward. 'Ah, sir, I understand you are the gentleman that managed to take control of the situation… Would you mind making a statement?'

The two wandered off to a quiet corner while Qssim dabbed at his head with the handkerchief. That bastard in the balaclava had actually made him bleed. The pristine white handkerchief now displayed an abstract pattern in dark red. In the corner, two embroidered characters stood out in dark blue. Qssim couldn't make them out. One looked vaguely like a back-to-front c. And then it dawned on him. They must have been Hebrew characters - initials for the Israeli's name.

CHAPTER FORTY-THREE

He hadn't been himself since that bloody phone call had interrupted their intimacy only days before. She knew it had been serious as he'd taken the phone into the bathroom and had been gone for ages.

He'd said it was nothing to worry about; some minor business problem that needn't concern her. But she knew otherwise. He wasn't a good liar. They had argued, and she had cried. And then they had had sex. Afterwards, he had held her and told her that she had been far too smart to outfox and that he had lied to her for good reason. She'd been right - it had nothing to do with the business. But he simply couldn't tell her too much for her own safety. That was the last thing she wanted to hear. It sounded like he was being blackmailed. But he reassured her that it was nothing like that. And it was only through her sheer persistence that he finally relented and reluctantly admitted that the whole thing revolved around his old friend Michael. The same Michael who had been a victim of the terrorist bombing in London and who was now under police protection having posed online as an Islamic fundamentalist. But try as she might, she couldn't get the whole story out of him. All he would tell her was that Michael was in trouble and he had to help him out by flying him to Scotland with a lightweight collapsible wheelchair.

Now she was sulking. She hated it when he wouldn't come clean and tell her everything he knew. It had been the same when he'd sold one of the restaurants last year.

The one in St John's Wood that she and the architects had worked tirelessly on over the interior design. He hadn't consulted her over it until it was a done deal.

But this was different. This thing sounded shady and potentially dangerous. Who the hell was Michael meeting in Scotland and why couldn't Hugo tell her? Were they the terrorists that Michael was in hiding from? He'd been evasive and said he didn't know. And that's when it started.

The palpitations were always a dead giveaway followed by dizziness and breathing difficulties. Hugo had only witnessed her panic attacks once before. But thanks to his quick-wittedness, he'd managed to calm her down. He cradled her in his arms and told her that he'd have his mobile on for the entire journey. That he'd call her every hour, and that if she didn't hear from him on the hour, to call the police immediately and tell them everything she knew. They'd know his location from the tracking device he'd fitted to the plane, as well as the GPS on his mobile.

Everything was going to be fine. He wouldn't be making the trip for some weeks anyway. And he'd only be gone for half a day. He'd be back before she knew it.

CHAPTER FORTY-FOUR

Lelah sat at her new desk gazing at the small family portrait that sat next to her computer. She had been no more than 12-years-old in that picture, and her parents looked so young and happy. They'd have been so proud of her now. But sadly, it wasn't to be. Her father had passed away a week before she'd learnt of her promotion, and her mother's dementia had now progressed to the stage that she could hardly remember her daughter's name.

Her promotion at *GCHQ* had come as a surprise. She had barely been in the job for a year, and now she already had a small team of young dedicated data encryption analysts to oversee.

She was obviously happy with the way her career was shaping up. Uncovering that short trail of emails that had resulted in the deaths of two terrorists had clearly played a part. But in truth, that whole episode had only been satisfying up to a point. The fact of the matter was that any further leads had simply dried up completely, which as far as she was concerned was a real bummer. After all, she'd had it on good authority that such golden nuggets would in usual circumstances, reveal many invaluable threads, and result in countless surveillance operations and even arrests. But in this instance, the entire chain of command had clearly gone underground, and as a result, the files had been removed from her desk and transferred to other sections of the intelligence community - most probably *MI5*.

To all intents and purposes, she'd been taken off this investigation. She now had other fish to fry. It was fair enough; and had no bearing on her abilities, but a little bit of her couldn't help feeling a touch miffed; pissed off even.

CHAPTER FORTY-FIVE

Michael couldn't sleep. And it had nothing to do with the discomfort in his legs. Since speaking to Hugo from The Angel Hotel's landline and then writing that long verbose letter to him giving his friend very specific instructions, his mind had been in overdrive.

He thought about telling Tash, but had then berated himself for even entertaining the idea. Of course, he couldn't tell her. She'd try and dissuade him, and failing that would almost certainly go to the police. Besides, it wasn't fair to involve her. He hated the idea of keeping his kids out of the picture, but he had little choice in the matter if he was going to succeed with his plan.

Hugo was a brick. He knew he would be. He had listened and taken everything he'd said on board. He didn't like Michael's plan. Of course, he didn't. Nobody in their right mind would like it. But it was, he had reluctantly admitted, probably Michael's only way of dealing with the mess he'd got himself into.

He had told Hugo that the pick-up point was going to be somewhere off the west coast of Scotland. He didn't yet know the precise location, or indeed the day and time of the rendezvous. This was to be finalised in the coming weeks. He would know only by receiving a curt note in the post via what seemed to be a convoluted string of third parties and post office box numbers. This bunch clearly didn't trust digital technology.

Hugo had agreed to sort out the money and more

importantly, to adapt a lightweight wheelchair that would meet all Michael's specific requirements. It would take him a little while to make the necessary adjustments but it wasn't going to be 'beyond the wit of man.' As for the mode of transport, well that was easy. Hugo had a bloody fleet to choose from, hadn't he? For this trip, he'd said that his *Evektor SportStar* would be ideal. It was a small two-seater, single prop, fixed-wing aircraft, classed as a microlight because its aluminium hulk was so incredibly lightweight. Nevertheless, it was a remarkably stable and reliable flyer. More importantly, it had an impressive range of 1300 kilometres, around 800 miles - easily enough to fly to the Hebrides and back on a single tank. And it was robust and happy enough to land in rough terrain if need be.

Then there was the question of whether they should carry a gun in the cabin. Hugo had a shotgun somewhere in his attic that his father had given him years ago, and Michael had urged him to bring it just in case. He certainly didn't want to carry one himself, but it was just an insurance policy for Hugo.

Finally but significantly, there was the problem of physically getting Michael into and out of the plane. Normally Hugo would employ a hoist for his wheelchair-bound flying students, but if he were to employ that, Michael was going to have to reach him in St Albans, since that piece of kit was far too heavy and cumbersome to fit in the hold. This said, getting to St Albans in a wheelchair undetected was clearly not going to happen. Any attempt to board a train would obviously end up with him being picked up by the police at St Albans station. Hugo was going to have to pick him up at night from a nearby field, and he was going to have to manhandle his friend into and out of the cockpit. It was going to be bloody challenging, but it was their only realistic option. Michael wasn't the largest of people but he still weighed at least nine stone.

Hugo had a lot to think about. His priority though had to be adapting a lightweight wheelchair to Michael's very specific requirements. It wasn't a job he was going to relish, but it was certainly something he was more than capable of turning his very able hands to. The money could wait.

CHAPTER FORTY-SIX

The Isle of Iona lies in the Inner Hebrides on the west coast of Scotland. This rocky hinterland with its 300-year-old abbey occupies a site that is one of the world's oldest Christian religious centres in Western Europe. Saint Columba had originally visited these shores in 560 AD and established a monastery here that would become one of the most influential centres for the spread of Christianity across Scotland.

The island's religious history was of little interest to Benazir. What interested her was the island's topography and its remoteness. Situated one mile from its far larger sister, the Isle of Mull, Iona wasn't easy to reach. In fact, vehicles weren't officially allowed on its hallowed ground. And it was pretty tiny - just one mile wide and four miles long with a population that barely got into three figures. The place was certainly remote, yet offered just about enough reasonably flat areas of grassland on which to illegally land a helicopter or small aeroplane. It was the ideal location for the pick-up and would be easy for a small look-out team to monitor for unwelcome convoys by air or sea.

◆

Michael was growing to like this place. Not just the cottage, but the slow pace of life and the air. It may have sounded like a terrible cliché, but the air really was better here than it was back in North London. That aside, it clearly wasn't to Natasha's liking. In truth, he was concerned for her wellbeing. She'd become noticeably moody and less chatty.

It was hardly surprising having been deprived of interaction with others her own age. But at least she was safe. He only wished he could say the same for Ben. Part of him just wanted to go straight to the police; reveal the entire contents of that filthy letter to Inspector Alexander, and get his son here with them where he'd be out of harm's way. Ben was everything to him. He loved his son more than anything in the world. But he simply couldn't come clean with the police. If he did, he'd be jeopardising the entire plan, and his kids would almost certainly end up spending the rest of their days in fear of their lives, constantly looking over their shoulders. And even if he were to contact Ben directly and persuaded him to leave university (which he wouldn't in a million years), there'd be the risk that his son would be followed here. And that would put all their lives at risk in one fell swoop. It was no good. He only had one feasible option: to hold his nerve and play those bastards at their own game.

He sliced the top off his boiled egg, causing the yellow yolk to dribble down the sides of the shell in rivulets, and as he dunked a toasted soldier into its glutenous core, the tall figure of Sergeant Alexander Bolzwinick appeared from the hallway.

'Good morning Michael... I'm afraid I shall be leaving you next week.' He parked himself on a chair and helped himself to a biscuit from a jar on the table. 'I've been selected to bolster security at the Palace of Westminster... I only have a couple of years to see out before I retire, so it'll be a nice way to end my career - not that I'd mind spending it here, of course. I'll miss this place; not to mention our little chats.'

Michael smiled. 'That is a shame. We'll miss you, too.'

'By the way, there were a few letters forwarded to you

that I left on the table in the hall. I'll fetch them for you if you like.'

'Thanks.'

Alexander rose from the table and returned with a small pile of mail, which he placed next to a jar of marmalade. On the top of the pile sat a manila envelope with a familiar-looking label. Michael froze and could sense his heart racing. He closed his eyes and took a deep breath.

'You ok there?'

Michael opened his eyes and forced a smile. 'Yeah. Just a bout of indigestion… It will pass.'

'Oh, I suffer with the same thing. Age-related I'm afraid. Peppermint tea… that's what you need. Works a treat for me.'

'Thanks. I'll get Tash to get some in.'

✦

Back in his bedroom, Michael closed the door and nervously peeled open the manila envelope. He could feel his shirt sticking to the cold sweat that had broken out on his back.

The letter was incredibly curt:

Proposed pick-up point: Isle of Iona. 56.33°N
6.42°W just north of the abbey
Landing strip will be marked with two rows of lights
Date: 2nd October
Time: 02.30 precisely
No-one to travel with you other than the pilot
The money to be arranged in £10,000 wads

CHAPTER FORTY-SEVEN

Hasan pulled into the forecourt next to a row of black *BMW*s. His partner was the quietly spoken and well built Gamal. Both men had been instructed to come unarmed. When dealing with the Russians you generally followed instructions to the letter. The last thing you could afford to do was piss them off.

Gamal pressed the intercom, which eventually came to life.

'Vwot is your name and who hev you come to see?'

'It's Gamal and Hasan. We have come to see Vladimir.'

'And vwot is de nature of your business plis?'

'We've come to collect the consignment of drill bits.'

There was an electronic buzzing sound and the door unbolted with a fairly chunky clunk from the other side. It opened onto a brightly lit corridor with white painted breezeblock walls and industrial rubber flooring. At the far end was another door and another intercom.

Again Gamal pressed the button and again the speaker sprang to life with the same voice.

'And now may I hev your order number?'

Gamal had written it on his wrist. He pulled up his shirt cuff. ' 1... 7... 5... 6... 5.... 2... K... B... S.'

The intercom went dead and the door eventually clicked open.

They were greeted by two burly bodyguards in black suits, and were led into a small bare side room where they were asked to face the wall, spread their legs and place both their hands on the wall while they were searched for concealed weapons. All they were carrying was the money split between them in two envelopes.

This indignity completed, the two men were frogmarched out of the room and along another corridor that led to a fire exit. One of the bodyguards led the way while the second followed at the rear. The fire escape door opened onto a steel platform from which a spiral steel staircase ran up the side of the exterior brickwork. The bodyguard leading the way pointed to the staircase. 'You follow me now. You understand?' Gamal and Hasan nodded, and Hasan who had a mild fear of heights avoided looking down through the see-through metal gridwork of the steel steps.

The staircase took them in concentric circles up to the very top of the building, and through another fire exit and into a lobby with a couple of leather sofas. One of the guards gesticulated towards the sofas. 'Plis…' Both men sank into the soft leather while the same guard punched numbers into his mobile and held it to his ear.

'Dey hev arrived… Yes… of course… Vwery vwell.' He slipped the mobile back into his breast pocket. 'Vladimir apologises for ze vwaiting. He comes soon.'

The two sat in silence while the figures in black suits left the room. Hasan reckoned that they were probably standing guard outside.

The room was pretty bare apart from a set of bookshelves that was stacked with old volumes that looked like a job-lot from the local charity shop and a solitary clock that had stopped at half-past nine and was hanging ludicrously high on the wall. The industrial black rubber flooring seemed to follow them everywhere they went; as did the brilliant white paintwork.

Hasan's mind turned to the plan of action and for the

first time since the meeting, he wondered how the fuck a wheelchair user was going to get himself into and out of an aircraft. Would there be some special piece of kit that would winch him in and out, or was his pilot some giant muscle man who'd be able to simply carry him? It wasn't his problem, but the question nevertheless was one that intrigued him, and it was surprising that no-one had thought of raising it at the meeting. Before he could give it any further thought, he became aware of a distinct rumbling sound as the entire bookcase started to slide magically into the wall, forming a doorway through which a diminutive though stocky man with thickset features and horn-rimmed glasses, appeared. It was laughably corny; sliding bookcases were straight out of James Bond for fuck's sake. Was this guy for real?

'Gentlemen. Gentlemen. Vwelcome. Step into my office plis.'

This, presumably, was Vladimir.

Hasan and Gamal rose from the sofa and followed their host into a large room that was completely out of keeping with the rest of the building. Gone were the whitewashed breezeblock walls, and in their place was rich mahogany panelling from floor to ceiling. Similarly, the industrial rubber had been replaced with a herringbone parquet floor and large Turkish rug. The furniture and lighting all looked like antiques, as did the sizeable oil paintings that hung from the walls in elaborate gilt frames that boasted their own delicate lights that arched gracefully above each subject.

'Gentlemen, plis be seated.' Vladimir gestured towards a chaise longue and seated himself behind a large desk. As he did so, two more men in black suits entered the room and sat silently at the back of the room, and the rumbling noise started up once more as the wall housing the bookcase on the other side slid closed. There was no other way out of the room.

Vladimir lit a cigar and offered his guests one. They politely declined the offer and Vladimir chuckled. 'Of course... Forgeeve me I vwas forgetteeng... So you have come about de consignment of drill bits... Dis is a vwery special consignment you understand. You must send my epologies to Benazir for de delay.' He took a long puff on his cigar and then looked Hasan squarely in the eye. 'You hev de payment?' Hasan nodded and pulled the envelope from his breast pocket, and Gamal did likewise. Vladimir clicked his fingers. 'Andrei, plis!' Andrei was the taller of the two men in black suits and had distinctive blonde hair. He stepped forward and extended his upturned palm to the two seated guests who handed him the two bulky packages. It was clearly the usual procedure as Andrei emptied the wads onto the desk and then fitted an eyepiece into his right eye and carefully inspected the money. This took several minutes and was conducted in complete silence. Once the inspection had finished Andrei counted out the money note by note while Vladimir smirked and enjoyed his cigar.

Eventually, Andrei's inspection was completed and he placed the eyepiece on the desk and looked at his boss.

'Is good.'

Vladimir smiled broadly and flicked a large piece of ash into a silver ashtray. 'Excellent... And now my friends, Andrei vill show you down to the warehouse... It vwas good to do business...'

The concealed door slid open once more and Andrei led the two visitors back into the world of industrial rubber flooring.

◆

The place was a rabbit warren of vast proportions.

The cavernous lift carried them at a snail's pace down to the bowels of the complex where several forklift trucks were trundling back and forth with wooden palettes laden with containers of varying size. Andrei led them down aisle after aisle of steel shelving units - a veritable cityscape of storage space that quite literally towered over them.

He finally stopped at an aisle that was labelled V22, and here he whistled loudly. Within seconds a forklift truck appeared and Andrei pointed to one of the shelves high up in the steel tower. 'Shelf 9 plis.'

The driver positioned the vehicle carefully in line with the shelves and then operated the hydraulic fork to rise and rise. The shelf must have been at least 30 feet above their heads, but the truck-driver had little trouble in sliding the crate off its housings and bringing it smoothly down to ground level.

The driver handed Andrei a crowbar, and he proceeded to prise open the wooden crate. Inside all one could see was straw, until, of course, Andrei began to rummage around inside, at which point he pulled out the first item and handed it nonchalantly to Hasan who had dreamt about holding one of these things. It felt solid and substantial. It was the first time he'd got to hold one and it felt good. It felt so bloody empowering. He just couldn't take his eyes off it.

Andrei smiled. 'Beautiful huh?'

Hasan nodded. It was a genuine *Vityaz - SN* 9x19 mm standard-issue Russian military submachine gun. Of course it was fucking beautiful.

CHAPTER FORTY-EIGHT

Benazir wouldn't normally have entertained the idea of going with, and her husband certainly wouldn't have approved, but something instinctively told her that she needed to be there. Besides, she didn't entirely trust Qssim; and it wasn't just over his clumsy sexual advances. There was something else about his general attitude that hadn't felt quite right of late. She didn't know what it was exactly, but she just felt that he wasn't as engaged and committed as he had been. And part of her - admittedly a very small part - wondered if he was, in fact, the real deal.

◆

Qssim pulled the bloodstained handkerchief from his pocket. It had been sitting in his trousers for days and he had completely forgotten about it. He hadn't forgotten about the Israeli though. That crazy Israeli who liked Palestinians and hated his government. It troubled him for the simple reason that it didn't fit in with his world view. In fact, it ran in the face of everything he'd been told about filthy Jews and the apartheid state called Israel. Not to mention the Jewish conspiracy to take over the world's media and banking institutions. So this guy had to be some kind of madman, right? He must have been an insane loony tune or something. But then, how on earth could a madman foil a gang of bank-robbers like he did? And if he wasn't insane, what could Qssim make of all that stuff he said about thousands of Israelis hating the way the Israeli government behaved? Could any of that have been true?

The whole episode was doing his head in, and it was making him question everything he'd believed in. Everything he stood for. Everything he thought was rotten to the core in this whole fucking world.

He dropped the handkerchief in the bin. But it was no good. The idea of Israelis speaking up for Palestinians; wearing the Palestinian flag on their lapels, and outwardly criticising their own government, just wouldn't go away.

✦

They had agreed on a possible pick-up point. He'd found it by chance when walking Ziggy the previous week. It was a small reasonably flat playing field that catered for football and cricket during their respective seasons.

Hugo had checked it out on an Ordnance Survey map and could see that a south-eastern approach would give him the best access, avoiding tall trees and telegraph wires. There was a small housing estate on the perimeter, but the houses were far enough away to give him comfortable clearance of at least 50 feet, if not more. He'd said as much when Michael had called him for the second time from The Angel Hotel. And that's when Michael had given him the final date, time and rendezvous on Iona.

Michael had read the exact wording of the letter over the phone, and Hugo had been relieved to hear that there were going to be lights illuminating the landing strip on the island. He possessed night vision goggles but had never tried landing in pitch black with them, and wouldn't want to do so out of choice. Flying a *microlight at night was actually in contravention of the British Microlight Aircraft Association*'s rules. But Hugo was always breaking them; most daringly when he'd flown under five London bridges for a charity stunt that later got him into the *Guinness Book of Records*. He'd flown several times at night and found that his eyes acclimatised to the low light conditions reasonably well. Landing, however, wasn't something he'd ever done without the assistance of some kind of lighting. No matter how well your eyes adjusted, low light conditions certainly affected your spacial awareness and would make an attempted landing in the dark exceptionally tricky and downright dangerous.

Hugo had then figured out that Iona was one of those tiny islands that didn't allow planes or indeed any forms of transport on its shores. So it would be prudent to approach the island from the West to avoid flying directly over its tiny residential areas. Bearing this in mind, his *Tomark Viper SD4* was going to be their best option simply because it had the quietest engine.

As for the question over a wheelchair, he had a couple of weeks to sort out a lightweight portable chair that would answer all Michael's needs, so he was going to have to put everything on hold and retreat to his workshop. He'd reassured Michael several times that he'd have it sorted in time. He'd built bloody aircraft in that damn workshop of his, so a wheelchair wasn't going to fox him one bit. Michael had laughed, but Hugo could tell that his friend knew that his request wasn't quite so simple. But he also knew that his friend trusted him wholeheartedly. Michael thought he was a bloody genius and had said as much. According to Michael, his 'extraordinary technical abilities knew no bounds.'

Then, of course, there was the case of money. Hugo was taking care of that at the same time. Everything was going to plan. Michael didn't have to worry about anything. He'd be there for him. He'd get him to those bastards if it was the last thing he did.

CHAPTER FORTY-NINE

Rebecca had seen him in this animated state before now. It was always the same. He'd get out of bed at some unearthly hour to fly and then lock himself away in his warehouse for hours on end; very occasionally coming out for a beer or a sandwich.

He'd started building his very first microlight two weeks after their honeymoon in Florence for crying out loud, and she had never really forgiven him for devoting so much of his time during that period of their lives to what she had called his 'stupid projects.' But then when he had finally opened those enormous double doors to his workshop and wheeled out the product of his labour, she could only gape with wonder. How anyone could single-handedly produce any kind of workable aeroplane, let alone one that looked so staggeringly beautiful, was completely beyond her. And the fact that this gleaming silver bird carried her name, painstakingly applied in a hand-rendered script below the cockpit, certainly helped to sweeten the pill.

Becks I had taken him no less than six months to complete from a kit supplied by a well respected Czech aircraft manufacturer; and their maiden flight had been back to Florence for a second honeymoon - that turned out to be even more special than their first. It was Hugo's way of apologising, and he knew how to apologise in style.

Over the years, they'd flown off to countless parts of the globe on a whim; Malta, Switzerland, Southern, France, Monaco ... she could go on ad infinitum. She'd grown to love that plane. It had come to symbolize a kind of freedom she had never known.

As the product of a broken marriage, Rebecca had enjoyed no real childhood to speak of. Her mother had struggled as a single mum with a string of low paid dead-end jobs, and long bouts of depression. They had lived in a succession of poky, damp flats in south London for which her mother could barely afford the rent.

Rebecca was naturally bright and realised from the outset that she was going to have to work hard at school to avoid following in her mother's footsteps. Her diligence would eventually pay off and against all the odds, she'd become the first pupil at her lousy comprehensive in Streatham to receive an offer to read Classics at Cambridge. Three years at Jesus College changed her irrevocably. Within the twinkling of an eye, she had lost all traces of that working-class south London twang and had fully embraced the worlds of literature and fine art - not to mention the delights of *Châteauneuf du Pape*, *Château Mouton Rothschild* and *Dom Perignon*.

She'd met Hugo after splitting up with Matthew, her erstwhile boyfriend from Cambridge who was clearly destined for great things in the world of politics but was, as far as she was concerned, completely up himself. She'd been taking time out after her graduation to get over him by aimlessly pottering around Devon in her old *Morris Minor* and had found one of those idyllic country pubs with low beamed ceilings and a real fire. And it had been here while nursing a *Pinot Grinot* and feeling a tad sorry for herself, that this larger than life character blustered into the place by chance in search of jump leads for his 'bloody *Land Rover*' that was apparently giving him grief. She was the only other person at the bar, and as it happened she did have a pair of jump leads in her boot, and for some curious, inexplicable reason had felt compelled to offer this stranger her assistance. Needless to say, the jump leads did the trick in more ways than one, and before too long friendship turned into something altogether more serious.

He was everything Matthew wasn't. He was self-effacing for starters and never took himself too seriously. But he was also quite brilliant despite the fact that he hadn't gone to university. And of course, he was decidedly posh, having been through the public school system at Marlborough College. But unlike so many public schoolboys she'd known, he wasn't in the least bit arrogant; confident, yes but never arrogant or conceited. Above all, he was genuinely sensitive and caring and possessed a mischievous sense of humour. In fact, there was nobody else she had ever known that could make her laugh quite like he did. He could get her to laugh like a frigging drain - it was embarrassing at times. For all these reasons she had come to love this far from perfect and less than handsome hunk of a man whose large, ungainly frame meant he had to stoop in old beamed pubs for fear of banging his head. She liked being with him; he was terrific company, and it got to the point that the idea of him not being around just didn't feel right.

◆

This whole business scared him to death, and he wasn't one to get scared easily. Michael had seemed so bloody calm about it all over the phone. But at the end of the day, Hugo was one of the very few people in this world who possessed the considerable technical skills to help Michael achieve his grand plan. And Hugo knew how much it meant to his friend; how much he loved his kids, and the fact that he'd do absolutely anything to protect them.

Hugo could fly him to Iona and design and build a lightweight motorised fold-up wheelchair that would answer all his friend's very specific needs while being compact and lightweight enough to carry onboard. None of that was a problem. The problem was the whole ghastly situation in which his friend now found himself. It was all so desperately sad. But there was absolutely nothing anyone could do about it - least of all, him. And Hugo had to admit that Michael's solution was, in fact, the only logical plan on the table. He'd had sleepless nights turning it over in his head, but there really was no other way out of this mess. If they pulled this off, Michael's kids would be safe, and he'd have every chance of getting to see Becks again; to feel her skin against his and fill his nostrils with her inimitable perfume. But it was a big if. Neither of them really knew what they were up against.

Michael had told him to take the shotgun in his attic, but Hugo had actually gone one better and got hold of a compact revolver - a *Ruger LCR* that was small enough to stuff into the top of his sock. Who would have thought that he'd find himself at this stage of life looking for illegal firearms? It was surreal.

Now he had two weeks to sort out everything. It was a tall order, but it was doable.

◆

Rebecca worried about him. It wasn't just his physical absence from the house; it was his mental absence when he occasionally materialised from the workshop. He was unusually quiet and introspective, and he'd stopped making her laugh. And whenever she'd broach the subject of his looming flight with Michael, and her deep concerns for his safety, he had held her close and looked directly into her eyes and reassured her that there was absolutely nothing to worry about and that he'd only be gone for half a day. But his reassurances did little to allay her fears.

Who was Michael meeting, and why was he meeting them on a remote Scottish island at two in the morning? As much as he wanted to, Hugo simply couldn't tell her.

CHAPTER FIFTY

Damien Lowry-Johnson had it all; good looks; a first-rate brain; monied parents; and the kind of privileges most young men would give their eye-teeth for. But unfortunately for Damien, he also possessed a deeply flawed nihilistic personality. He was, in short, a nasty piece of work who held grudges against anyone who deigned to be the least bit critical or disapproving of him. He was vindictive, arrogant and something of a racist into the bargain.

At Eton, his violent tendencies had come close to getting him expelled. On one occasion a particularly ugly spat with another boy had ended with Damien breaking the other boy's nose and administering two black eyes. Had it not been for his exceptional academic track record and his father's sizeable financial contributions to the school, he would certainly have been out on his ear.

Despite his shortcomings, he coasted into Worcester College Oxford to read History, and here he seems to have achieved a modicum of self-control and was able to form friendships with others who would ultimately carve successful careers in the spheres of politics and the media. For Damien, though, a 2:1 from Worcester wasn't going to cut the mustard. There was something about him that future employers just didn't like. It may have been his arrogance and air of superiority or his strange aloofness and coldness. Whatever it was, they had all, one after the other, turned him away at the last hurdle. Of course, the situation was only exacerbated by the fact that Damien was his own worst enemy and only applied for plum jobs. Anything less than a ridiculously high starting salary at the bluest of blue-chip institutions was quite simply beneath him. Needless to say, the longer this failure to secure employment continued, the more his superiority complex grew in intensity.

Things came to a head when his father who was a Lloyds of London 'name' in the city's insurance market took a massive financial blow in the late eighties when an extraordinary number of insurance claims forced him, along with others in his syndicate, to cover the firm's losses. The situation was compounded further when the government refused to bail out those who'd been left bankrupt. Damien viewed the entire episode as a vindictive act against his family and an indirect assault on his future inheritance. And as such, he took it personally and his hackles were raised. Lloyds, as far as he was concerned, had behaved appallingly and needed to be taught a lesson.

The lesson would be delivered with the assistance of one of his dubious friends with whom he conspired to rob the insurance underwriter through an elaborate insurance scam involving arson. The hair-brained scheme eventually unravelled at Snaresbrook Crown Court where the pair were found guilty of fraud and arson and sentenced to six years at Her Majesty's pleasure - a relatively light sentence in light of the recklessness of the crime.

Within five years of his sentence and a year before their son was due for release, both his mother and father died tragically in a car accident on a notorious stretch of country road on the outskirts of Stratford-upon-Avon. And as an only child, Damien came into a not-insignificant inheritance, despite the earlier Lloyds debacle. Upon his release from prison, he married his long-time girlfriend, sold the family home in Putney and led a reclusive lifestyle on the Isle of Man where he learnt to fly helicopters and set up his first legitimate business - *Heli Hire*, the Isle of Man's one and only private helicopter ferrying service.

His earliest clients had included shady characters from his time behind bars. He didn't care who they were and what they were up to. So long as they paid their bills, which they usually did in cash, he'd take them anywhere. After no more than three years of trading, the business was turning over in excess of five million pounds and even had one of London's leading commercial film production companies on its books for the purpose of filming aerial shots.

By the time, Benazir had been given the company's contact details, *Heli Hire* had acquired an impressive fleet of eight state-of-the-art helicopters and employed four full-time pilots. It was a company known among its clientele for its flexibility; one that was able and willing to bend the rules for a price.

CHAPTER FIFTY-ONE

She hated his tone on the phone. His voice had a supercilious, upper class and condescending air about it. And nobody had ever addressed her as 'sweetheart' before. Who the hell did he think he was?

'I'd rather you didn't call me that because I'm nobody's sweetheart - least of all yours.'

'Yup... No problem... And certainly no cause for getting one's female undergarments in a twist...' He sniggered to himself.

Benazir cringed. He really was a prick. She chose to ignore him.

'Now, you say you're looking to charter two-night flights to the West coast of Scotland... Where exactly did you have in mind?'

There was a pause. She could hear him breathing on the other end of the line.

'Iona. The isle of Iona... 56.33 degrees North 6.42 degrees West to be precise.'

'Fuck me sideways... You do realise that that would be classed as an illegal landing? Those fuckers don't even allow cars onto the island - let alone helicopters.'

'I am perfectly aware of that, Mr...'

'The name's Damien. Damien Lowry-Johnson '

'Well, Damien. This is the reason why I am talking to you today. I am reliably informed that you can sometimes accommodate irregular requests.'

'Are you now?' The line went silent again for a few

moments. Benazir closed her eyes. She wasn't going to say anything until he replied.

'You're not wrong, of course. We have been known to push the envelope, so to speak…'

Then in an altogether conspiratorial whisper. 'But this request of yours is a bit fucking left of field if you get my drift…'

She knew perfectly well what she was asking him, but had no intention of admitting it. Her source was reliable. She knew this twat's background; that he was as crooked as they come. He'd come round eventually.

'If I were to get caught touching down on that little pimple in the Atlantic I'd lose my license… It would be curtains for this business… Anyway, how did you find me?'

'Kenneth Ronald Betts assured me that you'd be interested.'

The next silence was palpable. He'd shared a cell with Ken who'd served ten years for fraud. Ken was sound.

Now his tone changed and became businesslike. 'Your request comes at a price, you understand?'

'Name your price, Mr Lowrey-Johnson.' The name suited this pillock.

'Two illegal landings on Iona at night for ten personnel? You're looking at 100k with a 50k advance.'

Benazir gulped. She knew this bastard was going to charge the earth. But this was absurd.

'That's quite some price.'

'As I say, the risk of my company losing its license is very real. So to keep things discreet, we will have to make some significant adjustments to our rotor blade configurations to keep the noise to an absolute minimum.

Such technical adjustments are perfectly feasible but pretty expensive I'm afraid. This said, we wouldn't want to wake the residents in the early hours, would we? I'd also point out that landing at night in such an exposed position also has its risks… If wind speeds exceed 50 knots we'll have to abort… The price also includes an advanced landing party to mark out landing positions with lights. I hasten to add that you won't find another outfit willing to flout the law quite so willingly, and quite as professionally. So take it or leave it.'

She had a good mind to get Hasan to put a bullet through this joker's head as soon as they returned. 'And when will we know if the wind is too strong?'

'We'll have a pretty good idea the day before. But the final decision will have to be made on the day.'

She bit her lip. 'In that case, Mr Lowry-Johnson, I think we have a deal.'

CHAPTER FIFTY-TWO

Michael had never suffered with depression prior to becoming wheelchair-bound. His black days had been at their peak while in rehabilitation at Stanmore when he had felt suicidal and had secretly stashed away countless tablets for a spontaneous overdose. If it hadn't been for his kids, he might have just done it. Thank God he hadn't. His life may have seemed terrible back then, but things had improved immeasurably since. He'd got himself into a new routine; he was still reasonably independent; he had a brilliant carer; the children had been fantastic; Ziggy had proved to be a loyal and loving companion; and life with all its complications was still bloody amazing. He'd started reading and cooking again - even if it did mean using a microwave because the hob was too high. And the simple things in life like smelling freshly cut grass or sipping a decent claret were as invigorating and life-affirming as they always had been. But now all that was going to end. It was hardly surprising he was feeling really low again.

He had started listening to Bach cello suites by Pablo Casals on his headphones. They were a wonderful antidote and had the effect of taking his mind off things. It was the best way he knew to blot out reality; to stop dwelling on his predicament. He couldn't put the clock back. He just had to get on with it and make the most of what little time he did have left.

CHAPTER FIFTY-THREE

Hugo poured a large glass of merlot and admired his handiwork. The lightweight frame made from carbon fibre tubing supported a canvas seat and back, and the all-important wiring was neatly concealed in the tubing. The wheels were detachable, and the whole thing folded down to a virtual flat pack. The heaviest component was the motor, which could be attached to the hub of the right wheel. All the controls were discreetly built into the right arm: a joystick on the upper side and a small switch on the underside that was completely out of view. It was no small feat of engineering, and it would perform precisely as Michael had asked.

He had also toyed with building a portable hoist but simply couldn't design anything that wouldn't exceed the restricted weight allowance. He'd just have to manhandle Michael into and out of the cockpit. He'd manage one way or another.

As he poured a second glass, Rebecca let herself in.

'Ah.., Perfect timing.' He handed her the glass. 'Chin chin.'

'Cheers… So you're done.'

'Certainly hope so. Doesn't look anything special, I know, but there's a lot of pretty fancy wiring inside her, and it boasts a fairly impressive torque.'

'I'll take your word for it.' She sipped the wine. 'May seem like a stupid question, but why couldn't Michael use his current wheelchair?'

'It's not a stupid question… As a matter of fact, he

wanted to use his own chair. But it's too cumbersome Becks, and being a manual chair, it would be really hard work for him to wheel himself over rough grassland. When I suggested building a lightweight electric model, he jumped at the idea. Besides, I've made it to fit in the hold.'

She lent over and kissed his forehead. 'You're a bloody good friend Huge.'

He took a large gulp. 'One tries one's best. But look Becks I really feel for Michael. He's got himself into the most awful mess. You really don't know the half of it.'

She looked at him with a determined gaze that made him blush. 'Well come on then. I've been trying to get to the bottom of this fucking thing for weeks. Are you going to tell me what's really going on here or what Hugo? For crying out loud. I deserve to know. I am your wife.' She had bottled up weeks of worry and frustration while he had tinkered in that damn workshop. Now it had all come flooding out. She suddenly felt so angry and scared that she was shaking.

He rose from his chair, strode over to the double doors and bolted them. Then he pulled down the blinds on all the windows. This completed, he returned to his seat and poured another glass of wine. Then he blew out his cheeks and expelled air, and Rebecca couldn't help noticing a tear forming in his right eye, which eventually found its freedom and rolled down his cheek.

'I'm sorry Becks. I should have told you all this earlier, but I just didn't want to involve you. I suppose I thought I was protecting you. But look, I'm going to tell you everything I know… But you have to promise me to keep this to yourself ok?'

She nodded nervously.

CHAPTER FIFTY-FOUR

This would be Michael's last visit to The Angel Hotel. It wasn't especially wheelchair friendly being a Georgian pile, but Michael liked it nonetheless. He'd have to alert someone from the rear entrance in the car park to set up a ramp at the front; a great big silver metal affair that required two strapping lads to carry it and lay it across the series of three steps up to the imposing double doors. The gradient was steeper than the legal requirement so one of the lads would have to push him up. But once inside, he could wheel himself to the back of the bar where there were three payphone booths left over from the 1970s.

He dialled and a woman's voice answered. It was Rebecca.

'Oh hi there Rebecca. It's Michael. I'm afraid I don't have long. I'm on a payphone. Is Hugo there?'

'Sure. I'll get him.'

Hugo must have been in the same room as he picked up immediately.

'Hi Michael.'

'How are we fixed?'

'All good. The chair is perfect. Everything will work.'

'Are you certain?'

'One hundred per cent.'

That was all he needed to hear. The man was a bloody perfectionist. If he was a hundred per cent certain, he knew that everything would go according to plan.

'And you've sorted the case of money?'

'Yep. It's an aluminium number with locks. Looks the part.'

Michael laughed. 'No expense spared, eh?'

'Michael. Are you one hundred per cent certain you want to go through with this thing?'

There was a short pause. 'Yeah. I'm afraid so... Wish I could say no but I can't.'

'I thought as much. Alright mate. I take it the time and date still stand?'

'As far as I know. Haven't heard anything to the contrary.'

'How are you going to give everyone the slip at your end?'

'I was waiting for you to ask me that.' Hugo didn't answer. 'Thought I'd use sleeping tablets. I'll have to drug the dog too.'

'Sounds like a good plan... Flying time will be around 54 minutes depending on wind direction. I suggest we give ourselves plenty of time. I'll aim to pick you up from the playing field at midnight precisely. How does that sound?'

'It sounds perfect Hugo. And well... I just... I wanted to say thank you. It means a lot...'

'Yeah, I know Michael. I know mate.'

◆

He made his way up in the lift to room 54. It was a simple room tastefully furnished with a large double bed. He wheeled himself to the window and gazed out, and for some inexplicable reason, his mind turned to his wedding reception all those years ago. It had been held in some swanky London hotel and his father-in-law had invited well over 400 guests, half of whom were his business associates. Louise had hated every minute of it. She had wanted a small intimate gathering, but her father had taken over the arrangements, and that was that. Michael had never smiled so much in his life and shaken the hands of so many complete strangers. Despite her annoyance, Louise had looked stunning in her silk wedding gown. He could picture her beaming face in his mind's eye. How life had changed.

The phone rang and he picked up the receiver.

'Oh thanks. Send her up please.'

He'd left the door open as it was too difficult for him to open from his wheelchair.

This was the second time he'd arranged to meet her. He'd originally expected her to be an Essex girl but had been pleasantly surprised that she'd been well-spoken and refined. She may not have been a raving beauty but she certainly wasn't unattractive, and was probably in her early thirties.

'Hello Michael. It's nice to see you again.'

'Likewise Samantha. I hope you like champagne. There's a bottle of Bollinger by the TV. Why don't you pour us a couple of glasses?'

She smiled radiantly and poured two glasses. 'Bottoms up.'

'Look, I know this must all seem a bit strange to you, but can we just do the same as last time?'

'It's not a problem Michael.' It wasn't the first time a client of hers hadn't wanted sex. There had been an elderly gentleman a couple of years ago who just wanted to sit and talk about his wife who had just passed away.

'I mean, it's not that I don't find you attractive, you understand.'

'Michael. It's fine. I understand.' She lined his wheelchair up with the side of the bed frame and he shuffled his backside onto the bed. Then she gently lifted his legs onto the mattress and deftly removed his trousers and unbuttoned his shirt. Michael was the first client she'd ever had any feelings for. And he was her one and only client who'd been in a wheelchair. He was a genuinely lovely man, and the sadness in his eyes moved her. She downed the champagne and visited the bathroom. 'I won't be long. Promise.'

By the time she returned, Michael was almost drifting off. He could just make out the silhouette of her shapely curves and her expensive silk lingerie as she slipped beneath the sheets. She smelt exquisite and her skin was warm and soft to the touch. They held each other in each other's arms - two lost souls in a world that barely made sense anymore. Then she did something she had never done to any of her clients. She kissed him passionately and squarely on the mouth.

✦

Rebecca now knew everything there was to know, and part of her wished that she didn't. This whole business was a living nightmare, and she feared for Hugo's safety more than ever.

She had pleaded with him not to go. But her desperate pleas had fallen on deaf ears. He said he had no choice. He was the only one who could help his friend in his hour of need. If he didn't act now, Ben and Natasha's lives would be in jeopardy.

All she could do was get her fill of him now, before she ran the very real risk of losing him forever. She rolled over and snuggled up to this big protective bear of a man. This big stubborn oaf. He was fast asleep. She'd exhausted him as usual. The thought of him not being with her made her feel physically sick and she clung to him like a limpet. His back formed a comforting pillow; a warm all-embracing cushion that now felt decidedly wet from her tears.

CHAPTER FIFTY-FIVE

Qssim sat on the bed where he'd placed his gun in its constituent parts, and started to clean the metal sections with an old toothbrush and a bore cleaning brush. It wasn't especially dirty, but there was something about taking the thing apart and brushing it that appealed to him; something he found strangely therapeutic.

For days now he'd been questioning his own judgement over all kinds of issues that had begun to trouble him. Until now, he'd seen things in black and white. Right and wrong; plain and simple. His father's murder, for instance, was something he never questioned or felt remorse for. He'd been beaten, sexually abused and mentally tortured by this sadistic and revolting excuse for a human being. But only now did he want to know what had shaped and influenced his father's behaviour.

It had been surprisingly easy to delve into the past with the assistance of the internet. Within a handful of clicks, he had managed to establish a few key facts. His father had been born in Deptford to a young girl by the name of Mollie Thackeray on 25 September 1949. There had been no mention of a father anywhere, so Mollie had clearly been a single mother at the age of just 24. Her death certificate was dated 1953, a mere four years after his father's birth. Cause of death at the tender age of just 28 wasn't entirely clear. There seemed to have been a catalogue of complicated medical conditions that had ultimately conspired to bring about heart failure. Further investigations revealed that his father had been farmed out to the enclosed Dr Barnardo's Village in Barkingside, Essex. And from here he had eventually been fostered to a string of families, one of which he had run away from. This family's surname was Temple and the father was one Maurice Cedrick Temple. A quick search brought up what Qssim had secretly feared all along. Maurice Cedrick Temple was sentenced to 15 years in prison for serial rape in 1966; two of his young victims being his own son and daughter. There was, Qssim realised, every chance that his father would have been another such victim, and it would have explained why he had run away.

While none of this could have excused his father's appalling behaviour, Qssim was now experiencing something he had never experienced in 40 years: guilt.

CHAPTER FIFTY-SIX

Benazir had arrived early and took the weight off her feet by making use of the leather armchair that had clearly been designated for members of the public. A middle-aged woman in an official beige polo shirt and lanyard around her neck smiled profusely at her. 'Good morning. Welcome to the dining room. Are you familiar with the house and its collection?'

Benazir smiled back. 'Yes thank you. I know the house well. I've come to specially view the Rembrandt and Vermeer.'

The woman smiled even more broadly and nodded in acknowledgement that this member of the public probably knew as much if not more about the place than she did.

In fairness, Benazir was familiar with Kenwood House, its history and its collection of old masters. In terms of contents insurance, she was clearly seated in the most expensive room in the house. Before her hung one of the most iconic self-portraits ever painted in the history of European art. The sad eyes of Rembrandt Harmenszoon van Rijn stared back at her as if to say, I may be a broken man; I may have lost three children and a wife, and I may be bankrupt, but I am still the greatest portrait painter the world has ever known. Look at me and you will see more than flesh and blood rendered in oil. You will see into my soul.

On the adjacent wall hung another treasure. Smaller, this exquisite little study of a woman playing a guitar was by the hand of Johannes Vermeer whose output in his home town of Delft was incredibly small. There are today only 34 paintings that have been attributed to him. And all of them without exception possess an indescribable ethereal quality where the angle of the light is such that it catches the folds of fabric or the iridescent sheen of a pearl earring in a way that only Vermeer was able to capture.

Benazir knew all this. She also knew that this particular Vermeer had been stolen back in 1974 by the IRA. But there was little anyone could have done with a genuine Vermeer other than to marvel at it. It was too iconic a painting to sell on the open market, and it was for this reason that it had been recovered in a cemetery in the city less than three months after it had been stolen.

At precisely 10.30, she left the house and made her way to the designated seat overlooking the heath uncannily close to where Mohammed had originally met Ibrahim, not that Banazir would have known that. Her contact was already there reading *The Times* obituary page. He was tall in his late fifties with a sallow complexion. 'You're late,' he said by way of a greeting without so much as turning his head in her direction.

'Hardly... Anyway, I have the details.'

'Good.'

She rose and headed back to the car park. As she did, he recovered a small piece of screwed up paper that she had left on the seat and unravelled it.

It read simply: *Heli Hire   Acc. No. 17590051   Sort Code: 45-54-90.*

◆

Benazir didn't know exactly how the money would be siphoned into that dickhead Lowry-Johnson's account, but she knew it would be far from straightforward. It would no doubt be transferred via a labyrinthine network of legitimate accounts in the names of charities and overseas businesses as well as offshore companies.

CHAPTER FIFTY-SEVEN

Michael had dreaded this day. He'd called Ben earlier and had tried his best to sound normal and cheerful on the phone, but it was difficult. He desperately wanted to see his son, but it wasn't even remotely possible. He just had to make do with the sound of his voice. It had been a short call as Ben had a lecture to attend, and he had tried to reassure his dad that he'd call him later. And with a lump in his throat, Michael had said 'ok son' and 'love you' knowing full well that there wouldn't be another conversation. It was gut-wrenchingly hard, and Michael despised himself for playing this deceitful game. He hated keeping things from anyone let alone his own children. But the tragedy was that he had no choice. Not if he was going to protect them.

◆

Ben felt guilty about putting the phone down on his dad. He couldn't say why exactly. It was just the tone of his father's voice. It sounded different to normal, and he somehow sensed that his dad wanted to tell him something. But it would be ok. He'd call him back in the morning.

He'd taken his bicycle out of the shed in the garden and wheeled it round to the front of the house where he put his cycle helmet on and clipped the strap below his chin. But that conversation was still going through his head. It was odd; his dad had never ended a conversation before with the words 'love you.'

◆

Zopiclone had always knocked him out when he needed to sleep. It had been a pretty reliable sleeping tablet. Now he'd have to rely on it to send the whole household to the land of nod in order to make his escape. There were only the three of them overnight, and they'd usually all eat together. Most evenings Natasha would prepare supper and ever since Alexander's tip about drinking mint tea to aid digestion, it had become something of a habit to make a large pot of fresh mint tea. All Michael had to do was prepare the tea and slip three tablets into the pot. He, of course, would refrain, and make a mug of coffee for himself instead.

The plan wasn't guaranteed, and Michael was half expecting Alexander to follow in his footsteps and opt for coffee. He even had visions of trying to ply him with whiskey nightcaps as an alternative. But as it turned out, he needn't have worried. Everything went to plan. Better still, Alexander had two full mugs of tea, and by 11 o'clock was snoring loudly on the sofa in front of *Newsnight*. And Natasha had made it upstairs, which remained quiet. He only wished he could get upstairs to kiss his sleeping daughter goodbye, but of course, he couldn't get upstairs; there was no lift.

Michael collected his stuff, most of which comprised his medication, and paraphernalia like catheter bags and his bowel irrigation system and stuffed them into a rucksack. The only other vital items were four torches to mark out a reasonably flat landing strip for Hugo. These he stuffed into his jacket pockets. Now he was ready to make his exit. But before doing so, he wheeled himself into the living room and turned the volume of Jeremy Paxman's voice down on the television. Alexander was slumped awkwardly on the sofa. He patted his friend's shoulder.

'Cheerio old friend. It was lovely to have known you. And good luck with your transfer to the Palace of Westminster where you'll be looking after far more important people than me.' And with those words, he swivelled his wheelchair round and made his way into the hall where he quietly opened the front door and let himself into the night air.

♦

Hugo had clung to her for what seemed like an eternity. She was inconsolable. It wasn't what he had planned at all. He knew she'd lose it and he had wanted to keep their goodbyes short and sweet. He really didn't need this. It was making his mission umpteen times harder, and, God knows, it was bloody hard enough as it was. He kept reassuring her that he'd be back in no time and that she could call him on the mobile. But it was no good. Nothing seemed to calm her. He hated leaving her like this, but he had absolutely no choice. He had to leave now if he was going to get to Michael at 12.00. He prised her shuddering body away from his and looked intently into her watery eyes. 'Becks. I have to go now… We'll speak later. I promise.' He kissed her on the forehead and then flew out of the front door.

♦

Damien had been pleasantly surprised to receive the money as quickly as he did. Payments had, it seemed, been made by a number of different organisations with registered offices overseas, and they had all flowed into his account on the same day. It was obviously a serious operation, but he had no idea who these guys were and what their business and modus operandi actually was. Normally, he wouldn't have wanted to fly any of his clients himself and hadn't done so for well over a year now, but there was something about this lot that made his adrenaline flow. And in all honesty, he was intrigued. He was used to dealing with the Marbella criminal fraternity. They were as typecast and predictable as you'd expect. But this organization fronted by that sophisticated bird on the phone was something else altogether. It was a class act. She'd impressed him, and he wanted to know more about her and what this particular outfit was up to.

It didn't take him long to discover that at least half of the organisations that had paid him were registered charities with Islamic connections and head offices in countries including Pakistan, Saudi Arabia, Afghanistan, as well as the US and UK. Many shared similar names like the *International Benevolence Foundation*, the *Global Relief Foundation*, *Humane International and International Relief*. This revelation took him completely by surprise. He was no fool. He knew instinctively that this was almost certainly laundered terrorist money. He'd read reports on how terrorists raised money through legitimate charities; many of which had had head offices in Saudi Arabia and other countries in the Gulf. He had originally thought the operation might have been part of a large arms or drugs deal. Terrorism hadn't registered on his radar for the simple reason that you'd never associate a woman of authority with an Islamic terror network. Those guys are sexist to the core. That was public knowledge. This put a whole new spin on the thing, and he didn't like it. He didn't like it one bit.

Having only just been toying with the idea of flying these monkeys himself, he was now desperately trying to figure out how he could get himself out of this mess. It was no good though. He was in too deep. There was no way he could pull out at this late stage. And if he was right, which he usually was, he and Donna his partner, were going to have to do a runner pretty sharpish if they valued their lives. Whatever these bastards were up to, there was every chance that they'd want him and his pilots out of the way for good. They wouldn't think twice about destroying any inconvenient evidence, even if it were in human form. He'd have to speak with James his business partner right away.

◆

'Hi James. It's Damien. Look, something's cropped up. Donna's mum has taken a turn for the worse. We're going to have to fuck off to Oxford and you're going to have to hold the fort. Is that okay mate?'

James mouthed 'Damien' to his girlfriend who was lying in a state of undress on the bed. 'Oh, that's fine. Not a problem. Sorry to hear that about Donna's mum.'

'Yeah. I know… Look this new client that wants to be flown to Iona… There's something fishy about them. Can't put my finger on it', he lied. 'Just call it a hunch. Make sure the boys who fly them are armed, just in case… Don't put the wind up them or anything… It's just an insurance policy.'

'Is everything alright Damien?'

'Yeah... It's fine. You know what I'm like. I'm just a bit paranoid... When I served time, I was always looking over my shoulder. Old habits die hard I guess... Just make sure the boys can look after themselves alright?'

'Okay. Yeah. It's not a problem. We have a couple of handguns in the safe.'

'Thanks James. Speak soon.'

'Yeah. Sure. Bye.'

James put down the phone and stood gazing into the middle distance while his girlfriend placed her arm around his neck.

'Is everything alright?'

'I don't know... Not sure.'

CHAPTER FIFTY-EIGHT

Michael reached the playing field in good time, switched on his torches and placed them as Hugo had instructed him on a reasonably flat section of grass - delineating a rectangle of around four metres by two. All he had to do now was wait, but naturally, his nerves had got the better of him and he desperately needed to empty his catheter leg bag. He wasn't in the least bit surprised that his bladder had gone into overdrive, and as he squeezed the contents onto the grass, the sound of a distant rumble greeted his ears. Typical. Hugo was ten minutes early. He was one of the few people he knew who was invariably early for meet-ups.

Michael wheeled himself well away from the torches and watched in awe as the silhouette of this graceful silver bird appeared against the light of the moon. It gently floated down and bounced lightly in the centre of Michael's home-made landing strip and came to a halt no more than a few metres beyond the illuminated strip. The engine eventually cut out and Michael could hear the canopy slide open, and within a few minutes the large frame of his friend came bounding out of the darkness.

'Michael. My dear Michael…' Hugo didn't quite know what to say in the circumstances. Instead of speaking any further he crouched down and hugged his friend. 'Christ! I think you're going to need a thicker jacket than this mate… Here, take mine. It should fit.' He ripped off his old leather flying jacket and placed it around Michael's shoulders.

'What about you?'

'I'm fine. I have a woollen fleece back in the cockpit… Now I'm going to push you up to the wing. And then my friend, I'm going to have to carry you over the bloody threshold.'

'But we haven't tied the knot yet.'

'Play your cards right, and who knows what'll happen?...'

As Hugo pushed Michael across the grass the two men giggled as if they had just left a pub after a good session. For a fleeting moment, it seemed just like the old days, but of course, it was anything but. They both felt the need to convince each other that everything was perfectly normal. It was, in truth, the only way they could keep their frayed nerves intact. And it was the only way they could carry this thing off.

Hugo placed his foot on both brakes and secured the chair. 'Right now, on the count of three, brace yourself and I will lift you onto the wing, ok?'

Michael nodded.

'One, two, three…' With what seemed strangely little effort, Hugo took Michael's limp legs beneath his right forearm and lifted his friend gently from the wheelchair. Initially, Michael's legs went into manic spasms, but these eventually passed, and Hugo was then able to somehow carry his passenger onto the wing and lower him gracefully into the passenger seat. This completed, he sunk into his own seat alongside Michael and slid the cockpit over their heads until it closed with a metallic click.

It felt very strange for Michael to be sitting in another seat, and looking out at his empty wheelchair on the grass. Strange but somehow liberating.

'Thanks Huge. I wasn't so sure how you were going to get me in...'

Hugo laughed. 'To be honest, neither was I... Now, before you ask me, your new chair is carefully packed in parts: wheels are behind your seat; the frame is folded flat beneath your seat; and everything else including all the pyrotechnics and a pretty nifty motor is carefully stowed away at the back of the plane - along with the case of money. We're just above the *MTOW*... Sorry, that stands for *maximum take-off weight*, which isn't meant to exceed 470 kg. But I'm not too concerned about that. Certainly not concerned enough to compromise on fuel. So you can rest assured that we'll still be flying on a full tank.'

None of this meant very much to Michael, and it wasn't really registering with him at all. He was far more focussed on the trip ahead and what lay in store for them.

'Did you bring a firearm?'

'Yep... Two actually. I have my old man's loaded shotgun below my seat and a very small revolver strapped to my ankle.'

'Good... I hope to God you don't have to use them... But you might have to.'

There was an awkward silence, and Hugo gave Michael one of his bewildered looks. 'I've never shot one of these buggers before. I'm probably a lousy shot.'

'Huge. You can turn your hand to anything... You built this bloody plane for crying out loud... You can fire a sodding gun. You'll be fine. But let's just hope you don't have to...'

'Yeah. Sure.' Hugo leant over and strapped Michael in. Then he strapped himself in. 'OK... You ready to go and meet these fuckers?'

Michael nodded. 'Wouldn't want to keep them waiting.'

Hugo pushed the fuel mixture knob in and slowly advanced the throttle. Michael swallowed nervously as the engine roared and reverberated and the aeroplane moved forward at a steady speed, which began to build momentum and shake the entire cockpit as they raced over the rough terrain of the playing field. Within seconds Michael noticed the nose of the plane lifting off the ground, at which point Hugo gently pulled back on the flight control. Now they had parted company with the ground and were soaring into a thick black velvet sky punctured with a million tiny pinpricks of glistening white light.

CHAPTER FIFTY-NINE

'Look I don't know any more than you do OK? All I know is what I'm telling you now.'

Stewart stared at James with incredulity. He had flown helicopters for over ten years and had been doing so for *Heli Hire* for almost a year now, but this was the first time he'd been asked to carry a gun. 'Why the fuck would that arsehole want me to carry a gun? There has to be a reason, James.'

James stood awkwardly in the doorway and shrugged., 'Like I say, all he said was that he had a strange feeling about this new client… Said it was down to his paranoia, which he'd developed in prison. And he wanted you boys to be able to look after yourselves… So just take it ok? It's no big deal. ' He extended his right hand with the semi-automatic *Browning* lying on his upturned palm and Stewart peevishly retrieved it.

'It's OK. It's unloaded. 'James thrust his hand into his jacket and produced a pre-loaded magazine. 'Here, you'll need this.'

Stewart took the magazine and slid it into the gun.

'Look, I'm sure everything will be fine… We've flown plenty of dodgy characters in the past, and nothing untoward has ever happened… You know what Damien's like. He doesn't trust a soul. Believe me Stew, it's just one of his crazy, hair-brained ideas…"

Stewart forced a smile. 'Yeah… I'm sure you're right… Anyway, I'd better get a move on. I have a helicopter to fly.'

✦

James could tell that Stewart wasn't a happy bunny. Perhaps there'd been a better way to break the news about the gun. But if there was, he couldn't for the life of him think what it would have been. It's all well and good for Damien to tell him not to put the 'wind up the boys' but it's a bit bloody tricky not to when you're asking them to carry a fucking gun.

Brian lived about half an hour's drive from Stewart, and James was hoping that this visit would be a little easier. Brian, after all, was ex-military and something of a hard nut.

Brian answered the door in his vest. You wouldn't want to pick a fight with this guy. He was well over six foot and with his bristling biceps, was built like the proverbial brick outhouse.

Unlike Stewart, he wasn't the least bit fazed about Damien's request.

'Look mate I'm happy to take the shooter, but I do usually take my own precautions... It's my army training... I'm always well prepared, me. And to be perfectly honest, I don't like *Brownings*. They're a bit crap. I'll stick with my own *Glock* if that's alright... I'll leave this one here in the drawer. But tell Dame, thanks for the warning. I'll keep an eye on those bastards, don't you worry...'

CHAPTER SIXTY

Benazir gazed out of the darkly tinted window into the moonlit field. They had arrived.

She had decided that it would be best for both parties to travel in convoy and fly from the same location. That way she'd be able to monitor everything with her own eyes. When it came to matters involving large sums of money and impressive firepower, you couldn't really trust anyone unreservedly. It would only take one bad apple to tip everything on its head.

Her worst suspicions about Qssim had already been corroborated when she'd had his laptop examined by one of her IT wireheads, who in a matter of hours had detected fifteen deleted pages of filthy Israeli propaganda. It didn't bode well, so she had been monitoring him closely, and had briefed Hasan to surreptitiously swap Qssim's personal stash of live ammunition for blanks.

The two helicopters sat close to the runway. They were the only visible aircraft on display and Benazir could make out the outlines of their respective pilots standing beside their machines. That wanker Damien was nowhere to be seen.

The two heavily tinted people-carriers parked by the side of a large corrugated aeroplane hangar and Benazir and Hasan let themselves out and strode over to the helicopters. Stewart stepped forward and shook their hands. 'Welcome to Bicknell Park. I trust you had a pleasant journey.'

Benazir smiled. 'It was tolerable. This is my colleague Hasan. We'll be flying separately. Is everything ready?'

'Yes. Rotor blades have been specially adjusted as promised to reduce noise. You'll be flying our most advanced models: our *EC135* and *A109S*. They are lovely machines designed to the highest specifications; and are highly manoeuvrable and fast... By the way, Damien apologises for not being here in person. He was called away at the last moment.'

Brian stood motionless in the shadows observing and listening to every word. He didn't like the look of these two. She clearly relied on this sidekick of hers to do her dirty work. And even in this low light, he could make out the contours of a gun holster strapped beneath Hasan's black jacket to the right-hand side of his chest. And the length of the contour suggested that this gun already had a silencer fitted. Damien may have been a tosser at times but he'd been right about this lot.'

Benazir turned to Hasan. 'Can you beckon the others across and help with the two holdalls?'

Hasan nodded. 'No problem.'

She turned back to Stewart. 'We have two large holdalls to transport; one in each helicopter.'

'That's fine. We have a reasonable amount of luggage space on each helicopter.'

As he spoke, the two flight parties emerged from the darkness grappling with two large holdalls resembling large cricket bags. They were clearly reasonably heavy items as four burly men weren't exactly making light work of lugging the bags across.

Brian stepped forward to help and was brushed aside by Qssim.

Benazir looked directly at Brian. 'That won't be necessary, thank you.'

Brian was half expecting them to react as they had. You could read these cunts like a book. They were carrying some seriously heavy kit; almost certainly semi-automatics. He felt his *Glock* strapped in its usual place just above his right ankle and the cold steel of the hunting knife just above it. He wouldn't be able to rely on Stewart if things kicked off. It would be every man for himself. But he had the advantage of knowing precisely what to expect from these clowns; while they had no fucking idea what he was capable of.

CHAPTER SIXTY-ONE

Qssim hadn't spoken a word since they'd set out for the pick-up point, and he sensed that Benazir had been keeping her beady eyes on him. It was his fault entirely. He'd been introspective and not particularly sociable for a while now. And they had no doubt noticed this change in him.

Islam had been his saviour when he'd been in prison. It had disciplined him; given him a focus; a set of rigid principles; it had even protected him and provided camaraderie. He hadn't questioned its precepts; its moralising; its dogma; and above all its radical political posturing. Who was he to challenge all this when it had saved him? But the incident with that Israeli had stalled him. It had prompted him to go online and find Israeli websites that supported the Palestinian cause; Jews who openly criticised the Israeli government in the strongest terms for its occupation of the West Bank and its human rights abuses. An Israeli musician had even formed an orchestra made up of Palestinians and Israelis, and demanded that the Israeli government act compassionately and responsively towards its Palestinian brethren.

The Imams would tell him that these Jews were the worst kind, and would refer to them as 'devious pigs who were just wanting to deceive our brothers and sisters.' They were nothing more than 'evil manipulators of the truth; vile opportunists who would murder our brothers and sisters in their beds given half the chance. They could never be trusted.'

But the more Qssim watched the videos on these websites, the less credible this line of reasoning became. In fact, it just seemed totally absurd. Why would anyone go to the lengths of holding protests on the streets and form orchestras to give worldwide tours as a form of deception? And the testimonies of both the Israelis and Palestinians in these videos didn't sound staged or in the least bit cynical. They had seemed genuinely heartfelt. And some of them even fucking moved him. Moved him as much as those films made by Hamas of Palestinian children with their artificial limbs.

Then, of course, there was all that shit he'd discovered about his father. Now he knew what his dad had been through: that he'd lost his mother at a stupidly young age and had been passed from pillar to post; and then been beaten and raped. His father was a scumbag of the lowest order, but it wasn't surprising was it? For the first time in his life, Qssim had understood why his father had been a vile piece of shit. He could never forgive him. But he could now at least understand him.

The long and short of it was that he didn't really know who the fuck he was anymore. He didn't even know if he really wanted to be here with this bunch of psychopaths who valued the cult of death more than life itself. But what he did know was this: he was going to have to snap out of this self-inflicted gloom and stop self-harming before someone noticed the scars on his arm. He was going to have to play the game; this whole fucking charade. Because if he didn't, he was going to end up like Ibrahim with a knife in his back.

CHAPTER SIXTY-TWO

Brian had discreetly placed his mobile in one of the many recesses in the instrument panel and brought up the link to the onboard CCTV. It was unlikely that he'd be in any kind of danger during the flight, but the first lesson he'd learnt from his army training was never to take anything for granted. So if nothing else, the display on his mobile now gave him a perfect view of the entire cabin behind him; he now had eyes in the back of his head.

As far as he could tell, all was quiet on the Western front. Three blokes, all of whom had beards and a swarthy Middle Eastern appearance, had their eyes closed. One was clearly listening to something on discreet earplugs, and the Hasan character was in conversation with the woman.

James had said to him that there was going to be some kind of rendezvous on Iona and that the party would plan to be back in the air within half an hour of touching down. The final destination was going to be somewhere on the Scottish mainland, and would apparently be revealed once they had landed on Iona. If he was right about the holdall, it might well have been an insurance policy against uninvited guests. It was obviously no accident that they were doing this thing on one of Scotland's most remote islands. The way he saw it, the greatest threat to him would probably come once they had landed. If one of these muppets could fly, they'd most likely want to assassinate him pretty swiftly. And his money was on the

Hasan character being the assassin, since he had the gun with the silencer. But Brian would be watching his every move like a hawk on his mobile, and would be ready to cut out the lights and take Hasan out with a death blow to the neck. Then he'd use Hasan's body as a shield and pick out the others in the half-light with Hasan's gun to avoid drawing the attention of the other party.

Stewart wouldn't stand a chance. But there was nothing Brian would be able to do about it, other than getting himself and the helicopter back to base in one piece.

◆

The headland was just about visible rising from the sea, a black jagged esplanade of ancient granite against a cobalt blue sky. The helicopter skimmed across the barren landscape from the Western coast, its only inhabitants amid this rocky hinterland being Common Sandpipers, Redshanks, Shags and Cormorants.

The rows of silver halogen lights twinkled like cat's eyes set into the turf, and Brian slowed the helicopter and began the gradual descent, lining up the nose of the aircraft with the rows of lights. It was a simple, vertical approach. There were no trees or obstacles to worry about.

The display on his mobile now told him that everyone had their eyes open. They were all alert, albeit pensive looking. The Hasan character was looking out of the side window and the woman was just gazing into the middle distance. She seemed deep in thought.

He brought them down gently onto the soft turf. It was a perfect landing.

And then he noticed it sitting no more than 100 yards

away to his right, its sleek silver lines glimmering in the moonlight. It was a fixed-wing single-engine two-seater: a nice looking aircraft by the looks of things. But who the hell was sitting in it?

✦

They'd touched down half an hour early. It had been a swift flight thanks to prevailing winds, which according to Hugo had been blowing in their favour. Surprisingly, Michael had actually nodded off for much of the journey and had only woken when the wheels made contact with the uneven grassland causing the aircraft to bounce ungainly across the field until its momentum dissipated and it finally settled into a very bumpy earthbound ride.

Hugo had been his usual organised self and had run through every detail of the chair for a second time. The joystick was simple to operate and the speed dial was set to medium speed but could be increased by turning it clockwise, and the all-important 'red button' as he had dubbed it, could be located directly beneath the right armrest. If anything should fail, Hugo could override the entire system remotely. He'd be watching him through night vision binoculars. If he needed him to intervene, all he had to do was pinch his nose with his right hand. The wads of money looked convincing enough and would give Michael those crucial extra seconds to bring the plan to fruition.

'Now, I think it would be prudent to get the chair ready and get you into it before our friends arrive. What do you say?'

Michael sighed. 'I was hoping we'd be able to sit here a bit longer, but you're probably right… Are your guns loaded and to hand?'

Hugo nodded. 'Yes... Don't you worry Michael. Those bastards won't stand a chance.'

Michael reached for his friend's hand and squeezed it. 'I know Huge... I know.'

✦

As the rotor blades came to a halt, he saw her unclip her safety belt and approach him. He'd remain vigilant, but he was relieved it wasn't Hasan.

'How far behind is our other party?'

'When we fly in convoy we usually leave five minutes between us.'

'Good. It looks as if our other visitor has already arrived.'

Brian chose to say nothing.

'The guys will take the holdall on their way out.'

She was about to say something else but was distracted by the distant rumble of rotor blades. Stewart was a little ahead of schedule. Within seconds, he was hovering over them.

As the dark shadow of the second helicopter descended and touched down no more than 50 yards in front of them between two rows of landing lights, she immediately produced a two-way radio from her pocket and spoke in Arabic. There was crackling and a gravelly male voice replied in Arabic. Brian's guess was that this was one of the back-up team on the ground. They'd have set up the landing lights and were more than likely monitoring the island for unwelcome visitors. She ended the call and turned to Hasan. 'OK, I need you and Qssim to cover us from the perimeter. You'll need to take up positions behind the dry stone wall to the north.

Brian was relieved to hear that Hasan was leaving the helicopter first. He'd only believe it though when the sod had moved his arse off the helicopter. But he couldn't make any sense of the logic here. How were these two muppets going to cover without night vision glasses and a marksman's rifle?

Benazir looked intently at Brian as if to say what are you waiting for?

This was his chance to eyeball this scumbag and his accomplice as he got up from his seat to open the side hatch. As the two men brushed passed him the muscles in his forearms tensed. Until they passed into the night, his whole body had been on standby, ready to spring into action at the merest hint of foul play. Thankfully, it hadn't been necessary.

CHAPTER SIXTY-THREE

'Two characters have just got out of the helicopter and are walking away from us.'

Hugo had been watching the two helicopters intently through his night vision binoculars. He had lifted Michael out of his seat and carried him out of the plane. But it had proved more challenging this time around, and at one point he had come close to dropping Michael when he lost his balance dismounting the wing. Fortunately, he managed to recover his balance and deposit Michael who now sat upright in his new chair with the case of money on his lap. Hugo had taken no time slotting and clicking his lightweight brainchild together, and it seemed to work perfectly.

The two men admired a particularly bright full moon.

'What do we do now?' The sweat was pouring off Michael's forehead and making his eyes sting; the anxiety was finally getting to him.

'We sit tight. Wait for them to make the first move.'

'What are those two others doing?'

'No idea… But they're not the only ones out there. I've spotted some other activity on the ground. They must have been responsible for the landing lights and are possibly monitoring the place for uninvited guests.'

Then almost as if on cue, a beam of light coming from one of the helicopters illuminated the entire plane and a well-articulated female voice with an impeccable English home counties accent rang out from the darkness.

'Welcome to the Isle of Iona, Mr Hollinghurst. I hope

you had a pleasant flight. First of all, can I ask your pilot to go back inside the aeroplane and close his cockpit please?'

'Looks like you're on mate.' Hugo stooped and clung his friend really tight. Michael could feel Hugo's stubble scrape the side of his cheek and could swear that the side of his face had now become unmistakably moist in the cold air… Hugo was crying.

✦

Qssim knew instinctively that this notion of covering the others was complete bollocks. There was already a back-up team on the ground. He'd seen them from the helicopter. He didn't trust Hasan, and something deep within him told him that this just didn't feel right.

As they approached the dry stone wall, Hasan took Qssim by the shoulder and immediately pointed his gun with the silencer at his forehead and pulled the trigger but the gun, by some curious stroke of fate, failed to fire.

How had Qssim been so stupid? He wasn't going to let this prick get a second chance. He got the first punch in, smacking Hasan squarely in the centre of his face, breaking his nose with a sickening click. There was blood everywhere, but Hasan was by no means a spent force. He was a big bastard, and he was fit. Now Hasan had come back at him with a vengeance, pummeling the side of Qssim's head with his bare knuckles, and then gripping Qssim's neck with both of his enormous hands. Qssim couldn't breathe. He could feel his life literally being squeezed away and he was becoming faint. It was the second time in his life that someone had wanted to strangle him to death.

As he took in what felt like his last view of the world: a

moonlit sky and the heavens above, his fingertips fell on cold steel - a small dagger he had strapped to his ankle. He could barely summon any energy but somehow managed to pull the knife from its home-made holster, and then with what little strength he had, plunged the blade through Hasan's fleshy thigh.

Hasan's pained scream came as music to Qssim's ear, and as the other man's hands fell away, Qssim gasped for air and instinctively twisted the knife further to inflict maximum damage before pulling the blade out. Hasan may have been in pain, but he wasn't out for the count and had managed to retrieve the gun and fired it in desperation. Qssim had only just anticipated Hasan's move in time but had been unable to completely dodge the bullet, which caught him in the shoulder and shattered his shoulder blade. Both men were now in considerable pain and were both losing blood as they struggled over the gun.

Qssim was determined to survive as he forced the gun out of Hasan's hand and then thrust the other man's left index finger into his mouth and bit hard with his back molars. Hasan screamed and Qssim could taste warm, salty blood in his mouth as he chewed unmercifully on the raw flesh and pulled his head clean away with a violent jerk. He spat out the fleshy appendage as Hasan writhed in agony, and then retrieved the gun with the silencer still attached, pointed it at Hasan's head and fired it three times.

◆

Hugo wiped away the tears from his eyes. He couldn't quite believe what was unfolding. It was the kind of thing that happened in far-fetched potboilers - not real life. He had closed the cockpit but could still hear the woman's voice on the megaphone. She had instructed Michael to move forward towards the helicopters and the spotlight had highlighted an area midway between the aircraft and the two helicopters in which the woman had now instructed him to park himself.

Michael moved the joystick forward and traversed the bumpy terrain slowly in order to avoid spasms in his legs, which could so easily be set off by an excessively bumpy ride. He eventually parked himself in the pool of light. Luckily, his legs hadn't succumbed. He'd always enjoyed hogging the limelight when treading the boards in those amateur dramatic productions of his youth, but this was a different kind of limelight; one he'd have done anything to stay well out of.

He sat there motionless and nervous with the case of money on his lap.

✦

All eight of them appeared out of the darkness. The woman was wearing a headscarf and was flanked either side by men carrying serious looking guns that wouldn't have looked out of place in the hands of the counter-terrorist forces.

They moved as one into the pool of light and Benazir stepped forward. She was visibly irritated. Hasan had agreed to be by her side. He was meant to be her personal bodyguard. This was shoddy behaviour. She was also furious to have misjudged Qssim. He had seemed so credible. And white Muslim converts were like gold dust for the cause… She should have known better than to have invested so much time and resources on this charlatan who had clearly spent hours watching filthy Israeli propaganda videos. In normal circumstances, she'd have had him interrogated, but since his unwelcome sexual advances, and his surly bloody nature of late, she'd lost patience. She just wanted him dead. He was too much of a threat.

She stepped towards Michael and as she did so, all eight of her henchmen trained their semi-automatics on him.

Michael wasn't expecting to be greeted by a woman. She was obviously of Arabic extraction and wasn't unattractive. Her eyes were cold though. There wasn't the merest trace of humanity in their hard steely gaze.

'Thank you for meeting our demands Mr Hollinghurst. As you can see, my men are well equipped, so it is imperative that you do not make one false move, otherwise you might get sprayed with several hundred bullets. Do you understand me Mr Hollinghurst?'

Michael nodded. 'I understand you perfectly well.'

'Good... What I'd like you to do now is to very slowly take the case of money off your knees with both hands and drop it on the ground.'

Michael nodded again and slowly raised the metal case and dropped it onto the ground just in front of his footplates. Then he nonchalantly placed both his hands on the armrests.

While one of her lackeys now came forward to retrieve the case, Michael slowly placed a solitary right finger beneath his right armrest.

Now another armed guard was fiddling with the lock on the case while his colleague held it aloft.

Michael closed his eyes. He could see his kids now.

They were beaming at him. It was Ben's 5th birthday party and he had provided the entertainment - a puppet show with marionettes that were old family heirlooms. They had loved every minute of it... Now he was in the maternity ward and Louise looked up at him. She seemed so radiant caressing that little bundle swathed in white cotton that was their newly born daughter; their very first child. He had never known such joy... Then it was his father's turn to make an appearance. It was his graduation day at Cambridge, and his father was standing there looking so proud. He had worked so damn hard running that shirt factory to scrape enough together to get his son into a decent private school and to gain an education that he himself had been so unfairly deprived of. His father raised his glass of champagne and blew him a kiss in that inimitable way of his. He was one hell of a beautiful man...

The steel case had now been duly opened, and the woman had reached inside and pulled out a wad. She looked at Michael with that steely inhuman gaze and he looked back at her, tears now streaming down his cheeks.

And that's when that finger of his ever so gently pushed the button beneath his right armrest.

CHAPTER SIXTY-FOUR

Joy Mullen loved this place. It was her idea of heaven on earth. She couldn't remember exactly how long she'd been coming here as a member of this very special ecumenical Christian community of men and women who were all seeking to live out the Gospel in a way that was radical, inclusive and relevant to life in the 21st century. It must have been well over 20 years.

Besides being part of the most wonderful community, the tranquillity and rugged beauty of the place was infectious. It had become so much a part of her that she simply loathed taking her leave of the island and spending time in the real world. But she was a realist. She knew she couldn't just stay here and bury her head in the sand. That would have been a derogation of duty to her fellow man and to her God; not to mention the International Ecumenical Peace Convocation and the World Council of Churches. But she had learnt to treasure the time that she did spend here. And there was nowhere on earth where she could sleep so soundly. Though this particular evening was to be the exception to the rule.

◆

The blast had quite literally shaken her bed, and the sound of the explosion itself had been so enormous and incongruous that it had come as an almighty shock to her system.

She grabbed her spectacles from the bedside table and

hurried across the stone floor. At the window, she eagerly pulled back the curtain and opened the sash window.

What she saw in the middle distance was a scene straight out of hell itself. An enormous fireball lit up the night sky and the smell of fuel was almost intoxicating.

She felt physically sick, and then she was.

CHAPTER SIXTY-FIVE

The heat from the explosion was like nothing Qssim had ever experienced. He had been dragging Hasan's body in an attempt to conceal it in a thicket of gorse when it happened.

The fireball was huge and both helicopters now seemed to be on fire, so he ducked down behind the wall anticipating further explosions. Within a couple of minutes, there was a second explosion followed closely by a third.

His shoulder had become excruciatingly painful but for a brief moment, all this excitement had distracted him from the pain.

It looked as if their so-called *Chair Man* had played them at their own fucking game. He chuckled to himself, and then he noticed the plane. It seemed to have been unscathed.

◆

Hugo had been taken aback by the size and ferocity of the explosion. He wasn't expecting it to be quite as seismic.

His friend, God bless him, had finally achieved the kind of retribution he was seeking, and Hugo had played a truly significant part in helping him pull it off. In the circumstances, everything about Michael's plan made sense. It was watertight. And like any legal contract that had been properly drafted, you couldn't argue with it. But that didn't stop him feeling like a complete and utter shit.

How could he have allowed himself to be complicit in this hideous plan? Michael was his best friend for Christ's sake.

The two further explosions had distracted him, and that's when he spotted the figure of a man who looked injured coming towards the plane. Michael had made him promise to bring his old man's shotgun, and use it if necessary. 'It was vital that all the terrorists perished, otherwise Ben and Natasha's lives would be in jeopardy.' Those had been the exact words of his friend, and he was buggered if he wasn't going to carry them out to the letter.

He retrieved the gun from under his seat, slid open a small sliver of the cockpit and placed the bore of the gun discreetly through the aperture. He took aim at this demented looking figure who seemed to be waving his arms in the air, and as soon as he was in close enough range he pulled the trigger.

CHAPTER SIXTY-SIX

It was Natasha who discovered the letter. She'd been the first to wake from her slumber as she had drunk less of the drugged tea.

It had looked innocent enough in its brown manilla envelope, but its contents had left her ashen-faced and in an extreme state of shock.

When Alexander came into the kitchen a little while later, she could barely string a sentence together. He knew straight away that something awful had happened and instinctively ran into Michael's room. As he feared, it was empty. He'd gone.

CHAPTER SIXTY-SEVEN

Ben was just about to leave for a lecture when his letter arrived. Normally he'd have just left it for later, but for some curious reason, he didn't. Perhaps it was because he recognised his father's handwriting on the envelope. Or perhaps he just wanted an excuse not to go to his lecture. In any event, he unclipped his cycle helmet and opened it in the kitchen.

CHAPTER SIXTY-EIGHT

Dear Ben and Tash,

There's no easy way to write you this letter. And if I'm honest, a part of me hates myself for not telling you all this in person.

The thing is, I'm dying. There, I've said it on paper. I just didn't have the guts to tell you face to face. I guess I just didn't want to see you cry.

I received the prognosis from Dr Baxter six months ago. Stage four prostate cancer I'm afraid, and it's too advanced to effectively treat.

Truth is there is another reason I couldn't tell you. You see, I'm being blackmailed by the individuals I am now in hiding from. Don't ask me how they tracked down our address in London. The fact is they have. Worse still, they seem to know your names. And that fact alone terrifies me. It terrifies me beyond words. I may not have been the best dad in the world. I buggered up our family life by screwing up my relationship with your mother. We did love each other once, of course. But human relationships are wonderfully strange and unpredictable. Some of us are lucky enough in life to know everlasting happiness. But with your mum and I, it just wasn't to be. And for that, I remain deeply sorry. That said, on an entirely different level, our marriage was an unmitigated bloody success -

because it produced you.

Dr Baxter reckons I have anything between six and eight months. But the second thing that terrifies me is the prospect of a long, lingering and painful death. I saw it when dad died. He didn't deserve that. Nobody in this world deserves that.

So instead of visiting a Swiss clinic to be put to sleep painlessly and in a dignified fashion, I have decided to end my life and those of my tormentors in one fell swoop. I will accept their blackmail demands. But I am certainly not going to part with a single penny of real money. I will stuff a case with photocopied banknotes while also stuffing my wheelchair with high explosives - and thereby employing their own filthy tactics. This way I avoid a terrifyingly slow and painful death from cancer, while the threat that these vile individuals pose to you and the rest of the civilised world will be eliminated altogether. I will in effect be killing two birds with one stone.

It's a macabre, surreal and pretty insane plan, I know. But it's also one that makes infinite sense. It's also one I could never carry out without the assistance of one man: Hugo Manningtree. In fairness to Hugo, he wasn't keen to help from the outset, and I had to win him round. And it took a fair bit of arguing believe me. So don't think ill of him. He's a good man and a dear friend. He will feel bad about what he's done. So I implore you, if you can, to reassure him that he did the right thing. It will mean a lot coming from you.

To borrow the words of one of this country's most brilliant and prolific authors, 'It is a far, far better thing that I do, than I have ever done; it is a far, far better rest that I go to than I have ever known.'

Naturally, it pains me not to be able to see you grow up and raise families of your own. I think I would have made a good fist of becoming a grandpa.

So what words of wisdom can I impart now that I haven't already? I'm not the best-qualified person to talk about relationships as I haven't exactly set the best example in this respect. But let me tell you this: when you both do eventually enter into the most meaningful relationship you've ever known; and believe me, you will, that relationship can be whatever you decide it to be. I can also tell you that it's quite something to remain attractive and be loved by your partner who has heard you snore; seen you at your worst, unmade up or unshaved; and who has washed your dirty underwear. If you can do that then you will be in nirvana. As someone far wiser than me once said: 'There is no greater happiness in this world than approaching a door at the end of the day knowing someone on the other side of that door is waiting for the sound of your footsteps.'

I do hope your lives pan out as well as they possibly can.

I love you so very much,

Dad

EPILOGUE

She had never let on to him that she was actually a mature student in her second year at university studying for a Masters in Genetic Engineering. She had kept both sides of her life totally separate. Two totally different compartments. It was best that way. After all, she simply couldn't afford to let the word get out on campus that she did this kind of thing on the side just to pay her way. It wouldn't have gone down at all well with her faculty. It might even have got her kicked out full stop.

She'd only seen him twice. They'd never had sex. He was a tetraplegic. And yet, he was her only client that she had harboured genuine feelings for. She couldn't say why exactly. But she knew instinctively that there was no bad bone in his body. She just warmed to him, end of.

She'd been thinking a lot about him of late. So it was a tad spooky that the letter had appeared that morning. She'd given him her address because he said he wanted to send her a little something for her birthday. That little something turned out to be something of a bombshell. She lit another cigarette and read it once more.

Dear Samantha,

I'm afraid we won't be seeing each other ever again.

This will come as a shock to you, but I am actually dying. I have stage four prostate cancer.

And in two days time, I shall be travelling with a dear

friend who will help me with an assisted suicide programme. I simply can't face a long and painful death.

I'm sorry to upset you with this news. Please, please forgive me. The last thing I want to do is upset you.

I just wanted to say how much I appreciated your company. You are a very special and bright young lady.

Had circumstances been different, we may have been able to get to know each other a little better, but life I'm afraid can be a cruel master.

As promised, I have enclosed a belated birthday present. Please use it as best you can. I don't wish to pry but I don't quite understand why you do what you do. You have a fine brain and there is I'm sure a very bright future ahead for you. Nothing would give me greater pleasure if you used this present to study at a university.

With all my love,

Michael

Attached to the letter was a cheque for £30,000.

◆

'So tell me, why you feel this way?'

Dennis looked at the psychiatrist in dismay. 'That's one fucking stupid question if you don't mind me saying so.'

The psychiatrist removed his glasses and began to polish the lenses. 'No I don't mind you saying so… But is it such a stupid fucking question?'

Dennis's right leg suddenly went into a violent spasm and he had to grip the leg above the knee to stop it. Then he unlocked the brake and wheeled himself round to the window and looked out at young boys playing football.

'That is why I feel as I do. I will never be able to do what they are doing. I'm going to be stuck in this fucking chair for the rest of my life.'

The psychiatrist smiled and placed his glasses back on his nose. 'And if there was something you could do to alleviate these feelings, what do you think that might be?'

Dennis had had enough of this bullshit. 'Look there's only one thing that would actually make me feel better, and that would be seeking out those arseholes that think it's fine to kill innocent men, women and children willy nilly in the name of Allah, and blow the lot of them to kingdom come. Ok?'

If you enjoyed *The Chair Man* and would like to read a sequel, please feel free to encourage the author to get his finger out and get back to his writing desk by penning an enthusiastic review on Amazon and Goodreads.
Thank you.

Sleeping with the Blackbirds is the highly acclaimed YA fiction from author, Alex Pearl.

Eleven-year-old schoolboy, Roy Nuttersley has been dealt a pretty raw deal. While hideous parents show him precious little in the way of love and affection, school bullies make his life a misery. So Roy takes comfort in looking after the birds in his garden and, in return, the birds hatch a series of ambitious schemes to protect their new friend. As with the best-laid plans, however, these get blown completely off course - and as a result the lives of both Roy and his arch tormentor, Harry Hodges are turned upside down - but in a surprisingly good way.

Available in paperback and ebook from Amazon

About the author

Back in the distant mists of time, Alex spent three years at art college in Maidstone; a college that David Hockney once taught at, and later described in a piece for *The Sunday Times* as the 'most miserable' episode of his life. Here, Alex was responsible for producing - among other things - the college's first theatrical production in which the lead character accidentally caught fire. Following college, he found employment in the advertising industry as a copywriter. He has turned to writing fiction in the twilight years of his writing career. *Sleeping with the Blackbirds,* a modern-day urban fantasy written for children was published in 2011 and has since become a Kindle bestseller. Alex is also quite possibly the only person on this planet to have been inadvertently locked in a record shop on Christmas Eve.

alex-pearl.net

Printed in Great Britain
by Amazon